STATE OF TERROR

Hillary Rodham Clinton is the first woman in US history to become the presidential nominee of a major political party. She served as the 67th Secretary of State after nearly four decades in public service advocating on behalf of children and families as an attorney, First Lady and US Senator. She is a wife, mother, grandmother and author of seven previous books.

Louise Penny is an international award-winning and bestselling author whose books have hit number one on the *New York Times*, *USA Today* and *Globe and Mail* lists. Her Chief Inspector Armand Gamache novels have been translated into thirty-one languages. In 2017, she received the Order of Canada for her contributions to Canadian culture. Louise Penny lives in a village south of Montréal.

ALSO BY
HILLARY RODHAM CLINTON

The Book of Gutsy Women
(with Chelsea Clinton)

What Happened

Hard Choices

Living History

It Takes a Village

Dear Socks, Dear Buddy:
Kids' Letters to the First Pets

An Invitation to the White House:
At Home with History

ALSO BY
LOUISE PENNY

The Madness of Crowds

All the Devils Are Here

A Better Man

Kingdom of the Blind

Glass Houses

A Great Reckoning

The Nature of the Beast

The Long Way Home

How the Light Gets In

The Beautiful Mystery

A Trick of the Light

Bury Your Dead

The Brutal Telling

A Rule Against Murder

The Cruelest Month

A Fatal Grace

Still Life

STATE OF TERROR

HILLARY RODHAM CLINTON

and

LOUISE PENNY

MACMILLAN

First published 2021 jointly by Simon & Schuster and St. Martin's Press

First published in the UK 2021 by Macmillan
an imprint of Pan Macmillan
The Smithson, 6 Briset Street, London EC1M 5NR
EU representative: Macmillan Publishers Ireland Ltd, 1st Floor,
The Liffey Trust Centre, 117–126 Sheriff Street Upper,
Dublin 1, D01 YC43
Associated companies throughout the world
www.panmacmillan.com

ISBN 978-1-5290-7970-8

3 5 7 9 8 6 4

A CIP catalogue record for this book is available from the British Library.

Printed and bound in India by Replika Press Pvt. Ltd.

MIX
Paper from responsible sources
FSC® C016779

To the courageous men and women who protect us from terror and stand up to violence, hatred, and extremism no matter the source. You inspire us every day to be braver, to be better.

The most amazing thing that has happened in my lifetime is neither putting a man on the moon nor Facebook having 2.8 billion monthly active users. It is that in the 75 years, 7 months, and 13 days since Nagasaki, a nuclear bomb has not been detonated.

—*Tom Peters*

STATE OF TERROR

CHAPTER 1

Madame Secretary," said Charles Boynton, hurrying beside his boss as she rushed down Mahogany Row to her office in the State Department. "You have eight minutes to get to the Capitol."

"It's ten minutes away," said Ellen Adams, breaking into a run. "And I have to shower and change. Unless . . ." She stopped and turned to her Chief of Staff. "I can go like this?"

She held out her arms to give him a good look at her. There was no mistaking the plea in her eyes, the anxiety in her voice, and the fact she looked like she'd just been dragged behind a piece of rusty farm equipment.

His face contorted in a smile that seemed to cause him pain.

In her late fifties, Ellen Adams was medium height, trim, elegant. A good dress sense and Spanx concealed her love of eclairs. Her makeup was subtle, bringing out her intelligent blue eyes while not trying to hide her age. She had no need to pretend to be younger than she was, but neither did she want to appear older.

Her hairdresser, when applying the specially formulated coloring, called her an "Eminence Blonde."

"With all due respect, Madame Secretary, you look like a hobo."

"Thank God he respects you," whispered Betsy Jameson, Ellen's best friend and counselor.

After a twenty-two-hour day that had started with Secretary Adams hosting a diplomatic breakfast at the American embassy in Seoul, and included high-level talks on regional security and efforts to salvage an unexpectedly crumbling and vital trade deal, the endless day had ended with a tour of a fertilizer plant in Gangwon Province, though that had been a cover for a quick trip to the DMZ.

After that, Ellen Adams had trudged onto the flight home. Once in the air, the first thing she'd done was remove the Spanx and pour a large glass of Chardonnay.

She'd then spent several hours sending reports back to her deputies and the President, and reading the incoming memos. Or at least trying to. She'd fallen asleep facedown on a report from State on staffing in the Iceland embassy.

She woke with a jerk when her assistant touched her shoulder.

"Madame Secretary, we're about to land."

"Where?"

"Washington."

"State?" She sat up and ran her hands through her hair, making it stand straight up, as though she'd had a scare or a very good idea.

She was hoping it was Seattle. To refuel, or take on food, or perhaps there was some fortuitous in-flight emergency. There was that, she knew, though it was neither mechanical nor fortuitous.

The emergency was that she'd fallen asleep and still needed to shower and—

"DC."

"Oh God, Ginny. Couldn't you have woken me up sooner?"

"I tried, but you just mumbled and went back to sleep."

Ellen had a vague memory of that but had thought it had been a dream. "Thanks for trying. Do I have time to brush my teeth?"

There was a ding as the captain put on the seat belt sign.

"I'm afraid not."

Ellen looked out the window of her government jet, which she jokingly called Air Force Three. She saw the dome of the Capitol Building, where she'd soon be seated.

She saw herself in the reflection. Hair askew. Mascara smeared. Clothing disheveled. Eyes bloodshot and burning from her contacts. There were lines of worry, of stress, that hadn't been there just a month earlier at the inauguration. That bright, shiny day when the world was new and all seemed possible.

How she loved this country. This glorious, broken beacon.

After decades of building and running an international media empire that now spread across television networks, an all-news channel, websites, and newspapers, she'd handed it over to the next generation. Her daughter, Katherine.

After the past four years of watching the country she loved flail itself almost to death, she was now in a position to help it heal.

Since the death of her beloved Quinn, Ellen had felt her life not just empty but callow. Instead of diminishing with time, that sense had grown, the chasm widening. She increasingly felt the need to do more. To help more. To not report on the pain but do something to ease it. To give back.

The opportunity had come from the most unlikely source: President-Elect Douglas Williams. How quickly life could change. For the worse, yes. But also for the better.

And now Ellen Adams found herself on Air Force Three. As Secretary of State for the new President.

She was in a position to rebuild bridges to allies after the near-criminal incompetence of the former administration. She could mend vital relationships or lay down warnings to unfriendly nations. Those that might have harm in mind and the ability to carry it out.

Ellen Adams was in a position to no longer just talk about change, but to bring it about. To turn enemies into friends and keep chaos and terror at bay.

And yet . . .

The face that looked back at her no longer seemed quite so confident. She was looking at a stranger. A tired, disheveled, spent woman. Older than her years. And perhaps a little wiser. Or was it more cynical? She hoped not and wondered why it was suddenly difficult to tell the two apart.

Bringing out a tissue, she licked it and wiped the mascara away. Then, after smoothing her hair, she smiled at her reflection.

It was the face she kept by the door. The one the public had come to know. The press, her colleagues, foreign leaders. The confident, gracious, assured Secretary of State representing the most powerful nation on earth.

But it was a facade. Ellen Adams saw something else in her ghostly face. Something ghastly she took pains to hide even from herself. But exhaustion had allowed it to swarm over her defenses.

She saw fear. And its close kin, doubt.

Was it real or counterfeit? A near enemy whispering she was not good enough. Not up to the job. That she would screw it up, and thousands, perhaps millions of lives would be jeopardized?

She shoved it away, recognizing that it was unhelpful. But it whispered, even as it receded, that that didn't mean it wasn't true.

After the plane landed at Andrews Air Force Base, Ellen had been hurried into an armored car, to read more memos, reports, emails. DC glided by, unseen now, as she got caught up.

Once in the basement garage of the monolithic Harry S. Truman Building, still called Foggy Bottom by longtime denizens, maybe even with affection, a phalanx formed to get her into the elevator and up to her private office on the seventh floor as quickly as possible.

Her Chief of Staff, Charles Boynton, met her at the elevator. He was one of the people assigned to the new Secretary of State by the President's own Chief of Staff. Tall and gangly, his slender frame was due more to excessive nervous energy than exercise or good eating habits. His hair and muscle tone seemed to be in a race to jump ship.

Boynton had spent twenty-six years rising through the political ranks, finally landing a top job as a strategist on Douglas Williams's successful presidential campaign. A campaign that had proven more brutal than most.

Charles Boynton had finally reached the inner sanctum and was determined to stay there. This was his reward for following orders. And being lucky in his choice of candidate.

Boynton found himself designing rules to keep unruly cabinet secretaries in line. In his view, they were temporary political appointments. Window dressing to his structure.

Together Ellen and her Chief of Staff rushed down the wood-paneled corridor of Mahogany Row toward the Secretary of State's office, trailed by aides and assistants and her Diplomatic Security agents.

"Don't worry," said Betsy, racing to catch up. "They're holding the State of the Union address for you. You can relax."

"No, no," said Boynton, his voice rising an octave. "You can't relax. The President's pissed. And by the way, it's not officially a SOTU."

"Oh, please, Charles. Try not to be pedantic." Ellen stopped suddenly, almost causing a pileup. Slipping off her mud-caked heels, she ran in stocking feet along the plush carpet. Picking up her pace.

"And the President's always pissed," Betsy called after them. "Oh, you mean angry? Well, he's always angry at Ellen."

Boynton shot her a warning glance.

He didn't like this Elizabeth Jameson. Betsy. An outsider whose only reason for being there was because she was a lifelong friend of the Secretary. Boynton knew it was the Secretary's right to choose one close confidante, a counselor, to work with her. But he didn't like it. The outsider brought an element of unpredictability to any situation.

And he did not like her. Privately he called her Mrs. Cleaver because she looked like Barbara Billingsley, the Beaver's mother in the TV show. A model 1950s housewife.

Safe. Stable. Compliant.

Except this Mrs. Cleaver turned out to be not so black-and-white. She seemed to have swallowed Bette "Fuck 'Em If They Can't Take a Joke" Midler. And while he quite liked the Divine Miss M, he thought perhaps not as the Secretary of State's counselor.

Though Charles Boynton had to admit that what Betsy said was true. Douglas Williams had no love for his Secretary of State. And to say it was mutual was an understatement.

It had come as a huge shock when the newly elected President had chosen a political foe, a woman who'd used her vast resources to support his rival for the party nomination, for such a powerful and prestigious position.

It was an even greater shock when Ellen Adams had turned her media empire over to her grown daughter and accepted the post.

The news was gobbled up by politicos, pundits, colleagues, and spit out as gossip. It fed and filled political talk shows for weeks.

The appointment of Ellen Adams was fodder at DC dinner parties. It was all anyone at Off the Record, the basement bar of the Hay-Adams, could talk about.

Why did she accept?

Though by far the greater, more interesting question was why had then President-Elect Williams offered his most vocal, most vicious adversary a place in his cabinet? And State, of all things?

The prevailing theory was that Douglas Williams was either following Abraham Lincoln and assembling a Team of Rivals. Or, more likely, he was following Sun Tzu, the ancient military strategist, and was keeping his friends close but his enemies closer.

Though, as it turned out, both theories were wrong.

For his part Charles Boynton, Charles to his friends, cared about his boss only to the extent that Ellen Adams's failures reflected badly on him, and he was damned if he'd be clinging to her coattails as she went down.

And after this trip to South Korea, her fortunes, and his, had taken a sharp turn south. And now they were holding up the entire fucking not–State of the Goddamned Union.

"Come on, come on. Hurry."

"Enough." Ellen skidded to a stop. "I won't be bullied and herded. If I have to go like this, so be it."

"You can't," said Boynton, his eyes wide with panic. "You look—"

"Yes, you've already said." She turned to her friend. "Betsy?"

There was a pause during which all they could hear was Boynton snorting his displeasure.

"You look fine," Betsy said quietly. "Maybe some lipstick." She handed Ellen a tube from her own purse along with a hairbrush and compact.

"Come on, come on," Boynton practically squeaked.

Holding Ellen's bloodshot eyes, Betsy whispered, "An oxymoron walked into a bar . . ."

Ellen thought, then smiled. "And the silence was deafening."

Betsy beamed. "Perfect."

She watched as her friend took a deep breath, handed her big travel bag to her assistant, and turned to Boynton.

"Shall we?"

While she appeared composed, Secretary Adams's heart was pounding as she walked in stocking feet, a filthy shoe dangling from each hand, back down Mahogany Row to the elevator. And the descent.

"Hurry, hurry." Amir gestured to his wife. "They're at the house."

They could hear the banging behind them, the men shouting, commanding. Their words heavily accented but their meaning clear: "Dr. Bukhari, come out. Now."

"Go." Amir shoved Nasrin down the alley. "Run."

"You?" she asked, clutching the satchel to her chest.

There was the splintering of wood as the door to their home in Kahuta, just outside Islamabad, was shattered.

"They don't want me. It's you they need to stop. I'll distract them. Go, go."

But as she turned, he grabbed her arm and pulled her to him, clutching her to his chest. "I love you. I'm so proud of you."

He kissed her so hard their teeth collided and she could taste blood from her cut lip. But still she clung to him. And he to her. At the sounds of more shouts, closer now, they parted.

He almost asked her to let him know when she was safely at her destination. But didn't. He knew she could not contact him.

He also knew, as did she, that he would not survive the night.

CHAPTER 2

There was a murmur as the Deputy Sergeant at Arms announced the arrival of the Secretary of State. It was ten past nine, and the rest of the cabinet had already been seated.

There had been speculation that Ellen Adams was missing because she was the Designated Survivor, though most believed President Williams would choose his sock before he'd choose her.

As she entered the chamber, Ellen appeared not to notice the deafening silence.

An oxymoron walked into . . .

She held her head up and followed her escort, smiling to Representatives gathered on each side of the aisle, as though nothing were wrong.

"You're late," hissed the Secretary of Defense when she took her place in the front row, between him and the Director of National Intelligence. "We held the speech for you. The President's furious. Thinks you did it on purpose, so the networks would be focused on you and not him."

"The President would be wrong," said the Director of National Intelligence, the DNI. "There's no way you'd do that."

"Thank you, Tim," said Ellen. It was a rare show of support from one of President Williams's loyalists.

"Given the shitshow that was South Korea," Tim Beecham continued, "I can't imagine you'd want the attention."

"What in God's name are you wearing?" asked the Secretary of Defense. "Have you been mud wrestling again?"

He grimaced and scrunched up his nose.

"No, Mr. Secretary, I've been doing my job. And sometimes that means getting down and dirty." She gave him the once-over. "You're looking as pristine as ever."

On her other side, the DNI laughed, and then they all stood as the Sergeant at Arms announced, "Mr. Speaker, the President of the United States."

Dr. Nasrin Bukhari ran down the familiar alleys, swerving to avoid the crates and cans that littered the area and if kicked would give her away.

She never paused. Never looked back. Not even when the gunfire began.

She decided that her husband of twenty-eight years had escaped. Had survived. Had eluded those sent to try to stop them. To stop her.

He hadn't been killed or, worse, captured, to be tortured until he gave up what he knew.

When the gunfire stopped, she took that as a sign that Amir had gotten safely away. As she now must.

Everything depended on it.

Half a block short of the bus stop, she slowed down, caught her breath, and walked with a calm, measured pace to join the line. Her heart pounding, but her face placid.

Anahita Dahir sat at her desk in the Bureau of South and Central Asian Affairs at the State Department.

She paused in what she was doing to walk over to the television on the far wall, tuned to the President's speech.

It was nine fifteen. The address was late, held up, the commentators said, by the absence of the Secretary of State, Anahita's new boss.

The camera followed the newly elected President as he arrived in the ornate chamber, to wild applause from his supporters and muted clapping from the still-bruised opposition. Since he'd only been sworn in weeks earlier, it was difficult to believe President Williams actually knew the true state of the union, and that he was likely to admit it even if he did.

The speech would be, the pundits agreed, a balancing act between criticizing the previous administration for the mess left behind, though not too overtly, and sounding a hopeful note, though not too optimistic.

This was about tamping down the extravagant expectations raised in the election, while deflecting any blame.

President Williams's appearance before Congress was political theater, a kind of Kabuki. More about appearances than words. And Douglas Williams certainly knew how to look presidential.

Though, as Anahita watched him glad-hand his way into the chamber, greeting and smiling at political friends and foes alike, the camera kept cutting away to the Secretary of State.

This was the real drama. The real story of the night.

The commentators were giddy with speculation on what President Williams would do when he came face-to-face with his Secretary of State. Ellen Adams, they were pleased to point out, and repeat, and repeat, was just off the plane from a disastrous first outing, where she managed to alienate an important ally and destabilize an already fragile region.

The moment the two met, here in the chamber, would be seen by hundreds of millions internationally and replayed over and over on social media.

The chamber was crackling with anticipation.

The commentators leaned forward, anxious to decode whatever message the President might send.

The young foreign service officer was alone in the department, except for the supervisor in his corner office. She stepped closer to the screen, interested to see what would happen between her new President and her new boss. She was so captivated that she failed to hear the ping of a message coming in.

While President Williams made his way forward, stopping to chat and wave, the political commentators filled the time by discussing Ellen Adams's hair, her makeup, her clothes, which were disheveled and smeared with what they hoped was mud.

"She looks like she just came from a rodeo."

"And into a slaughterhouse."

More chuckling.

Finally one of the commentators pointed out that Secretary Adams probably hadn't planned to arrive looking like that. It was a testament to how hard she was working.

"She's just off the plane from Seoul," he reminded them.

"Where, we understand, talks broke down."

"Well," he admitted, "I said she was working hard, not effectively."

Then they discussed, in grim tones, just how disastrous her failure in South Korea might prove. For Secretary Adams, for the nascent administration. For their relations in that part of the world.

This too was political theater, the FSO knew. There was no way one unfortunate meeting would lead to permanent damage. But as she watched her new boss, she knew that damage had been done.

While fairly new to the job, Anahita Dahir was astute enough to know that in Washington, appearances were often far more powerful than reality. In fact, so strong were they that they could actually create reality.

The camera lingered on Secretary Adams as the commentators picked her apart.

Unlike the pundits, what Anahita Dahir saw was a woman about her mother's age standing erect, straight-backed, head high, attentive. Respectful. Turned toward the man coming her way. Calmly awaiting her fate.

Her disheveled state only seemed to add, in Anahita's eyes, to her dignity.

Up until that moment, the young FSO had been happy to absorb what the commentators and her fellow analysts said. That Ellen Adams was a cynical political appointment by a crafty President.

But now, as she watched President Williams approach and Secretary Adams brace herself, Anahita wondered.

The FSO hit mute on the television. There was no need to listen to more.

She walked back to her desk and noticed the new message. Opening it, she saw that where the sender's name would be, there were just random letters. And in the message itself there were no words, just a series of numbers and symbols.

As the President approached, Ellen Adams thought he was going to ignore her.

"Mr. President," she said.

He paused and looked beyond her, through her, nodding and smiling at the people on either side. Then he reached past her, his elbow almost hitting her face, to take the hand of the person behind. Only then did he slowly, slowly bring his eyes to hers. The animosity was so palpable that both the Secretary of Defense and the Director of National Intelligence retreated a step.

"Pissed" didn't begin to describe how he was feeling, and they did not want to be hit with the splash.

To the cameras and the millions watching, his handsome face was stern, more disappointed than angry. A sad parent looking at a well-meaning but wayward child.

"Madame Secretary." *You incompetent shit.*

"Mr. President." *You arrogant asshole.*

"Perhaps you can come by the Oval Office in the morning before the cabinet meeting."

"With pleasure, sir."

He passed on, leaving her to look after him warmly. A loyal member of his cabinet.

Taking her seat, she listened politely while President Williams began his address. But as it progressed, Ellen felt herself drawn in. Not by the rhetoric, but by something far more profound than words.

It was the solemnity, the history, the tradition. She was swept up in the majesty, in the quiet grandeur, the grace of this event. In the symbolism, if not the actual content.

A powerful message was being sent to friends and foes alike. Of continuity, of strength, of resolve and purpose. That the damage done by the former administration would be repaired. That America was back.

Ellen Adams felt an emotion so strong it overwhelmed her dislike of Douglas Williams. It pushed her distrust and suspicions away, leaving only pride. And amazement. That somehow, life had brought her here. Had put her in a position to serve.

She might look like a hobo and smell like fertilizer, but she was the American Secretary of State. She loved her country and would do everything in her power to protect it.

Dr. Nasrin Bukhari took her seat on the back row of the bus and forced herself to look straight ahead. Not out the window. Not at the satchel on her lap, held in a white-knuckled grip.

Not at her fellow passengers. It was vital to avoid eye contact.

She forced her face to look neutral, bored.

The bus started up and began to bump its way toward the border. It had been arranged that she would fly out, but without telling anyone, including Amir, she'd changed the plan. The people sent to stop her would expect her to try to get out as quickly as possible. They'd be at the airport. They'd put people on all the flights if need be. They'd do anything to prevent her reaching her destination.

If Amir was captured and tortured, he'd reveal the plan. So it had to change.

Nasrin Bukhari loved her country. She would do whatever was necessary to protect it.

And that meant leaving all she loved behind.

Anahita Dahir stared at the computer screen. Brows drawn together, she took just a few seconds to decide the message was spam. It happened more often than anyone would guess.

Still, she wanted confirmation. Knocking on her supervisor's door, she leaned in. He was watching the speech and shaking his head.

"What?"

"A message. I think it's spam."

"Let me see it."

She showed him.

"It's definitely not from any of our sources?"

"Definitely, sir."

"Good. Delete it."

Which she did. But not before jotting down the message. Just in case.

19/0717, 38/1536, 119/1848

CHAPTER 3

"Congratulations, Mr. President. That went well," said Barbara Stenhauser.

Doug Williams laughed. "It went very well. Better than I could have hoped."

He loosened his tie and put his feet up on the desk.

They were back in the Oval Office. A bar had been set up, along with light snacks for the family, friends, and affluent supporters invited back to celebrate the President's first address to Congress.

Williams, though, wanted a few moments alone with his Chief of Staff, to decompress. The speech had done everything he'd wanted, and more. But it was something else that was making him almost giddy.

He entwined his hands behind his head and rocked, while a steward brought him a scotch and a small plate of bacon-wrapped scallops and deep-fried shrimp.

He gestured to Barb to join him and, thanking the steward, he indicated he should leave.

Barb Stenhauser sat and took a long sip of red wine.

"Can she survive this?" he asked.

"I doubt it. We'll let the media have at her. From what I saw before your speech, they'd already begun. She'll be dead before she gets home. Just to be sure, I've lined up a few of our own Senators to start expressing guarded concern about her fitness for the job, given the shitshow in South Korea."

"Good. Where's she heading next?"

"I have her scheduled to go to Canada."

"Oh God. We'll be at war with them before the week's out."

Barb laughed. "Let's hope. I've always wanted a place in Québec. Early reports are extremely positive about your speech, sir. They're citing your dignified tone, your reaching across the aisle. But there are rumblings, Mr. President, that the appointment of Ellen Adams, while courageous, was a misstep, especially after the debacle of South Korea."

"A little blowback in our direction is to be expected. As long as most of the shit lands on her. Besides, it'll give critics something to focus on while we get on with the job."

Stenhauser smiled. Rarely had she seen so accomplished a politician. One with the courage to take a flesh wound if it meant killing off an opponent.

Though she knew he was in for far more than a flesh wound.

The fact that Douglas Williams made her skin crawl was something she could ignore, if it meant finally implementing an agenda she believed in with all her heart.

Leaning across the desk, she handed him a sheet of paper. "I've prepared a short statement supporting Secretary Adams."

He read it, then tossed it back. "Perfect. Dignified, but noncommittal."

"Faint praise."

He laughed, then sighed with relief. "Flip on the television. Let's see what they're saying."

He tipped forward and placed his elbows on the desk as the large monitor lit up. He'd been tempted to tell his Chief of Staff just how clever he'd really been. But he didn't dare.

"Here."

Katherine Adams handed her mother and her godmother large glasses of Chardonnay; then, grabbing the bottle by the neck, she took her own glass to the large sofa and sat between them. Three pairs of slippered feet were up on the coffee table.

Katherine reached for the remote.

"Not yet," said her mother, laying a hand on her daughter's wrist. "Let's pretend for a few more moments that they're talking about my triumph in South Korea."

"And congratulating you on your new hairstyle and dress sense," said Betsy.

"And perfume," said Katherine.

Ellen laughed.

As soon as she'd gotten home, she'd showered and changed into sweats. Now the three women sat, side by side, in the comfortable den. The walls were covered in shelves, filled with books and framed photographs of Ellen's children and her life with her late husband.

It was a private space, a sanctuary reserved for family and the closest of friends.

Wearing glasses now, Ellen had pulled out a folder and was reading, shaking her head.

"What's wrong?" asked Betsy.

"The talks. They shouldn't have collapsed. The advance team did good work." She held up the papers. "We were prepared. The South Koreans were prepared. I'd had conversations with my counterpart. This was supposed to be a formality."

"So what happened?" asked Katherine.

Her mother sighed. "I don't know. I'm trying to figure that out. What time is it?"

"Eleven thirty-five," said Katherine.

"Twelve thirty-five in the afternoon in Seoul," said Ellen. "I'm tempted to call, but won't. I need more information." She glanced at Betsy, who was scrolling through messages. "Anything?"

"Lots of supportive emails and texts from friends and family," said Betsy.

Ellen continued to look at her, but Betsy shook her head, knowing what Ellen was asking, and not asking.

"I can write him," offered Katherine.

"No. He knows what's happening. If he wanted to get in touch, he would."

"You know he's busy, Mom."

Ellen pointed to the remote. "Might as well turn on the news. Get it over with."

What appeared on the television would serve, both Betsy and Katherine knew, as a counterirritant, taking Ellen's mind off the message that had not appeared on her phone.

Ellen Adams continued to read through the reports, trying to find some clue as to what had gone wrong in Seoul. Only half listening to the so-called experts on the television.

She knew what they'd be saying. Even her own company's media outlets, the internationally syndicated news channel, the papers, the online sites, would be taking a run at their former owner.

In fact, in an effort to prove they were unbiased, they'd be first to pile on. And pile high. Ellen could already smell the opinion pieces.

When she'd accepted the position of Secretary of State, Ellen had divested herself of her holdings, turning them over to her daughter with the express, and written, order that Katherine Adams not personally interfere in any coverage of the Williams administration generally, or Secretary Adams specifically.

It was a pledge her daughter had found easy to make. After all, she wasn't the journalist in the family. Her degree, her expertise, her interest was only in the business side. She took after her mother in that.

Betsy touched Ellen's arm and nodded toward the television.

Looking up from her papers, she watched for a moment, then sat up straighter.

"Oh, fuck," said Doug Williams. "Are you kidding me?"

He glared at his Chief of Staff as though expecting her to do something about it.

What Barb Stenhauser did was change channels. Then again. And again. But somehow, between President Williams's State of the Union Address and his second glass of scotch, something had shifted.

Katherine started laughing, her eyes gleaming.

"My God, every channel." She clicked through them all, resting on each just long enough to hear the pundits and political yobs congratulating Secretary Adams on her hard work. Her willingness to show up at the Capitol unkempt, with the muck of her job still clinging to her.

Yes, the trip had been an unexpected debacle, but the larger message was that Ellen Adams, and by extension the US, was unbowed. Willing to get into the trenches. To show up. To at least try to undo the damage done by four years of chaos.

Her failure in South Korea was being blamed on the mess left behind by an inept former President and his own Secretary of State.

Now Katherine let out a hoot. "Look at this." She shoved her phone in front of her mother and Betsy.

A meme had gone viral on social media.

After being introduced, Secretary Adams walked down the aisle toward her seat for the address, the television camera picking up a rival Senator who'd looked at her with disdain and muttered:

"Dirty woman."

"What the hell!" said Doug Williams, tossing a shrimp onto his plate so hard it bounced onto the Resolute desk, then jumped ship and landed on the carpet. "Shit."

Lying in bed, Anahita Dahir had a thought.

Suppose the strange message was from Gil?

Yes. It could have been Gil. Wanting to get back in touch. To touch.

She could feel his skin, moist with perspiration from those hot, hot, sticky close Islamabad afternoons. They'd stolen away to her small room, almost exactly midway between his desk at the wire service and her desk at the embassy.

She was so junior no one would notice she was missing. Gil Bahar was so respected a journalist no one would question his absence. They'd assume he was off chasing a lead.

In the close, close, claustrophobic world of the Pakistani capital, clandestine meetings were held all day and all night. Between operatives and agents. Between informants and those who trafficked in information. Between dealers and users, of drugs, of arms, of death.

Between embassy staff and journalists.

It was a place and time where anything could happen at any moment. The young journalists and aid workers, doctors and nurses, embassy staff and informants met and mingled in underground bars, in tiny apartments. At parties. They bumped up against each other. Ground up against each other.

Life around them was precious and precarious. And they were immortal.

Her body moved, rhythmically, in her DC bed, feeling again his hard body against hers. His hard body inside hers.

A few minutes later Anahita got up. And though she knew she was asking for trouble, still she reached for her phone.

Did you try to message me?

She woke up now and then through the night to check her phone. No reply.

"Idiot," she muttered, even as she smelled again his muskiness. Felt his naked white skin as it slid against her dark, moist body. Both luminous in the afternoon sun.

She could feel the weight of him on top of her. Lying heavy on her heart.

Nasrin Bukhari sat in the departure lounge.

A weary guard at the border had checked her passport, failing to pick up on the fact it was fake. Or perhaps he didn't really care anymore.

He'd looked down at the document, then into her eyes. He saw an exhausted middle-aged woman. Her traditional hijab washed out and frayed where it framed her lined face.

Surely no threat. He'd moved on. To the next passenger desperate to cross the frontier from threat to fragile hope.

Dr. Bukhari knew that in her satchel she carried that hope. In her head she carried that threat.

She'd made it to the airport with three hours to spare before her flight. It was, she now realized, perhaps a little too much time.

Nasrin Bukhari positioned herself to be able to see, in her peripheral vision, the man lounging against the wall across the concourse. He'd been at security as she'd checked through. He'd followed her, she was almost certain, to the waiting area.

She'd been looking for a Pakistani. An Indian. An Iranian. Surely they'd be the ones sent to stop her. It never occurred to her they'd send a white man. The very fact that he stood out was his camouflage. Dr. Bukhari would not have credited her enemies with this stroke of genius.

Though it was possible she was imagining things. Too little rest, too little food, too much fear were creating paranoia. She could feel her reason drifting away. Light-headed from lack of sleep, she seemed at times to be floating above her body.

As an intellectual, a scientist, Dr. Bukhari found this the most frightening event so far. She could no longer trust her mind. Nor could she trust her emotions.

She was adrift.

No, she thought. Not that. She had a clear direction. A clear destination. She just had to get there.

Nasrin Bukhari looked at the battered old clock on the wall of the filthy waiting area. Again. Two hours and fifty-three minutes until her flight to Frankfurt.

In her peripheral vision, she saw the man take out his phone.

The text came in at one thirty in the morning.

Didn't write glid you did. You might be album to help me with something. Need info on scientist.

Ana clicked it off. He couldn't even be bothered to check for typos before sending the message.

She'd walked into that propeller, knowing, or at least suspecting, that she was just a source to him. Nothing more. And probably had been all along. Her value to him was as his insider at the embassy and now the State Department. His source in the Bureau of South and Central Asian Affairs.

Anahita wondered how much she really knew about Gil Bahar. He was a respected journalist with Reuters. There had been rumors, though. Whispers.

But Islamabad was built on whispers and rumors. Even the veterans couldn't separate truth from fiction. Reality from paranoia. In that cauldron, the two melded and became one. Indistinguishable.

What she did know was that Gil Bahar had been kidnapped in Afghanistan by the Pathan family network a few years earlier and held for eight months before escaping. Known as "the family," the Pathan were the nom de guerre of the most extreme, the most brutal of the terrorists in the Pakistani-Afghan tribal area. Closely aligned with Al-Qaeda, they were feared even by other Taliban groups.

Where other journalists had been tortured, then executed, beheaded, Gil Bahar had gotten out unscathed.

And why was that? was the whispered question. How had he escaped the Pathan?

Anahita Dahir had chosen to ignore the nasty innuendo. But now, as she lay in bed, she allowed herself to go there.

The last time Gil had contacted her was shortly after she'd been transferred out of Pakistan to take up her job in DC. He'd called her personal number and, after some pleasantries, had asked for information.

She hadn't given it to him, of course, but three days later there'd been an assassination. Of the very person whose movements Gil had been asking about.

And now he wanted more information. About some scientist.

CHAPTER 4

Yes?" said Ellen, surfacing immediately from a deep sleep. "What is it?"

As she answered her phone, she noted the time. Two thirty-five a.m.

"Madame Secretary," came Charles Boynton's voice. Deep, somber. "There's been an explosion."

She sat up and reached for her glasses. "Where?"

"London."

She felt a guilty wave of relief. Not US soil, at least. But still. She swung her legs out of bed and turned on the light.

"Tell me."

Within forty-five minutes Secretary Adams was in the Situation Room of the White House.

To cut down on confusion and unnecessary noise, only the core of the National Security Council had been called. Ranged around the table were the President, the Vice President, the secretaries of State, Defense, Homeland Security. The Director of National Intelligence and the Chairman of the Joint Chiefs of Staff.

Various aides and the White House Chief of Staff sat in chairs against the wall.

The faces were grim, but not panicked. The Chairman of the Joint Chiefs had been through this before, even if the President and his cabinet had not.

The media was just beginning to report on what had happened. What was happening.

A map of London took up the entire screen at the far end of the room. A red dot, like a splotch of blood, showed the exact location of the explosion.

Along Piccadilly. Just outside Fortnum & Mason, Ellen noted, going through what she knew of London. The Ritz just down the street. Hatchards, the oldest bookshop in London, was lost under the red mark.

"There's no question it was a bomb?" asked President Williams.

"None, Mr. President," said Tim Beecham, the Director of National Intelligence. "We're in constant touch with MI5 and MI6. They're scrambling to get a handle on what happened, but given the destruction, it couldn't be anything else."

"Go on," said President Williams, leaning forward.

"It appears to have been on a bus," said Army General Albert "Bert" Whitehead, the Chair of the Joint Chiefs. His uniform was misbuttoned. His tie hastily thrown around his neck, undone. A loose noose.

But his voice was strong, his eyes clear. His focus complete.

"Appears?" asked Williams.

"The damage is too great to get a precise read right now. It could've been a car bomb or a truck that exploded just as a bus went by. There's debris everywhere, as you can see."

General Whitehead tapped his secure laptop, and a still photo replaced the map. It had been taken from a satellite. The image unexpectedly clear, even from miles in space.

They all leaned toward it.

There was a crater in the middle of the famous street, and around it was littered twisted metal. Smoke rose, suspended, from vehicles; facades of centuries-old buildings that had survived the Blitz had disappeared.

But no bodies, Ellen noticed. Blown, she suspected, into pieces too small to easily identify as human.

The blast zone was only confined by the buildings on either side; otherwise who knew how far out it would have gone.

"My God," whispered the Secretary of Defense. "What did that?"

"Mr. President," said Barbara Stenhauser, "we've just received video."

At a nod, she brought it up. It was taken from one of the tens of thousands of security cameras around London.

There was a time code generator at the bottom right of the picture.

7:17:04

"When did the bomb go off?" President Williams asked.

"Seven seventeen and forty-three seconds, GMT, sir," said General Whitehead.

Ellen Adams brought her hand to her mouth as she watched. It was the beginning of rush hour. The sun was trying to break through the gray March morning.

7:17:20

Men and women were streaming along the sidewalk. Cars, delivery vans, black cabs waited at the stoplight.

As the time counted up. Counted down.

7:17:32

"Run, run," Ellen heard the Secretary of Homeland Security, sitting next to her, whisper. "Run."

But, of course, they didn't.

A bright red double-decker pulled up to a stop.

7:17:39

A young woman stepped aside to let an elderly man on first. He turned to thank her.

7:17:43

They watched over and over, from different angles as more videos came in, projected onto the large screen at the end of the Situation Room.

In the second one, they could see the bus more clearly as it arrived at the stop. The angle allowed them to make out faces. Including a little girl in the front seat of the upper deck. The best seat. The one all the children, including Ellen's own, had rushed for.

Try as she might, Ellen couldn't take her eyes off the girl.

Run. Run.

But of course, in every video, no matter the angle, the little girl remained. And then was gone.

The confirmation, when it came from the UK, was academic. It was clear that this was a bomb. Planted on the bus. Timed to go off at the worst possible moment, in the worst possible place.

Rush hour in central London.

"Has anyone taken responsibility?" President Williams asked.

"Not yet," said the DNI, checking and rechecking his reports.

Information was pouring in now. The key, they all knew, was to manage it. To not let themselves be overwhelmed.

"And no chatter?" asked President Williams.

He looked around the gleaming long table at the shaking heads, stopping at Ellen.

"Nothing," she confirmed. But still he stared at her, as though the failure were hers, and hers alone.

And a simple truth was brought home.

He doesn't trust me, she realized. She probably should have realized it sooner, but she'd been so caught up in trying to get a handle on her new job, she hadn't paused to think.

In her hubris, Ellen Adams had assumed he'd chosen her as his Secretary of State, despite their obvious antagonism, because he knew she'd be good at the job.

Now she saw he not only disliked her, he distrusted her.

So why had he appointed someone he didn't trust to such a powerful position?

And part of the answer was clear, in that room, in that moment.

Because President Douglas Williams hadn't expected an international crisis to hit so early in his, or her, tenure. He hadn't expected to have to trust her.

So what had he expected?

All this came to her in a flash, but she hadn't time to linger on it. There were far more immediate and important concerns.

President Williams dragged his eyes from her and settled on the DNI. "Isn't that unusual?" he asked. "To not hear anything?"

"Not necessarily," said Tim Beecham. "Not if it's a one-off. A lone wolf who blew himself up with the explosion."

"But even so," said Ellen, looking around the table, "don't those people normally want the world to know? Don't they put out a statement, a video, on social media?"

"There is one reason no one has— " General Whitehead began before being interrupted by the President's Chief of Staff.

"Sir, I have the British Prime Minister on the line," said Barb Stenhauser.

Like everyone else there, her clothes had been thrown on. Her grave expression was not masked by makeup. Though no amount could have hidden it.

The carnage on the screen was replaced by the stern face of Prime Minister Bellington, his hair askew, as always.

"Mr. Prime Minister, the American peop—" Douglas Williams began.

"Yes, yes, whatever. You want to know what happened. So do I. And frankly, I have nothing to tell you."

He glared off camera at what they could only guess were representatives of MI5 and MI6. British Intelligence.

"Was there a specific target?" asked Williams.

"Can't tell yet. We've only just been able to confirm that the bomb was on the bus. We have no idea who was on it, or nearby. The passengers and pedestrians were blown to bits. I can send you the video."

"No need," said Williams. "We've seen it."

Bellington raised his brows. It was unclear if he was impressed or annoyed. But he quickly decided to let it go.

The Prime Minister, three years into his first term, was immensely popular with the right wing of his party and the Conservative voting public because he'd promised national security and independence from other nations. This bombing would not help his reelection campaign.

"It'll take a long time to get definite identification," Bellington said. "We're going over the videos to see if facial recognition flags anyone. A possible terrorist, or a target. Any help you can give would be appreciated."

"Could the target have been a building and not a person? Like the 9/11 attacks?" asked the DNI.

"Could be," admitted the Prime Minister. "But there're more obvious targets in London than Fortnum & Mason."

"Though it's possible someone objected to paying a hundred pounds for afternoon tea," said the Secretary of Defense, and looked around the table for appreciative smiles.

There were none.

"But the Royal Academy of Arts is there too," said Ellen.

"Art, Madame Secretary?" said Prime Minister Bellington, turning to her. "You think someone would create such carnage to disrupt an exhibition?"

Ellen tried not to bristle at the patronizing tone, though she admitted that all British accents sounded patronizing to her American ear. When they spoke, she heard an implied *You idiot.*

She heard it now. But he was under pressure and was releasing some of it in her direction. She would allow him that. For now.

And, to be fair, Prime Minister Bellington had been a favorite target of her media outlets for years, painting him as woefully inadequate. A hollow man, an upper-class twit, with any guts he might have had replaced by entitlement and random Latin phrases.

It wasn't surprising he'd look at her like that. In fact, Ellen conceded, he was showing surprising restraint.

"Not just art, Mr. Prime Minister," she said. "There's the Geological Society right there."

"True." His eyes now probing, piercing even. Far more intelligent than she'd thought possible. "You know London well."

"It's one of my favorite cities. This is a terrible, terrible event."

And it was. But the implications might go far beyond the dreadful loss of life and destruction of part of that city's rich history.

"Geology?" said the Secretary of Defense. "Why would anyone want to blow up a place that studies rocks?"

Ellen Adams didn't answer. Instead she looked at the screen, meeting the thoughtful eyes of the British Prime Minister.

"Geology is far more than rocks," he said. "It's oil. Coal. Gold. Diamonds."

Bellington paused there, holding Ellen Adams's eyes, inviting her to do the honors.

"Uranium," she said.

He nodded. "Which can be turned into a nuclear bomb. *Factum fieri infectum non potest.* It's impossible for the deed to be undone,"

Bellington translated himself. "But maybe we can prevent another attack."

"You think there'll be another, Mr. Prime Minister?" asked President Williams.

"I do, sir."

"But where?" muttered the DNI.

When the meeting broke up, Ellen made sure to walk out beside General Whitehead.

"You began to say there was a reason someone might not take responsibility. That is what you were about to say, isn't it?"

He nodded.

The head of the Joint Chiefs of Staff looked more like a librarian than a warrior.

Interestingly, the Librarian of Congress looked like a warrior.

General Whitehead's face was kindly, his voice gentle. His eyes looked at her from behind owlish glasses.

But she knew his record, as a combat soldier. A Ranger. He'd risen through the ranks having led from the front, gaining not just the respect but also the loyalty and trust of the men and women under him.

General Whitehead stopped, letting the others pass by, and studied her. His gaze was searching but not antagonistic.

"What is that reason, General?"

"They didn't claim responsibility, Madame Secretary, because they don't need to. Their goal was, is, something else entirely. Something more important than terror."

She felt the blood run from her face, pooling in her core, her heart.

"And what would that be?" she asked, surprised and relieved to hear her voice more composed than she felt.

"Assassination, maybe. Perhaps it was surgical, to send a message to only one person or group. No announcement necessary. They might know too that their silence would tie up our resources far more effectively than claiming responsibility."

"I'd hardly call what happened in London 'surgical.'"

"True. I meant surgical in terms of purpose. A narrow, defined goal. We see hundreds dead, they might see only one. We see horrific destruction, they see a single building gone. Perception." His hand went to his tie, and he seemed surprised to find it undone. "I can tell you one thing, Secretary Adams. From my experience, the greater the silence, the greater the goal."

"You agree with the Prime Minister, then? That there'll be a second attack?"

"I don't know." He held her eyes, opened his mouth, then closed it.

"You can tell me, General."

He smiled, slightly. "What I do know is that, in strategic terms, this is a pretty great silence."

By the time he finished speaking, the smile was gone. His face grim.

The predator was out there. Somewhere. Hiding in a vast silence.

They didn't have to wait long.

It was closing in on ten in the morning when Ellen Adams returned to her office at the State Department.

There was frantic activity. Before she could even get through the elevator door, she was scrummed by her press aides asking for something they could feed the ravenous media. Once out of the elevator, she was hurried to her office. Men and women ran up and down the corridor, jumping in and out of offices. Not trusting to text messages or even phone calls. There were shouted questions, demands, as aides chased down every possible lead.

"We're talking to all our sources," said Boynton, walking rapidly beside her. "Intelligence organizations internationally are on it. We've also contacted counterterrorism think tanks. Strategic studies departments."

"Anything?"

"Not yet. But someone knows something."

Once at her desk, she went through her contacts list. "I have some names for you. People I've met in my travels. Some journalists. Some gadflies who say little but take in a lot." She forwarded him a series of contact cards. "Use my name. Apologize and explain."

"I will. We need to move to the secure videoconference room. They're waiting."

Once she was there, faces appeared on the screen.

"Welcome, Madame Secretary."

The meeting of the Five Eyes had begun.

Anahita Dahir sat at her desk in the State Department.

Every foreign service officer worldwide had been tasked to forward any intelligence, anything at all, that might have bearing. The place was throbbing with near-frenzied energy as messages were sent and received. Coded and decoded.

Anahita went through the messages that had come in to her desk overnight while also monitoring the news on television.

It felt, more and more, as though journalists had a better network than the CIA or NSA. Or State.

That reminded her of Gil, and she was tempted once again to contact him. To see if he knew anything. But she also suspected this idea came not so much from her brain as considerably farther down. And now was not the time to indulge that.

As a junior FSO on the Pakistan desk, she was not privy to the high-level communications. The more mundane intelligence, from marginal informants, came in to her. Things like where various government ministers had lunch, with whom, and what they ate.

But even those messages had to be read more carefully.

Five Eyes was the name for an alliance of intelligence agencies from Australia, New Zealand, Canada, the UK, and the US. Ellen had not heard of this organization of English-speaking allies until she'd become Secretary of State.

Because of their strategic positions, the Five Eyes essentially covered the planet. But even they had heard nothing. No whispers beforehand. No triumphant declarations in the hours after the explosion.

Secretary Adams was joined on the video call by her cabinet counterparts and their chief intel officers from each country. The five spies and five secretaries quickly, succinctly, shared what they knew. What their networks had picked up. Which was nothing.

"Nothing?" demanded the UK Foreign Secretary. "How's that possible? Hundreds are dead. Many more injured. Central London looks like the Blitz. This wasn't a firecracker, this was a goddamned fucking massive bomb."

"Look, Your Lordship," the Australian Foreign Minister said, putting undue emphasis on the last word. "There's nothing. We've gone back over intel out of Russia, the Middle East, Asia. We're continuing to dig, but so far only silence."

A great silence, thought Ellen, remembering the General's words.

"It has to have been a single nutjob with expertise and a grievance," said the New Zealand Foreign Minister.

"Agreed," said the CIA Director, who was the US Eye. "If it was an FTO, like Al-Qaeda or ISIS—"

"Al-Shabaab," said the New Zealand Eye.

"The Pathan—" said the Australian Eye.

"Are you going to list them all?" asked the UK Foreign Secretary. "Because time is not on our side."

"The point is—" the Australian Eye began.

"Yes, what is the point?" demanded the UK Foreign Secretary.

"All right," the Canadian Eye jumped in. "Enough. Let's not turn on each other. We all know the point. If any one of the hundreds of known terrorist organizations set off the bomb, they'd have taken responsibility by now."

"And the unknown?" asked the US Eye. "Suppose a new one has sprung up?"

"Well, they don't just spring up, do they?" said the New Zealand Eye. She turned to her Australian counterpart for support.

"A new one that managed to pull this off," said the Australian Eye, "wouldn't remain unknown for long. They'd be shouting it from the rooftops."

"Is it possible," Secretary Adams said, "that no one has taken responsibility because they don't need to?"

All Eyes and eyes turned to her as though surprised an empty chair had learned to talk. The UK Foreign Secretary huffed his annoyance that the new American Secretary of State would waste their time by thinking she had anything worthwhile to say.

The US Eye looked embarrassed.

Ellen forged ahead, explaining what General Whitehead had said. The fact it came from a General and the head of the Joint Chiefs of Staff meant they gave it far more credibility than if she'd made the suggestion herself. Ellen didn't care. She didn't need their approval or their respect, just their attention.

"Madame Secretary," said the UK Foreign Secretary, "the whole point of a terrorist is to spread terror. Staying schtum isn't part of the playbook."

"Yes, thank you," said Ellen.

"Maybe they're fans of Alfred Hitchcock," said the Canadian Eye.

"Yes, yes," said the UK Foreign Secretary. "Or Monty Python. Let's move on—"

"What do you mean?" Ellen asked the Canadian.

"I mean that Hitchcock knew that the closed door is much more frightening than the open. Think of when you were a kid, at night. Staring at the closet door. Wondering what was really in there. We filled the void with our imaginations. And we almost never thought that it was a kind fairy holding a puppy and some pudding." She paused, and it seemed to Ellen that she looked straight at her. "Those with a truly catastrophic agenda never let us open the door. It opens when they're ready to release it. Your General is right, Madame Secretary. The true nature of terror is the unknown. The truly terrible thrives in silence."

Ellen felt herself grow very, very still, very quiet. And then the silence was shattered. Ellen jolted in her chair as all their encrypted phones went off at once.

On the UK screen, they could see an aide say something in the Foreign Secretary's ear.

"Oh Christ," he whispered, then turned to the screen, stricken, just as Boynton bent down next to Ellen Adams.

"Madame Secretary, there's been an explosion in Paris."

CHAPTER 5

The flight landed at the Frankfurt airport ten minutes late, but still with plenty of time to make the bus connection.

As the plane taxied to the terminal, Nasrin Bukhari checked her watch and reset it to 4:03 in the afternoon. She didn't dare carry a phone, even a burner. She couldn't take the risk.

Nuclear physicists, she'd often told her schoolteacher husband, were by nature extremely risk-averse. Which made him laugh and point out that there was no more risky work than what she did.

It also made what she was doing now so far out of her comfort zone she might as well be on another planet.

Or in Frankfurt.

Around her in the plane, as fellow passengers turned on their phones, there were murmurs, then moans, then cries. Something had happened.

Not daring to speak with anyone, Dr. Bukhari waited until she was inside the terminal, then went to one of the television monitors. A crowd had gathered, and she was too far back to hear what was being said, even if she could have understood the language.

But she could see the images. And read the crawl at the bottom of the screen.

London. Paris. Scenes of near-apocalyptic destruction. She stared, paralyzed. Wishing Amir were there. Not to tell her what to do, but to slip his hand in hers. So she wouldn't be alone.

This was, she knew, a coincidence. Nothing to do with her. Couldn't be.

And yet, as she backed away and turned, she caught the eye of the young man who'd gotten off the plane with her and now stood a few feet away.

Not watching the screen. Not looking at the scenes of carnage. He was looking at her with, she was pretty sure, recognition. And contempt.

"Sit down," commanded President Williams, looking up briefly from his notes, then back down.

Ellen Adams took the chair across from him in the Oval Office. It was still warm from the head, or bottom, of the DNI.

Behind her, the bank of monitors was tuned to different channels, all with either talking heads or shots of the atrocities.

In the car on the way over, sirens howling on the Diplomatic Security escort, Ellen had read the brutally short messages from international intelligence agencies. Most asking for, begging for, not offering, information.

"There'll be a full cabinet meeting in twenty minutes," said Williams, taking off his glasses and staring at her. "But I need to get a handle on what's happened, and whether we're at risk. Are we?"

"I don't know, Mr. President."

His lips thinned, and even across the Resolute desk, she could hear his long intake of breath. He was trying, she suspected, to inhale his anger.

But it was far too great to be contained. Out it shot, in a cloud of spittle and rage.

"What the fffffuck do you mean?"

The words, the word, exploded out of him. Ellen had heard it many times, but never had it been directed at her with such force. Or unfairness.

Though this was not a day to parse fairness.

His shout was propelled by fear, that much she knew, even as she forced herself not to wipe the moisture from her face.

She was afraid too. But his was magnified by the certainty that if he wasn't careful, wasn't fast enough and smart enough, the next images would be of New York or Washington. Chicago or Los Angeles.

Just weeks into the job, still trying to find his way back to the White House bowling alley, and this happened. Worse. He was saddled with a new administration. Smart men and women, but without depth in this arena.

And, worse still, he'd inherited a bureaucracy crippled by, populated by, the incompetents of the previous administration.

He wasn't just afraid. The President of the United States had been thrust into a near-perpetual state of terror. And he wasn't alone.

"I can tell you, Mr. President, what we know. I can give you facts, not speculation."

He glared at her. His most political of appointments. And that made her the weakest link in a very weak chain.

On her lap she balanced a dossier, which she now opened. Adjusting her glasses, she read, "The Paris blast occurred at three thirty-six local time. It was on a bus headed along the Faubourg Saint-Denis in the Tenth—"

"Yes, I know all that. The world knows all that." He gestured toward the bank of television screens. "Tell me something I don't know. Something that will help."

The second explosion was less than twenty minutes old. They hadn't had time to collect information, she wanted to say. But he knew that too.

Now she took off her glasses, rubbed her eyes, and looked at him.

"I have nothing."

The air crackled with his rage.

"Nothing?" he rasped.

"You want me to lie?"

"I want you to be something close to competent."

Ellen took a deep breath and searched her mind for something to say that wouldn't enrage him further. And waste precious time.

"Every allied intelligence agency is going over posts, over messages. They're scouring the dark web for hidden sites. We're examining video to see if we can identify either the bomber or a possible target. So far, in London, we've identified one possible target."

"That is?"

"The Geological Society." As she spoke, she saw the face of the girl. In the upper window. Looking forward, down Piccadilly. Looking into a future that didn't exist.

President Williams was about to speak. To say, Ellen could see, something dismissive, when he stopped to think. Then nodded.

"And Paris?"

"Paris is interesting. We'd have expected an explosion to be at a known site. The Louvre, Notre-Dame. The President's residence."

Williams leaned forward. Interested.

"But the number 38 bus was nowhere near any likely target. It was just going along a wide avenue. Not even that many people around it. It wasn't rush hour. There doesn't seem to be a reason for it. And yet there was."

"Could the bomb have gone off by mistake?" he asked. "Too soon or too late?"

"It's possible, yes. But we're developing another theory. The number 38 bus goes to several train stations. In fact, it was on its way to the Gare du Nord when it blew up."

"Gare du Nord. That's where the Eurostar from London comes in," he said.

Douglas Williams was proving smarter than Ellen had assumed. Or at least better traveled.

"Exactly."

"You think there was someone on that bus heading to London?"

"It's a possibility. We're going over video from each of the stops, but Paris isn't nearly as well covered by CCTV as London."

"You'd have thought after what happened in 2015 . . . ," said Williams. "Anything more out of London?"

"Not yet. No hits on a possible target of assassination, and unfortunately almost everyone getting on the bus was carrying a package or a knapsack or something that could be an explosive. In addition to the regular channels, I've asked my former colleagues at the news agencies to pass along what their journalists and informants have heard."

There was a pause before the President spoke. It went on just long enough for Barbara Stenhauser to look over from the sofa, where she was monitoring both the conversation and the deluge of information.

"Does that include your son?" said Williams. "From what I remember, he's well-connected."

The air between them froze. Any fragile entente that had been reached cracked, then shattered.

"I don't think, Mr. President, you want to bring my son into this."

"And I don't think, Madame Secretary, you want to ignore a direct question from your Commander-in-Chief."

"He doesn't work for any of my former outlets."

"That wasn't the question, or the issue." Williams's voice was brittle. "He's your son. He has contacts. Given what happened a few years ago, he might know something."

"I remember what happened, Mr. President." If his tone was brittle, hers was positively glacial. "I don't need a reminder."

They glared at each other. Barb Stenhauser knew she should probably interrupt. Bring civility back to the conversation. Return it to something useful and constructive.

But she did not. She was curious to see where this would go. If it wasn't constructive, it might at least prove instructive.

"He'd tell me if he knew anything about the bombings."

"Would he?"

The wound between them had opened to a chasm. And both, teetering on the edge, fell headlong in.

Barb Stenhauser had assumed the President disliked Ellen Adams because she'd used her formidable media might to support his rival for the party nomination. In the process, she'd humiliated Doug Williams at every opportunity. Belittling him, painting him as incompetent, manipulative. Unready.

A coward.

She'd even created a contest, inviting readers to come up with anagrams for his name.

Doug Williams became "Aglow Dim Luis." And, after his loss in the Iowa caucus, "Glum Iowa Slid."

The anagrams still followed President Williams around, muttered in stage whispers by his political enemies. Of which Ellen Adams had been one. And it seemed her elevation to Secretary of State might not have changed anything.

"Al Go Mud Swill."

Now Stenhauser realized she'd been so focused on her boss, she hadn't stopped to wonder why Adams disliked Williams so much.

Watching them, she realized she'd underestimated the feelings. It wasn't mere dislike. It wasn't even anger that filled the Oval Office. It was a hatred so strong the Chief of Staff half expected the windows to be blown out by the force of it.

Now she wondered what they were remembering. What had happened a few years ago?

"Contact him," President Williams all but snarled. "Now. Or you're fired."

"I don't have his coordinates." Ellen felt her cheeks burn as she admitted that. "We're not in touch."

"Get in touch."

Asking the head of her Diplomatic Security detail, who was standing just outside the door, for her phone, she sent a message to Betsy. Asking her to contact her son and see if he had any information, anything at all, on the bombings.

Within moments a reply came in.

"Let me see it," said Williams, holding his hand out.

Ellen hesitated, then gave him her phone. He looked at the message, his brows drawing together.

"What does it mean?"

It was her turn to hold her hand out for the phone. "It's a code my counselor and I use. One we worked out as children, to make sure we are who we say we are."

On the screen were the words: *A non sequitur walks into a bar . . .*

He gave back her phone, muttering, "Intellectual bullshit."

Ignorant ass, thought Ellen as she typed, *In a strong wind, even turkeys can fly.* Then she placed the phone on the desk. "It might take a while. I don't know where he is. He could be anywhere in the world."

"He could be in Paris," said Williams.

"Are you suggesting—"

"Mr. President," said Stenhauser. "It's time for the cabinet meeting."

Anahita Dahir glanced up now and then to see the images, but mostly to read the crawl at the bottom of the television screen on the wall of the large open office. She wanted to see if the reporters had more information than she did, which would not be difficult.

The first bomb, in London, had gone off at 2:17 that morning. The second bomb, in Paris, less than an hour ago, at 9:36.

But as she watched the scenes, the endless loop of the bombs exploding, Anahita realized that didn't make sense. It was light in London, so it couldn't have been in the middle of the night. And in Paris, it didn't look like rush hour.

Then she shook her head and muttered to herself, realizing her mistake. The American news nets had translated the time to US eastern time. The time in Europe would have been . . .

She did the quick calculations, adding the necessary hours, then sat stock-still. Staring ahead.

And then, to her horror, she saw what should have been obvious.

Anahita started sweeping papers off her desk.

"What're you doing?" the FSO at the next desk asked. "Something wrong?"

But Anahita wasn't listening; she was muttering to herself, "Please, oh please, oh please."

And there it was.

She clutched the piece of paper. But her hands were shaking so badly she had to place it on the desk to read it.

It was the message that had come in the night before. The code. Grabbing it, she ran to her supervisor's office, but he wasn't there.

"In meetings," said his assistant.

"Where? I need to see him. It's urgent."

The assistant knew how junior the FSO was and looked unconvinced. She pointed up, toward heaven, or the next thing to it, the seventh-floor Mahogany Row offices. "Look, you know what's happening. I'm not going to interrupt a meeting with the Chief of Staff."

"You have to. It's about a message that came in last night. Please."

The assistant hesitated, then seeing the near panic on the young woman's face, she placed a call. "I'm sorry, sir, but Anahita Dahir is here. Junior FSO on the Pakistan desk, yes. She says she has a message, something that came in last night." The assistant listened, then looked at Anahita. "Is it the one you showed the supervisor?"

"Yes, yes."

"Yes, sir." She listened, acknowledged, then hung up. "He says he'll speak with you when he gets back."

"When will that be?"

"Who knows."

"No. No, no, no. He has to see this now."

"Then leave it with me. I'll show him when he returns."

Anahita clutched it to her body. "No. I will."

She returned to her desk and looked down at it again.

19/0717, 38/1536

The numbers of the buses that had exploded, and the exact times.

It wasn't code. It was a warning.

And there was one more.

119/1848

A number 119 bus was going to explode at 6:48 that evening. If it was in America, they had eight hours.

If it was in Europe . . . She looked at the bank of clocks showing different times in different zones.

It was already four thirty in much of Europe. They had just over two hours.

Anahita Dahir had been raised to do as she was told. A good Lebanese girl, she followed rules. Had all her life. It wasn't just drilled into her; it came naturally.

She hesitated. She could wait. Should wait. Had been ordered to wait. Except it couldn't wait. And they didn't know what she did. Orders based on ignorance could not be legitimate. Could they?

She took a picture of the numbers, then sat for a moment staring at them. Another moment. And another. The seconds hands on all the clocks around the walls, all the time zones around the world, ticked. Ticked. As the planet counted down.

Tick. Tick.

Admonishing her for her indecision. Tsk. Tsk.

Then Anahita Dahir stood up so quickly her chair fell over. The activity in the large room was so frantic only the FSO next to her noticed.

"Ana, are you all right?"

But she was speaking to Anahita's back as she headed for the door.

CHAPTER 6

Nasrin Bukhari watched as the number 61 bus from the airport into downtown Frankfurt drew up.

It was clear now that the man was following her. But there seemed little she could do about it. She almost certainly couldn't shake him. She just had to hope that, once she reached her destination, the people there would know what to do.

She was close now. Against all odds, she'd gotten this far. How she wished she could call Amir. Hear his voice. Tell him she was safe, and hear that he was too.

She took her seat and allowed herself to glance back. There he was, a few rows behind.

So intent was she on the now familiar man, Nasrin failed to notice the other one.

Anahita waited by the bank of elevators. Just one opened directly to Mahogany Row. Paneled, not surprisingly, in mahogany, it could be entered only with a special key.

There was no other way up, and Anahita certainly did not have the key. Or the clearance.

But the woman waiting for the elevator almost certainly did. She was bent over her phone, typing quickly and looking stressed.

Everyone looked stressed, from the security guards to the senior officials.

Anahita turned her ID around so her name could not be seen, and hurried over with a determined step. She stopped and, looking at the closed door, heaved a sigh of impatience and muttered something under her breath.

Then she took out her own phone and looked intently at it, trying to appear focused. Head down. Absorbed.

"Excuse me—" the other woman began, clearly wondering who this stranger was. And why she wanted to go to the seventh floor.

Anahita looked up and raised her hand as if to say, *Just give me a moment.* Then went back to her apparently vital message.

To make it look legit, she typed, *Where are you? Have you heard the news?*

The elevator arrived, and the woman, now back on her phone, got on, with Anahita following.

Everyone frantic here, she continued to write as the elevator doors closed. *Any thoughts?*

Once on, they were whisked up to the seventh floor.

Gil Bahar's phone vibrated with an incoming message.

Shifting in his seat, he read it; then, annoyed, he clicked his phone off without replying. He didn't have time for this bullshit.

A few minutes later, as the bus left the station and it was safe to take his eyes off his target, he opened the phone again and sent a quick reply.

In Frankfurt on bus. More later.

Betsy forwarded the reply, without comment, just as Ellen was going into the cabinet meeting.

She read it, then surrendered her phone to the Secret Service agent at the door, where it joined the others in cubbyholes.

As Secretary Adams entered the room, a few cabinet colleagues looked at her and said, "Dirty woman."

She smiled, acknowledging the joke. Some, she knew, were laughing with her. Others at her.

The phrase had gone viral, and "Dirty Woman" had quickly been adopted and co-opted by women's groups as a rallying cry against toxic masculinity.

Looking around the table, Ellen would hardly call any of her colleagues particularly toxic.

What they were, she knew, was a collection of some of the finest minds the country had produced. In finance, in education, in health care. In national security.

None had been tainted by the absurdity of the previous four years. But as a result, none had recent experience at the highest level of governance. They were smart, some even brilliant, committed, well-meaning, and hardworking. But there was not a depth of knowledge, an institutional memory. Contacts and vital connections hadn't yet been made. Trust had not yet been forged between this administration and the world outside these walls.

It still had to be established within the walls, for God's sake.

The previous administration had purged anybody who criticized policy. It punished dissenting voices. It silenced all critics, from Senators to members of Congress, from cabinet secretaries to chiefs of staff to janitors.

Total loyalty to President Dunn and his decisions, no matter how ego-driven and uninformed and outright dangerous they were, had been demanded.

Competence was replaced by blind loyalty as the determining factor for employment by an increasingly deranged administration.

Secretary Adams, on entering as SecState, had quickly realized there was no such thing as the Deep State. There was nothing "deep" about it. Nothing hidden. Career employees and political appointees wandered the halls and sat in meetings and shared bathrooms and tables in the cafeterias.

Those left behind by the Dunn administration had the thousand-yard stare of combatants finally detached from the horrors around them. The horrors they themselves had perpetrated.

And now, one month in, this crisis happened.

"Ellen," said President Williams, turning to his Secretary of State on his left, "what can you tell us?"

Looking at his smug expression as he lobbed the grenade at her, Ellen knew that not all the viciousness came from the opposition.

Not everyone wanted to heal old wounds.

Anahita allowed the other woman off first, holding her hand out and saying with both deference and confidence, "Please."

Please. Please.

She paused at the elevator, supposedly to read another vital message, but in reality to give the woman time to disappear into a room.

Then she looked down the long hallway.

Tick, tick, tick.

The famous Mahogany Row. It looked like she'd alighted into some men's club in New York or London. The corridor in front of her was wide and dark-paneled, the portraits of former Secretaries lining the walls. Anahita could almost smell the cigars.

What she actually smelled was the slightly cloying scent of the oriental lilies in an exuberant arrangement on a gleaming side table partway down the corridor.

Mahogany Row was magnificent. It was meant to be magnificent. To impress visitors, both foreign and domestic. It spoke of power and permanence.

Two Diplomatic Security agents stood on either side of tall double doors halfway down Mahogany Row. The SecState's office, Anahita guessed.

That she did not want. She needed the conference room. But which of the doors was it? She could hardly open all of them.

The agents were beginning to turn in her direction.

Anahita made a decision. This was not the time to be her mother's daughter. Or her father's. This was the time to be someone else.

She decided to channel Linda Matar, her personal hero.

Clicking her phone off and leaving it with security, she walked decisively down the corridor, straight to the agents.

"I'm an FSO from the Pakistan desk. I've been told to deliver a message to my supervisor in person. Where can I find the conference room?"

"Your badge, ma'am?"

Ma'am?

Turning it around, she showed it to him.

"You shouldn't be on this floor."

"Yes, I know. But I've been told to deliver a message. Look, frisk me, stay with me, do whatever, but I need to deliver the message. Now."

Tick, tick, tick.

The officers exchanged glances. At a nod from the senior of the two, the female agent gave Anahita a quick pat-down, then walked with her down the corridor to a door without a number or a plate.

Anahita knocked. Once. Twice. Louder. Harder.

Linda Matar. Breathe. Linda Matar. Breathe.

The door flew open. "Yes," demanded a lean, ferret-faced young man. "What is it?"

"I need to speak with Daniel Holden. My name is Anahita Dahir. I'm in his bureau. I have a message for him."

"We're in a meeting. He can't be dist—"

Linda Matar.

Anahita pushed past him.

"Hey," he shouted.

All faces around the table turned. Anahita stopped and put her arms out in a gesture of surrender. Showing she meant no harm. She scanned the faces for—

"What the hell are you doing here?" Daniel Holden stood up, glaring at her.

"The message."

The agents closed in on her, just as her boss said, "I know her. It's all right." Then he focused on Anahita. "I know you believe your message is important. Everything today is important, including, especially, what we're discussing. You need to leave. I'll speak with you later."

His tone was calm but firm.

Linda Matar would not stand to be patronized.

But Anahita Dahir was not actually her. She nodded, her face burning, and backed up. "I'm sorry, sir."

Then, pushing past her mother and father and her need to please, Anahita turned, grabbed his hand, and shoved the crumpled paper into it.

"Read it. For God's sake, read it. There's going to be another attack."

He watched as Anahita was rushed out the door, tempted to call her back. Then, glancing at the paper, he saw there was no mention of another attack, just numbers and symbols. The FSO was just another panicked junior operative, trying to make herself more important than she was. He didn't have time for that now.

Placing the paper in his jacket pocket and resolving to look at it later, he returned to his seat, apologizing for the interruption.

Tick, tick, tick.

Outside, security escorted Anahita down the hall to the elevator and watched her leave.

Anahita returned to her desk several floors below, knowing she'd failed.

By the look on her supervisor's face, she knew he wouldn't read the message. Not in time, anyway.

Well, she'd tried. She'd done her best.

She looked at the screens, the scenes from Paris and London. Of wounded men and women, covered in ash and dust and blood. Of passersby trying to staunch unstaunchable wounds. Kneeling down and holding the hands of the dying. Looking up. Seeking help.

They were scenes of terrible destruction, of carnage. The endless loop of CCTV footage of men and women, Prometheus-like, being murdered over and over.

There were just over two hours left before the next explosion, if that message, that warning, was to be believed.

There was, Anahita knew, one more thing she could try. Something she was loath to do, but now had to.

Going on Facebook, she found a former classmate. And from him, she got another name, and from her, another.

Until, twenty precious minutes later, she had the one she needed. The one she loathed.

Secretary Adams left the cabinet meeting early and was driven, for what felt like the hundredth time since she'd been roused from bed at 2:35 that morning, between the White House and Foggy Bottom.

Once at State, she went directly to the Secretary's private conference room, where she was joined by Charles Boynton, her Chief of Staff, and other aides.

Calls were put through to contacts, to counterparts, to security analysts.

Faced with a vacuum of information, the hive mind that was the cabinet had decided there would not be another attack. And if there was, it probably wouldn't be on American soil.

So, while tragic, this was not a matter of national security. They would help their allies in any way possible, but what they needed to project to the American people was confidence that they were secure.

When pressed by Ellen, her head of State's Bureau of Intelligence and Research said they had no proof either way, but that since no organization had taken responsibility, it seemed reasonable to assume the two explosions were by lone wolves working in unison.

"How is that possible?" Ellen had asked. "By definition, lone wolves don't work in unison."

"Maybe it was a small pack."

"Ahhh," she said, and decided not to waste time or breath on this.

Now, as she sat in the private conference room, listening to reports revealing nothing new, she wondered how big a mistake it had been to leave the cabinet meeting.

At that level of politics, Ellen Adams was appreciating, if you weren't at the table, you were on the menu.

But let them do their worst. This was the table she needed to be at.

"Get the Director of National Intelligence on the line," she said. "I have some questions."

CHAPTER
7

The first bomb had only gone off a few hours earlier, but already accountants were sitting in Katherine Adams's office, warning her of their own looming crisis.

"We can't just wire money to our overseas bureaus willy-nilly," the head of accounting for International Media Corp was explaining. "We need justification. At this rate, we'll have sent a million dollars by noon."

"Willy-nilly?" demanded Katherine's head of the news division. "Have you pulled your head out of your ass long enough to notice . . ." He waved at the silent monitors streaming the grisly images broadcasting on IMC stations domestically and internationally. "Isn't that justification enough? My journalists need support, and that comes in the form of money. Now."

"If we could get receipts— " one of the accountants began.

"Right. Written in blood work for you?" he yelled.

They both looked at Katherine, exasperated.

She'd only been the CEO for a couple months, and this was her first real test. But she'd been raised in a media family, watching her mother navigate journalistic issues, political issues. Fairness issues. Juggling egos and personalities, which loomed large in both journalists and politicians. Often blotting out the sun. And reason.

All this had been discussed with her parents at the dinner table. All her life. She had apprenticed for this job. All her life.

While her half brother took after his own father and was the journalist, she took after their mother and was the manager.

But nothing had prepared her for managing this. What she had learned was the art of looking confident when all she wanted was to duck and cover under the desk and let someone else make decisions.

"We have to remain rational," the head accountant appealed to her. "If we're audited and we have no proof of where the money went . . ."

"What will happen?" demanded the journalist. "Will you be blown up? You don't seem to understand. Journalists are on the front line. They're getting information on these bombs faster than intelligence agencies. And how do they do it? By asking politely? By saying please and thank you? By offering milk and— "

"I get the point, but you need to impress on your journalists that this isn't their money. They need to be grown up— "

He looked at Katherine Adams.

Say something, thought Katherine. *Take charge. For God's sake, say something.*

"Grown up? Do you have any idea what it takes to cover wars, insurgencies," said the chief journalist. "To spend years grooming contacts in terrorist organizations, never mind the intelligence agencies, which can be far scarier. It takes two things. Courage and money. They provide the courage, since you have none of that to offer, and you can at least provide the money. Now."

He turned to Katherine in frustration. "You explain. I'm leaving."

The room shuddered as the door slammed shut behind him. The accountants turned to Katherine and waited. And waited.

"Just do it," she said.

"We're bleeding money, Katherine."

Katherine looked over his shoulder, at the bank of monitors. At the scenes in London and Paris. Then she refocused on the chief accountant. A lifelong friend of the family.

"Do it."

When he'd gathered his papers and people and left, she looked at the email from her mother. She'd copied Katherine on her request to the head of news to share with the State Department any information their journalists gathered that might help.

Before it went to air.

Katherine hadn't asked the head of news if he planned to do it. And the head of news had not volunteered to tell her.

Best to not be seen trying to influence. Or be influenced.

What was clear was that her mother was throwing a wide net, trying to get as much information as possible. There'd even been the rumor, broadcast on their all-news channel, that Secretary Adams had reached out to her immediate predecessors, asking for any insight they might have.

That was alternately interpreted by the pundits as a bold initiative by a SecState who could put aside ego and party for the sake of the country or, alternatively, a stupid waste of time by a desperate and incompetent Secretary of State way out of her depth.

There was a knock; then Katherine's door opened and her assistant entered, along with a blast of frantic activity. "You might want to see this. It came in on your old email address." She handed the phone to her boss. "Looks like she knew you from school."

"I don't have time—"

"She works at the State Department now."

"Great, thanks."

When her assistant left, Katherine glanced at the message. It was short. Abrupt even.

We were at high school together. I need to speak to you. It was signed, *Anahita Dahir, FSO, South-Central Asia Bureau, Department of State.*

Katherine sat back in her chair. She remembered an Ana Dab-something. Mousy little girl who'd rat on anyone who smoked or toked, who tried to sneak in late or cheat on an exam.

A teacher's pet who even the teachers despised.

They'd taken pleasure tossing balls at her, not to her, in basketball. Tripping her in soccer. Hitting her shins in field hockey.

Not bullying. It was payback. Not punishment, the young Katherine Adams knew. It was a consequence. Ana Dab-something brought it on herself.

But now, fifteen years on, Katherine Adams knew something else. It had been cruel.

What in the world could Ana want with Katherine now? Today of all days.

She hit reply and asked for Ana's number. It appeared in seconds. She placed the call, and it was immediately picked up.

"Ana?"

"Katie?"

"Listen, Ana, I've been meaning to try to get in touch for a while. I'm sorry—"

"Be quiet and listen," said Ana. Katherine's brows shot up. This was not the Ana Dab-something she remembered. "I need to speak to your mother."

"What? Where are you? Is that a toilet?"

It was.

As soon as she'd received Katherine's email, Anahita had left her desk and gone to the women's bathroom. She was in a stall and had flushed the toilet to cover her words.

"I'm begging you. Can you get me in to your mother?"

"Why? What's this about? Is it to do with the bombings?"

Anahita knew she'd be asked, and knew that Katie, now Katherine, Adams had taken over from her mother as head of the massive and powerful news organization.

The last thing Ana wanted was to have what she knew leaked all over the news.

"I can't tell you."

"Well, you're gonna," said Katherine. "I'm not sure even I can get in to see her. Why should I get you in?"

"Because you owe me."

"What? I owe you an apology, which I've tried to give. And I am sorry. But I don't owe you this."

"Please. Please. I have something she needs to see."

"What?"

Flush. "I'm not going to"—flush—"tell you!"

Flush.

"Oh, for God's sake, before you empty the Potomac, meet me outside the State building, 21st Street entrance, northeast corner."

"Be quick."

"Yeah, well, now I have to go to the bathroom."

Tick. Tick.

Anahita looked at her phone. She'd set her alarm to go off at 12:48 p.m, 1848 in Europe. When the bomb would go off.

Her phone said 12:01. A minute past noon. They had forty-seven minutes.

"Ana?"

Anahita turned and saw a vaguely familiar woman running across the street. She wore an on-point tweed coat, boots that looked like they were made for riding. She had long chestnut hair and deep brown eyes.

The grown woman to the girl Ana had last seen turning her back on her that last day of school.

Katherine saw almost exactly the same girl she'd last seen fifteen years earlier, sucking up to the principal on the last day of school. Without purpose, but just because.

Prettier than Katherine remembered. Her long hair jet-black, her skin tawny and clear. Her brown eyes as intense as ever. But now they held a confidence, a determination that hadn't been there before.

"Katie?" said Anahita. "Thank you for meeting me."

"What do you have?"

Anahita hesitated. "I can't tell you. You have to trust me."

"I can't just get you in. Can you imagine what my mother's up against? To interrupt her—"

"I know exactly what Secretary Adams is up against. Even better than she does. Look, I have information." When Katie looked not just skeptical but concerned that she was dealing with a madwoman or worse, Anahita said, "Have you ever known me to be anything but straight? Too straight sometimes. I never lie. I never cheat. I never break the rules. I've tried to show this information to my supervisor, but I don't think he's taking it seriously. Please."

Katherine looked at the face in front of her. There was real fear there. She took a deep breath, then exhaled, and bringing out her phone, she sent a message.

A moment later there was a ding.

"Come on. We can at least get up to the seventh, but I can't guarantee my mother will see you."

Ana hurried after, her shorter legs taking two quick steps to Katherine's one.

Tick. Tick.

An older woman met them in the lobby. She looked like Mrs. Cleaver from the *Leave It to Beaver* reruns Anahita watched on late-night television when she couldn't sleep.

"This is my mother's closest friend and now counselor," said Katherine. "Betsy Jameson, Ana Dab—umm—"

"Dahir."

"I have your passes." Betsy handed them out. "What the hell is this about? You've chosen a shitty time to visit."

Anahita raised her brows. Mrs. Cleaver's script seemed to have changed.

"I don't know what this's about," Katherine admitted as they followed Betsy to the wood-paneled elevator that was waiting for them in the lobby. "She won't tell me."

Only when the doors whisked closed and there was no turning back did Anahita remember the two security agents and prayed there'd been a shift change.

She looked at her phone.

Forty-one minutes left.

Gil stood in line at the bus terminal, no longer bothering to hide. In fact, he wanted her to see him. To know. To feel that hot breath.

By now the woman certainly knew he was following her. But he also knew she could not deviate from her plan. And neither could he.

Nasrin let two buses come and go. When the third pulled up, she got on. Holding Amir's worn satchel tight to her chest, she inhaled his musky scent.

The leather case was, she now admitted, almost certainly all she had left of him. They'd risked everything to get it, and her, out.

She'd lost everything. He'd lost more.

But with that came an unexpected calm, and freedom. The worst had happened. She was no longer afraid.

Nasrin settled into the back corner. She could, at least, watch him this time, instead of the other way around.

Gil got on and sat across and one row down from her.

The other man sat, unnoticed, immediately in front of Nasrin.

And then the number 119 bus pulled out.

"Halt!"

Anahita did.

"What the hell is this?" demanded Betsy. "She's my guest. Let her by."

"Do you know this woman?" the female agent demanded, her hand resting on her gun.

"Of course I do," Mrs. Cleaver lied. "And do you know her?" Betsy pointed to Katherine.

The agents nodded.

"Good. Let us through."

Anahita's heart was pounding so hard she thought they could surely see it throbbing through her thick winter coat.

The woman agent glared at her, then nodded. One firm jerk of her head.

"Thank you," said Anahita, though that only seemed to further infuriate the agent.

They entered the outer office. It was not at all what Anahita had imagined. She'd expected more dark paneling. Large leather chairs. Some thick-pile rug that looked impressive, if not examined too closely.

Like so much else in government, she was learning something new every day. Magnificent, if you didn't get too close.

But Secretary Adams's waiting room was not like that at all. It was worse.

There was scaffolding. Tarps. The worn and patched wood floor was exposed and covered in a layer of plaster dust. It was a construction site. Secretary Adams was remaking the office of the Secretary of State. In every way.

"Wait here," said Betsy. "You"—she pointed at Katherine—"come with me."

"Hurry, please," said Anahita.

Betsy stopped, turned, and Anahita expected some sharp reply. Instead she saw a tired, worried, sympathetic face.

"We will. You can relax, you've done it. You're in. Secretary Adams will be with you in a moment."

Anahita watched Betsy and Katherine disappear into the next room.

She did not relax. Mrs. Cleaver meant well, but she didn't know what Anahita knew.

She checked her phone.

Thirty-eight minutes left.

The bus bumped along toward the far side of Frankfurt, stopping to let men and women and children off.

To let men and women and children on.

CHAPTER 8

Ellen Adams appeared with her Chief of Staff hard on her heels.

Anahita's eyes involuntarily widened. She'd only ever seen the Secretary at a distance or on television.

She was taller than Anahita had thought. But just as intense.

"You have information?" said Secretary Adams, walking right up to her.

"Here."

Anahita shoved her phone at the Secretary of State, who took it, looked, then passed the phone to Boynton.

"What is that?" Ellen demanded.

"A photograph I took of a message that came in to my station last night. I'm an FSO on the—"

"Pakistan desk, yes. What does it mean?"

"This's a waste of time, Madame Secretary," said Boynton, holding up the phone. "She's a junior FSO. We have senior intelligence staff in the boardroom, waiting. She"—he gestured toward Anahita—"can't possibly know anything our intelligence service doesn't."

Ellen rounded on him. "Which, from all I've heard, is nothing. She can hardly do worse." She turned back to the junior FSO. "Explain."

Anahita grabbed the phone from Boynton and stepped beside Secretary Adams, leaning into her. Their shoulders touching.

"Look at the numbers, Madame Secretary."

"I am—" Ellen began, then fell silent as the numbers separated and regrouped and formed something terrifying.

The thing in the closet. The thing under the bed. The thing down the dark alley that no amount of singing could drive away.

All the unimaginable horrors came together, in those figures.

"They're the bus routes and times of the two previous explosions," said Ellen. "And there's a third." Her voice was barely more than a whisper, as though anything louder would set it off. "This was sent to you last night?"

"Yes."

"What?" demanded Boynton, stepping forward to look.

Betsy and Katherine also crowded around.

Then Boynton, Betsy, and Katherine spoke at once, but Ellen put up her hands for silence.

"Where will it happen?" she asked.

"I don't know."

"Who sent it?"

"I don't know."

"Great," said Boynton. No one was listening to him. Or appeared to be listening.

But Secretary Adams took it in and filed it away with the rest of his behavior.

"If I had to guess, I'd say the next target is also in Europe," said Anahita.

Ellen gave a quick, decisive nod. "Agreed. Since we have to narrow it down, that seems reasonable. If that's the case—" She checked the time and did the calculations. "Oh God." She looked at Betsy. "There're twenty-four minutes left."

Betsy, lost for words, blanched.

"Come with me," said Ellen.

They followed her into her private conference room. All the chairs were occupied, and all eyes turned to them.

Secretary Adams explained succinctly what they had and what was about to happen.

"I want this code sent to every allied intelligence organization. And I want a list of European capitals with number 119 bus routes. You can leave out London and Paris. I want it in five minutes."

There was a moment's pause, as though they'd been suspended, and then the place burst into activity.

"Get the head of Intelligence for the European Union on the line," Ellen said to Boynton as she headed quickly back into her private office. Standing at her desk, about to sit down, she looked at him.

Her Chief of Staff was standing at the door.

"What?" she said.

He looked behind him, into the conference room and the hive of activity. Then he stepped into her office and closed the door.

"You didn't ask why her."

"I'm sorry."

"The young FSO. Why her? Why did the warning come in to her?"

Ellen was about to say that it didn't matter, but stopped herself. Realizing that it probably did.

"Get the EU Intelligence Director on the line, then find out what you can about Anahita Dahir."

Sitting down, she brought out her phone and sent a message to her son: *Please contact me.*

Her finger hovered over the heart emoji, then moved over and hit the send arrow.

Then she waited. Waited.

Tick. Tick.

There was no reply.

"We have it," said the senior intelligence analyst for the State Department, rushing into Ellen's office.

She was just off the phone with the head of EU Intelligence, informing her of what they had.

The analyst put the list in front of her. The others were ranged behind him, watching as she read. It didn't take long. It was a surprisingly short list.

London and Paris could be stricken off. That left Rome, Madrid, and Frankfurt.

"Is one more likely than the rest?" she demanded.

There were six minutes left.

"Not that we can tell, Madame Secretary. We have calls in to the transport departments of each city, but it's now past six, and the offices are closed."

They were staring wide-eyed at her. Ellen turned to Boynton. "Get Interpol. Tell them to alert the police in each of these cities. Katherine!"

"Yes?" her daughter called, appearing at the door, phone to her ear.

"Rome, Madrid, Frankfurt. Get the word out."

"Got it."

"What's happening?" asked Anahita as she watched a group of senior analysts rush from the room toward the Secretary of State's office.

"They have the list of cities with number 119 buses," said an aide.

"What are they?"

The aide shoved the list down the table.

As Anahita read it, her brows knitted in thought. And then they unfurrowed as her eyes widened.

"Jesus, Frankfurt," she muttered and brought out her phone.

There were four and a half minutes left.

Her hands shaking, she tapped. Brought up the wrong message. Tapped again. And Gil's message from that morning appeared.

On way to Frankfurt.

She typed, *You in Frankfurt? On a bus? Now?* And hit the urgent icon.

Yes, Gil replied as he relaxed in his seat. It had been a long twenty-six hours, but they were almost there.

Why? Anahita wrote.

Following lead.

What kead. Anahita, fingers trembling, had hit send before noticing the typo. She was in the process of correcting when he replied.

Can't say.

Where are you in F?

She waited. Staring at her screen. *Please. Please.*

Three minutes and twenty seconds . . .

On bus.

Which bus?

Does it matter?

!!!!!

#119

Gil put his phone in his pocket and settled back, watching the kids in front of him poke and shove each other. Across the way, an older woman watched them, no doubt grateful they weren't her children or grandchildren.

The bus was packed, and Gil wondered if he should offer his seat to someone, but he needed to watch Dr. Bukhari, to see where she'd get off. And if his informant was right.

Get off! Bomb!!

But there was no reply.

Anahita stared at the screen. *Come on. Come on.*

Nothing.

She tried calling.

Nothing.

She got up and ran to the Secretary of State's office. Security tried to stop her, but once again she pushed past.

"A friend," she shouted. "A friend is on the number 119 bus in Frankfurt. He's following a lead. I tried to tell him there was a bomb, but he didn't reply."

"A lead?" said Betsy. "He's a journalist?"

"Yes."

Betsy swung around and stared at Ellen.

As Secretary Adams pulled out her phone, Betsy turned back to Anahita. "What's his name?"

Ellen looked at the last personal message she'd received. From her son.

In Frankfurt on bus. More later.

"Gil," said Anahita. "Gil Bahar." She looked from Betsy's shocked face to Ellen's. Her mouth open, her eyes wide.

Ellen, trembling, hit the phone icon and held Betsy's eyes.

"What?" demanded Anahita.

"Gil Bahar's her son," said Charles Boynton.

All the air had been sucked out of the room.

There were three minutes and five seconds left.

Everyone stared at Ellen.

Katherine entered and stopped. "What's happened?"

Betsy went over to her. "Gil's on the number 119 bus in Frankfurt. Your mother's calling him."

"Oh God," she said, and could manage no more.

The bus stopped, and the kids in front, noticing the stop, screamed, and, leaping up, they got off. Just as the man sitting in front of Nasrin left.

But he left something behind.

A few families got on. Some teens. An older couple.

Gil felt his phone vibrate with an incoming call but ignored it. He needed to focus on Dr. Bukhari at each stop, to make sure she didn't get off at the very last moment.

The bus started up, and he pulled out the phone.

"Fuck," he said and hit the red decline.

"He declined," said Ellen.

"Use my phone," said Katherine. She dialed and handed it to her mother.

There was a minute and ten seconds left.

Once again, his phone vibrated.

Gil took it out, expecting to see his mother's picture.

Instead the photograph he saw was of his half sister, Katherine.

"Hi, Katie—"

"Listen to me closely," said his mother, her voice stern, calm.

"Oh, shit," said Gil and went to hit End Call.

"There's a bomb," said Ellen, her voice rising.

"What?"

"There's a bomb on your bus." The calm was shattered. Her voice rose to almost a shout. "You have just over a minute. Go!"

It took him a split second to register the words, the panic, the meaning.

He stood up and yelled, "Stop the bus! There's a bomb!"

The other passengers looked at him, then cringed away from the American madman.

He reached out for Nasrin, grabbing her arm. "Get up! Get off."

She pushed him away and lashed out with Amir's satchel. Battering him and calling for help.

So this was how he planned to get her off, she thought, her mind and adrenaline racing.

Leaving her, Gil ran to the front and shouted at the driver.

"Stop! Get everyone off."

He turned and looked down the long bus, at the faces staring at him. The men, women, children. Terrified. Not of a bomb, but of him.

"Please," he begged.

Tick. Tick.

They watched as the wall of clocks in the magnificent office counted down. In the background, muffled, they could hear Gil yelling, begging.

Nineteen.

Eighteen.

"Gil!" his mother shouted. "Get off!"

Finally the bus shuddered to a stop. The door opened and the driver got up.

"Thank—" Gil began before he felt the driver's hands grip his jacket.

And he was tossed out.

Ten.

Nine.

Their eyes wide. Their breathing stopped.

"Eight," Anahita whispered.

Landing on the hard pavement, bruised and winded, he looked up as the bus drove away. Staggering to his feet, Gil ran after it; then, realizing he could never catch up, he turned to the pedestrians.

Three.

Two.

"Get back, get down. It's—"

Tick . . . tock.

Ellen's face went white just as Anahita's alarm went off.

CHAPTER 9

The phone slipped from Ellen's hand and dropped to the floor.

Light-headed, she reached behind her, trying to steady herself. To keep herself upright.

Framed photos, mementos, a lamp crashed down.

Then, in a panic, she stooped to retrieve the phone.

"Gil?!" she shouted into it. "Gil??"

But the line was dead.

"Gil?" she whispered into the monstrous silence.

"Mom?" said Katherine, stepping toward her.

"It exploded," she muttered, her eyes wide, staring at her daughter, then at Betsy.

And then, pandemonium, as everyone in the room burst into action, shouting orders.

"Stop!"

They did. All turned and looked at Secretary Adams. Betsy was on one side of her now, Katherine on the other.

Ten seconds had passed since the explosion.

"Do we know the exact location of the bus?" Ellen demanded.

"Yes. It can be traced from the phone connection," said Boynton. He grabbed the phone, hit some keys, and nodded. "Got it."

"Send that to the Germans," Secretary Adams commanded. "And call emergency services in Frankfurt. Now!"

"Yes, Madame Secretary."

Aides were told to inform all the intelligence services about what just happened, and to contact the American consulate in Frankfurt and get people there.

"And tell them to find Gil," Ellen called after them. "Gil Bahar." She spelled it out, the letters chasing the hurrying aides down the hall.

She turned to Katherine, who was trying to raise Gil on the phone. Katherine shook her head. They looked at Anahita, who was also trying.

Her eyes were wide, her phone to her ear. Nothing.

"I'm calling our bureau in Frankfurt. They can get there fast," said Katherine, her finger pounding the screen of her phone. "You," she said to Anahita, "keep trying my brother."

Ana nodded.

Phones began ringing, dinging, alerting.

Betsy turned on the monitors and stared as Dr. Phil interviewed a woman whose husband was transitioning into a woman, and who had to break it to her that she herself was transitioning into a man.

Click.

Judge Judy was adjudicating a case where a neighbor kept stealing a tea towel from a clothesline.

Click. Click.

Nothing yet. It had been just over a minute.

Click.

"Madame Secretary, I've informed the German Chancellor and sent the coordinates to their intelligence and emergency services," Boynton reported. "Should we inform the President?"

"President?" asked Ellen.

"Of the United States."

"Oh God, yes. I'll do that."

Ellen sat heavily, all but collapsing into her chair, and dropped her head into her hands. Her fingers clutched her scalp. When she raised her head, her eyes were bloodshot, but there was no other indication she might have just heard her son murdered.

"Get President Williams on the line, please."

Reports were coming in fast and furious as aides passed on what they had.

"Mr. President, there's been another bombing."

"Hold on."

Doug Williams indicated to his Chief of Staff that she should end the meeting with representatives of the Small Business Administration and clear the Oval Office.

When he was alone, Williams turned and looked out across the lawn.

"Where?"

"Frankfurt. Another bus."

"Shit." *At least not here*, he couldn't help but think.

Sitting down at his desk, he put her on speaker and rapidly typed into the secure search engine on his laptop. "I see nothing online."

Barb Stenhauser returned, her body language asking the question. But all she got was a quick gesture she took, rightly, to mean she needed to scroll through the channels on the monitors.

"Another explosion," he called to her across the Oval Office. "Frankfurt."

"Shit." Leaving the channel on CNN, she grabbed her phone.

"When did this happen?" he asked Ellen.

She looked at the clock and was surprised to see it had been only a minute and a half. "Ninety seconds ago."

It seemed forever.

"We've informed the German government and the international intelligence community," said Secretary Adams. "Alerts have gone out over secure channels."

"Wait a minute. You told the Germans? Not the other way around? How did you find out so quickly?"

Ellen paused, not wanting to tell him. But she knew she had to.

"My son was on the bus."

That was met with silence.

"I'm sorry," he said, and almost sounded it.

"He might've gotten off," she said. "It sounds . . ." She gathered herself. ". . . like he might've."

"You were talking to him? At the time?"

"Can I come and see you, Mr. President, to explain the sequence of events?"

"I think you'd better."

By the time Ellen arrived at the White House clutching her phone, refusing to give it to the Secret Service in case Gil should call, the Director of National Intelligence, the Director of the CIA, and General Whitehead, the Chair of the Joint Chiefs, were already in the Oval Office.

"Homeland Security and Defense should be with us soon," said President Williams, "but we won't wait."

He didn't mention Gil, which was a relief. Though Ellen suspected it wasn't to spare her pain. More likely it was either emotional cowardice, or he'd forgotten.

Ellen went quickly, succinctly, through what had happened. By then the world knew about the explosion. The images were all over the news. TV hosts were near hysterical with either anxiety or excitement. Journalists were at the scene, getting closer than they should have been allowed as the normally efficient German police tried to regain control of the area. Ambulances, firetrucks were trying to get through.

"Are you saying a junior FSO received a warning?" demanded

Tim Beecham, the DNI. "No one else in the world, in our sophisticated intelligence network, all our seasoned operatives, no one else picked it up. Instead someone sent her the message?"

"Yes," said Ellen, who'd just told them exactly that.

"But who?" asked the President.

"We don't know. She erased the message."

"Erased?"

"It's protocol. She thought it was spam."

"Was it from a Nigerian prince?" asked the Director of Homeland Security, who had just arrived. No one laughed.

"Why her?" asked the President. "This Ana . . ."

"Anahita Dahir. I don't know—"

"Anahita Dahir," mumbled the head of the CIA, and looked at National Intelligence.

"I didn't have time to ask," Secretary Adams was saying. "I'm just grateful she reacted."

"Too late," said the Secretary of Defense. "All the bombs went off."

Ellen was silent. It was, after all, true.

The Director of National Intelligence excused himself, then returned a minute later.

General Whitehead watched that, his head tilted slightly. He slid a glance over to Secretary Adams and gave her a small smile that should have been reassuring, but had the opposite effect.

Now she too studied Tim Beecham.

"Everything all right?" Doug Williams asked.

"Fine, Mr. President," said Beecham. "I just needed to alert some of my people."

Ellen Adams wondered why that brief absence had worried the head of the Joint Chiefs of Staff. And she thought she knew.

Tim Beecham did not need to leave the room to make that call. The only reason he would was to keep it from the rest of them.

Now why would that be?

Ellen glanced again at General Whitehead, but his attention was refocused on the President.

Secretary Adams answered their questions while Gil's mother had her back to the monitors. Not daring to look. In case . . .

It was General Whitehead who finally asked.

"Your son?"

"No word." Her voice hard, brittle. Her eyes pleading with him not to ask more.

He gave a curt nod and did not.

"And still no one has taken responsibility?" asked the President.

"No. This's clearly beyond lone-wolf territory, sir," said Defense. "This's a pack."

"I need answers, not clichés." President Williams looked around the room at his blank-faced advisors.

The moment elongated.

"Nothing?" he all but shouted. "Nothing? Are you fucking kidding me? We're the greatest nation on earth. We have the best surveillance equipment, the best intelligence network, and you bring me shit?"

"With all due respect, Mr. President—" the Director of the CIA began.

"Fuck that. Just tell me." He glared at him.

The head of the CIA looked around the room for support. His eyes settled on the Secretary of State. Ellen sighed.

Since she was already on the outs with the President, she had the least to lose. Besides, Ellen Adams no longer cared about these politics.

"You're four years out of date, Doug."

The use of his first name slipped out.

"What's that supposed to mean?"

"You know perfectly well," she snapped and looked over at Barb

Stenhauser, his Chief of Staff. "And so do you. I don't have time to waste, so here are the bullet points. The former administration screwed up everything it touched. It poisoned the well, poisoned our relationships. We're the leader of the free world in name only. That effective intelligence network you're so proud of no longer exists. Our allies distrust us. Those who'd do us harm are circling. And we let it happen. We let them in. Russia. The Chinese. That madman in North Korea. And here, in the administration, in positions of influence? And even the lower-level workers? Can we really trust that they're doing a good job?"

"Deep State," said the Director of National Intelligence.

Ellen rounded on him. "It's not depth we need to worry about, it's width. It's everywhere. Four years of hiring, of promoting, of rewarding people who'd say and do anything to prop up a deranged President has left us vulnerable." She looked at her phone. Still nothing. "Not everyone's incompetent, and those who are probably aren't malicious. They're not undermining us, they just have no real idea how to do the job well. Look, I come from the private sector. I can tell if people are motivated, inspired. We've inherited thousands of workers who've spent four years in fear. They just want to keep their heads down. That includes my department. And that extends into"—she looked at Barb Stenhauser—"the White House."

"Does it include me?" General Whitehead asked. "I worked under the previous administration."

"And from what I hear you spent most of your time throwing yourself on grenades," said Ellen. "Trying to stop or at least lessen the impact of the more insane military and strategic decisions."

"Not altogether successfully," admitted the Chairman of the Joint Chiefs of Staff. "I begged the President and his supporters not to encourage further nuclear development, and you know what he said?"

Ellen, too afraid to ask, remained silent.

"He said, 'What good are nukes if you can't use them?'" Whitehead actually paled as he said it. "If I'd spoken out more forcefully . . ."

"At least you tried," said Ellen.

Whitehead gave a small grunt. "That'll be on the tombstone. 'At least he tried' . . ."

"It matters," said Ellen. "Most didn't. I'm sorry, Mr. President. I need to get back to State. Actually, I need to get to Germany. Is there anything else you need from me?"

"No, Ellen." President Williams hesitated. "The trip to Germany. Is it a personal visit?"

She stared at him, hardly believing what he was saying. What he meant.

General Whitehead stepped forward. "I can get you on one of the military transports already scheduled out of Andrews within the hour."

"No," said President Williams. "It's all right. Even if it's not official business, you can take your government plane. I'm sure the German Chancellor will understand the last-minute nature of the trip and not see it as a breach of protocol."

"She's a human being." Ellen glared at Williams. "You should try it."

CHAPTER 10

Nothing?" asked Ellen as she rushed into her office.

She knew if there had been news of Gil, she'd have heard. But still, she had to ask.

"No," said Boynton.

Betsy and Katherine had left to pack for Frankfurt, and now Ellen strode into the conference room. She'd been fielding urgent questions from her international counterparts, and now she sat down and stared at her Chief of Staff, senior aides, and security analysts.

"Report."

"The Germans say the same organization is clearly behind all three explosions," a senior aide said. "But they don't know which organization."

"Could be Al-Qaeda," said a security analyst. "ISIS—"

"ISIL."

"Stop." Ellen put up her hand. "The explosions were hours apart. You'd have thought if the point was terror, they'd be timed to pretty much happen simultaneously. Like 9/11." She looked around the table at the brain trust. "Wouldn't you?"

There were shrugs and silence.

"Madame Secretary, the truth is," said a senior analyst, "we just don't know what the purpose was. Is."

"Is? It's not over?" she said.

She could feel hysteria mounting. A giddy, near-overwhelming desire to start laughing. To run out of the room, waving her arms, and race screaming down the hall, out the front door, down the middle of the street. Not stopping until she reached the plane.

They were looking at each other, as though daring each other to talk.

"Just say it," she said.

That was met with more silence. Ellen couldn't read these people yet. They were schooled in hiding their true feelings, certainly their true thoughts. This was partly because of their diplomatic and intelligence training and partly as a result of four years being punished for revealing anything resembling a fact, never mind the truth.

"We think there's a larger purpose," said the woman who seemed to have drawn the short straw. "That these bombs were sent as a first warning."

She narrowed her eyes and turned her head slightly away. Bracing herself. Expecting to be lambasted for presenting bad news.

Instead Secretary Adams absorbed what she heard and nodded.

"Thank you." She looked around the table. "And what is that warning?"

"That something bigger is planned. That this was just a taste of what they're capable of," said one of the security analysts, encouraged by his boss's reaction.

"That they can and will do whatever they want," said another. "Wherever, whenever they want."

"That they're willing to kill innocent men, women, and children anywhere in the world," said another.

"That they're professional," said yet another. By now Ellen was sorry she'd encouraged such honesty. "No underwear bombers. No shoe bombers. No nail bombs in knapsacks. Whoever did this is in a whole other league."

"They will be successful, Madam Secretary, whatever they choose to do," agreed another.

"Are you finished?" asked Ellen.

They looked at each other, and to a person gave a long sigh. Letting out years of frustration. And along with it, a long litany of worry.

"What do we know about the message Ms. Dahir received?" Ellen asked.

"We've found it on the server," said one of the intelligence officers. "There's no IP address. Nothing to show where it originated. We're working on it."

"Good. Where is Ms. Dahir?" asked Secretary Adams. "I'm leaving for Germany in thirty-five minutes, and I want to speak with her before I go."

They looked around, as though expecting Anahita to materialize.

"Well?" asked Ellen.

"I haven't seen her for a while," said Boynton. "She's probably back at her desk. I'll get her up here."

A minute later he reported that she wasn't there.

Ellen felt a chill slide from the base of her skull down her spine. "Find her."

Had she disappeared of her own volition? Had she been disappeared?

Neither was good.

Ellen remembered the whispered "Anahita Dahir" and the look between the Director of the CIA and Ted Beecham, the DNI.

She knew that look. It was reserved for anyone not named Jane or Debbie, Billy or Ted. It had angered her at the time, but now she found herself thinking the same thing.

Anahita Dahir. Where was she from? What was her background? What was her allegiance?

Where is she?

And Ellen heard, again, that simple statement of fact. Despite the early warning, the bombs had exploded. Because Anahita Dahir had brought the message to them too late.

Her phone rang. The private line. It was Katherine.

"He's alive." Her voice, jubilant, shot down the line.

"Oh God," moaned Ellen and leaned over until her head touched the conference table.

"What?" asked Boynton, his eyes wide in concern. "Your son?"

Ellen looked up and met eyes that, unlike the President, actually cared. And she thought, at that moment, that she loved Charles Boynton.

She loved everyone.

"He's alive." Speaking into the phone now, she asked Katherine, "How is he? Where is he?"

"He's hurt, but not critical. They say he'll recover. He's at the *zum heiligen . . . Geist—*"

"Never mind," said Ellen. "We'll be there soon enough. Meet me at Andrews."

As she hung up, Gil's mother closed her eyes and took a deep breath. Then Secretary Adams opened her eyes and looked at her smiling aides.

"He's fine. He'll recover. I'm heading there. You're coming with me," she said to her Chief of Staff. "Is there anything else we know?" They shook their heads. "Anything we suspect?"

"These were definitely coordinated terrorist attacks, Madame Secretary," said the senior intelligence analyst in the room. "But as to who, we can't tell. As we said, it could be anyone from an extremist far-right group to a new Islamic State cell. Fortunately, if the message the FSO received is to be believed, it's likely the last."

"For now," said an aide. "What I don't understand is why they'd warn us about the bombs. Why send that message at all?"

"They didn't," said the analyst. "Whoever planned the bombings wanted them to go off."

"Then who sent the warning?" asked Ellen. When there was silence, she said, "Speculate."

"A rival group?" said the senior intelligence analyst. "A mole maybe, within the organization. Someone who doesn't share their ideology and wanted to stop the explosions. We're working blind."

"No, you're looking in all the predictable places," said Ellen. "Use your imaginations. There can't be many who could pull together the people and expertise. I want a list." She stood up. "We need to find out whose brainchild this is, and we need to abort it."

"We still have no idea why those buses?" asked Boynton. "Why those cities? Was it random?"

Again, all heads, like dogs on a dashboard, shook.

Ellen stood up, and the others followed suit. "I want to speak to Ms. Dahir before I leave. Find her."

At the door, she stopped. Remembering that look. The one that passed between the CIA Director and Tim Beecham.

"Get the Director of National Intelligence on the line," she said to Boynton.

By the time she got to her desk, the call had come through.

"Tim."

"Madame Secretary."

"Do you have my FSO?"

"Why would I?"

"Don't mess with me. You might have intelligence reports, but I have whole embassies."

"Technically—"

"Just tell me."

"Yes, Madame Secretary. We have her."

Anahita had never dreamed this was possible. Not here. Not in a civilized country.

Not in her country.

She sat at a metal table across from two men in uniform but without insignias or name tags. Military intelligence. Two others, even larger, stood at the door. In case she made a run for it.

But even if she could get through that wall of solid flesh, where would she run?

Back to wherever she came from was their suspicion, she'd realized early on. As though she hadn't come from Cleveland.

She could tell by how they repeated her name. Anahita.

They said it as though it translated into something ugly. Terrorist. Alien. Enemy. Threat.

Anahita, they sneered. Anahita Dahir.

"I was born in Cleveland," she explained. "You can check."

"We have," said the younger of the two officers. "But records can be forged."

"Can they?" She didn't mean to sound as clueless as she did, and she could tell it only added to their suspicions. In their experience no one was that naïve. Or innocent.

Certainly no one with the name Anahita Dahir.

"Dahir." From "*dabir*." Arabic meaning "tutor." "Teacher."

And "Anahita," from the Persian, for "healer." For "wisdom."

But it was no use telling them that. They'd stop listening after "Persian."

Which translated into "Iranian." Which meant enemy.

No, best to say nothing. Though privately Anahita Dahir wondered if they weren't right, and they were not, in fact, on the same side. It was hard to believe she was allied with people like this.

"What's your ethnic background?" the younger of the two demanded.

"My parents are from Lebanon. Beirut. They escaped during the civil war and came here as refugees. I'm first generation."

"Muslim?"

"Christian."

"Your parents?"

"My father's Muslim. My mother's Christian. One of the reasons they had to leave. Christians were targeted."

"Who sent you the coded message?"

"I have no idea."

"Tell us."

"I am. I honestly don't know. As soon as it came in, I showed it to my supervisor. You can ask him."

"Don't tell us our job. Just answer the questions."

"I'm try—"

"Did you tell your supervisor what the message meant?"

"No, I didn't—"

"Why not?"

"Because I didn—"

"You waited until two bombs had gone off, and it was too late to stop the third."

"No, no!" She felt herself getting confused and fought to regain equilibrium.

"And then you deleted it."

"I thought it was spam."

"Spam?" the older of the two asked, his voice more reasonable. And far more frightening. "Explain that, please."

"We get it sometimes. Bots cycle through different addresses, sending out messages at random. Most are stopped by the State Department firewall, but some sneak through—" As soon as she said "sneak," she regretted it, but forged ahead. "It happens about once a week." She was about to say, *You can ask any of the other FSOs*, but stopped herself. She was learning. "When some get through, they can seem to be nonsense. Like this one. If I can't understand it, I ask."

"Are you blaming your supervisor?" the younger demanded.

"No, of course not. I'm just answering the questions," she snapped.

Her anger was now stronger than her fear. She turned to the senior officer.

"If we know something's junk, we can delete it or show it to our supervisor for his or her opinion, and then erase. Which is what I did."

The senior intelligence officer paused, then leaned forward.

"That's not all you did. You wrote down the numbers. Why?"

Anahita went quiet. And still.

How to explain.

"It just seemed strange."

That landed in the small, close room with a thud. The younger agent shook his head and leaned back, but the older one continued to watch her.

"I know that's not much of an explanation, but it's the truth," she said, now speaking solely to the older man. "I'm not completely sure why I did."

That sounded even worse. She could tell because the senior officer did not react at all. Nothing. From what Anahita could tell, he wasn't even breathing.

Just then there was a commotion at the door.

And even so, the senior intelligence officer didn't react. He trusted the guards to do their job while he did his. Which seemed, now, to be staring at her.

"Step aside."

Now the senior officer turned to look at the door, as did Anahita. It was a voice she recognized. A moment later Charles Boynton entered, followed by the Secretary of State.

Everyone sprang to their feet, though the senior officer more slowly than the rest.

"Madame Secretary," he said, and when Anahita began to say something to Ellen, he silenced her with a look.

"You have my FSO," Ellen said, looking briefly at Anahita to make sure she was all right.

The young woman looked anxious, but not harmed.

"Yes. We have some questions for her."

"As do I. Tell me your name, please."

He hesitated for just a beat. "Jeffrey Rosen. Colonel, Defense Intelligence Agency."

Ellen put out her hand. "Ellen Adams. Secretary of State, United States of America."

Colonel Rosen took her hand and smiled, very slightly.

"Can we talk, Colonel? Privately, please."

He nodded to the junior officer, who led Anahita out of the room, but not before she said, "Madame Secretary, Gil? Is he . . . ?"

"In the hospital. He'll recover."

Anahita gave her a small nod, her shoulders sagging, releasing hours of anxiety. "You know I didn't . . . I wasn't involved."

Ignoring that, Ellen nodded to the others to leave her and the Colonel. Only Charles Boynton stayed, standing by the door.

"What has she told you?"

"Just what you probably already know." He recapped the sequence of events from the moment the message appeared in the FSO's box to when the bomb exploded. "What we don't know is—"

"Why she wrote the numbers down," said Ellen.

She tried not to take his raised brows as an insult. Ellen Adams was used to people underestimating her. Accomplished middle-aged women were often diminished by small men. Though she didn't think this Colonel Rosen was one.

He would have been equally surprised had General Whitehead gotten to that answer so quickly.

"And?" she asked.

"She had no explanation."

"Don't you think, Colonel, if she was a foreign agent, if she was involved in this, she'd have had an explanation?"

That surprised him, and he considered it. "She appears innocent."

"And that makes her guilty? You'd have done well in the witch trials." Ellen walked to the door. "I'm going to Germany."

He followed her. "I hope you get answers, Madame Secretary. I'm relieved to hear about your son. He's a brave man."

That stopped Ellen. She paused to look at this Colonel in military intelligence and wondered if he knew how brave. Not just that day, but in those horrific days in Afghanistan. Rosen's face was a cipher, giving nothing away.

"We'll be working from this end. Anahita Dahir knows something."

"If she does, I hope to get it out of her on the flight over."

Ellen knew she should probably not have gotten such pleasure from the surprised look on Colonel Rosen's face. But she did.

"That would be a mistake." No *Madame Secretary* this time. Just a bald, bold statement. "Ms. Dahir is involved in this. I don't know how, but she is. Even you must see that."

"Even me?" Ellen's eyes were as hard as her tone. "I'm your Secretary of State. You might disagree with me. Clearly you do. But you will respect the office."

"Apologies." He paused but didn't back down. "I think you are making a mistake, Madame Secretary."

Ellen examined him for a long moment. He'd spoken his mind. His truth. Which was more than most would do in the vacuum that had become the upper echelons of the government.

"Let me tell you something else, Madame Secretary. Anahita Dahir is not to be trusted."

"Yes, you've made that clear, Colonel. And believe me, I've taken what you say seriously. But Ms. Dahir is still coming with me."

What the Colonel hadn't seen was the look on the junior FSO's face when she'd been trying to convince Secretary Adams that a third attack was imminent.

There was sheer panic there. This was a young woman desperate to stop the explosion.

Ellen also knew that, without Anahita, her son would be dead. She owed her. But did she trust her?

Not completely. That look on the FSO's face as she'd pleaded with Ellen to believe her, to do something, could have been an act, a ruse to get into the inner circle. To manipulate them while a much larger attack was planned.

Ellen knew that Colonel Rosen thought she was far more naïve than she was. And for now, until she could separate ally from enemy, that suited Ellen just fine.

Besides, if Anahita Dahir was involved, Ellen wanted to keep her close. To watch her. To perhaps lull her into making a mistake.

Unless, thought Ellen as she led the way to the waiting limousines to take them to Andrews, she was the one making the mistake.

While on the flight, Anahita tried to get in to see Secretary Adams, to thank her for rescuing her. For trusting her. For bringing her with them to Germany. Where she could see Gil.

She wanted to explain that she knew nothing, was hiding nothing. But then, that would have been a lie.

CHAPTER
11

It was near dawn by the time Gil Bahar drifted up to consciousness. He felt his limbs heavy, constrained. As though he were tied down.

It brought back vague memories.

And then, with a rush of panic, they were no longer vague. Or memories. He could feel the filthy ropes cutting into his wrists and ankles. Smell the stench of shit and urine and rotting food and flesh.

Facedown, breathing in the dirt from the floor.

The thirst. The thirst. And the terror.

And then he jerked awake, rising quickly to the surface, struggling to sit up. In a sudden and overwhelming panic.

"It's OK," came the familiar voice, and with it a familiar scent both comforting and unsettling. "You're safe."

He struggled before finally focusing. "Mom?"

What're you doing here? Have they kidnapped you too?

"It's all right," she said gently. Her face close, but not too close. "You're in the hospital. The doctors say you'll be fine in a few days."

And then it came back. His bruised mind working. Leaping, stumbling back, back. Frankfurt. The people, the pedestrians. The bus. The faces of the passengers staring at him. The children.

The woman with the satchel. What was her name. Her name.

"Wie heißen sie?"

A bright light was shone in his eyes. A hand placed on his head, holding him still, holding him down. Holding his lids open.

"What?" Gil said, starting to thrash.

Then the woman, a doctor, stepped back. "Sorry. Your name. What is your name, *bitte*?"

He had to think for a moment. "Gil."

"For Gilbert, *ja*?"

He paused for just a beat before agreeing. Not able to meet his mother's eyes.

"Your family name?" The doctor's voice was soft but firm, with a heavy German accent.

That took longer. Why couldn't he remember?

"Bukhari," he blurted out. "Nasrin Bukhari."

The doctor looked at him, then turned to his mother. Both looked worried.

"No, no," he said, trying to sit up. "My name is Gil Bahar. Her name is Dr. Nasrin Bukhari."

"My name is Dr. Gerhardt."

"I don't mean you. The woman on the bus." He looked beyond the doctor to his mother. "I was following her."

Ellen was standing just off to the side. She'd asked the others to wait outside while she sat with Gil. When he'd stirred, she'd pressed the button for the doctor.

Now she stepped forward. "Let the doctor do her exam, then we can talk."

She held Gil's eyes, letting him know the less he said in front of anyone else, the better.

He agreed. Besides, it would give him time to sort through the jumble. To dredge up specifics. Why did that name, Nasrin Bukhari, give him the willies?

Who was she?

Dr. Gerhardt finished her exam and seemed satisfied. She

told him that he had a concussion, broken ribs, and bruises. "And a deep gash on your thigh. You were lucky. It would have been life-threatening if bystanders hadn't applied pressure so quickly. We've put in stitches, but you need to rest for a few days."

By the time she left, Gil had his answer.

It wasn't Dr. Bukhari who scared him. It was the person standing in the shadows behind her.

Ellen watched the heavy door close behind the doctor, then turned to her son. She reached for his hand, but he pulled it away. Not sharply. Instinctively.

Which made it worse.

"I'm so sorry," she began, but he interrupted, gesturing for her to bend down. She thought, for a brief moment, maybe he was going to kiss her cheek. But instead he whispered.

"Bashir Shah."

She turned her head and stared at him. Ellen Adams hadn't heard that name in years. Not since those long meetings with the corporate lawyers, when they'd warned her not to air the investigative documentary on the Pakistani arms dealer.

It had taken their reporter more than a year of digging. It had led to threats against the reporter's family. More than one of his sources had disappeared.

There was no way, after that, they were not going to run the story.

Dr. Shah shrugged off the accusations of arms dealing, though he did issue a rare statement decrying the attacks on an upstanding Pakistani citizen. They were the same sort of false accusations leveled against most of his predecessors and mentors, those brave and brilliant Pakistani nuclear physicists who'd blazed the path. People like AQ Khan.

Dr. Shah explained that Pakistan was the West's ally in the war on terror.

The fact that he *was* the terror had been the point of the documentary. And indeed, in his tepid denial was embedded a deeper truth.

Bashir Shah wanted the world to know he was a merchant of death.

To her horror Ellen Adams realized she had, inadvertently and at the cost of lives, done his advertising for him. The Oscar-winning documentary let terrorists know where to get their biological weapons. Their chlorine. Their sarin nerve gas. Their small arms and their missile launchers.

And worse.

"Was he on the bus?" she asked, incredulous.

"No. But he's behind it."

"The bombs?"

Now Gil shook his head. "Not the bus bombs. Something else. I don't know who's behind the bombs."

"You said you were following a woman. Nasrin . . ." Ellen tried to remember her last name.

"Bukhari," said Gil. "An informant told me Shah had recruited three Pakistani nuclear physicists. Dr. Bukhari's one of them. I wanted to see where she was going. What Shah was up to. Where he was, if nothing else."

"But we know where he is," said Ellen. "He's under house arrest in Islamabad. Has been for years."

The Pakistanis had also taken the precaution of censoring Dr. Shah's access to the internet. Unlike other arms dealers, Bashir Shah was both a businessman and an ideologue. He'd been born in Islamabad but raised in England. Now in his fifties, he'd been radicalized while studying physics at Cambridge, and subsequently deeply influenced by jihadist sites on the internet.

While he'd admired the previous generation of Pakistani nuclear physicists, he'd grown to believe they had not gone far enough. But he would.

There was no line Bashir Shah would not cross.

"The Pakistanis released him last year," said Gil.

"They wouldn't," she said, raising her voice, then lowering it again at a warning look from her son. "They couldn't," she whispered, almost a hiss. "We'd know about it. They'd never go behind our backs. American agents were the ones who found him in the first place."

"They didn't go behind our backs. The previous administration agreed."

Ellen pulled back, staring at her son. Trying to grasp what he was saying. She'd been confused about why they were whispering. Now she knew.

If what he said was true . . .

She looked around the private room, as though expecting to see Bashir Shah standing in a corner, watching them.

Her mind raced, pulling disparate pieces together. Trying to fill in the cracks, the blanks.

Ellen Adams knew from reading State Department briefings that there were many bad actors out there. Men and women who cared for nothing and nobody in pursuit of their aims.

Assad in Syria. Al-Qurashi of the Islamic State. Kim Jong Un in North Korea.

And though diplomacy would not allow her to say it officially, privately Ellen Adams would add Ivanov in Russia to that list.

But no one compared to Bashir Shah. He wasn't just bad, or wicked, as her grandmother might have said. Bashir Shah was evil. Intent on creating a Hell on earth.

"Gil, how did you know about Shah and the physicists?"

"I can't tell you."

"You must."

"It's a source. I can't." He paused, ignoring the anger in her eyes. "How many?"

Ellen knew what he meant. "There isn't a firm figure yet, but it looks like twenty-three dead on the bus and five on the ground."

Tears sprang to Gil's dark eyes as he remembered their faces. And wondered if he could have done more. Could have at least ripped that child from its mother's arms and . . .

"You tried," said his mother.

But was that good enough, he wondered. Or was that comforting thought actually a cobblestone on the road to Hell?

Katherine took her mother's place beside Gil's bed, sitting with her half brother while he slept, then woke, then slept again.

Anahita had also gone in to say hello to Gil. He smiled at her and held out his hand.

"I hear you saved my life."

"I wish I could have saved more."

She took his hand, so familiar. A hand that knew her body perhaps better than she herself did.

They talked for a moment, and when his eyes grew heavy, she left him. Almost bending down to kiss his cheek but stopping herself. Not just because Katherine was there, but because it wouldn't be appropriate.

They were no longer "that."

Once she was out of the room, Boynton gestured to her. "You're coming with us."

"Take us to the site of the bombing, please," Secretary Adams said to the Diplomatic Security driver when she, Boynton, Anahita, and Betsy got in the vehicle. "Then to the US consulate."

Another car with aides and advisors followed, all surrounded, front and back, by German police vehicles.

"I've told the Consul that you'll be there within the hour," said Boynton. "He and his people are gathering as much information as they can on what happened here. You have a meeting with him, then with the top US intelligence and security people in Germany, then a conference call with your counterparts. Here's the list of attendees, suggested by the French."

Ellen went through the countries and the names, striking some off, adding one. She wanted to keep it tight.

Handing the list of names back to Boynton, she asked, "Is the vehicle secure?"

"Secure?"

"Has it been swept?"

"Swept?" asked Boynton.

"Please stop repeating everything and just answer."

"Yes, it's secure, Madame Secretary," said Steve Kowalski, the leader of her Diplomatic Security detail, who was riding with them in the front passenger seat.

Boynton looked at her closely. "Why?"

"What can you tell me about Bashir Shah?" Despite the assurances, she'd lowered her voice.

"Shah?" asked Betsy.

When Ellen's media empire had grown out of all expectations, she'd asked Betsy to quit her job as a teacher and join her. In that testosterone-filled world, Ellen needed a close ally and confidante. It also helped that Betsy was fierce, in her brilliance and her loyalty.

It was Betsy who'd helped helm the documentary on the arms dealer.

"He's not behind this, is he?" she asked. "Tell me he's not behind this."

Ellen saw that Betsy was not just surprised; she was incredulous.

And then, as Frankfurt rolled by, Betsy's expression slid from doubtful to worried and settled into something close to horror.

"Who?" asked Charles Boynton.

"Bashir Shah," Ellen repeated. "What do you know about him?"

"Nothing. I've never heard of the man."

He looked from Secretary Adams, to Betsy, then back to the Secretary of State. He didn't bother to look at Anahita Dahir. But Ellen did. And what she saw was similar to the expression on Betsy's face.

Similar, but not quite the same. Anahita, at the mention of Bashir Shah, wasn't just afraid; she was terrified.

What Charles Boynton did see was his boss's expression aimed at him. Ellen Adams was angrier than he'd ever seen her, though, granted, he'd only known her a month.

"You're lying."

"I'm sorry?" he said, hardly believing what he just heard.

"You must know Shah," snapped Betsy. "He's—"

But Ellen placed a hand on her leg to stop her. "No. Don't say any more."

"This's ridiculous," he snapped back. Then he quickly added, "Madame Secretary. I honestly don't know who you're talking about. I'm new to State as well."

It was true. Barbara Stenhauser, with the President's approval, had selected Charles Boynton to be Ellen's Chief of Staff.

It had been a surprise to them both. Instead of allowing Ellen to choose her own Chief, or even appointing someone already in the department, they'd installed a top political aide from their campaign in the preeminent administrative job at State.

Ellen had suspected it was all part of President Williams's efforts to undermine her. But now she wondered if there was a darker purpose. Could Charles Boynton really be that ignorant? How could he not know Bashir Shah? Granted, Shah lived in the shadows. But wasn't it their job to see into those shadows?

"We're here, Madame Secretary," said Kowalski from the front seat.

Hundreds had gathered to look on, kept back from the scene of the explosion by wooden barriers. The onlookers turned to watch as she got out of the car. There was an eerie silence, broken by the soft click as the vehicle door closed.

She was greeted by the German police officer in charge, as well as the senior American Intelligence agent in Germany, CIA Station Chief Scott Cargill.

"We can't get too close," the American explained.

It was almost exactly twelve hours since the explosion. The sun was just coming up on what looked to be another cold, damp, gray March day. Bleak and uninviting. Frankfurt, that industrial city, was looking at its worst. And it was never great at the best of times.

Much of its historic center had been bombed out in the war. While it was considered an "alpha world city," that came down to its place as an economic hub. It lacked the charm of many smaller cities, and the excitement and youthful energy of Berlin.

Ellen looked behind her at the silent people gathered at the barriers.

"Relatives mostly," the German officer explained. Already there was a carpet of flowers. Teddy bears. Balloons. As though those could comfort the dead.

And for all Ellen knew, they could.

She looked around at the destruction. The twisted metal. The bricks and glass. The red blankets laid on the ground. Almost flat.

She knew the press was regarding her. Recording her.

But still, she continued to stare at the field of blankets, spread over such a distance, their corners lifting slightly in the breeze. It was almost pretty. Almost peaceful.

"Madame Secretary?" Scott Cargill said, but still Ellen stared.

One of those blankets could have covered Gil.

All of those blankets covered someone's child, mother, father, husband, wife. Friend.

It was so quiet, barely a sound. Only the now familiar clicking of cameras. Aimed at her.

"We are the Dead," she thought, remembering the war poem. *"Short days ago we lived, felt dawn, saw sunset glow, / Loved and were loved . . ."*

Ellen Adams looked behind her at the relatives watching her. Then back to the blankets, like a field of poppies.

"Ellen?" Betsy whispered, stepping between her and the journalists, shielding, even for a moment, her friend.

Ellen met those eyes and nodded. Swallowing her bile, tamping down her horror, Secretary Adams turned her revulsion into resolve.

"What can you tell me?" she asked the German officer.

"Very little, madame. It was a massive explosion, as you can see. Whoever did this wanted to make sure it would accomplish the goal."

"And what was that goal?"

He shook his head. He wasn't so much weary, though he must've been on the job for almost twenty-four hours straight, as drained.

"The same as the other two, I assume. In London and Paris." He looked around, then back to her. "If you have any insight, please tell me."

He studied her, and when there was only silence, he went on: "As far as we know, there's nothing here, in this spot, that any organization could consider strategic."

Ellen took a deep breath and thanked them.

She'd had to ask about the goal, though she already knew at least part of the answer. But she couldn't tell them about Dr. Nasrin Bukhari. The Pakistani nuclear physicist who'd been on the bus. Not yet. Not until she knew more.

And she wanted to keep Bashir Shah to herself, at least until she spoke to her counterparts.

Before returning to the car, Ellen took one last, long look. Had all this been done to murder one person?

And as the German officer had so succinctly said, the goal here was almost certainly the same as in London and Paris. Which meant . . .

"We need to get to the consulate," she said to Boynton.

But still, Ellen paused at the barrier to speak to the relatives. To look at the photographs they held. Of sons and daughters, of mothers and fathers, husbands and wives. Missing.

"If ye break faith with us who die, / We shall not sleep . . ."

Ellen Adams had no intention of breaking faith. Though as she sat in the vehicle as it sped through early-morning Frankfurt, she looked at Charles Boynton and Anahita Dahir, and wondered if, inadvertently, she already had.

CHAPTER 12

They had their answer by the time the meeting was convened.

On her screen Ellen saw foreign ministers from select countries, along with their top intelligence officials and aides.

"Your information was right, Madame Secretary," said the British Foreign Secretary, no longer quite so patronizing. "We've identified Dr. Ahmed Iqbal as a passenger on the London bus. He's a Pakistani national living in Cambridge and teaching at the Cavendish Lab, in the University of Cambridge Department of Physics."

"He was a nuclear physicist?" the German Foreign Minister, Heinrich Von Baier, asked.

"Yes."

"Monsieur Peugeot?" Ellen asked, turning to the French Foreign Minister on the upper right of the screen.

This always felt like *Hollywood Squares* to her, though it was no game.

"*Oui*, it's preliminary right now, we need to double- and triple-check, but it looks like among the dead on the Paris bus is Dr. Edouard Monpetit. Aged"—he checked his notes—"thirty-seven. Married. One child."

"Not Pakistani?" asked the Canadian, Jocelyn Tardiff.

"A Pakistani mother and French Algerian father," Peugeot explained. "He lived in Lahore and traveled to Paris two days ago."

"And from there?" asked Ellen. "Where was he going?"

"We don't know yet," admitted the French Foreign Minister. "We've sent agents to speak to his family."

"I take it you identified them from facial recognition," said the German Foreign Minister.

"Yes," agreed the Brit. "We picked Dr. Iqbal up on CCTV cameras as he got on the bus at the Knightsbridge tube station."

"Then why were they not identified before?" the German asked. "When you were looking for possible suspects and targets?"

Ellen leaned forward. It was a good question.

"Well now," said the UK, "our intelligence algorithms didn't consider him a target."

"The same is true in Paris," said France. "The first time around, our facial recognition program dismissed Dr. Monpetit."

"Why?" asked Italy. "Surely nuclear physicists would be a natural target, or at least make the short list."

"Dr. Monpetit is considered a journeyman physicist," explained France. "He worked in Pakistan's nuclear program, but in a low-level position, on the periphery. Mostly on packaging."

"Delivery?" asked Germany.

"No, just the casing."

"And Dr. Iqbal?" asked Italy.

"As far as we know right now, Dr. Iqbal was not associated with the Pakistani, or any, nuclear program," said the UK.

"But he was a nuclear physicist," said Canada, emphasizing the pertinent word.

She either had the worst dress sense any of them had ever seen or, more likely, she was wearing a flannel dressing gown. With moose and bears.

Her gray hair was pulled back and she was without makeup.

It was, after all, just after two in the morning in Ottawa, and she'd been yanked out of a deep sleep.

But while the rest of her looked unprepared, her expression told a different story. She was alert, composed, focused. And grim.

"Dr. Iqbal was an academic," said the UK. "A theorist. And even then, not very accomplished. Again, all this is preliminary, but a rudimentary check shows only"—he turned to his aide, who showed him a document—"a dozen publications to his name. All as secondary author."

The UK Foreign Secretary took off his glasses, and when the aide leaned in and started to say something, he snapped, "Yes, yes. I know." Turning back to the camera, he said, "We're searching his rooms in Cambridge and will interview his supervisor. We haven't yet contacted the Pakistanis."

"Neither have we," said France. "Best to wait."

The UK Foreign Secretary bristled. He did not take kindly to being told what to do by France. Or Germany. Or Italy. Or Canada. Or his own aides. Or probably, thought Ellen, his mother.

Ellen reflected that this was a loose-knit alliance that could tear apart at any moment. What held it together was not mutual respect but mutual need.

It was less like *Hollywood Squares* and more like a life raft. And you sure don't want to make war on a fellow passenger and risk all of them tipping over.

"Anything on Nasrin Bukhari?" Canada asked.

"All we know so far is that she worked at the Karachi Nuclear Power Plant for a time. We don't know if she still did," said Germany. "Canada helped set up that plant, no?"

Now it was Germany's turn to be disingenuous.

"That was decades ago," said Canada, stiffly. "And we pulled support when we realized what Pakistan's true intention might be."

"A little late—" said Germany.

Canada opened her mouth, then shut it again. Ellen tilted her head and thought she'd like to have a glass of Chardonnay with that woman. Such self-control.

What the Canadian Minister of Foreign Affairs did say was, "The Karachi facility is an energy plant. Not part of their weapons program."

"Well . . . ," said Germany, "that's what we think. What we hope. But Dr. Bukhari being targeted might suggest something else."

"Merde," muttered France.

"We have a long way to go," said the UK. "Including, of course, why these three were murdered. What were they up to, and who'd want to stop them?"

"Israel," they all said at once. It was the go-to answer whenever there was an assassination.

"President Williams has a call in to the Israeli Prime Minister," said Ellen. "We might know something soon, but while Mossad might target these scientists, I doubt they'd blow up buses to do it."

"True," admitted the UK.

"There is some good news," said Italy. "With these three dead, presumably whatever they had planned is also dead? No?"

"We don't know what they were up to," said France. "Maybe they stumbled onto something and were coming to tell us."

"All three?" asked Canada. "At the same time? Seems a bit of a coincidence."

Ellen shifted. She hadn't yet told them about Bashir Shah. That these scientists had been recruited by him.

"I don't think they meant to warn us," she said.

The German Foreign Minister stared at her. "Do you know something, Ellen? We've told you what we know so far. But you have not. You told our Chancellor that there would be a bombing in Frankfurt. You even knew the exact bus route and time. How was that?"

"And," said France, "how did you know about Nasrin Bukhari and to check for nuclear physicists from Pakistan on the other buses? I think we're owed answers."

Somehow, to Ellen's ears, their questions had the slight odor of accusations. But what could they possibly be accusing her of?

No, she thought. Not her personally. The Americans. And Secretary Adams realized that while these men and women were predisposed to trust the US—wanted to, were perhaps even desperate to, considering what was at stake—the fact was they did not.

Not anymore. Not after the debacle of the past four years.

And she realized that a huge part of her job as Secretary of State would be to regain that trust. She remembered her mother bending down, at the entrance to the schoolyard her first day, and saying, "Ellen, if you want to have a friend, you need to be a friend."

She'd met Betsy that day. Betsy, who even at the age of five looked like June Cleaver, though she sounded like a tiny sailor in the merchant navy.

And now, half a century later, Ellen Adams, the American Secretary of State, desperately needed to make friends.

She looked at the worried and wary faces of her colleagues and knew what she had to do. She had to tell them the truth. About the odd message that came in to the junior FSO. She had to tell them what Gil had said. About Bashir Shah.

They had a right to know.

Though perhaps not just yet.

When she'd arrived twenty minutes earlier at the American consulate in Frankfurt, she'd immediately gone to a secure room and contacted the Chairman of the Joint Chiefs of Staff back in Washington.

General Whitehead answered on the first ring. "Yes?"

"It's Ellen Adams. Did I wake you up?"

In the background she could hear his wife groggily asking who was calling at two in the morning.

"It's Secretary Adams," he said, his voice muted through the hand he'd obviously placed over the mouthpiece. "It's all right, Madame Secretary." He still sounded sleepy but was gaining strength with each word. "How's your son?"

It was the question a man who'd lost too many young men and women would think to ask.

"Recovering, thank you. I need to ask you a question. It's confidential."

"This line is secure." He'd obviously left his bedroom and gone into a private office. "Go on."

Ellen looked through the thick, reinforced window of the consulate, toward the park across Gießener Straße. But the weak morning sun revealed it wasn't actually a park. It just looked like one.

Much like the building she was in was the home of American diplomats but looked like a Stalag.

Things were not as they appeared.

That was no park she was looking at. Some bright light had decided to put the US consulate across from a massive graveyard.

"What can you tell me about Bashir Shah?"

Bert Whitehead sat down with a thud and stared across his office, at the photographs on the far wall.

This would be, he knew, his last campaign. He didn't have the heart, never mind the stomach, for it anymore.

Bashir Shah. Had she really just said that name?

"I think, Madame Secretary, that you know as much as I do."

"I think, General Whitehead"—her voice came surprisingly clear down the line from Frankfurt—"that might not be true."

"I've seen the documentary your journalist did on Dr. Shah."

"That was a while ago."

"True. I've also read the dossier that Intelligence has prepared for your confirmation. I know about the notes."

Ellen gave a small, unamused laugh. "Of course you would."

"You were wise to report them as soon as they arrived."

The notes he was referring to had started appearing shortly after the documentary had aired. Every year Ellen Adams received at her home, through the mail, a card. It was unsigned and wished her a happy birthday. In English and Urdu. It also wished her long life.

Ellen had given the first to the FBI, then forgotten about it. Until one arrived on Gil's birthday. Then on Katherine's.

And when Quinn, Ellen's second husband and Katherine's father, had died suddenly of a heart attack, another one arrived. Within hours. Before the official announcement had been made. A note of condolence. In English and Urdu.

This one hand-delivered.

She had no way to prove it, and the FBI came up empty, but she knew. As she'd held the note, her fingers growing cold as blood rushed from her broken heart, she knew.

It was from Bashir Shah.

They'd run a toxicology exam, and there was nothing to suggest Quinn's death was anything other than natural. Tragic. But natural.

Ellen wanted to believe that Shah had simply taken advantage of the tragedy to sow doubt. To add cruelty to grief. To play cat to her mouse.

But Ellen Adams was no quivering mouse. She'd stared the truth in the face.

Bashir Shah had killed her husband. And there was another terrible truth. He'd done it in revenge for the documentary she'd aired, which had led to a series of newspaper reports, which had led, after months of pressure from the then American administration on the Pakistani government, to Shah's arrest and trial.

Now she had Shah in her sights once again. But she needed information, and a lot of it.

"Pretend I know nothing," she said.

"May I ask why you want to know about Dr. Shah?"

"Please, just tell me. I was tempted to call Tim Beecham but decided to call you first."

There was, again, that pause. "I think, Madame Secretary, that was a good decision."

And with that, Ellen Adams had her answer. What that look of concern had meant in the Oval Office, a million years ago, when the Director of National Intelligence had left the room to make a call. And the Chairman of the Joint Chiefs had watched, with furrowed brow.

"Dr. Shah is a Pakistani nuclear physicist," General Whitehead began. Slowly opening the closet door to reveal what was inside. "He's one of the sons of their nuclear program, having inherited it from the first generation. But his weapons are much more powerful, much more sophisticated. He's brilliant. Undoubtedly a genius. He set up his own institute, the Pakistani Research Laboratories, that was a cover for Pakistan's efforts to progress their nuclear weapons program to compete with India."

"Efforts which were successful," said Ellen.

"Yes. We know that Pakistan is still expanding its arsenal. From what we can tell, it has one hundred sixty nuclear warheads."

"Jesus wept."

"Jesus will be sobbing soon. Our informants tell us by 2025, it will have two hundred fifty warheads."

"Dear God," sighed Ellen.

"This makes it extraordinarily dangerous in an unstable region, and they're determined to keep it that way."

"Israel has nuclear weapons too, doesn't it?" said Ellen and heard a chuckle down the line.

"If you can get them to admit that, Madame Secretary, the Yankees will hire you to pitch, 'cause you can clearly work miracles."

"I'm a Pirates fan."

"Ah, yes. I forgot you're from Pittsburgh."

"Between us, General, tell me. Israel does have nuclear warheads, right?"

"Yes, Madame Secretary. It's the only secret they're happy to let slip. But that's actually given the Pakistani nuclear program an excuse. They insist increasing their inventory is just like Israel's program. They want to provide a so-called balance of terror against India."

"Nice."

Ellen Adams was familiar with the concept, from the Cold War between the US and the USSR, when neither side wanted to hit the button, knowing it could lead to reprisals that could wipe out the human race.

It kept each from behaving especially badly. That was the theory.

What it in fact created wasn't a balance of terror, but a perpetual state of terror.

"And Iran's nuclear weapons program?" she asked.

She could almost hear him shaking his head. "We have suspicions, but we can't confirm. But yes, Madame Secretary, I think we need to assume Iran either has, or soon will have, its own nuclear weapons."

"All of this is public knowledge," said Ellen. "What can you tell me about Dr. Shah's private dealings? At some point he went into business on his own."

"True. He began trafficking in weapons-grade uranium and plutonium. But not just that. Others deal in that market, notably the Russian mob. But what makes Shah so dangerous is that he became a one-stop shop, a kind of Walmart of weapons, selling not just the materials but the technology. The equipment, the expertise, the delivery systems."

"The people."

"Yes. Clients could go to him and in one transaction they could buy everything they needed to develop their own nuclear bombs. From soup to nuts, so to speak."

"Clients. You mean other countries?" asked Ellen.

"In some cases. We think he supplied the North Koreans with the components for their nuclear weapons program."

"And the Pakistani government knew what Shah was doing?"

"Yes. He couldn't have gotten away with it without, if not their approval, then their willingness to turn a blind eye. They tolerated his dealings. Why? Because his goals lined up nicely with theirs."

"And those were?"

"To keep the region destabilized, to gain advantage over India, and to undermine the West. Shah has made billions supplying anything and everything to the highest bidder. Not just nuclear technology, but heavy weapons, chemicals, biological agents. More traditional weapons. You asked about his clients being other countries. That's not where the danger lies. We at least have some control over governments. The real threat is that nuclear weapons will fall into the hands of criminals and terrorist organizations. Frankly, the fact they haven't yet is shocking."

Ellen paused a moment to absorb that, her mind racing ahead. "Who supplies Shah with these components, these weapons? He doesn't make them."

"No, he's the middleman. There're all sorts of players, but one of his main suppliers seems to be the Russian mafia."

"And Pakistan allows this?" Ellen needed to be absolutely sure on this point. "They're our ally."

"They're playing a dangerous game. The Pakistani government

allowed us to operate military bases in the north during our long military presence in Afghanistan, but they also gave safe haven to bin Laden, Al-Qaeda, the Pathan, the Taliban. Their border with Afghanistan is porous. The country is riddled with extremists, terrorists, supported and protected by the government."

"And supplied by Shah."

"Yes, though to meet him you'd never suspect. He looks like your brother, your best friend. Scholarly. Benign."

"But things are not as they appear."

"Rarely are," said General Whitehead. "I was in those meetings with the Pakistani military. But I was also in those caves. I saw the weapons hidden there and supplied by Shah. If any of these groups ever actually did get a nuclear bomb—"

"Why haven't they, if he's been supplying them for decades?"

"Two reasons," said Bert Whitehead. "Most of these groups are cannibals. They fight among themselves. Kill their own. There's little organization, no continuity. It takes years and years, and stability, to actually build a bomb. And you can't do it in a cave on a mountainside. The other reason is that Western intelligence agencies stop them. Our intelligence and policing networks have broken up dozens of efforts to sell or obtain nuclear materials and waste since the collapse of the Soviet Union. And remember, it only takes a small amount to build a dirty bomb."

Secretary Adams didn't have to be reminded. That thought was never far from her mind.

"As you know," the General continued, "the American administration before this past one pressured Pakistan to arrest Shah. That was partly thanks to your documentary. Public pressure was put on the Pakistanis. We were hoping for a prison term, but all he got was house arrest. Still, that's better than nothing, I suppose. It limits his influence."

"Until now," said Ellen.

"What do you mean?"

"Didn't you know? He's out. The Pakistanis released him last year."

"For Christ's sake—I'm sorry, Madame Secretary." General Whitehead sighed. "Bashir Shah out. That's a problem."

"More than you think. It was apparently done with our blessing."

"Our?"

"The previous administration."

"That's not possible. Who'd be stupid enough . . . Never mind."

Former President Eric Dunn, that's who. Known to even, perhaps especially, his closest associates as Eric the Dumb. But this went beyond dumb into deranged.

"It was just after the election," said Secretary Adams.

"After the election? After they lost?" asked General Whitehead. "Now why would they do that?" he muttered to himself. "How do you know all this?"

"My son told me. He was following a nuclear physicist named Nasrin Bukhari who'd been hired by Shah."

Ellen explained what she knew. There was silence down the line as General Whitehead listened, absorbing every word. And what it meant.

Finally he said, "But why would Shah kill his own people?"

"He wouldn't."

"Then who?"

"I was hoping you'd tell me."

But all the Secretary of State heard was a great silence.

CHAPTER 13

"The Israeli Prime Minister denies they had anything to do with the bombings," Boynton whispered in Ellen's ear half an hour later as she sat in the virtual meeting with other foreign ministers, intelligence chiefs, and aides.

"Thank you," she said, then turned to the others on the video call and told them.

Boynton's interruption was welcome. It meant she did not have to answer the question of how she knew about the exact time of the bomb, the target, and the city.

This bought her a little more time to consider her answer.

"Do we believe the Israeli Prime Minister?" asked France.

"Have the Israelis ever lied to us before?" asked Italy.

That got a laugh.

But they also knew that while Israel might not be entirely truthful with them, the Prime Minister was less likely to lie to the American President. That was a friend Israel needed to keep. And starting off with a lie was not helpful.

"Besides," said the UK Foreign Secretary, "Mossad might be happy to kill Pakistani nuclear physicists, but not in such a messy, brutal way. They pride themselves on being precise. Clean. This was anything but."

He seemed to have forgotten that Ellen had said exactly that just a few minutes earlier.

"Madame Secretary," said the Canadian, "you haven't answered our question. How did you come to know about the Frankfurt attack and Dr. Bukhari?"

Ellen thought maybe she and the Canadian might not be friends after all.

"And that the targets on the other buses were probably Pakistani physicists?" asked Italy.

"As you know, my son was on the Frankfurt bus. He's a journalist. One of his sources had told him that there was a plot involving Pakistani nuclear physicists. The name he was given was Nasrin Bukhari. He was following her. It wasn't hard then to put it all together."

"Who was his source?" the Canadian asked.

Really, thought Ellen, this woman wearing moose and bears was getting quite annoying.

"He won't tell me."

"His own mother?" asked the German.

"The Secretary of State." Her tone discouraged any follow-up questions on her personal relationship with her son.

"What was the plot? What was planned?" France asked, leaning toward the screen, so that his nose appeared huge and they could see his pores.

"My son doesn't know."

France looked skeptical.

"Your son was kidnapped by the Pathan a few years ago," the German Foreign Minister said.

"That's true," said France.

"Be careful," the Canadian warned him. But France rarely listened to Canada.

"Where other journalists were executed, including three French, he managed to escape—" said France.

"Clément," snapped Canada. "Enough."

But it was not.

"And now I understand your son has converted to Islam. He's a Muslim."

"Clément!" said the Canadian. *"C'est assez."* That's enough.

But it was too late. And far too much.

"What're you saying?" Ellen's voice was filled with warning.

Though she knew perfectly well what the French Foreign Minister was saying. What others had suggested, but never to her face.

"He's not saying anything," said Italy. "He's upset. Paris just suffered a terrible attack. Let it go, Madame Secretary."

Now France's face was practically smashed up against the screen. "How do you know your son is not part of this plot? How do we know he didn't plant the bomb?"

And there it was.

"How dare you," snarled Ellen. "How dare you suggest my son would have anything to do with this. He tried to stop it. Risked his life to stop it. Almost died in the explosion."

"Almost," said the German, his voice maddeningly calm, infuriatingly reasonable. "But he did not. He survived. Just as he survived the kidnapping."

Ellen turned to him. Barely believing what she was hearing. "You can't be serious."

She looked at them all. Even Canada, in her silly moose-and-bear flannel, was waiting for her to answer the question.

How had Gil Bahar escaped his Islamic terrorist kidnappers when all others had been executed?

It was a question she herself had asked when she'd met him in Stockholm right after his escape. She hadn't meant to suggest anything. But Gil had heard an accusation. He always did.

Their relationship, already strained, had gotten worse after that, as the unanswered question festered.

Now they barely talked. Though Ellen had tried and tried, through

Betsy, through Katherine. Through phone calls and letters. To explain that she loved him. Trusted him.

And that she'd only asked thinking he'd want to talk about it.

Gil's kidnapping was also at the heart of the conflict between Ellen Adams and then Senator, now President, Douglas Williams.

That too had festered.

She looked at her colleagues. All frayed, all afraid. Secretary Adams could not yet tell them about the coded message that had come in, not until they had a better handle on it, and on Anahita Dahir.

But she had to throw them something. And she knew what.

"His source did tell him who was behind it," she offered. "He was able to tell me this morning from his hospital bed."

She thought she'd throw that in. Gil had not escaped unharmed, thank you very much.

"And?" said Germany.

"Bashir Shah."

It was as though some black hole had torn open and sucked all the life, all the light, all the sound from their rooms. Leaving them senseless.

Shah.

And then, all at once, with a whoosh, they began talking. Shouting questions.

But it boiled down to one question, asked several different ways.

"How could it be Shah? He's under house arrest in Islamabad. Has been for years."

She went through exactly what she'd discussed with General Whitehead, to stunned silence once again.

"Shit."

"Merde."

"Scheiße."

"*Merda.*"

"Fucking hell," said the Canadian.

Ellen retooled her thinking. Maybe a bottle of Chardonnay with this woman after all, when this was over.

"Are you saying we have no idea where Shah is?" asked France.

"Yes." She searched their faces and came to the conclusion they were equally ignorant. And equally outraged. Equally angry.

At her.

"You let this happen?" said Germany. "You let the most dangerous arms dealer escape— *Nein*, not escape, walk out the front door?"

"I think he probably took the back," said Italy. "So no one would see—"

"The door is immaterial," snapped Germany. "The point is, he's free, with the blessing of the US government."

"But not this administration, and not my blessing," said Ellen. "I hate him as much as you do, maybe more."

Because the truth was, Ellen Adams did suspect Shah had killed Quinn. A man she loved with all her heart. In retaliation for that documentary. And just because he could.

And then he taunted her, to this day, with those cheery cards.

Now he'd been freed, and was free to do whatever he pleased, with the protection of some in the Pakistani government and the blessing of a delusional American President and his flying monkeys in the cabinet.

Including, Ellen Adams now suspected, Tim Beecham, their own acting Director of National Intelligence.

That was why General Whitehead didn't trust him.

Tim Beecham was a holdover from the previous administration, one of a flurry of political nominations sent to the Senate in the waning days of the Dunn Presidency. The Senate hadn't voted on him, and the new President had left him as "acting" DNI until he could decide whether to keep him in place. From his time in the

Senate, Williams knew Beecham as a right-wing conservative intelligence professional, but that was all.

The President was left to hope his Director of National Intelligence was loyal. Which he certainly was. But to whom?

"What's Shah up to?" asked the Canadian. "Three nuclear physicists. That can't be good."

"Three dead physicists," said Italy. "Doesn't that mean someone did us a favor?"

Ellen saw again the faces of the families, the photographs they held. The teddy bears and balloons and the flowers dying on the pavement. Some favor.

And yet Italy had a point.

"What I don't understand is why he'd recruit second-rate nuclear physicists?" asked Canada. "Presumably he could buy just about anyone."

That had been worrying Ellen too.

"You have to pressure your son, Madame Secretary," said Italy. "He needs to tell you who his source is. We have to know what Shah is up to."

At Ellen's request, Betsy flew back to DC.

Once at her window seat on the commercial flight out of Frankfurt, she opened the letter Ellen had given her. Written in her easily identifiable scribble.

Despite the fact Ellen herself had handed it to her, slipped into a copy of *People* magazine, and there was no mistaking the handwriting, Ellen had still opened the letter with, *A mixed metaphor walks into a bar . . .*

The seat belt sign was turned on, and the announcement was made to please put phones on airplane mode. Which Betsy did, right after sending a quick email to Ellen.

. . . seeing the handwriting on the wall, but hoping to nip it in the bud.

Then she sat back and read the rest of the short note, while just behind her and off to her right, in the business-class seat in the middle of the cabin, a nondescript young man read a newspaper.

He probably thought that she hadn't spotted him.

After reading the note, Betsy slipped it into the pocket of her pantsuit. Someone might steal her purse, but they were less likely to get her pants off.

The letter would be safe there.

All the way across the Atlantic, while other passengers ate and slept in their lie-flat beds, Betsy Jameson looked out the window and considered how she'd accomplish what Ellen had asked.

"I'll see her now," Ellen said.

She was in an office provided by the American Consul General and watched as Charles Boynton left the room and returned with Anahita Dahir.

"Thank you, Charles. You can leave us."

He hesitated at the door. "Can I get you something to eat or drink, Madame Secretary?"

"No, thank you. Ms. Dahir?"

Even though Anahita was starving, she shook her head. She sure wasn't going to eat an egg salad sandwich in front of the Secretary of State.

Boynton closed the door, a worried expression on his face. He was being frozen out, and he had to find a way back in.

Ellen waited until the door clicked softly shut; then she waved Anahita to an armchair across from where she was sitting.

"Who are you?"

"I'm sorry, Madame Secretary?"

"You heard me. We don't have time to waste. People have died, there's every reason to think worse is coming. And you're involved. So answer me now. Who are you?"

As Anahita watched, Ellen slowly placed her hand, splayed, over the closed cover of a folder resting across her knees. It was, Ana knew, an intelligence briefing. Much like the one her interrogators had in the basement of the State Department.

She lifted her eyes from that to the Secretary of State.

"I'm Anahita Dahir, a foreign service officer. You can ask anyone. Katherine knows me. Gil knows me. I'm exactly who I say I am."

"Now that's not true, is it?" said Ellen. "I believe that's your name and job, but I also think there's more to it. That message came in to you. Specifically. We now know there's a connection to Pakistan. All three nuclear physicists are from there. You spent two years in our Islamabad embassy. You're on the Pakistan desk. Who sent you the message?"

"I don't know."

"You do," snapped Ellen. "Look, I got you out of that interrogation. Probably shouldn't have, but I did. Brought you with me so you'd be safe. Again, probably shouldn't have, but did. You saved my son's life and I owed you that. But there's a limit, and we've reached it. Security agents are right outside that door." She didn't bother to look in that direction. "If you don't answer me now, I'll call them in and hand you over."

"I don't know." Ana's voice was high, straining out of her constricted throat. "You have to believe me."

"No, what I have to do is get at the truth. You copied out the message before you erased it. Do you normally?"

Anahita shook her head.

"Then why this one?"

By the miserable look on the FSO's face, Ellen knew she had her. While she might not get the answer, she at least had the question.

But when the answer came, it wasn't at all what Ellen expected.

"My family is Lebanese. Loving but strict. Traditional. A good Lebanese girl lives at home until she's married. My parents gave me far more freedom than my friends ever got. I was allowed to move out of our home, to leave the country even, for the job. They were proud that I was working for the State Department, serving my country. And they trusted me never to cross a certain line."

Ellen listened closely, her mind racing ahead, then skidding to a stop.

"Gil."

Anahita nodded. "Yes. When that message came in, I really did think it was spam. At first. That's why I showed it to my supervisor and then erased it. But just before I did, I wondered if, maybe, it was from Gil."

"Why would you think that?"

There was a pause, and Ellen realized this grown woman was blushing.

"We'd always meet at my small apartment in Islamabad. When he wanted to get together, he'd send a text with the time. Nothing else. Just the time."

"Charming," said Ellen, and saw Anahita smile slightly.

"He was, actually. That makes it sound bad, but he did it for me. I wanted to keep our relationship secret so that nothing could get back to my parents. And it was—"

Fun. Heady. Exciting. Sneaking around in a city filled with deception, duplicity. Those steamy, sultry days and nights in Islamabad. Everyone so young, so vital, so firm, so certain. Life teeming all around them while Death waited in the marketplace.

The work they were doing felt so important. As translators, security, journalists. Spies. They felt themselves so important. Immortal in a place where violence and death struck others. Never them.

And those texts. *1945. 1330.* And her favorite, *0615.* To wake up to that. To Gil.

Watching Anahita's physical reaction to the memory forced Ellen to suppress a smile. It was, she could tell, exactly the same way she'd felt about Gil's father. Cal had been her first love. Not her soul mate. That was Quinn, Katherine's father.

But man, was Cal Bahar fun. And firm.

And even now, thinking of him . . .

She stopped. If there was a less appropriate time for this, she didn't know it.

Ellen cleared her throat, and Anahita blushed again, and returned to the cold, gray, featureless room in Frankfurt. "I'd hoped the message was from Gil. I wrote it down, then erased it. Later that night I sent off a message to Gil asking if it was from him."

"Did you know where he was?"

"No. We hadn't been in touch for a while. Not since I returned to DC."

Ellen nodded, and suspected had Anahita told those security officers all this, they wouldn't have believed her. They wouldn't have understood the yearning, the burning, a young woman could have for her first love. How it could lead her to overinterpret, misinterpret, reread, and reinterpret a message.

How hope could blind even the most intelligent of people.

But it made perfect sense to Ellen Adams. She too had been dazzled, by Gil's father. Blinded to what others saw all too clearly. What Betsy had seen and tried, gently, to say. All the reasons she and Cal could never work.

"That's how you knew he was in Frankfurt," she said.

"Yes."

"But if it wasn't Gil who sent the message, who did?"

"I don't know. I don't think whoever sent it meant for it to come to me specifically. Just anyone who happened to be on the desk."

"What do you know about Bashir Shah?" Ellen saw the FSO's face freeze. "You know something. I saw your reaction in the car. You were terrified."

There was a long silence as Anahita fidgeted. "When I was in Islamabad, I was working on nuclear proliferation issues, and some of my Pakistani contacts would talk about him. Almost in awe. He was mythical. In a terrible way. Like one of the gods of war. Is he behind this?"

Instead of answering, Ellen got up. "Is there anything else you need to tell me?"

Anahita also got to her feet and shook her head. "No, Madame Secretary. That's all."

Ellen walked her to the door. "I'll be going back to the hospital to see Gil before we leave. Would you like to come?"

Anahita hesitated, then lifted her chin and put her shoulders back. "Thank you, but no."

As Ellen closed the door, she wondered if Gil had any idea what he'd lost.

As Anahita walked back down the hall, she considered how far she could get if she just kept going. How long before they noticed she was gone?

Before they realized she'd lied. Again.

CHAPTER 14

As Betsy Jameson waited in the taxi line at Dulles, she wondered if she should ask that nice young man if he'd like to share a ride.

He was so clearly following her it was almost sweet. She hoped he wasn't a spy, because he'd have quite a short career, and perhaps a short life, if even she could spot him. But Betsy suspected he wasn't so much following her as guarding her.

Sent by Ellen to make sure she was safe.

It was both comforting and disconcerting. It hadn't occurred to Betsy that what she was about to do could be dangerous. Difficult, yes, but not dangerous.

Betsy Jameson was used to difficult. Her upbringing, on the south side of Pittsburgh, had made her a fighter. The difficulty was that she grew up believing life was a struggle, people were shitty, no one was to be trusted. Family was there to abuse her, men were rapists, and women were bitches. Cats were sneaky. Dogs were OK. Except the small yappy ones. And don't get her started on birds.

In her experience, monsters didn't come out of the closet; they came in through the front door. Invited in.

Betsy Jameson, at the age of five, in the playground of the new school, had learned not to let anyone in.

She'd retreated into her own cave, on the side of an emotional mountain. Where no one and nothing could find her. Could hurt her.

When playing Red Rover, she never invited anyone over. And the other kids learned, when racing toward the line, to never try to break through Betsy Jameson's grip.

But on that first day of school, sitting with her back to the wall, Betsy had watched a little blond girl, with knock-knees, huge thick glasses, and a sweater too warm for the day, stand at the entrance to the playground. Her mother was bending down, whispering something. The solemn little girl looked at her, nodded; then they kissed.

Betsy couldn't remember the last time anyone kissed her. Not like that, anyway. Fleeting, on the cheek, gently. Kindly.

Then the little blond girl, who looked so fragile, had stepped across the threshold into the yard and, unexpectedly and irrevocably, deep into the cave. Where Betsy Jameson kept her heart.

From that day forward, Ellen and Betsy were almost inseparable. Ellen taught Betsy that goodness existed, and Betsy taught Ellen how to kick attackers in the nuts.

Ellen and Betsy had gone to university together, Ellen studying law and political science and Betsy taking a degree in English literature and becoming a teacher.

It was an achievement that went uncelebrated by her family, but by then it no longer mattered. Betsy Jameson had left her cave behind and emerged into a world where danger still lurked, but so did goodness.

Now, in the March chill of the DC airport, she remembered Ellen's long embrace in the lobby of the American consulate in Frankfurt and her whispered "Watch yourself."

Of course, at the time, she hadn't yet opened her letter. The one still in her pants pocket.

The one asking her to quietly, secretly, look into Tim Beecham.

He was now President Williams's acting Director of National Intelligence. He had been, at least officially, a senior national security advisor in the previous administration. But what had he really done? That's what Ellen wanted to, needed to, know. And fast.

On the surface, what Ellen asked her to do was straightforward enough. But it wasn't the surface that they were interested in.

Betsy glanced at the young man, who was studying the same newspaper he'd spent eight hours reading on the flight. She almost took pity on him. But then decided it would just embarrass him if she approached and offered him a lift. Besides, she wanted time on the drive into Foggy Bottom to think.

The next taxi was hers.

As it pulled away, Betsy saw the agent jump the ropes and get into a car already waiting at the curb, in the red zone. Vehicles were not normally allowed to wait there, unless they had government tags.

Betsy sat back and considered her next move.

"Have you eaten?"

"Not yet," said Katherine.

"Go grab something, I'll sit with him," said Ellen.

Their flight to Islamabad was scheduled to take off in less than an hour. Ellen had cleared it with the President and her fellow foreign ministers. There'd been some pushback, but it was obvious that while the UK, France, and Germany had been the targets of the bombing, the US had the best chance of getting answers out of the Pakistanis.

It was also decided that, until they were in the air, no one else, including Islamabad, would be told of the imminent arrival of the US Secretary of State.

Gil's breathing changed. There was a slight groan as he shifted in his hospital bed and began to wake up. Ellen took his hand, feeling it both familiar and unfamiliar. It had been so long since she'd held it.

She watched his handsome, bruised face as he struggled up through the morass of painkillers.

Opening his eyes, he focused on his mother and smiled. Then full consciousness hit and the smile disappeared.

"How are you?" she whispered, leaning close to kiss his cheek. But he pulled back.

It was subtle but enough.

"OK." His brows lowered as the memory of what had happened came back. "The others?"

Seventeen bystanders were also in the hospital. Secretary Adams had spoken to some, briefly. Those with the most minor injuries. The doctors advised against disturbing the others, many of them still sedated. Many fighting for their lives, their families sitting vigil.

In an instant everything had changed as they'd walked along, driven along, cycled along a road they took every day.

Limbs lost. Brains irreparably damaged. Blinded, maimed, paralyzed.

Scars, visible and invisible, were created that would never heal.

The hospital door opened, and Charles Boynton looked in. "Madame Secretary, you're wanted."

"Thank you, Charles. I'll be with you in a minute."

Her Chief of Staff hovered for a moment before withdrawing.

Ellen turned back to Gil. "I'm on my way to Islamabad."

"Are the Pakistanis cooperating?"

"That's why I'm going. To make sure they do. I suspect they know exactly where Shah is."

"So do I."

"Gil, I have to ask you again." She held his gaze. "We need to know your source."

He smiled. "And here I thought my mother was visiting to make sure I was all right. I didn't realize I'm talking to the Secretary of State."

Ellen bit back a few replies that had appeared fully formed and had almost escaped.

It was a cheap shot, and Gil knew it.

"I can't tell you," he said, his voice softer. "You know that. You ran a media empire. You went to court to defend journalists who wouldn't reveal their sources, and now you ask me to reveal mine?"

"Lives are—"

"Don't tell me that lives are at stake," he snapped.

There were some memories that lived, forever young, in his mind. Photographs, stills, that floated up unexpectedly on gloomy nights and sunny days. When he was walking, or eating, or in the shower. In the most mundane of moments, they appeared.

The beheading of his friend the French journalist. Gil's captors had made sure he saw it, and that he knew he was next. Jean-Jacques had looked straight at him, held his eyes, as the blade was applied to his throat.

There was the image of the young Black woman at the moment the truck, driven by a far-right extremist in Texas, had hit the crowd of peaceful protesters he was covering. The last moment of her life.

There were others, but those were the most frequent visitors. The uninvited guests. The uninvited ghosts.

And now another image took its place alongside the other horrors. The rows of passengers on the bus, their faces upturned, staring at him. Afraid of him. They were about to die, and he couldn't save them.

"The only reason we have a hope of stopping more deaths," he said, "is because my source trusted me. That'll stop the moment I tell you who it is. No, Ellen. I won't tell you."

The use of her name, rather than "Mom" or even "Mother," always hurt her. And she suspected that was why he did it. Partly to cause pain, but also as a warning.

Go no further.

Still, her relationship with her son was less important than the lives of perhaps tens of thousands of other sons and daughters. Mothers and fathers. If this tore her family apart completely, so be it. It would be less horrific than the loss many families had suffered in the past few hours.

"We need more information, and your source must have it. He doesn't need to know you told us."

"Are you kidding me?" He glared at her. "He'll know when they kill him."

"They?"

"Shah and his people."

"Does he work for Shah?"

"Look, I want to help. I want to find Shah too. To stop him. But I can't tell you any more."

Ellen took a deep breath and tried to calm herself.

She regrouped. "Do you think your source knows what Shah has planned?"

"I asked, of course. He said he doesn't know."

"Do you believe him?"

Gil's father, Cal Bahar, had instilled in his son the conviction that journalists, investigative reporters, war correspondents, were heroes. The Fourth Estate, keeping democracy's feet to the fire.

Gil Bahar had been raised knowing that was what he wanted to do, was meant to do. He didn't want to be in a conflict; he wanted to cover one. Whether that conflict was Afghanistan or Washington.

To witness. To report. To find out why. And how. And who.

To tell the truth. No matter how ugly. How dangerous.

His mother, on the other hand, had always been the businessperson. The bureaucrat who ran the empire. The rational one who never looked beyond the figures on the spreadsheet.

The bean counter, his father called her, sometimes even with affection. He liked beans, he'd add with a laugh.

Gil, the budding journalist, could see the truth behind the jest, even as a child.

But now he thought maybe something had changed. Either his father had been wrong all this time and perhaps didn't know his mother as well as he thought, or she'd developed the facility of asking not just what people knew but also, more importantly, what they believed.

And now, finally, she was asking him what he believed.

"I think maybe he does know what Shah has planned," said Gil. "But it was all I could do to get Shah's name out of my source. He was terrified, and for good reason. He probably regrets telling me that much."

"If he won't tell you Shah's plan, can you at least try to find out if the deaths of the physicists put an end to it, or if it's still on?"

Gil hauled himself up in bed, wincing slightly, and stared at his mother. The Secretary of State.

"Are you tracing my messages?"

She hesitated. "I'm not. I trust you to give me anything important that you find out. But others . . ."

He nodded. "In that case, I can't contact my source." He'd spoken loudly, verging on the unnatural, before dropping his voice to a whisper. "But there might be another way."

"Madame Secretary, you're needed."

Ellen looked toward Boynton, standing at the door, and wondered how much he'd heard.

"The plane will wait," she said.

"Is Ana here?" Gil glanced toward the door.

For just a moment, he looked like her little boy again. Afraid to ask a painful question but, like a good journalist in a conflict zone, determining that the need to know outweighed the fear.

"No. She was invited, but . . ."

He nodded. That was enough truth for now.

"Madame Secretary," said Boynton, an edge to his voice now. "It's not the plane."

As soon as Ellen stepped out of the limousine at the American consulate in Frankfurt, she was met by a middle-aged man, the same one she'd spoken to at the scene of the bombing. The head of American Intelligence in Germany.

"Scott Cargill, Madame Secretary."

"Yes, I remember you, Mr. Cargill." She turned to the slightly younger woman with him, even as they rushed her into the building.

"This is Frau Fischer. She's with German Intelligence," he explained as Marine guards held the doors open.

"We have a suspect," said Fischer, in excellent English.

Their footsteps echoed on the marble floor as they crossed the lobby to the elevators, one of which was being held for them.

"In custody?" asked Ellen.

"Not yet," said Frau Fischer as the elevator doors whisked closed. "All we have so far is an image from the security cameras along the route, and the one inside the bus."

Ellen and Boynton were led into a windowless room that had a bunker-like quality. Ellen was surprised to see the German Foreign Minister was there in person, from Berlin.

"Ellen," he said and extended his hand.

"Heinrich."

He indicated a comfortable swivel chair beside him. "You need to see this video we found."

As she took her seat, she smiled slightly at the "we." Ellen suspected Heinrich Von Baier had as much to do with the find as the coffee cup did.

He gave a sign and a video appeared on the screen at the front of the room.

It showed the number 119 bus pulling up to a stop and a man getting off. Then, at a click, the image froze.

"This," said Scott Cargill, "is two stops before the explosion."

"Our bomber," said Von Baier, and Ellen smiled again, this time at the "our." She wondered how long his ownership would last if they were wrong.

On the screen she saw a slight young man wearing jeans, a jacket, and around his neck, a checkered keffiyeh.

She turned to Cargill. "How do you know this is him? It looks like racial profiling to me."

"We know because of two other pieces of evidence," Cargill said. Once again, a video appeared, this time taken from inside the bus.

And once again, they froze the image on the screen.

She saw Gil, sitting apparently perfectly relaxed near the back of the bus.

"That," Frau Fischer said, pointing to the woman behind Gil and off to his left, "is Nasrin Bukhari."

"The physicist."

"*Ja*, Madame Secretary. You recognize your son, of course. And that"—the finger pointed to a passenger just in front of Dr. Bukhari—"is our suspect. Watch what happens next."

The tape rolled again, and they saw the man bend down so that he was hidden by the woman in the seat in front of him. Then he sat up, stood up, and walked to the front of the bus. The next view was the one they'd already seen, taken as he exited.

The image froze, and then Fischer zoomed in on his face. He was dark-skinned, clean-shaven, and appeared to be looking straight at the CCTV camera.

"From the blast pattern of the explosion, we know that it originated at the very back and on the left side of the bus," said Fischer. "Where he sat."

Ellen stared at the face.

What was he thinking as he left the bus? Left the people? What had he been thinking as he sat there, watching the children squirm in their seats? The teenagers on their phones? The exhausted workers on their way home? How had he felt, knowing . . . ?

What did any bomber think, feel, knowing innocents would die?

Ellen was not insensible to the fact, to the truth, that American military personnel, on orders from their leaders, had pressed buttons sending missiles aimed at enemies, but sometimes also sending innocent civilians from this world.

Now she leaned forward, staring at the young man. "Why is he alive?"

"Well, he left the bus, Madame Secretary," said Von Baier.

"Yes, I got that. But aren't they normally suicide bombers?"

There was silence, as the question sat there. Finally Cargill answered.

"That's often true, but not always."

"When is it true?" Ellen asked.

"When the people involved are radicalized. Religious fanatics," he replied. "And when their handlers, those who groomed them, want to make absolutely sure the bomb will go off."

"You mean, when it's a rudimentary device?" asked Ellen, looking at the two intelligence officers. "Probably homemade by amateurs. It could fail unless manually triggered."

"Ja."

"And when is it not true? When do they just leave the bomb, like he did?" She gestured to the man on the screen.

Now the German and American officers were nodding, thinking. Assessing.

"When they are sure of the device," said the German.

"And when they are not fanatics," said the American.

"Go on," said Ellen.

"When they're too high-value an asset to waste on a senseless act of self-destruction.

"Or when he decides he doesn't want to die," said Frau Fischer.

Everyone stared at the screen, at the face. Of the killer. Who was still alive, and out there.

"We'll get this to the international intelligence network," said the German Foreign Minister. "If he's been recruited and groomed, he'll be in the system somewhere."

"But facial recognition didn't pick him up," said Ellen.

"No. That's true," said Cargill. "He might be an asset they've kept clean. We'll alert the airports and train stations. Bus terminals and car-rental agencies."

"And get it on social media and to the networks," said Frau Fischer. "Even if we can't identify him, the publicity will hamper his movements. Someone might see him and report."

Cargill nodded to an agent, who quickly left the room.

"There is something else that's a little, ummm . . ."

Ellen and Von Baier waited while the American Intelligence officer searched for the right word.

". . . unusual."

"Great," muttered Ellen while beside her the dignified Von Baier mumbled, *"Scheisse."*

"More than a little," said Fischer. "Look."

She pointed to the screen and the image they had been looking at for some minutes now.

"What?" asked Ellen.

"No hat."

Ellen shifted her gaze to the German officer, then to Von Baier, who was as baffled as she. This young woman could not possibly be worried about the bomber catching cold in chilly Frankfurt in early March without a . . .

And then she had it at the same moment Von Baier got it. His brows arching as his blue eyes opened wide.

"He's not trying to hide who he is," said Ellen.

"Exactly," said Fischer. "He practically paused so we'd get a good look at him."

Ellen was quiet. Staring at the face. Getting a good look at him. Was it her imagination? Was there sorrow in those eyes? A plea even? For understanding? For help? Surely not. No one sets off a bomb, killing so many innocent people, and expects to be understood.

"Theories?" asked Von Baier.

"This could be a good thing," said Cargill. "He might be cocky. Overconfident. He either doesn't believe we'll figure out that he placed the bomb, or he wants us to know."

"Why?" Von Baier asked.

"Well, that's what we don't know," admitted Cargill. "Ego? Brashness?"

"Look at his expression," said Ellen. Was she the only one who saw it? "He's sorry."

"Oh, come on, Madame Secretary, you can't believe that," said Von Baier. "He's about to murder innocent civilians. He's not sorry at all."

Ellen looked over at Cargill, who obviously agreed with the German Foreign Minister. Then she shifted her gaze to Frau Fischer, who was staring at the face of the bomber, her brows drawn together.

Then she looked at Ellen. Shaking her head.

"I think he's afraid," said Frau Fischer.

Ellen studied the young face again and nodded. "I think you're right."

"Of course he's afraid," said Von Baier. "Of being blown up by his own bomb and meeting a maker who actually isn't all that happy about what he did."

"No, it's something else," said Ellen; then her face cleared. "He wasn't supposed to survive."

"Maybe that's why his handler didn't insist on trying to hide his identity," said Frau Fischer. "Because it wouldn't matter."

Ellen's mind raced. "We need to stop the publication of his picture."

"Why?" said Cargill. And a split second later understood. "Oh, shit."

If the bomber was supposed to die, best his handlers believed he did.

"Verdammt," snapped Fischer. "We need to find him. Fast. Before they do."

"Get Thompson," Cargill was shouting into the phone. "Tell him to stop. Do not put the picture of the suspect—"

Cargill sat with a thud. "OK. Then limit the release." He hung up. "Too late. It's already gone out. But we might be able to stop some publications."

"Nein," said Frau Fischer. "The damage is done. We need to use it if we can. Get it out far and wide. Someone will know who he is. I'll contact the intelligence chiefs in other countries, in case he's crossed a border." She headed for the door. "We'll find him."

Ellen started to get up. "If there's nothing else, I need to call the President and report, then get to my plane—"

"There is one other video we'd like to show you, Ellen," said Heinrich Von Baier.

She sat back down and looked at the screen as the interior of the bus once again appeared.

The bomber had already left. His seat was empty. Ellen watched as Gil answered his phone, listened, then stood up and started shouting.

She watched, her hands closing into fists, as Gil tried desperately to stop the bus. To get people off. He was almost weeping with panic and frustration. Grabbing at people, trying to yank them to their feet. Including Nasrin Bukhari, who batted him away with a satchel.

Ellen watched, every muscle in her body tight, as the bus finally stopped. The driver got up and threw Gil out.

The video flickered, and they saw the street view as Gil landed hard on the sidewalk and the bus pulled away.

Ellen leaned forward, her hand now clasping her mouth, as her son picked himself up and ran after the bus. There was no sound, but it was clear he was shouting. Screaming. Then he stopped, turned, and tried to get people off the sidewalk.

And then, the explosion.

She closed her eyes.

"Madame Secretary." Heinrich Von Baier had stood up and now turned to her. His face grave, his manner formal. "I owe you an apology. I was wrong to suggest your son could have been involved. He did all he could to save lives and would have been killed had the driver not thrown him out."

He dropped his head in a small bow, acknowledging his mistake.

And privately she acknowledged hers, in underestimating his integrity. He took ownership of the mistakes as well.

"Danke," she said. Getting to her feet, she held out both hands toward the diplomat. He took them and squeezed gently. "It was a natural mistake," she said. "One I would probably have made too."

"Thank you," he said, though they both suspected that was not true.

Von Baier dropped his voice and said to Ellen, "Good luck in Islamabad. Be careful. Shah will be watching."

"Yes." She turned to Boynton, who'd been sitting quietly watching all this. "I'll call the President from Air Force Three."

"There's still your meeting."

"This wasn't the meeting you meant?"

"No, Madame Secretary. There's another."

CHAPTER 15

"You need to repeat that, please," said Ellen.

Boynton had shown her into yet another dim, windowless, featureless room. It was in the sub-basement. They'd had to go through a number of security checks and reinforced doors to get there.

Once they were inside, a technician tapped a keyboard then said, "Could you put in your security code please, Madame Secretary."

"My Chief of Staff can use his, can't he?"

"No, I'm afraid not. This needs the highest clearance."

Unsure what "this" was, Ellen typed in the series of numbers and waited.

A large monitor sprang to life, and there was Tim Beecham, the Director of National Intelligence.

After greetings, formal and without a hint of warmth, Beecham began to explain, but when it became clear what this meeting was about, Ellen stopped him and turned to Charles Boynton.

"Get Scott Cargill in here, please. He needs to hear this."

"Madame Secretary, the fewer—" Beecham began, but she stopped him with a look.

"Yes, of course," said Boynton, returning a few minutes later with Cargill, who pulled up a chair beside her.

There was no need for introductions. The DNI knew the CIA's Station Chief in Germany well.

"Anything?" she whispered, and Cargill shook his head.

At Ellen's request, Tim Beecham repeated what he'd said earlier.

"We've gone over the message that came in to Ms. Dahir. The one she says she erased."

The wording wasn't lost on Ellen. "Well, she must've erased it if you found it buried in the trash file. That is where it was found?"

"Yes."

"And it must have a time code attached, showing when it was dumped?"

"Yes."

"One that corresponds to the timeline she explained."

"Yes."

"So Anahita Dahir was telling the truth." Best, Ellen thought, to establish facts and authority early. And without ambiguity.

She didn't like this sly man, and she suspected General Whitehead felt the same way. And now, watching Beecham squirm, Ellen thought of Betsy and her commission to her friend to find out more about the DNI.

She'd heard nothing since Betsy's quick text to say she'd arrived back in DC and was on her way to the State Department.

"So what's your news, Tim?"

"We've found out where the message originated."

"You did?" She leaned so close to the monitor she could feel the heat radiating off it. "Where?"

"Iran."

Ellen sat back as though scalded and took a slow, deep breath in, then a long exhale. Beside her, she heard Cargill say, "Huh." The soft grunt a person made when hit in the solar plexus.

Iran. Iran.

Her mind raced. Iran.

If Shah was selling both nuclear secrets and nuclear physicists,

Iran would want to stop it. Iran had its own nuclear program, which it publicly denied while making sure every power in the region and beyond knew the truth.

Ellen connected the dots. The bloody trail of explosions and assassinations throughout the Middle East. All in aid of Iran stopping anyone else in the region from getting nuclear capability.

"Iran would absolutely want to stop Shah's physicists from reaching their destination," she said.

"That's true," said Beecham. "Except—"

"Whoever sent that message to your FSO didn't plant the bombs," said Cargill. "They tried to prevent the murders."

Ellen's eyes opened wider. That was true. She looked from him to the monitor. While Beecham looked even more annoyed, this time at having his great reveal stolen, he also looked troubled.

"That's what we don't understand," said Beecham. "Why would the Iranians try to stop the bombings? Why would they want to save Shah's physicists? We considered the possibility they're the ones who'd bought the physicists from Dr. Shah, but dismissed it."

"There's no way the Iranian government would trust, never mind hire, Pakistanis," agreed Cargill. "And they sure wouldn't deal with Bashir Shah. He's too enmeshed with the Saudis and other Sunni Arab countries."

"And he wouldn't deal with Iran, would he?" asked Ellen.

"Unlikely," said Beecham. "Besides, Iran has its own highly skilled nuclear physicists and its own program in place. No, this makes no sense."

"So where does that leave us?" asked Ellen.

Nothing.

"Are we sure it came out of Iran?" she asked. "Can't messages be misdirected? Sent off different towers and IP providers? Surely whoever's behind the bombings is sophisticated enough to hide where they are." She paused. "Damn. I keep making the same mistake. It just makes far more sense that Iran is behind the bombings. Not that they tried to stop them."

"It was definitely from Iran," Beecham confirmed. "But there does seem to be some urgency behind the message, otherwise I think they would have tried harder to hide where it came from. And there's something else."

He was looking smug, and Ellen felt something crawl along her spine. As though a huge spider was making its way up.

"Go on."

"We know where the message came from."

"Yes, you've said. Iran."

"No, more precise. We tracked it to a computer in Tehran, belonging to a"—he checked his notes—"Professor Behnam Ahmadi."

"You're kidding," said Cargill. But it was just a figure of speech. He knew, they all knew, that the Director of National Intelligence was far from kidding.

"You know him?" Ellen asked Cargill.

He nodded, putting his thoughts in order. "He's a nuclear physicist."

"Is it possible he knew these people and wanted to save them?" she asked.

"It's possible," said Beecham. "But unlikely."

"Why?"

"Dr. Ahmadi's one of the architects of Iran's nuclear program," said Cargill. "At least that's what we believe. It's difficult to get precise information on a weapons program they deny having."

"We know they have one, what we don't know is if they've managed to develop a bomb yet," said Beecham.

"So what does this mean?" Ellen looked from one to the other, searching their faces. "Why would Dr. Ahmadi try to stop the murders of these physicists?"

"We considered the possibility he's a foreign agent in the employ of another country," said Beecham. "The Saudis, for instance, who are desperate to develop a nuclear weapons program. They'd pay well. Or even the Israelis. They've killed Iranian scientists working on Iran's nuclear program."

"But Dr. Ahmadi would never work for the Israelis, would he?" asked Ellen.

"Depends how much they pay and how desperate he is. We can't rule anything out."

Cargill was shaking his head. "I don't believe it. There's no way Ahmadi would collaborate with another country."

"Why do you say that? What sort of man is he, this Professor Ahmadi?" asked Ellen.

"You might remember when the US embassy in Tehran was occupied by the students and American hostages taken?" asked Beecham. "Back in 1979."

Ellen glared at him. "Yes, I believe someone mentioned that."

"Well, Behnam Ahmadi was one of the students. We have photographs of him holding a gun to an American diplomat's head."

"I'd like to see those."

"I'll send them to you, Madame Secretary," said Beecham. "Behnam Ahmadi is a true believer. A follower of Khomeini and a devotee of the hard-line cleric Mohammad Yazdi."

"But both are dead," said Ellen.

"True, but it proves Dr. Ahmadi's loyalties and beliefs," said Beecham. "He's now clearly aligned behind the current Grand Ayatollah, Khosravi."

"Didn't Khosravi issue a fatwa against any nuclear weapons program?" asked Ellen. With some satisfaction, she saw Beecham's surprise that she'd know so much.

"Yes," said Cargill. "But we don't believe it was sincere. As long as Iran was part of the Joint Comprehensive Plan of Action and allowed in UN inspectors, we were pretty sure their program had stopped. But since the Dunn administration threw it out . . ."

"Iran has been free to move forward," said Ellen.

"It's made it far more difficult to verify anything," said Beecham.

So the question remained. "Why would an Iranian hard-liner try to save three Pakistani nuclear physicists whose work could hurt his country?" Ellen asked.

There was silence. Clearly they had no idea. For a moment she thought the screen had frozen.

"There is one more piece of important information, Madame Secretary," the DNI finally said. "You might not like it."

"There's almost nothing about the past twenty-four hours I have liked. Let's have it, Tim."

"After you left DC and took the FSO with you, we did a deep dive into Anahita Dahir's background."

The spider had crawled up to the base of Ellen's skull.

"She told us that her parents are Lebanese and they came here as refugees fleeing Beirut during the civil war. We checked, and that's what their application for refugee status says."

But, thought Ellen. *But* . . .

"But at the time, during the war, there was no way to thoroughly check. Now we can. And did. Ms. Dahir's mother is a Maronite Christian from Beirut. A professor of history."

But, thought Ellen. *But* . . .

"But her father is not Lebanese," said Beecham. "He's an economist. From Iran."

"Are you sure?"

"I wouldn't be telling you this if we weren't."

And Ellen thought that was probably true.

"This's the FSO who's traveling with you?" asked Cargill. "How much access has she been given?"

Ellen turned to Charles Boynton, who'd been silent and all but invisible during the meeting. He had, she noticed, that rare ability to disappear while still being present. Not a great advantage in social situations, but a huge advantage if hoping to mine secrets of State.

"The FSO doesn't have top secret security clearance or access codes," said Boynton.

"But she does have ears and a brain," said Ellen. "She managed to talk her way into my meeting yesterday. Find her. Bring her here."

When Boynton left, Ellen turned back to the screen in time to see an aide speaking quietly to Beecham and showing him something. He'd put his monitor on mute, but they could see he was both interested and annoyed.

He turned back to her and unmuted. "When were you planning to tell me that you have a suspect in the Frankfurt bombing?"

"I was coming to it."

"Well, no need now. A junior aide just told me. She got it off CNN." His face was almost purple.

"Would you excuse us, please?" Ellen asked Cargill, knowing this was going to get ugly.

When he left, Tim Beecham rounded on her. "You do know that the President is also getting this from the television and not from us."

"Enough, Tim," said Ellen, raising a hand. "I understand your frustration, but the fact is we only just found this out ourselves and I came straight here. You didn't give me a chance to say anything."

She knew that was probably unfair, but the truth was, Ellen was in no hurry to tell this man anything.

In case . . . In case the DNI was the bogeyman.

She again wondered how Betsy was getting along and if it had been a mistake to send a retired schoolteacher to dig up information on a possible traitor.

She also wondered why she hadn't heard from Betsy yet. But

then her phone was in the hands of the Diplomatic Security agent outside the door. Betsy might have tried.

"Tell me now," snapped Tim Beecham.

So Ellen did, and finished by saying, "We now think it's possible he was supposed to be a suicide bomber. London and Paris have gone back over recordings. They think they've ID'd the bombers from cameras inside the bus. Both died in the explosions."

"So why didn't this one?"

"We think he went against orders."

"Which makes him extremely valuable to us," said Beecham. "And extremely dangerous to whoever planned all this."

"Yes."

Ellen watched a senior aide slide a paper to Tim Beecham, who read it, a fleeting glance of genuine puzzlement crossing his face.

"We've found out more about your FSO and her family." He tapped the paper in front of him. "When her father arrived in Beirut from Iran after the revolution, he changed his name to Dahir. Before that it was Ahmadi."

Now it was Ellen's turn to freeze. "Ahmadi? As in Behnam Ahmadi?"

"His brother."

Anahita Dahir's uncle ran the Iranian weapons program.

CHAPTER 16

Scott?"

Cargill looked up from the messages pouring in. It was getting more and more difficult to manage the flood of information. To separate the important from the trivial. The facts from false reports.

The bomber had been sighted all over Europe and even Russia.

"Yes? What is it?"

"Bad Kötzting."

"Are you sure?"

"Positive. He lives there. Local police recognized him. Sent his ID."

She showed it to her Station Chief.

And there he was. Aram Wani. Age twenty-seven. And his address in the small Bavarian town.

"He has a wife and child."

"Is he there now?"

"We don't know. I've asked that Spezialeinsatzkommandos be sent to his home. They're on their way from Nuremburg, but it'll take a while. In the meantime, I've instructed the local cops to send someone in to quietly check."

"Good. We need to get there."

"I have a helicopter waiting."

"Ja?"

The young woman opened the door a sliver.

"Frau Wani?"

"Ja."

She had a child in her arms and looked wary but not actually afraid.

The female cop was in civilian clothes and old enough to be Frau Wani's mother. Almost her grandmother.

"Oh, good. I hope you don't mind my dropping by without calling first."

"No, but who are you?" The door opened wider.

"My name's Naomi. Cold day." The officer brought her shoulders up and her elbows in, to indicate a chill. The door opened wider, and she was invited in. *"Danke."*

"Bitte."

"Really, it's more the damp, isn't it?" Naomi smiled warmly and looked around. The home was small, immaculate. The child, an eighteen-month-old girl, was almost impossibly beautiful, with the light brown complexion and blue eyes of a child from a German mother and Iranian father.

Frau Wani had been born and raised in Germany of European heritage, the officer knew, having done a quick check before heading over.

"Didn't your husband tell you?" she asked.

"No."

The officer shook her head as if to indicate, *Men.*

"As you know, a regional lottery has been created to offer fast-tracked citizenship to immigrants. Because your husband married a German"—she smiled even more warmly—"and has a child, his name appeared as someone who's eligible." Now she paused and looked concerned. "He is Aram Wani, isn't he?"

"Oh, yes." Frau Wani's face opened in a huge smile. She stepped aside completely and, shutting the door, indicated that her visitor should go into the kitchen. "I've never heard of this lottery. But it's true?"

"It is. But I need to ask him a few questions. Is he here?"

Aram Wani sat slouched at the back of the bus.

If he saw any irony in this, he didn't show it. In fact, he showed nothing. Nothing. Because if he let anything out, he'd burst into flames.

He had to get home. Get to his family. Get them out. Get across the border into the Czech Republic. He'd hoped to do it before anyone found out he was still alive. But in the bus station he'd seen his face all over the screens.

They knew. The police, yes, but also Shah and the Russians.

He'd considered turning himself in. Then he'd have at least a chance of survival. And he could beg the German authorities to protect his family. But there wasn't time. He had to get to them first.

Betsy Jameson walked down Mahogany Row carrying a bag with chicken salad on a croissant. It was a prop, to give the impression that all was normal.

A few staffers stopped in their rushing around to greet her and ask if she'd heard anything from Secretary Adams. And what she was doing back.

"The Secretary wanted me here, in case anything should come up," she said.

Fortunately, people in the State Department were too busy to care about her vague answers. And most knew not to ask too many questions.

The place was hopping. News of the bomber's photograph had

shot through the offices, raising hopes that a breakthrough might be coming soon.

The State Department in Washington was used to crises. There was always at least one place in the world that had gone into the crapper and demanded a response. But this was different. Not simply because the terror attacks had succeeded so spectacularly well, but that no one in that building, no one in the intelligence community anywhere, had heard even a whispered warning.

Nothing.

And if they'd heard nothing about those attacks, what else was about to happen? That was the nightmare these people lived with.

The National Terrorism Advisory System had issued an alert, warning citizens that another attack, this one on American soil, could be imminent.

In every office, on every floor, men and women of the State Department were contacting colleagues and informants. Mining information. Digging deep. And when a nugget came in, they tried to discern the gold from the fool's gold.

Using her pass card, Betsy heard the locks on the thick door into the Secretary of State's suite of offices clunk and saw the door pop open a crack, but before she could enter, she heard someone say, "Mrs. Jameson."

She turned and saw a woman approach, wearing the deep green uniform and insignia of a captain in the Army Rangers. Special Forces.

"Yes?"

"General Whitehead heard you were back and sent me over. He says if you need anything, to call me. My name is Denise Phelan." Betsy felt something arrive in her jacket pocket. "Don't hesitate."

Then Captain Phelan smiled engagingly and walked back toward the elevators, leaving Betsy to wonder why she would possibly need the help of an Army Ranger.

Once into Ellen's suite of offices, she was greeted by the men and women who supported the Secretary. They all knew she was Secretary Adams's counselor. An honorary position, they believed. There to morally support the Secretary of State, but not to do any serious work.

They were courteous, friendly, and vaguely dismissive.

For her part, Betsy chatted away, making small talk, even perching on the corner of a desk. Apparently settling in for a nice long chin-wag.

After decades of teaching high school, Betsy Jameson had become fluent in body language. Especially that of people who'd completely lost interest.

When she was pretty sure she'd annoyed everyone to the point of near explosion, she went into Ellen's private office and closed the door. Knowing those outside would rather gnaw their hand off than risk more inane chatter from someone who clearly did not grasp that they were in the middle of a crisis.

Betsy Jameson knew she would not be disturbed.

She sat on the small couch in Ellen's office, took the croissant out of its bag and placed it on some papers, then brought up Candy Crush on her phone, and after playing a game and a half, she turned off the screen saver mode so it would continue to show the game.

Anyone who entered would see it on her phone and think she had nothing better to do than play and eat. They certainly would never suspect she was gathering information on the Director of National Intelligence.

Then she went through the connecting door into Charles Boynton's office. Turning on his computer, she put in his password. If anyone traced what she was doing, it would come back to that ferret Boynton. Not her. Not Ellen.

As she settled into the chair, she felt something hard and rectangular in her pocket.

Even before she pulled it out, Betsy knew what it was. A phone. A burner. Slipped into her jacket by Captain Phelan.

Pressing it on, she saw it was fully charged with just one number preprogrammed. Replacing it, Betsy looked at Boynton's screen. Took a deep breath, and went to work.

Those who underestimated teachers did so at their peril.

"OK, you shithead," she muttered as she typed. "I'm coming for you."

She hit enter, and up came the confidential files on Timothy T. Beecham.

Anahita took the chair indicated in the bunker-like office in the basement of the Frankfurt consulate.

She and Secretary Adams had been joined by Charles Boynton. Tim Beecham, the DNI, and the two officers who'd interrogated her were on-screen from DC.

The senior officer began to talk but was politely and firmly silenced by the Secretary of State.

"If you don't mind, I'll lead this interview. If, when I've finished, you have questions, you may, of course, ask them."

She had deliberately called this an interview and not an interrogation. She wanted to put Anahita Dahir at ease. And she could see it was working.

Already the FSO looked less stressed, seeing that Secretary Adams and not the others would lead the questioning.

She thinks I'm her friend. She's wrong.

Anahita forced her face to relax. Forced her body to relax.

Just enough to give the impression she'd been taken in. But she had not.

The FSO's guard was as high as ever. Though she suspected it was not high enough. And that it was far too late.

They knew.

What Anahita Dahir didn't know was just how much they'd found out. They'd swarmed over her walls, that much was obvious, but how deep into her life had they managed to get?

Betsy's hand hovered an inch over Boynton's keyboard.

She'd heard something. Someone was in the outer office.

She glanced at the door. It was closed but not locked.

Cursing herself, Betsy realized she didn't have time to log out and close down. Reaching behind her, she grabbed the power cord and yanked it from the wall.

She didn't wait around to see the screen go blank. Scooping up her notes, she leapt back through the door into Ellen's office and got to the couch just as Barb Stenhauser appeared.

The White House Chief of Staff stopped suddenly and stared at Betsy.

"Mrs. Jameson, I thought you were in Frankfurt with Secretary Adams."

"Oh, hello." Betsy put down her sandwich. "I was, but . . ."

"Yes?"

But what? What? Betsy racked her brains. She hadn't expected to run into Barb Stenhauser. It was unusual in the extreme for the White House Chief of Staff to come to Foggy Bottom.

Stenhauser was waiting.

"Well, this's embarrassing . . ."

For God's sake, Betsy begged her brain, *now you're making it worse. What could possibly be embarrassing? Come up with something.*

"We got into a fight," she blurted out.

"Oh, that's a shame. Must've been quite bad. What was it about?"

Oh, for Christ's sake, thought Betsy. *What was it about???*

"Her son. Gil."

"Really? What about him?"

Was it Betsy's fevered mind, or had Stenhauser's tone changed? From mild surprise to mounting suspicion.

"Pardon?"

"The fight. What was it about?"

"Well, that's personal."

"Still," said the Chief of Staff, taking a step deeper into the room. "I'd like to hear. You can trust me."

"I think you can probably guess," said Betsy. *Please. Please guess.*

Barb Stenhauser stared at her, and Betsy realized, with some surprise, that she was actually trying to guess. The White House Chief of Staff never wanted to appear ignorant. Her currency was knowing everything. Her Achilles' heel was not being able to admit when she did not.

"The kidnapping." Stenhauser said it with such authority, even Betsy believed it for a moment.

Barb Stenhauser had in fact hit on the one, the only thing that could possibly fracture Betsy's friendship with Ellen.

The kidnapping of Gil Bahar three years earlier.

And then Betsy hit on the one thing Stenhauser really, always wanted to hear. The words that released the arrow. The only thing that might bring down the White House Chief of Staff.

"You're right." She saw Stenhauser relax. Like a junkie with a fix.

She was wrong, of course, but now Betsy had the path forward.

"I told Ellen I thought then Senator Williams had been right not to negotiate for Gil's release."

"Really?" said Stenhauser, taking a step closer to Betsy and glancing toward the game of Candy Crush up on the phone. Betsy quickly turned it off, in apparent embarrassment.

"You agreed with the Senator?" his Chief of Staff asked.

"I did. I thought it was a courageous stand."

"That was my idea, you know."

"Ahhh, I should've guessed." To her surprise, Betsy was able to keep the revulsion out of her voice.

Those long weeks, when Gil was missing in Afghanistan. Then that photo. Filthy, disheveled. Matted hair and beard. Almost unrecognizable, except to a mother. And a godmother.

Those eyes, haunted. Near empty.

Brilliant, vibrant, troubled Gil. On his knees, two Pathan Taliban fighters standing behind him, AK-47s slung across their chests, as though he were a buck and they the hunters.

"Senator Williams wanted to negotiate at first, but I pointed out that a successful run for the White House depended on our showing strength and resolve."

Betsy forced a thin smile, trying to keep her eyes on the long view and not on this piece of crap.

"Wise."

It had been a nightmare.

Every night on the news, on Ellen's own channels, there were images of the beheadings. And photographs of Gil Bahar, the celebrated journalist. The only US hostage and a prize one at that.

His own death was threatened every day.

Ellen had begged, literally gotten on her knees and begged Senator Williams to use back channels to get him released. Officially, the US could not be seen to negotiate with terrorists, and certainly not the Pathan, the most brutal offshoot of the Taliban. But privately, it happened all the time.

Sometimes even successfully.

But this time, despite Ellen prostrating herself, then Senator Williams, the chair of the Senate Intelligence Committee, refused.

Ellen never fully recovered from the terror of that time. And never forgave him. Never would.

Neither would Betsy Jameson.

And Doug Williams would never forgive Ellen Adams for the merciless campaign her media empire had then waged to stop him from winning the party nomination.

"At the time, I told Ellen I agreed with her when she called Senator Williams an arrogant, power-drunk maniac."

Ellen had gone after him with all the resources at her command, intent on performing her own political beheading.

Unfortunately, it hadn't quite worked, and Ellen's political enemy, her nemesis, had actually been elected president. And, to everyone's astonishment, had picked Ellen Adams as his Secretary of State.

But Ellen knew why. And Betsy knew why. President Williams had his own execution planned.

First he'd pluck Ellen Adams from her media perch and put her in his cabinet, where Secretary Adams would become his hostage. Then he'd draw the sword across her throat.

If Ellen or Betsy had had any doubts about his motives, the trip to South Korea had put them to rest. It was a failure that should not have happened. It had been a public execution, orchestrated by the US President, who would, apparently, stop at nothing to ruin his own Secretary of State.

"On the flight over to Frankfurt," Betsy said to the White House Chief of Staff, "I had a few too many and told Ellen that I thought President Williams wasn't a vacant asshole with shit for brains. That he certainly wasn't a prick who'd escaped from a bag of idiots. And he sure wasn't a dumb-as-dirt egotist who got his law degree by mailing in tops from Cap'n Crunch boxes."

Betsy was now enjoying herself. It had been a while since she'd taken rogue Mrs. Cleaver out for a spin.

But it was time to move on.

Almost gagging on the next thing she knew she had to say, Betsy looked Barb Stenhauser in the eyes and lied. "I told her I thought he'd done the right thing in not rescuing Gil. He'd had no choice."

"And she sent you home for it."

"I was lucky she didn't throw me out of Air Force Three. So I'm sitting here, eating a sandwich, playing Candy Crush, and trying to get up the courage to call her and apologize. Even if I believe that Doug Williams is a narcissistic shithead."

OK, that felt good.

"Is or isn't?"

"Pardon?"

"You said he *is* a narcissistic you-know-what."

"What?"

"Never mind."

"What are you doing here?" Betsy asked. "Can I help you?"

"No. The President sent me over to see if Secretary Adams or her Chief of Staff left any notes behind, from their meeting. In all the excitement, the stenographer seems to have missed some points."

"Good luck. As you can see, her desk is a dump and his is far too neat for any real work to exist." Betsy hesitated. "You worked together before, didn't you? You and Boynton?"

"Briefly."

"On the Intelligence Committee, when Senator Williams chaired it."

"Yes. And on the campaign."

It had been a guess on Betsy's part, but hadn't been that difficult to put together since Stenhauser herself had assigned Charles

Boynton as Ellen's Chief of Staff. As she watched Stenhauser walk into Boynton's office and close the door, she wondered just how crowded that bag of idiots was. And who else had escaped.

Betsy shot off a quick email to Ellen saying she'd arrived at State and thanking her for the young agent she'd sent to guard her.

The subjunctive would have walked into a bar . . .

Twenty minutes later she tried the door into Boynton's office. It was unlocked and empty.

Barb Stenhauser had left.

Sitting at Boynton's desk, she reached behind her for the power cord. Her heart skipped a beat.

Charles Boynton's computer had already been plugged back in.

Scott Cargill did up his seat belt and indicated to the pilot that they should take off.

His number two handed him her phone. He read the message quickly, his face revealing nothing. "The others?"

"We're checking. Should have news in minutes."

Cargill gave a curt nod and sent off a message to the Secretary of State, then looked out over Frankfurt as the helicopter banked and headed east. To Bavaria and the charming medieval village of Bad Kötzting, where a terrorist had made a home.

The Diplomatic Security agent handed Ellen her phone. An urgent flagged message had come in from Scott Cargill.

Nasrin Bukhari's husband found murdered. Checking other families. Have tracked bombing suspect to Bavaria. On way.

Cargill looked at the reply. *Good luck. Let me know.*

Ellen handed her phone back to the security agent and turned to Anahita.

"We don't have much time, Ms. Dahir," said Secretary Adams, her voice brusque, formal. "You've lied to us over and over. Now you need to tell us the truth."

Anahita sat bolt upright in the chair and nodded.

"What's your involvement in the bombings?"

Anahita's surprise was evident. "Madame Secretary?"

"Enough. We know about your father."

"What about him?" She kept her voice level.

It was ridiculous to not tell them everything. They obviously knew, and to deny it would just make things worse.

And yet Anahita Dahir found that she could not tell them the truth. It was the one thing her parents had asked of her. The one thing she'd promised never to tell. Anyone.

Not a living soul, her mother, who believed in souls, had said.

Her father, who did not, had placed her on his knee and told her not to be afraid. That everything would be fine if she kept just this one secret. And then he told her he loved her more than life itself.

He believed in life, in the sanctity of life.

When she was old enough to understand, he'd told her why their big secret could never leave their little home in the DC suburb.

In a calm voice he explained that their entire family had been murdered. Wiped out in a bloody frenzy by Iranian hard-liners in the revolution because his family, her family, were intellectuals who could not, apparently, be trusted.

Because education led to questioning, which led to independent thought. Which led to a desire for freedom. Which the ayatollahs could not control.

"I was the only one to escape."

His voice was strong, almost matter-of-fact, but his grief showed in his eyes.

"You're afraid the Iranians will come after you," she'd said.

"No. I'm afraid they won't have to. If the Americans find out I lied on my refugee application, if they find out I'm actually Iranian . . ."

"They'll send you back?" By then she was old enough to know what that would mean. "I will never, ever tell," she'd promised.

And she hadn't. And she wouldn't.

"This's ridiculous," said Beecham. "You can see she's not going to cooperate. It's clear who she's working for, and it isn't us. Arrest her. Charge her."

The security agent in the room took a step toward Anahita.

"With what?" asked Ellen, staying the agent with a motion of her hand.

"With sedition, with mass murder, with terrorism. With conspiracy," said Beecham. "If you don't like those, I have more."

"You're forgetting," snapped Ellen. "The Iranian message was meant to stop the bombs. If anything they helped."

"The message was out of Iran?" Anahita asked.

"Look," said Ellen, losing all patience. "Enough of this. We know your father's Iranian. He lied on his refugee application. We know his name was Ahmadi—"

"Why did your uncle send the message?" Beecham cut in.

Anahita looked from one to the other. "What?"

Ellen brought her hand down so hard on the table the bang made Anahita jump and even startled Beecham all the way across the ocean.

Secretary Adams leaned forward so that she was right up into Anahita's face. "Enough. Time is short. We need answers."

"But you're mistaken. I have no uncle."

"Of course you do," snapped Beecham. "He lives in Tehran. His name's Behnam Ahmadi and he's a nuclear physicist. He helped create Iran's weapons program."

"That's not possible. My whole family was killed in the revolution. My father was the only one to—"

She stopped, but it was too late. She'd let it out.

Anahita waited. Waited. For the monster, the Azhi Dahaka, to get her. So powerful was the imprinting, so deep her promise to her parents, that even as a rational adult Anahita Dahir believed if she let that secret escape, disaster would immediately follow.

She waited, her eyes wide, her breathing erratic.

But nothing happened. Though Anahita wasn't fooled. The monster had been released and it was coming for them. Hurtling toward the modest family home in Bethesda.

She needed to call them. To warn them. To what? Run? Hide? Where?

"Ana?" The voice came to her from far away. "Ana?"

Anahita came back to the bunker room in the basement of the US consulate in Frankfurt.

"Tell us," Secretary Adams said softly.

"I don't understand."

"Then just tell us what you know."

"I was told they'd all died. My father's whole family. Killed by the extremists. That I had no family left." She held Ellen's eyes.

"That's bullshit," said the senior intelligence officer, on the screen from DC. "The message came in to her station. Her uncle knew where and how to find her. She must know him."

"But I don't," said Anahita, looking at them.

"Then you need to call your father," said Ellen. Her voice crisp. Decisive.

"Is that such a good idea, Madame Secretary?" asked the senior agent.

"It's a goddamned awful idea," said Beecham. "Why don't we

just let the terrorists join our group? Come on in." He waved his arms. "We'll show you what we have and don't have."

He glared at Ellen. Who returned the stare.

"They're on their way," reported the junior intelligence officer, looking up from his phone. "Should be in Bethesda any minute."

"Who?" asked Anahita, feeling panic rising.

But she knew the answer.

The monster. The one she'd released.

"Good," said Beecham, getting to his feet. "I'm going there too."

Betsy Jameson stared at the screen in Charles Boynton's office at the State Department. Her eyes were wide, her hand was over her mouth.

"Darn."

Betsy's friends and family had noticed years ago that when things were bad, her language was filthy. But when things were nearing catastrophe, her language cleaned right up.

"Oh gosh," Betsy whispered, through her splayed fingers as she stared at the screen.

Barb Stenhauser had seen what Betsy had been doing. Up on the screen was her search of the records on Timothy T. Beecham.

Oddly truncated files.

Then Betsy started laughing.

What Stenhauser would know was that Charles Boynton had been researching the Director of National Intelligence. Not Betsy Jameson, who was too busy playing Candy Crush and eating her emotions.

She sat back in the chair and took a deep breath, calming herself.

Then she leaned forward and got to work again. Clearly a deeper dive was necessary.

An hour later Betsy took off her glasses, rubbed her eyes, and stared at the screen. She was getting nowhere. Just when she thought she was onto a promising lead, she hit a dead end. It was like being in a maze. With the real Tim Beecham in the center, but no way to get there.

But there must be. She was just missing it.

She'd tried university records. She knew he'd gone to Harvard Law, but there was nothing there. Just confirmation he'd graduated, nothing else.

His military records had been similarly expunged.

He was married with two children. He was forty-seven years of age. Republican family from Utah.

That much could not be kept secret.

It would be easier to find information on her mail carrier, Betsy knew, than on the DNI. She couldn't even find out what the *T* in "Timothy T. Beecham" stood for.

What she needed wasn't the right path to the heart of the maze. What she needed was a chain saw.

She put her coat on and went for a walk. Clearing her head. Thinking. Thinking.

Sitting on a park bench, she watched a few hardy joggers go by, then spotted the young man from the plane. Her bodyguard. He was discreetly standing by a small shed.

Betsy brought out her phone and saw the reply from Ellen.

The subjunctive would have walked into a bar . . . had it only known, the message started.

Progressing here, Ellen's note continued. *Glad you're home.*

P.S. What bodyguard?

Betsy gathered her things, and without looking toward the shed, she began walking casually away. Her heart running ahead, almost catching up to her racing mind.

Strolling through the increasingly bitter day, she could feel the eyes on her back.

The bus pulled into the small station in Bad Kötzting.

"Are you leaving?" the driver called, his voice annoyed, impatient.

Aram had waited until everyone else had gotten out. And then waited a little longer, to see if anyone was loitering in the station.

He saw no one.

"Das tut mir Leid," he said. As he brushed past the driver, he pulled the wool hat he'd bought in Frankfurt farther down his face. "Sorry. I was asleep."

The driver didn't care. He just wanted to get to the tavern for hot food and warm beer.

"Another message, sir," Cargill's second-in-command shouted over the rotor noise.

She showed him her phone and the brief text.

The wives, children, parents of the other bombers and physicists, all murdered.

"Oh Christ," he whispered. "Shah's cleaning up." He leaned forward and said to the pilot, "Faster. We need to get there faster."

Then he said to his second-in-command, "Warn the police in Bad Kötzting."

There was the sound of the front door opening.

"Oh, that must be Aram now."

Frau Wani got up as Naomi reached behind her and brought out her gun.

CHAPTER 17

Irfan Dahir picked up the phone and smiled.

"Dorood, Anahita. Chetori?"

There was a pause, but then he knew his daughter was in Frankfurt. Overseas connections could sometimes lag.

The word *Farsi* appeared at the bottom of Ellen's screen in the bunker room in Frankfurt, written by the translator.

Then quickly more words appeared: *Hello, Anahita. How are you doing?*

Ellen looked at Anahita and nodded, indicating she should reply. But the young woman looked stricken. Paralyzed.

"Ana?" the voice, deep, warm with just a slight edge of concern now, came over the speaker. *"Halet khubah?"*

Are you OK? the translator typed.

Ellen gestured toward Anahita to say something. Anything.

"Salam," she finally said.

Hello.

Irfan felt his heart stop; then it threw itself against his rib cage. Trying to escape.

"Salam." The simple word he'd taught his daughter when she was young enough to talk and old enough to understand.

"Hello"—but in Arabic. It would be, he'd explained to the solemn little girl, their code. If there was trouble, if anyone ever found out, then she should use the Arabic word for "hello." Not the Farsi.

He looked toward the living room window, which opened out onto the quiet street.

A black car, unmarked, was pulling into the drive, and another was parked by the curb.

"Irfan?" said his wife, coming in from the kitchen, bringing with her the fragrance of mint and cumin and coriander from the kaftas she was making. "There're men in the backyard."

He exhaled a breath he'd held for decades.

Bringing the phone back to his ear, he said, in softly accented English, "I understand. Anahita, are you all right?"

"Daddy," she said, her chin dimpling, "I'm sorry."

"That's all right. I love you. And it will all be fine, I know it."

Listening to this dignified man, and watching his devastated daughter, Ellen Adams felt a pang of shame. But then she remembered the red blankets fluttering in the breeze, and the photographs of the sons and daughters, husbands and wives and children, clutched in trembling hands.

And she no longer felt shame. She felt outrage. Ellen Adams would not break faith with those who died.

Through the speaker they heard the distant ring of a doorbell.

Irfan Dahir motioned to his wife, now standing stock-still in the middle of the living room, to just stay there.

When he unlocked the door and began to open it, it was suddenly thrust open. As he stumbled back, heavily armed men grabbed him, throwing him to the floor.

"Irfan!" his wife screamed.

Anahita's eyes widened in panic.

"Daddy? Mommy?" she shouted into the phone. "What's happening?"

The knee on Irfan's back gave one last sharp shove, pressing the breath out of him; then it lifted.

He felt himself hoisted like a rag doll to his feet, where he swayed.

"Irfan Dahir?"

He turned and focused on an older man in plain clothes. Clean-shaven, short gray hair, suit and tie. He looked, thought Irfan in his slightly confused state, like a high school principal.

"Yes," he whispered, his voice hoarse.

"You're under arrest."

"On what charge?"

"Murder."

"What?"

His astonishment traveled down the phone line, across the Atlantic, and landed in the US consulate in Frankfurt, where it found the ears of his daughter. And the American Secretary of State.

Betsy Jameson took her double-strength espresso to the round bistro table in the corner. She'd also bought a muffin. Something to justify her taking up a table, even though the place was almost empty.

But it was at least public.

The young man was no longer making any pretense. It was clear he was following her.

She felt the phone, still in her jacket pocket. Bringing it out, she stared at the number. It belonged, almost certainly, to Captain Phelan, the Army Ranger sent by General Whitehead.

Her finger hovered over the button.

"Don't hesitate," Denise Phelan had said, her eyes intense.

But now Betsy did. How did she know the Ranger had been sent by the Chairman of the Joint Chiefs? She just had Phelan's word. And today, that was not good enough.

She made up her mind. Replacing the phone in her pocket, Betsy brought out her own and dialed. After jumping through innumerable hoops, she heard a man's deep voice.

"Mrs. Jameson?"

"Yes. I'm sorry to disturb you, General."

"What can I do for you?"

"We've never met—"

"True, but I know who you are. Did you get my package?"

Betsy exhaled. Relieved but also suddenly exhausted. "So she was from you."

"Yes. But wise of you to check. Is there a problem?"

"Well . . ." Now she felt embarrassed. But when she looked across the coffee shop to the man sitting and watching, any embarrassment disappeared. "I'm wondering if you'd join me for a drink."

"Absolutely. When and where?"

The speed with which he agreed both reassured and troubled Betsy. It was clear he was worried.

She told him and, after jumping in a taxi and giving the address of a random hotel, she got out, walked to a side door, and hailed another taxi. Something she'd seen on TV shows to "lose a tail." And something she never thought she'd have to do in real life.

To her astonishment, it seemed to work.

Minutes later she walked into Off the Record. The bar in the basement of the Hay-Adams hotel was a familiar haunt for Washington insiders, with its dim lights and plush red velvet upholstery.

Right across the street from the White House, it was where journalists and political aides whispered in dark corners. Where confidences were exchanged, and deals struck.

Inside the Beltway it was considered neutral ground.

Betsy took one of the private half-moon booths and watched the door for the General, and also for her shadow.

It took her a moment to recognize General Whitehead when he did arrive. The fact that he slid into the booth and introduced himself was, it must be admitted, a clue.

If Betsy looked like June Cleaver, this man looked a bit like Fred MacMurray, from *My Three Sons*. Lanky, kindly. A man more at home in a cardigan than a uniform.

While Betsy had seen him on television many times, and in person from a distance, they'd never actually met. Nor had she any desire to, until now.

Betsy Jameson had a suspicion of the higher ranks in the military, believing they were, at heart, warmongers. And no one was of a higher rank than the Chairman of the Joint Chiefs.

And no one was more deserving of her suspicions than General Albert Whitehead, who'd also served in the Dunn administration.

But Ellen trusted him. And Betsy trusted Ellen.

Besides, she didn't know who else to turn to.

The helicopter landed, and Cargill sprinted to the waiting car.

He sent a quick message to the Secretary of State.

On ground in Bad Kötzting. On our way to house. Update later.

A camera had been set up, and now Anahita, in Frankfurt, saw her parents sitting side by side at the family dining room table in Bethesda.

It was a room she knew well. It was where birthdays were celebrated. Where holiday meals were shared with friends. Where she'd done her homework every day for fifteen years.

Where she'd scratched the initials of a boy she'd had a crush on.

Her mother had given her hell for that.

And now she was seeing something she'd never have thought possible growing up. The Director of National Intelligence for the United States had joined her parents at the modest table. But it was as far from a social occasion as it was possible to get.

As Tim Beecham studied the Dahirs, so did Secretary Adams. Their faces were washed out by the harsh lights of the camera. But one thing could not be washed away.

They were terrified. As scared as if the head of the Iranian secret police was sitting across from them.

Ellen tried to banish that comparison, but it kept creeping back via Abu Ghraib and Guantánamo and a host of black sites she was just learning of.

"Tell us what you know about the bombings," said Tim Beecham.

"The ones in Europe?" asked Maya Dahir.

"Are there others?" demanded the DNI.

Now Mrs. Dahir looked confused. "No. I mean, I don't know."

"One hundred and twelve dead and counting," said Beecham, turning his glare from Maya to Irfan. "Hundreds more injured. And the trail leads back to you."

"Me?" Irfan Dahir looked genuinely shocked. "I had nothing to do with it. Nothing."

He turned to Maya for support. She looked equally stunned, and equally frightened.

"But your brother, Behnam, does," said Beecham. "Perhaps you should ask him."

Irfan closed his eyes and lowered his head. "Behn," he whispered, "what have you done?"

In Frankfurt, Anahita sat beside the Secretary of State and stared at the monitor.

None of this seemed possible.

"Tell us about your family in Tehran, Mr. Dahir."

After taking a moment to gather himself, Irfan began to talk. To say the words he'd kept locked tightly away for decades.

"I have a brother and sister still in Tehran."

"Daddy?" said Anahita.

"My sister is a doctor," he continued, not yet willing or able to face his daughter. "My brother, younger brother, is a nuclear physicist. Both are loyal to the regime."

"More than loyal," said Tim Beecham. "We have pictures of your brother holding a gun to the head of a senior American diplomat when the hostages were taken."

"That was a long time ago. He and I were very different."

Beecham leaned forward. "Maybe not quite so different. Does this look familiar?"

He held up a grainy newspaper photo, the line under it just readable.

Students holding Americans hostage in Tehran.

"Well, Mr. Dahir?"

Had Irfan Dahir been capable of saying, *I'm fucked*, he would have. And he was.

So Tim Beecham said it for him.

"You're fucked, Mr. Dahir. That's you in the photo, isn't it. Next to your brother."

Irfan stared, his shoulders sagging. He'd had no idea such a picture existed. He'd even managed to forget that that young man raising a rifle over his head in triumph had existed. Once.

"Yes. It is." He took several rapid shallow breaths, as though he'd finished a race that was far too long. And far too far.

"By our records, you didn't leave Iran for another two years. Hardly the act of a man fleeing for his life."

Irfan considered for a moment before quietly saying, "Have you ever heard of the Secretary's Dilemma, Mr. Beecham?"

CHAPTER 18

After their drinks arrived, a ginger ale for Betsy Jameson, a beer for himself, General Whitehead turned to her.

One of the reasons she hadn't immediately recognized him was because he wasn't in uniform. Bert Whitehead had taken the time to change into a regular suit.

"Less conspicuous," he'd explained with a smile.

Betsy appreciated the point. It would be hard to be more conspicuous than a four-star General in uniform, covered in insignias and medals. He looked like the Tin Man from *The Wizard of Oz*. Who'd been searching for a heart, thought Betsy.

Was this man also missing a heart? An arsenal of weapons at his disposal and no heart. It was a terrifying thought.

But out of uniform Bert Whitehead looked like any one of thousands of government bureaucrats. If the government had been staffed by Fred MacMurray.

And yet there was about him an unmistakable aura of quiet authority. She could see why men and women would follow this man. Would do what he said, unquestioning.

"What can I do for you, Mrs. Jameson?"

"I'm being followed."

He lifted his head in surprise but didn't look around. There was, though, a heightened sense of attention.

"Is the person here?"

"Yes. He arrived just before you. I thought I'd lost him, but apparently not. He's behind you. By the door."

"What's he look like?"

After Betsy described the young man, Bert Whitehead excused himself and, as Betsy watched, walked straight over to him.

Bending down, he said a few words; then the two left together, Whitehead's hand on the man's arm. It looked friendly, but Betsy knew it was not.

An eternity later, though by the clock on her phone it showed just over two minutes had passed, Bert Whitehead returned to the booth.

"He won't be bothering you again."

"Who is he? Who sent him?"

When Whitehead didn't answer, Betsy said it for him. "Timothy T. Beecham."

He looked at her for a moment. "Did Secretary Adams say anything to you?"

"She sent me back here to see what I could dig up on Beecham. To find out what he might be involved in."

"I told her not to do anything."

"Well, you don't know Ellen Adams."

He smiled. "I'm beginning to."

"What can you tell me about Beecham? I can't find anything in the files. It's all been moved."

"Or erased."

"Why would anyone do that?"

"I guess because there's something in there they don't want anyone to see."

"What?"

"I don't know."

"But you know something."

Bert Whitehead looked unhappy. Even, perhaps, annoyed at being put in this position. But finally he relented.

"All I know is that against all sensible advice, against my own arguments, the Dunn administration pulled out of the nuclear accord with Iran. It was a terrible mistake. It closed Iran to all inspection, all scrutiny, of their weapons program."

"What does that have to do with Beecham?"

"He was one of the ones pushing President Dunn to do it."

"Why would Beecham do that?"

"The better question is, who benefited?"

"All right, let's pretend I asked the better question."

The General smiled. Then it disappeared. "The Russians, for one. When we pulled out, it gave them free rein in Iran. It's too late now to change that. It's done." He looked down at the coasters on the table and smiled. " 'When thou hast done, thou hast not done, for I have more.' "

General Whitehead looked up and met her eyes. He had, unexpectedly, quoted the English poet John Donne. Why?

And then she saw what he'd been looking at. One of Off the Record's famous coasters, caricatures of political leaders.

General Whitehead was looking at the one of Eric Dunn.

He wasn't saying, "When thou hast done." He was saying, "When thou hast Dunn."

Eric Dunn.

Secretary Adams listened as Beecham continued to question Irfan Dahir, though she was becoming more and more focused on her phone.

Finally she picked it up and sent off a message to Scott Cargill. *Any news?*

Nothing.

"What do you mean?" Betsy asked. "What more does Eric Dunn have? I need to know. Ellen needs to know."

General Whitehead sighed. "For one, a desire to get back into power."

"What politician doesn't?" Betsy pointed to the coasters on the table. Amusing images of various presidents and cabinet ministers, as well as some foreign leaders.

The Russian President. The Supreme Leader of North Korea. The Prime Minister of Britain. All recognizable from the nightly news.

"True," said General Whitehead. "But it goes far deeper than Eric Dunn. There are elements inside the United States unhappy with the direction the country is moving in. They're using him. They see Dunn as the only chance to stop the erosion of the American way. Not because he has a vision, but because he can be manipulated. First, though, they need to get him back into power."

"How?"

He paused for a moment, finding, choosing, his words. "What would happen if there was a catastrophe on American soil? A terror attack so horrific it would wound this nation for generations? And it happened during this administration?"

"It would be blamed on Doug Williams. There'd be calls for his administration to step down."

"Now, suppose the President did not survive the attacks?"

Betsy felt a weight on her chest so heavy she could barely breathe. "What are you saying? Is that about to happen?"

"I don't know."

"But you're afraid."

He didn't answer, but his lips were compressed, and his knuckles turned white in an effort to control his fear.

The hard-right media was already blaming the bus bombs, and the failure to stop them, on American Intelligence and, by extension, this new administration. And even the more moderate outlets were beginning to whip up fears of another attack. A bigger attack. On American soil.

And if one happened . . .

"Are you saying the former President would knowingly allow terrorists to get their hands on a bomb, maybe even a nuclear weapon and use it in order to get back into power?" asked Betsy.

"I don't think it's something Eric Dunn would consciously, knowingly agree to. I think he's being used, not just by the Russians, but by other elements closer to home.

"In his party?"

"Yes, probably, but it goes far beyond party affiliation. There are those who hate America's diversity and the changes it's brought. They see it as a threat, to their livelihoods, to their way of life. They think of themselves, see themselves, as patriots. You must've seen them at demonstrations. True believers, neo-Nazis, fascists."

"I have seen them, General, and I can't believe those people with placards are orchestrating all this."

"No, they're the visible symptom. The disease is deeper. Those with power and wealth, who want to protect what they have. And who want more."

For I have more . . .

"They've found the perfect vehicle in Eric Dunn."

"Their Trojan horse," said Betsy.

Whitehead smiled. "A good analogy. Hollow. An empty vessel into which these men and women have poured their ambitions, their outrages, their hatreds and insecurities."

As she watched him, as she listened to his tone, something struck her. "Did you like Eric Dunn?"

General Whitehead shook his head. "I neither liked nor hated him. He was my Commander-in-Chief. I suspect he was a decent person once. Most people are. Few grow up hoping to destroy their country."

"But you're saying the ones behind this don't think they are destroying the country. Just the opposite. They think they're patriots, saving their country."

"Their country. That's how they see it. Us and Them. They're as radicalized as Al-Qaeda. Domestic terrorists."

Was this man crazy? Betsy wondered. Too many knocks on the head? Too many crisp salutes? Was he seeing conspiracies where none existed?

She didn't know what to hope. That the Chair of the Joint Chiefs of Staff was a delusional lunatic, or that he was saying what others were too afraid to acknowledge.

That there was a genuine threat against the country. From within.

Betsy drifted her finger up and down her perspiring glass of ginger ale and wished it was whiskey.

"And Beecham? How does he fit into this?"

When Whitehead's mouth tightened so that his lips were barely visible, she said, "You've come this far. I need to know. What's his role in all this?"

"I don't know. I've tried to find out, through back channels, but haven't managed anything yet."

"But you suspect."

"What I do know is that Tim Beecham was in charge of intelligence analysis of the Iranian nuclear program. He knows a great deal about the movement of arms in that region. He knows people."

"Shah?"

"Why did the Dunn administration agree to Shah's release?" asked Whitehead.

"Don't look at me."

"Within months, the administration withdrew from the pact, giving Iran free rein with its nuclear program, and then it allowed a Pakistani trafficker in nuclear arms to be freed."

"Are the two related?" asked Betsy.

"Insofar as both increased the risk of nuclear proliferation, yes. But what, specifically, is the endgame?"

"Again," said Betsy, "wrong person to ask. Give me another John Donne quote and I'll be able to help."

Whitehead's smile was short-lived. "What I do know is that the constant in both decisions was Tim Beecham."

"You know what you're saying?"

"I'm afraid I do." And General Whitehead looked afraid. "There's more."

"'For I have more,'" said Betsy, quietly. And waited for it.

"It's what's called a 'wicked problem.' The Middle East was already a cauldron, though fairly stable. And then President Dunn withdrew all our troops from Afghanistan with no plan or conditions required from the Taliban. President Williams inherited that decision."

Betsy paused, studying the military man. Was her initial impression right? Was he a warmonger with Fred MacMurray's face?

"I know it was controversial, but we had to leave sometime," she said. "Bring our troops home. I thought it was the one good thing he did."

"No one wants to see them out of harm's way more than I do, believe me. And I agree, it was time. That wasn't the issue."

"Then what was?"

"It was done without a plan, without getting anything in return. Nothing was put in place to make sure all the gains, the hard-won stability, our intelligence and counterintelligence and counterterrorism capabilities would be maintained. Under the Dunn plan a vacuum was created. One the Taliban is happy to fill."

Betsy sat back. "Huh. You're saying after more than two decades of fighting, the Taliban is back in control of Afghanistan?"

"It will be. And it will bring with it not just Al-Qaeda, but the Pathan. Do you know them?"

"They're the ones who kidnapped Gil."

"Secretary Adams's son, yes. They're an extended family of extremists, with claws in every organization, legitimate and otherwise, in the region. The current so-called democratic government of Afghanistan was propped up by us. Remove us, without a plan . . ." He opened his hands. "All the rats come streaming back. All the ground lost. All the rights withdrawn."

"The women, the girls . . ."

"Who believed they were safe to get an education and a job?" said Whitehead. "Will be punished. But there's more."

Betsy was beginning to hate John Donne.

"Go on."

"The Taliban will need support. Allies in the region. And who better than the Pakistanis, who'd do just about anything to keep Afghanistan from turning to India for support."

"But Pakistan is our ally. So wouldn't that be a good thing? I know there are lots of moving pieces, but still . . ."

"Pakistan is playing a complex game," said General Whitehead. "Where was Osama bin Laden found?"

"Pakistan," said Betsy.

"Not just Pakistan, not in a cave on some remote mountainside. He was living in a massive, luxurious compound just outside the city of Abbottabad. Well inside the border. You can't tell me the Pakistanis didn't know he was there.

"I've been trying to see the connective tissue between these moving parts," said Whitehead. "Only one thing makes sense. Dunn was convinced that, politically, it was a win to pull the troops out of Afghanistan—"

"Yes. We were all tired of that war."

"Agreed. He's astute enough not to want to see Afghanistan descend into chaos. It wouldn't look good if all the gains, all the sacrifices, were seen to have been for nothing. So what does he do?"

Betsy considered, then smiled, but without amusement. "He approaches Pakistan."

"Or they quietly approach him. They promise to keep Afghanistan under control, but they want something in return. Something truly terrifying."

"Ah, thank God. Truly terrifying. Unlike what you've already said. OK, what did they want?"

General Whitehead was staring at her, willing her to see what he saw.

"Bashir Shah," she said. "They released the dog of war."

"He's the linchpin around which all this revolves. Pakistan would save the Dunn administration from making a political blunder. Even if the Taliban returns, it would keep the terrorist organizations under control. In return, Pakistan wanted the US to accept the release of Bashir Shah."

"And Dunn didn't know or care who Shah was," said Betsy. "All he saw and cared about was getting reelected."

"And when he didn't—"

"Those behind this panicked," she said. "Are panicking. They need to get him back in."

The Chair of the Joint Chiefs nodded. He looked solemn, sad, as he studied the middle-aged schoolteacher who looked like a 1950s housewife.

Lowering his voice, he said, "You need to stop your investigation. These are unpleasant people doing unpleasant things."

"I'm not a child, General Whitehead. No need to talk to me as though I am one."

He smiled slightly. "I'm sorry. You're right. I'm just not used to talking to civilians about this. To anyone, for that matter."

Without moving his head, his eyes shifted to the bar area, where a man who was vaguely familiar to Betsy had taken a seat and was beginning to cause a commotion, as people moved away from him.

Whitehead's gaze returned to her, and he lowered his voice even further. "These people are killers."

"Yes. I got that much." Betsy saw, again, the devastation on the quiet Frankfurt street. "Just say it. What's the nightmare?"

"Bashir Shah was released knowing he could sell nuclear expertise and materials to other countries. He has powerful allies inside the Pakistani government, the military. They'd all get rich. But—"

"Let me guess. There's more."

"The real nightmare is that Bashir Shah will sell nuclear weapons to terrorists."

That bald statement sat on the worn table between them. A table that had heard many secrets, many plots, many terrible things. But none so terrible as this.

"Can you imagine," he said quietly. "A terrorist organization, Al-Qaeda, ISIS, with nuclear bombs? That's the nightmare."

"That's what this's about?" Betsy's voice was barely audible. "The physicists? The bus bombings?" She studied him for a moment. "And Tim Beecham's a part of it?"

"I don't know. All I know is that he was involved in all those decisions that appear unrelated but are, in fact, interlocked. To withdraw the US from the Iran nuclear accord, to take the troops out of Afghanistan without a plan and therefore ensure terrorists get back in on the coattails of the Taliban, and to release Shah. I suspect that's why you can't find anything on Beecham. There are documents, emails, messages, notes taken in meetings, proving this. All needed to be hidden."

"So it goes deeper than just Beecham?"

"Much. It would have to. I suspect Tim Beecham, if he is involved, is a puppet. A tool. There are far more powerful people behind this."

"Who?"

"I don't know."

This time she believed him. But there was more. She could tell. Betsy Jameson remained quiet, for an eternity, until General Whitehead could finally say it.

"My fear is that those physicists were killed not at the beginning of a job, but at the end."

"Oh dear."

CHAPTER 19

The door to the home in Bad Kötzting was open a crack.

Even before he entered, Scott Cargill knew what he'd find. The acrid smell of automatic weapons discharge seeped out the door and brought with it something else unmistakable. The slightly metallic scent of blood.

His gun grasped firmly in his hand, he signaled his number two to go around back. Then he entered quietly, carefully.

In the hallway he found the bodies of the woman. And child.

Stepping carefully around them, he looked into the front room.

Empty.

Down the dark hall again, he entered the kitchen. And there he found the body of an older woman. Her police-issue gun still in her hand. Her eyes open wide. Glazed.

He stood perfectly still. Listening.

This had happened recently.

Were the gunmen still in the home? He didn't think so.

And Aram Wani? The bomber? Had they killed him too?

Cargill climbed the stairs, his gun at the ready. Going in and out of the small bedrooms. The scent of violence hadn't made it up there. All he could smell was baby lotion.

Returning down the stairs, he saw a shadow fall across the threshold of the open front door.

He stopped.

It stopped.

Cargill heard a small noise. A sob.

He bounded down the stairs and landed at the bottom in time to see the back of a young man, fleeing.

He ran out the door after him, shouting to his second-in-command. Not sure if she heard.

Aram Wani ran. He ran knowing his life depended on it. Even as he knew he no longer cared if he lived or died.

The running was instinct. Nothing more. And yet he ran away, from death. From the man with the gun. The man who'd murdered his wife and child.

Aram Wani ran.

Scott Cargill gave chase. Running with all his might. As the CIA Station Chief for Germany, he hadn't actually had to run in a while.

But now he did. His knees thrusting forward, his feet pounding on the cobblestones. His lungs gasping in the cold air.

He ran.

Wani skidded around a corner.

Cargill slowed down very slightly, to avoid falling as he turned. And tried to work out if he could shoot Wani without actually killing him. Just to stop him. To bring him in. So they could question him. Find out about the network that had organized the attacks.

And, maybe, what this was all about.

As he turned the corner, he slid to a stop.

"Oh, shit."

Anahita's parents were arrested and taken into custody. But as they were being led away, Ellen stopped them.

"Just one more question, Mr. Dahir. What's the Secretary's Dilemma?"

"It's a mathematical problem, Madame Secretary."

"What sort of problem?" She sat in Frankfurt and looked at him on the monitor.

"It's about when to stop," said Irfan.

"Stop what?"

"Stop looking for a house, a spouse, a job. A secretary," he said. "Knowing when you've found the right one. The best one. Or do you always question if a better one is out there? As long as you're doing that, no progress is possible. A decision must be made, even if it's imperfect. When I was in Tehran, during the revolution, I saw too much. Too many things that didn't line up with all I'd been taught about Islam. But at what stage do I leave? Iran was my home. All my family and friends were there. I loved Iran. So how far is too far? When do I make that commitment to leave, knowing there was no going back?"

"And when did you?" asked Ellen.

"When I saw that the new regime was as bad, if not worse, as the old. And if I stayed, I would be too."

Out of the corner of her eye, she saw Tim Beecham shift, as though anxious for this conversation to end.

"There's actually an equation for that?" she asked Dahir.

"Yes. Though as with many things, we can do the sums, and those might be helpful, but finally it comes down to instinct." He paused, and his dark, sad eyes held hers. "And courage, Madame Secretary."

The Secretary's Dilemma, thought Ellen.

She understood.

When the Dahirs had been led away and the screens had gone blank, Anahita turned to Ellen.

"They've done nothing wrong. Yes, he lied, decades ago. He's been a proud American, a model citizen, ever since. You know they had nothing to do with what's happening."

"I know no such thing," said Ellen. "What I do know is that someone in your uncle's household sent you a message. Someone knows who you are, even if you don't know them."

Anahita's brow cleared. "You believe me, then. And you believe them."

"I wouldn't go that far. But you saved Gil's life. You tried to save the others. I don't think you're involved, but as for your parents . . ." She wondered whether to say the rest, but decided she might as well. "Gil cares for you. He trusts you, and he doesn't trust easily."

"He cares for me? He said that?"

"I don't think that's the lede here, do you?"

As she left the bunker room in the Frankfurt consulate, Secretary Adams thought about Gil. He'd been so angry at her for asking about the informant. So adamant about not telling her. So determined to protect that informant.

And then his whispered "There might be another way . . ." Just before asking if Anahita was there.

Ellen had assumed he asked because he had feelings for the young woman. But now she wondered.

Was it possible that the informant was the petite, slender woman walking slightly behind her, who smelled of rose and protested her innocence? And ignorance? But whose family was in it up to their necks? And perhaps even over their heads?

An urgent message, flagged red, appeared on her phone.

Scott Cargill. Finally.

Ellen opened it and saw it wasn't from Cargill but from Tim Beecham.

Just heard from assets in Tehran. There is a daughter. Zahara Ahmadi. 23. Student. Physics.

Ellen turned to Boynton, who she'd forgotten, yet again, was there.

"Get the President on a secure line." Then she typed to Beecham, *Is she the one?*

We believe so. She's apparently less hard-line.

Believe, or know?

Can't know for sure without bringing her in.

No, don't. Do nothing. I have another idea. Ellen turned to Anahita. "You need to get a message to your cousin."

"I have a cousin?"

"Yes."

"A cousin?" said Anahita.

"Focus. You need to contact her."

That got Anahita's attention. "Me? How? I had no idea I had a cousin until you just told me."

Ellen let that ride. "If she could get a message to you, you can get one to her. Cargill will help." Then she remembered he'd left to get the bombing suspect.

"We have the IP address for the sender in Tehran, Madame Secretary," said Boynton. "We can use that."

Ellen considered. "No. That computer is probably monitored by the Iranians." She stopped herself. If that was true, the Iranian authorities would soon find out about the message to the US State Department. They'd think it was the uncle who sent it. At least at first. And he might protect his daughter. At least at first.

They had to get a message to this Zahara Ahmadi, fast.

"The President will join you in three minutes," said Boynton.

"Thank you. Take Ms. Dahir up to Cargill's section," Ellen told Boynton. "They're working on getting through to the cousin. I want to hear other options in ten minutes."

They were back upstairs now. Where there was sunshine and a nice view of the graveyard.

She checked her phone again. Still no message from Bad Kötzting.

"Bit messier than I would have wanted," said the man by the pool. He was in his fifties, slender and fit, and he'd made a point of getting even fitter while under house arrest. "But at least the job is done."

"Yes, sir. And it might even be to our advantage," suggested the aide who'd brought him the news.

"And how is that?" Bashir Shah asked.

"It will get their attention."

"I think we already have their attention, don't you?" He motioned the aide to sit down so he needn't shield his eyes from the glaring sun as he spoke. "There were two failures that I don't want repeated."

Though Shah's voice was cordial, the aide, already terrified of bringing the news about the suicide bomber who did not actually commit suicide, felt himself turning to stone. His body was rigid. Prepared. His boss's body was tight, coiled, like a predator preparing to leap.

"Do you know what those failures are?" Shah asked.

"The bomber escaped, though we've—"

Shah raised his hand. "And?"

"And the son wasn't killed."

"Yes. The son escaped. A lot of effort went into making sure Gil Bahar was on that bus. How is it he got off?"

"That was the other thing, sir. Our informant sent a video."

Shah watched the video taken from inside the number 119 bus in Frankfurt. When it was over, Shah turned to the aide.

"He had a phone call. He was warned. Who called?"

"His mother."

Shah took a deep breath. It was both the answer he expected and the one he least wanted.

"And how did the Secretary of State come to know about the bomb?" Now his voice was hard. Anger licking at the words. "Who warned her?"

The aide looked around, but the others had taken a step back.

"I don't know, sir. We think it was someone within the State Department. A foreign service officer."

"And how did that person find out?"

Now the aide looked upset. "We'll know soon, sir. There is"—he closed his eyes and said a short prayer—"one other thing."

"Go on."

"They know about you."

"Ellen Adams knows those nuclear physicists were working for me?"

"Yes, sir." He wondered how it would happen. Shot? Stabbed? Or just thrown into the swamp for the alligators? Dear God, not that.

But instead he saw his boss smile. And nod.

Bashir Shah got up. "I have drinks at the club and need to change. I want answers by the time I return."

The aide watched Dr. Shah walk around the pool and into the large home he was borrowing from a close friend in Palm Beach.

The American Consul General in Frankfurt had lent Secretary Adams his office.

She sat at his desk. The President of the United States' unhappy face was on the secure phone in her hand. It felt, for a giddy moment, as though she held him in the palm of her hand.

If only . . .

And then the moment passed as Tim Beecham's even less happy face appeared on the other half of the split screen, looking squished up against the President's.

Though Ellen was surprised he'd been invited to join the call, she chose not to show it, or question. There was nothing she could do about it now anyway. But she'd have to step carefully. Choose what to say. What not to say.

"OK," said President Williams. "What's wrong now?"

"Nothing, Mr. President," said Ellen. "In fact, we've made good progress."

She brought him up to speed, careful to tell the President only what Beecham already knew.

"So, you think this Zahara Ahmadi is behind the warnings," said Williams. "What do we know about her, Beecham?"

"I just received a report on her. She's studying physics at the University of Tehran."

"Like her father," said the President.

"Not completely. Her field is statistical mechanics."

"That's probability theory, right?" said Williams.

It was a good thing, Ellen thought, that she'd trained herself not to show surprise because otherwise she'd have fallen off her chair.

It seemed Doug Williams might be brighter than she'd thought.

"Yes, Mr. President. But what's interesting is that she belongs to a student organization that's progressive. Pushing for more openness. For connections with the West. The only red flag is that she seems quite religious."

"I'm quite religious," said President Williams. "Is that a cause for suspicion?"

"In Iran it is, sir."

"Does she belong to a mosque?" Ellen asked.

"She does."

"Same one as her father?" she asked.

"No. Hers is attached to the university. We're checking on the cleric to see if he's radical."

"What're you thinking, Ellen?" President Williams asked.

"We're now pretty sure Iran was behind the attacks, Mr. President. That always made the most sense. They saw the Pakistani physicists as threats. Now, if Zahara Ahmadi is the one who sent the message to my FSO, then she wanted to stop the bombings. As to why? I can't say until we speak to her. We have people trying to work out how to get a message to her."

She had to admit this much in front of Beecham. It was his department, after all, that was working on it and he'd been part of that decision.

The fact that he knew about Zahara and the efforts to contact her was, at the very least, problematic. But there was nothing Ellen could do about it now.

"How did she find out about the bombings?" asked the President, then paused. "Her father? The physicist?"

"We think it's possible, Mr. President," said Beecham.

"Tim, are you saying her father told her?" asked Williams. "That he also wanted it stopped?"

"No. Dr. Ahmadi's a hard-liner, a supporter of the regime. But she might've overheard something, or seen something among his papers."

"We're speculating. Not helpful. How can we be sure of any of this?" asked President Williams, leaning forward so that his face was distorted. "Ellen?"

"I've been trying to establish a relationship with the Iranian Foreign Minister since we took office. There's a lot of damage done, but he's an educated, cultured man who seems to see the advantage of an entente between us."

"They murdered innocent people on those buses," said President Williams. "Not the act of a cultured man looking for peace."

"No," Ellen agreed. "The thing is, if we've figured out where the warning came from, I suspect the Iranians aren't far behind. It's possible her father will protect Zahara for a while, but maybe not. If she's picked up . . ."

"So we need to get to her first," said Williams. "How?"

"If the FSO, her cousin, can get a short message to my people on the ground," said Beecham, "they might be able to approach her. Slip it to her. Let her know we are aware and will protect her."

"But how can we promise that?" asked Williams. "We can't exactly kidnap her. Can we?"

He actually looked hopeful.

"I have another idea," said Ellen. She hadn't wanted to say this in front of the Director of National Intelligence but felt she had no choice now. Things were moving too quickly. "I want to go to Tehran."

Doug Williams opened his mouth, then shut it again, before saying, "Excuse me?"

"Tehran. Air Force Three is ready. The plan was to fly to Pakistan, but we can change the flight plan en route. Fly covertly to Tehran."

"In honking great Air Force Three?" demanded Williams. "Don't you think someone might notice?"

Beecham, though silent, looked like his eyes were about to pop out of his head.

"Yes. But we can be in and out before the press finds out. There's not exactly freedom of information in Iran. I might even be able to bring Zahara Ahmadi out with me."

"Really, Wile E. Coyote. That's your plan?" said Williams. "Suppose they don't let you out? Though that would be one way to get rid of my now lunatic Secretary of State."

"Too many variables," said Beecham. "They might not want to keep her."

"Who would blame them? And if they did, someone here might notice she was missing. Would take a while, but eventually—"

"OK," said Ellen. "I get the point. But I think I should meet with the Iranian Foreign Minister face-to-face and discuss this. It would establish a rapport, if not a trust. And it might help distract them long enough to get that message to Zahara Ahmadi. So far they don't seem to realize anyone tried to stop the attacks."

"Tim?" asked President Williams.

The DNI shook his head. "If Secretary Adams does that, then the Iranians will know that we know they're behind the attacks. It's never a good idea to let them in on how much intel we have. Or don't have."

"If the Iranians killed those physicists, that means they might know what's going on," said Ellen. "What Shah has planned. Maybe, even, where he is." She held President Williams's eyes. "Isn't it worth the risk?"

He gave a curt nod. "Do it. But not Tehran. Meet in Oman. It's a neutral country. I'll call the Sultan and let you know if he agrees. Tim, you and Ellen work together to get a message to the daughter."

"Sir, I don't—" Beecham began.

"Enough," snapped Williams. "I can see you don't like each other, but unfortunately for you, you two do seem to get results. Like Lennon and McCartney. So, you will continue. Work it out. I want an *Abbey Road* by the end of the day. Good luck in Oman, Ellen. And let me know as soon as your people have picked up the bomber in Germany."

"I will, sir," said Ellen.

His screen went blank. Leaving Ellen Adams and Tim Beecham to glare at each other.

"I get to be McCartney," she said.

"Fine. Lennon was the better musician anyway."

Ellen was about to argue the point but realized there were more important issues.

"I guess we'd better come together, right now," she said, and saw a thin smile.

"He just do what he please," she hummed to herself.

Ellen decided to go down to Cargill's section to get an update, but as soon as she arrived, she saw something was wrong.

The room, normally a hive of activity, was silent. No one moved except to turn shocked faces to her.

"What?" she asked. "What's happened?"

A senior analyst stepped forward. "They're dead, Madame Secretary."

Ellen felt herself grow cold and still. "Who?"

Though she knew the answer.

Scott Cargill. His second-in-command. And Aram Wani.

All three gunned down in a back alley in Bad Kötzting.

CHAPTER 20

Betsy answered on the first ring.

"How goes it?"

"Not so good," said Ellen.

She sounded exhausted. And not surprising. It was after six p.m. in DC, which made it after midnight in Frankfurt.

Even more than exhausted, Ellen sounded dispirited.

"Tell me," said Betsy.

She sat up on the couch Ellen had in her office. She'd been trying to catch a nap before tackling Timothy T. Beecham again. She wished she had some news, any news, for Ellen.

Listening to her friend's voice, drained of most of its vigor, Betsy decided not to tell her about the man who'd been following her. Besides, General Whitehead had taken care of him. And Ellen might've forgotten that brief exchange that ended with *What bodyguard?*

"First, tell me about that bodyguard thing," said Ellen, and Betsy smiled.

Of course she wouldn't forget.

"It was a joke. There was this handsome young guy trying to pick me up. At least, I'm pretty sure he was. He couldn't have been trying to catch the eye of the beautiful young woman beside me on the flight."

"Of course not." Ellen gave a short imitation of a laugh. "Did you have your way with him?"

"Sadly, my way is now a whole cheesecake and a bottle of Chardonnay."

"Oh God, that sounds good," said Ellen.

"I did meet with General Whitehead. He had some thoughts on what's happening. And going to happen."

"Tell me."

And Betsy did. "He thinks the Pakistanis, supported by the Russians, convinced Dunn to agree to the release of Shah as part of a deal."

"What deal?" Ellen's voice was filled with apprehension.

"Dunn would pull our troops out of Afghanistan with no conditions from the Afghans, and Pakistan would ensure stability there. In exchange, the Pakistanis demanded the US agree to the release of the most dangerous arms dealer in the world. And Dunn was too dense to know what he was agreeing too."

Too dense, Ellen thought, or myopic. Only seeing approval ratings. Or dollar signs.

"And Beecham?" she asked.

"Was involved in both decisions," said Betsy.

"The Iago whispering in Othello's ear."

"I prefer to see him as Lady Macbeth," said Betsy.

"Proof?"

"None so far. There's more." *For I have more*, thought Betsy. "General Whitehead thinks Beecham isn't alone. That there's a plot by people who consider themselves patriots to bring down a government they consider illegitimate and install Dunn. Because he'll do what they want."

Unseen by Betsy, the Secretary of State was nodding. The fact that this wasn't a complete shock was, in itself, shocking.

Ellen was alone in her hotel room in Frankfurt. It was coming up on one in the morning, and she was too tired, too wired, to sleep. Though she was desperate to.

She was waiting for a message to tell her the Oman trip was on. Then she could contact her Iranian counterpart. She'd already sent out small, private feelers.

If Iran had arranged for the bus bombs and the bombers, then they'd also arranged for the murder of Aram Wani in Bad Kötzting. And with him, Scott Cargill and his second-in-command.

Yes, Secretary Adams was anxious to have a word or two with the Iranians.

"I need to know who to trust," said Ellen. "And who not to. I need proof."

Betsy heard fear in that familiar voice.

"You be careful, Elizabeth Anne Jameson," said Ellen.

"No worries. Bert Whitehead's sent a Ranger to watch over me. I haven't called her yet."

"Please, promise me you will."

"I promise. Now it's your turn. Tell me what's happened."

And Ellen Adams did. She told her best friend, her counselor, everything. And when she'd finished, Betsy said, "I'm so sorry. It was the Iranians who killed Scott Cargill and his number two."

"And the bomber. I think so. I'm heading to Oman, to meet with the Iranian Foreign Minister."

"Are you insane?" demanded Betsy, sitting up straight now. "You can't do that. They might kill you. Or even kidnap you."

Unexpectedly, there was a laugh down the line. "Doug Williams did suggest that when he okayed the trip."

"Asshole."

"No, it was a joke. I'll be fine. The Iranians aren't exactly our friends, but they are smart. There's no advantage in hurting or kidnapping me. I initially suggested Tehran—"

"For God's sake—"

"So that Tim Beecham would know I'm the idiot he thinks I

am," said Ellen. "I also knew if I first suggested Oman, Williams would turn it down."

"Wait a minute. You played that same mind game about my first husband. Is that how . . ."

"No. He was never my idea."

"I wish I was going with you."

"So do I."

"Who is?"

"Besides Boynton and Diplomatic Security, I've decided to bring Katherine and Anahita Dahir, the FSO. She speaks Farsi. It'll be helpful to have someone who knows what the Foreign Minister is really saying."

"Can you trust her after what you found out about her family?"

There was a pause. "No. Not completely. That's another reason I want her close. We have put her to good use, though. The CIA has figured out how to get a message to Zahara Ahmadi, and we need Anahita for that. Her cousin won't trust an American operative, but she might trust Anahita. The Iranians probably monitor communications from Dr. Ahmadi's computer. We need to get to Zahara before the Iranian secret police."

"Are you sure she's the one who sent the message?"

"No, but it's the most likely answer." Ellen breathed a long sigh. "I've approved the operation. They'll approach Zahara Ahmadi as soon as she leaves home for classes."

Betsy had long known that while she had bravado, Ellen was the brave one. She was glad she didn't have to make decisions like this.

"Before I hang up, how's Gil?"

"I called the hospital a few minutes ago. He's sleeping, and the doctor on duty said he's much better. I'll drop in on my way to the airport."

"Still no word on his informant?"

"No, none."

There'd been a pause. Betsy didn't know if Ellen had hesitated on purpose, or if it was fatigue. She decided not to ask. The sooner she got off the line, the sooner her friend could get some sleep.

"Be careful, Ellen Sue Adams."

It came to Betsy with a start an hour later, waking her out of her nap.

Who she'd seen in the basement bar of the Hay-Adams hotel. The one the General had also seen. The one making the commotion.

She hadn't seen him in years. He'd looked younger then. Almost dewy.

But that afternoon, at Off the Record, he was almost unrecognizable. In fact, thought Betsy as she leapt off the couch and into the shower, he'd looked a lot like a chain saw.

The call came at close to three in the morning in Frankfurt, waking Ellen out of a fitful sleep.

The Oman trip was on.

Ellen sprang out of bed, and within two hours she had a commitment from the Iranian Foreign Minister to meet at the Sultan's official residence in Old Muscat.

"I can give you an hour, Madame Secretary," he'd said. He spoke beautiful English, though he often preferred to go through an interpreter.

This time, though, they spoke directly. Simpler. Easier. And more discreet.

After calling Charles Boynton, and having him call Anahita Dahir, she woke up Katherine.

"We're going to Oman," she said. "Wear modest dress."

"Right. I'll leave my leather chaps behind."

Her mother laughed. "Plane leaves in forty minutes. Cars leave in twenty."

"Got it. Anahita?" Katherine asked.

It seemed the two young women had forged a friendship. Ellen didn't know if she was happy about that or not.

"Is coming with us."

Sure enough, twenty minutes later the armored vehicles left for the airport.

"Can you please stop at the hospital first?" asked Ellen.

Within minutes she was standing by Gil's bed. He was asleep, his bruised face at peace. "Gil?" she whispered. She hated to do it, but there was so much about all this Ellen Adams hated, this was just one more to add to the list. "Gil?"

He stirred and opened puffy eyes. "What time is it?"

"Just after four in the morning."

"What're you doing here?" He struggled to sit up, and she helped, placing a pillow behind his back.

"I'm on my way to Oman to speak to the Iranian Foreign Minister. The Iranians were behind the bombings."

Gil nodded. "That makes sense. They wouldn't want Shah to sell nuclear secrets, or scientists, to anyone else in the region."

"Your informant—"

"I told you, I'm not going—"

She held up her hand to stop him. "I know. I'm not asking who it is." She dropped her voice. "When I was last here, you were about to say something. You told me there might be another way to find out more from your informant. More about Shah."

"I can't tell you," he whispered.

"But how will you do it? You're in the hospital."

"I've worked it out. You do what you need to, and let me do my thing. I was the one blown up. I'm the one who'll forever see their faces. I have a stake in this too. You have to trust me."

"It's not that I don't trust you. It's that I don't want to lose you." She made up her mind to say it. To see. "I'm taking Anahita to Oman with me. She's outside now."

Ellen waited to see Gil's reaction. If Anahita was his informant . . .

But there was no reaction. Except, "Say hi from me, will you?"

"I will. We should be back later today. I'll stop in then."

"Good luck."

Twenty-five minutes later Air Force Three was hurtling down the runway in the dark, beginning its seven-hour flight to the Gulf State.

Once they were at cruising altitude, Ellen went into her office to prepare. There she found a lovely arrangement of flowers. Her favorite. Sweet pea. Delicate and fragrant.

Bending over to smell them, Ellen noticed a note.

"Did you order these?" she asked her Chief of Staff as Boynton came in with a steward who had coffee and a light breakfast.

Boynton put down the files he was carrying and looked at the bouquet. "No. But they're nice. Probably from the American Ambassador."

"I wonder how she knew these are my favorite."

"She's very thorough," said Boynton, who had not known his boss had a favorite flower. But then, he'd been a bit busy finding out other things about the new Secretary of State. "Must've done her research."

"Thank you," Ellen said to the steward, who'd poured her a large black coffee, then left.

Opening the note, she felt the coffee cup begin to slip off her finger. She stopped it just in time, but not before a small drop landed on, and scalded, her thigh.

"What is it?" asked Boynton, walking over.

"Who sent these flowers?" she asked, her voice now brusque.

"I told you, Madame Secretary," he said. "I don't know." He seemed genuinely perplexed by her reaction. "What's wrong?"

"Find out, please."

"I will."

He hurried from the room as Ellen placed the note on her desk. Careful not to handle it more than she already had.

It was a scan of the note she'd passed to Betsy, before her friend and counselor had flown back to DC. It was the one asking her to look into Tim Beecham. And to not, whatever happened, let anyone else see it.

And yet here it was. On its way to Oman, on board Air Force Three, shoved into a bouquet of sweet peas, which no longer seemed so lovely.

There was no other writing on it. And no signature. But she knew who was behind it. Who was behind all those unsigned notes over the years. The birthday cards. Christmas cards. The message sent after Quinn died.

She picked up the secure line and called Betsy, her heart pounding in her throat.

CHAPTER 21

The bar was packed now.

It was just after ten in the evening, and DC had come out to play.

Betsy looked around, her eyes adjusting to the dim light. She made straight for the bar itself, where she'd last seen Pete Hamilton. He was no longer there, though she was tempted to look under it, since that seemed to be where he was headed.

"What can I get you?" the bartender asked.

A vat of Chardonnay, thought Ellen Adams's best friend.

"A diet ginger ale, please," said the SecState's counselor. "With a maraschino cherry if possible," Betsy added.

While she waited, she felt her phone vibrate.

"What are you doing up? It must be—" she asked before being cut off.

"A simile walks into a bar," said Ellen, her voice strained.

"What? As a matter of fact, I have just walked into a bar."

"Betsy, a simile walks into a bar!"

Betsy's mind froze for a moment . . . simile. Simile.

"As parched as a desert. Ellen"—she dropped her voice—"what's this about? Where are you? What's that noise?"

"You're all right?"

"Yes. I'm in Off the Record. Did you know they already have a coaster with your caricature on it?"

"Listen, Betsy, that note I gave you just before you left, where is it?"

"In my pocket." She put her hand in. It wasn't there. "Oh, wait. I remember. I took it out and put it on your desk when I got to your office. I wanted to keep it safe." Betsy grew still. "Why?"

"Because there's a copy of it here."

"In Frankfurt? How—"

"No. On Air Force Three."

"Shit." Her mind raced, going back over her actions that day. "I left it on your desk when I went into Boynton's office to use his computer to research Beecham."

"Did anyone come in?"

"Yes. Barb Stenhauser. Jesus, Ellen."

Dear God, thought Ellen. The DNI was bad enough, but the President's Chief of Staff?

"Why would she take it, then scan it to you?"

"Whoever took it sent it to Shah. He had it placed in an arrangement of sweet peas on the plane."

"The flowers Quinn used to send you. As a warning?"

"As a taunt. He wants me to know he's close. So close, he can do anything he pleases. Reach me anywhere."

"But they'd need someone in Frankfurt, someone with access to your plane. Ellen—"

"I know."

It could be anyone. A member of her security team. One of the stewards. The pilot even.

Or—Ellen looked toward the closed door—her own Chief of Staff. The near-invisible Charles Boynton.

"My God," said Betsy. "If Stenhauser . . . Does that mean Williams . . . ?"

"No," said Ellen. "I think he's many things, but not in league with Bashir Shah. What I do know is we need clarity. So far we suspect everyone. That has to stop."

"Agreed, but what do we do?"

"Again, we need facts, proof. Information. Are you sure no one else went into my office?"

"I'm sure . . ."

"What is it?" said Ellen.

"I suppose someone might've gone into your office when I came here to meet General Whitehead. This means Shah knows you're onto Beecham."

Ellen Adams found herself growing very still, very calm. Like most women, unlike the myth, she was good in a crisis. And this was a crisis. "Which means time is short. They must be trying to decide what to do about it. Have you found anything yet?"

"No, nothing yet. That's why I'm here."

"In the bar?"

"With a diet ginger—"

"And maraschino?" asked Ellen.

"The best part. Listen, Ellen, when I was here this afternoon, I saw Pete Hamilton."

"Dunn's former press secretary?"

"Yes."

"Young, idealistic. Kinda endearing," said Ellen. "He did a good job selling Dunn's lies."

"He was so convincing," agreed Betsy.

"Probably because he actually believed what he was saying. The propogandist is his own first customer."

It was something she used to drum into any green journalist hired by her media empire, along with the Buddhist monk Thubten Chodron's advice: "Don't believe everything you think."

"Hamilton was doing a good job," said Ellen. "But then he was replaced by Dunn's son."

"That numbskull," said Betsy. "Did we ever hear why they got rid of Hamilton?"

"It was never explained, but the rumor was he had a drinking problem. Couldn't be trusted with state secrets. Why do you want to meet him?"

"Because I need someone from inside the Dunn administration. Someone who can help us find the information we need. Everyone else is afraid to talk, but Hamilton might."

"Hard to trust the word of an embittered addict. But maybe he's better."

Betsy remembered the loud, belligerent voice, and the men and women moving away from him.

"Maybe not," admitted Betsy. "I don't need someone quotable. I need someone who can get us the proof we need. Besides, I'm now obsessed with finding out what the *T* in 'Timothy T. Beecham' stands for."

"Please don't come back with only that."

Betsy laughed, and so did Ellen. After the day she'd had, she hadn't thought she'd be able to laugh, but Betsy could always lighten her heart.

"Be careful," Ellen said. "You said General Whitehead had a Ranger contact you, right? Call her. If Shah's read my note to you, he knows you're onto Beecham. If you get close . . ." Ellen paused. It didn't bear thinking of. But she had to. "I wouldn't put it past him to . . ."

"Hurt me?"

"Please, just for my peace of mind. There's so little of it left."

"OK. I will. But I want to contact this Pete Hamilton first. Don't need some Army Ranger scaring him off. You're on your way to Oman?"

"Yes."

"Give my love to Katherine. Hope she left her leather chaps behind."

Ellen laughed again, then considered. She'd thought her daughter had been joking, but maybe . . .

"Oh, and Ellen?"

"Yes?"

"You be careful."

Ellen hung up and looked at the sweet peas. So delicate, such cheerful colors. Such a gentle fragrance. They always reminded her of Quinn's kindness.

She picked up the bouquet and was about to drop it into the garbage can, then stopped and replaced them on her desk.

Shah was not going to take that from her.

And dear God, don't let him take Betsy.

"Yeah, that was him," said the bartender when Betsy asked. "Pete Hamilton. Comes in about every two weeks. In case."

"Of what?"

"In case anyone actually wants to talk to him. Hire him maybe."

"Does anyone?"

"No, never." The bartender eyed her, this woman who looked like the Beaver's mother.

"So he left?"

"Was asked to leave. He was drunk or high or something when he arrived. Started harassing some customers, so he was shown the door." He studied her. "Why're you looking for him?"

"I'm his aunt. His family lost track of him after he left the White House. His mother's sick and I need to talk to him. Do you know where he lives?"

"No. Not exactly. Someplace in Deanwood, I think. I wouldn't go there now. Not after dark."

Betsy paid for her diet ginger and gathered her things. "Unfortunately, his mother's really sick. I need to find him fast."

The bartender caught up with her at the door. "Listen, you

shouldn't just hang around that neighborhood." He gave her a card. "He left this a few months back, in case anyone needed a PR guy."

She looked at the grubby slip of paper, obviously printed off on his home computer.

"Thank you."

"If you see him, tell him not to come back here. It's just embarrassing."

The taxi pulled up to the address. Deanwood, in the northeast of DC, was twenty minutes and a world away from the Hay-Adams. And the White House.

Betsy stood at the door of the apartment building. There was no buzzer, just a hole where one might have been.

She tried the door. The handle was broken, leaving it unlocked. When she entered, Betsy was met with a smell she could almost see.

Urine. Feces. Rotten food and something, or someone, decomposing, she thought.

Up the rickety stairs she climbed, to the top floor, and knocked on the door.

CHAPTER 22

Fuck off."

Betsy held a tissue to her face in an attempt to block out the odors.

"Mr. Hamilton?"

Silence.

"Pete Hamilton? I, ahhh"—she looked at the grubby card in her hand—"need a PR person."

"At midnight? Fuck off."

"It's an emergency."

Silence. Then the squeal of a chair on wood.

"How did you find me?" The voice now was just on the other side of the door.

"I got your address from the bartender at Off the Record. I saw you there today."

"Who are you?"

On the ride over, Betsy had wondered how she'd answer this question.

"My name is Elizabeth Jameson. My friends call me Betsy."

If she wanted, needed, him to be honest, she needed to be. No good starting with a lie.

She heard one, two, three locks turn and a bolt withdraw. And the door swung open.

Betsy braced for a noxious wave. It took her a couple of breaths to realize the place didn't smell. Or, more accurately, it smelled of aftershave. The faint scent of pleasant masculinity.

And baking. Specifically, chocolate chip cookies.

She expected the man standing in front of her to be bleary-eyed. Caked in vomit. Wearing sagging, filthy underwear. She'd prepared for that. In fact, much of her childhood had prepared her for that.

Betsy Jameson had not prepared for this.

Pete Hamilton stood in front of her clean-shaven, clear-eyed, in sweats that looked like they might've been ironed. His dark hair still moist from a shower.

He was only slightly taller than she, with what looked like a layer of baby fat. Not thick but soft. Chubby-faced, he looked like the Gerber baby in a tenement.

"You're the counselor."

"I am. And you're the former press secretary."

He stepped aside. "You'd better come in."

The door opened right into a small living room whose walls had been painted a soothing gray-blue. The wood floors looked like they'd been sanded and refinished.

There was a sofa, opened to a bed, and what looked like a comfortable armchair. A table by the window had an open laptop with papers beside it. Along with a glass of water and a cookie.

In a corner was a kitchenette.

In the few seconds it took to absorb this, she heard the locks being put back in place.

"What do you want?" he asked. "Not a PR person, I'm guessing."

"Well, yes, I do need a PR person. More specifically, I need you."

He stared at her and smiled. "Let me guess. This has something to do with the bus explosions." He tilted his head. "You don't suspect me, do you?"

He gave her the same cherubic smile he'd used to such effect at the podium, peddling Dunn's lies. It was disarming, and Betsy struggled to keep her defenses up.

But faced with the cherub and the scent of chocolate chip cookies, it was a battle she worried she could not win. And then she remembered the faces of the families, in Frankfurt, and her defenses rammed into place.

"I think you can help me, Mr. Hamilton."

"Why would I want to?"

She looked around the apartment, then settled her eyes on his.

"You think I hate it here and long to escape?" he said. "It might not look like much, but it's home. And this is actually a community, with broken but decent people. I fit right in."

"But it would be nice to have a choice, wouldn't it? I think that's what you long for. Don't we all. You can choose to live here, but not have to. Like I said, I saw you this afternoon at Off the Record. You appeared pissed out of your mind. Messy, pathetic."

"You do need a PR person," he said, and she smiled.

"Why the act?" When he didn't answer, she walked across to the table and looked down at the notes by his computer. She got just a glimpse before he splayed his hand over them.

"Please leave."

"You're writing a book. On Dunn."

"No. Please leave. I can't help you."

She held his dark eyes. "You don't fit in here at all."

He snorted. "You elitist Democrats are all the same. You pretend to care for the downtrodden while actually despising them."

She raised her brows. "You misunderstand me. You said your neighbors are decent. That's why you don't fit in. You're indecent. I'm offering you a chance to help find out who's responsible for the bombings. Maybe even prevent another. And all you care about is your book, your revenge."

"It's not revenge, it's justice. I'm not writing a book. I'm trying to find evidence, proof."

"Of what?"

"Of what they did to me. Of who did it."

"Madame Secretary?" Charles Boynton stood just inside the cabin of Air Force Three. "They're ready in Tehran. They just need your go-ahead. Would you like me to contact Mr. Beecham?"

"No, that won't be necessary."

"But—"

"Thank you, Charles. Can you ask Ms. Dahir and Katherine to come in?"

After he left, Secretary Adams picked up the secure phone.

The agent on the ground in Tehran was clearly surprised to hear the voice of the US Secretary of State.

"You're in place?" she asked.

"Yes, Madame Secretary. We can see the Ahmadi home. She should be leaving for classes at the university anytime now."

"You're confident Iranian security isn't onto you?"

There was a soft chuckle from the woman on the other end. "As confident as we can ever be. But that's why we need to move quickly. The longer we wait, the more chance they'll find out."

Ellen paused, thinking of Scott Cargill. Of the other intelligence agent. Gunned down just hours ago in Bad Kötzting.

How brave these people were, while she sailed above it all, with hot coffee and pastries and the scent of sweet pea.

"Do it. May Allah bless you."

"Inshallah."

"May I use your washroom?" Betsy asked.

When she returned, she found him in the kitchen making a pot of tea, the cookies on a plate on the counter. He nodded toward them.

She did as she was told, picking up the plate and taking a cookie as she walked to the armchair. The bed had been converted back into a sofa.

"May I be mother?" he asked when he joined her, indicating the teapot. Handing her a mug, he said, "Find what you were looking for?"

"Actually"—she took it—"I did not."

No drugs except aspirin. It didn't surprise her now. This man was not the drunken addict he wanted people to believe.

"I need an insider, Mr. Hamilton. Someone who knows things, who can find things out. Someone willing to talk."

"About the bus bombs? I know nothing about them."

"About the dirty little secrets of the Dunn administration."

That was met with silence.

"Why would I do that?" he finally said.

"Because you're trying to dig them up yourself."

"No, I'm just trying to find my own evidence."

"May I? They're delicious." She nodded toward the cookies.

"Would you like a sandwich? Are you hungry?"

She smiled. "No, I'm fine. But thank you." She leaned toward him. "What did they do to you?"

When he was quiet, she decided to help him along.

"They fired you without cause, so they had to invent cause. They mocked up emails, messages, something showing you're an addict."

As she spoke, she watched him. He'd lowered his eyes.

No, she thought, there was more. *"For I have more . . ."*

"There was the suggestion you were trafficking."

He raised his eyes and took a long, deep breath. "I wasn't."

"But you did do drugs."

"Who didn't? I was a kid, they were our form of a martini. But I didn't—"

"—inhale?"

He smiled. "I didn't traffic. I never would. And I didn't do anything stronger than grass. But they made it sound like I was some drug-addled danger to the administration, that I was possibly going to sell secrets to fund my habit. That I was a danger to national security."

His eyes now pleaded with her. No, not her. Betsy realized while he was looking at her, he was seeing his accusers. In the closed-door meeting. As they placed the evidence in front of him.

His shock. His denials. His pleading. His weeping. They had to believe him.

And the tragic thing was that, of course, they did.

"Why did they do that to you?" she asked.

He brought his laptop over to her and clicked some keys, bringing up a file with a photo.

"That's the closest I can come to a reason. It came out three days before I was fired."

It was from a newspaper report. No, not a report. A DC political gossip column. The picture showed Pete Hamilton, looking so much younger than the young man in front of her. He was laughing with some White House correspondents. They were in Off the Record.

The line under it said, *Pete Hamilton, White House press secretary, clearly in on the joke.*

Betsy looked up. "That's it? They fired you for meeting with reporters? Isn't that what you're supposed to do?"

"Loyalty was the most important thing in that White House. Anyone who looked like they might say anything at all critical was let go."

"But you're just laughing. It could've been about anything."

"Didn't matter. Those are journalists from CNN. The President thought I was laughing at some joke about him. The seed was planted. Weeds grow quickly. I had to go."

"Go, OK, maybe at a stretch. But they made you look like a national security threat. A trafficker. They ruined you."

"As an example. It was early in the administration, they needed to show everyone what would happen to anyone even suspected of being disloyal. I'm lucky they didn't put my head on a spike."

"They might as well have. You're unemployable."

"Yes. They never made a statement, never publicly accused me, nothing that I could defend or take to court."

"They? Eric Dunn?"

She could see him hesitate. "I hope not, but I don't know. Not much happened in that administration that he didn't know about."

"And now?" She looked at the table and the files. "You're trying to clear your name. Find proof it was manufactured."

"Took me a while to get this angry. At first I was shocked. Then I actually thought I deserved it. I believed in Eric Dunn. In the goals of the administration. But as time went by, and I saw the damage they'd done to me, I got angry."

"You have a long fuse."

"Attached to a big bomb."

"What was that performance at Off the Record today? You were just pretending to be drunk or high. Why?"

"You need to tell me why you're here, Mrs. Jameson. And you need to know that, no matter what happened to me, I'm a conservative, through and through. I might not be a big fan of Dunn anymore, but I also think your man is a fool."

Betsy surprised him with a laugh. "If you really do still follow politics, you know you won't get any argument from me, or from Secretary Adams." Then she grew serious. "Our man might be a fool, but at least he's not dangerous."

"A President who's a fool is, by definition, dangerous."

"What I mean is that he's not outright plotting to overthrow the government by helping to support, maybe even arm, terrorists. You asked what I'm doing here? We think Eric Dunn, or people loyal to him, are involved in the bus bombings, and what's coming next."

Pete Hamilton stared at her. Surprised, perhaps, but not, she thought, shocked.

"And what makes you think that?"

"Because he allowed the release of Bashir Shah, the Pakistani—"

"I know who he is. He's out of house arrest?"

"And has disappeared."

"You think Shah's behind the bombings?"

"No. It's not yet public, but there was a Pakistani nuclear physicist on each of those buses, recruited by Shah."

It was eerie to see his face. He still looked like a cherub, but a cherub who'd swallowed a monster.

"What do you know?" she asked. "You know something. You've heard something."

"You asked why I go to Off the Record and pretend to be drunk. I go there to prove to them that I'm no threat. I'm so far gone, no one needs to worry about me. And they don't. So I sit there glassy-eyed, mumbling to myself, while they talk to each other. I hear things. If they're going to make me a drunken nonperson, I might as well take advantage of that."

Betsy looked at this man-child and realized she might be in the presence of a modern Mozart. A boy genius.

"And what have you heard?"

"Whispers. People are always scheming, always exaggerating in DC. Always promising big things, but this's different. This's quiet. None of the regular political bullshit and posturing. I've tried to find out, but my problem is, I know where to look and how to look. I've spent years listening, hearing things. I know where they keep their confidential records. What I don't have is access. I can't get through the White House cybersecurity."

Betsy smiled.

At just after seven in the morning, Zahara Ahmadi left her home for the short walk to the University of Tehran.

A rose-colored hijab framed her face and fell to her feet.

Her mother always wore black, and her father had insisted his daughters also wear the more somber hijab, out of respect. But once she was in her twenties and at university, Zahara, who adored her father, indulged in this one act of personal rebellion.

Her hijabs were bright and cheerful. Because, she'd explained to her father, Islam made her happy. Allah brought her joy and peace.

While her father could see that was true, he did not approve or agree. Dr. Ahmadi worried that his elder daughter, who he adored, did not have the proper respect or reverence or even fear of their God, never mind their government.

He knew what both could do, if displeased.

As Zahara Ahmadi walked the familiar route, she became aware of someone behind her. In a shop window she saw not one but two people. A man and a woman. Both in deepest black, the woman in a full burqa.

Zahara knew VAJA agents, members of the secret intelligence service, when she saw them. They'd visited her home, her father, all her life. Sitting in his messy study and questioning him. Instructing him. He took it all in and did as he was told.

Not, she knew, because he was forced to, but because he wanted to.

She'd never been afraid of these people. Zahara saw them as her father did. Extensions of a government intent on protecting its citizens against a hostile world. But now she knew differently. Ever since that last visit. That last conversation that had drifted up the vent into her room.

She picked up her pace.

The streets were empty except for some vendors beginning to put out their wares.

The man and woman sped up, their footsteps getting closer.

She sped up.

They sped up.

She broke into a run.

They ran after her. Gaining. The faster she ran, the more panicked she became.

She'd always thought she was brave. Now she realized she'd just been naïve.

Zahara raced down an alley and out the other side, her cheerful bright pink robes flapping behind her. Marking her. Making her impossible to miss.

"Stop," one of them yelled. "We don't want to hurt you."

But of course, what else would they say? *Stop, so we can kill you*? *Torture you*? *Disappear you*?

Zahara didn't stop. But as she turned the next corner, she ran straight into the man. Actually bumping into him so hard she stumbled backward and would have fallen if the woman coming up behind hadn't caught her.

Zahara struggled, but the man held her tight, a hand over her mouth, while the woman reached into the pocket of her burqa.

"No," Zahara tried to plead. Her voice muffled by the hand. "No, don't."

Something was thrust into her face.

"Zahara?" came a voice.

Slowly she stopped twisting and stared at the mobile phone as it spoke to her in accented Farsi. It was a young woman's voice. An American voice.

"It's Anahita. Your cousin. These people are here to help."

In the office of Air Force Three as it soared toward Oman, Secretary Adams, Katherine, and Anahita all stared at the phone on the desk.

Waiting for a reply. The moments ticked by.

"Anahita?" came the tinny voice.

The people gathered around looked at each other and smiled. Relaxing.

"How do I know it's you?"

They were prepared for this question. In anticipation, they'd asked Irfan Dahir to tell his daughter something only he and his younger brother could have known.

Ellen nodded to Anahita.

"My father used to call your father 'little shithead,' and your father called my father 'dumbass' because he didn't study physics but went into economics."

A small moan of relief, and even amusement, came out of the speaker.

"It's true. I now call my little sister that. She's studying theater."

"I have another cousin?" asked Anahita, staring at the small box on the desk as though it contained the family she'd longed for all her life.

"I have a brother too. He really is a shithead."

Anahita laughed.

Ellen made a rapid circle with her finger.

Anahita nodded. "I got your message but couldn't stop the bombings. Listen, those people are there to help if you get into trouble. They can get you out."

"But I don't want to leave. Iran's my home. I did it to help, not to hurt Iran. Killing innocent people isn't the way forward."

"Yes, all right, but you don't want to end up in the hands of the secret police. Listen, we have to know how your father found out about the physicists. Do you know about Bashir Shah? What does he have planned? If—"

There was, then, a shout. The sound of a scuffle.

And then the line went dead.

CHAPTER 23

I'm sorry, Madame Secretary," the Iranian Foreign Minister said. "Bus bombs? I have no idea what you're talking about."

"You surprise me, Minister Aziz. Does President Nasseri not take you into his confidence?"

They were sitting in a huge reception room, having been met at the entrance to the palace by the Sultan himself.

The tall, gracious man had walked Ellen to the room overlooking the Gulf of Oman, making polite conversation about the art and culture of Oman on the way.

And then he'd left them.

The room was covered floor to ceiling in near-blinding white marble. Out the double doors, which opened onto a wide terrace, Ellen could almost see Iran across the water. Had he wanted to, the Iranian Foreign Minister could have boated over to their meeting.

Now, as she leaned forward, Aziz leaned back. Up until that moment she'd done everything the cultural attachés had advised.

When meeting with the Iranian Foreign Minister, there should be no touching.

Use his formal title.

Her hair must be covered in a modest headscarf.

Never turn your back on him, she was told, and never look at the time. And a hundred other small things that would not cause offense.

While she'd certainly avoided insult, doing all those things had not actually gotten her anywhere. And though she had no desire to cause more damage to a relationship on life support, neither did she have time for this posturing.

"I can assure you, if there was something to know," he said, "I would."

All of this was said through his interpreter.

Ellen had asked the Iranian Foreign Minister if they might share his.

"That's quite an act of trust, Secretary Adams," Minister Aziz had said in perfect English during their phone conversation.

"You're not suggesting there's a risk your interpreter might misrepresent me?" she said, her voice filled with amusement.

"If he does, we will just have his tongue torn out by eagles. That is what your press says about us, isn't it? That we are barbarians?"

"Our own mistruths," admitted Ellen. "There's a lot we don't actually know about each other's culture and reality. Perhaps now's the time for honesty." She paused. "And transparency."

Though tempted to demand to know what had happened to Zahara Ahmadi, she did not. It would only make things worse.

Instead, they sat across from each other, the bright sun gleaming off the vast ocean of white marble in the Al Alam Palace, with Mutrah Harbor of Old Muscat in front of them.

Of course, Ellen didn't tell him that the young aide behind her spoke Farsi.

Anahita had been instructed not to say anything, and certainly not to say anything in Farsi, but to just listen and let her know later what the Foreign Minister actually said.

Aziz had regarded Anahita, then spoken to her in Farsi. Asking where she was from.

Anahita had looked blank.

He'd smiled.

Ellen wasn't sure if he'd been convinced, but as the meeting went on, she could see that he'd forgotten about Katherine, Anahita, and Charles Boynton, sitting quietly behind her, as he focused on the American Secretary of State.

"You say President Nasseri tells you everything of importance, and yet," said Ellen, "you do not know about the bus bombs? The ones your own government planted?"

She was intrigued by this man. He clearly believed in the goals of the revolution, but also appeared to believe that an isolated Iran was a weakened one.

And he'd been sending subtle signals to her that he no longer trusted the Russians, Iran's neighbor and ally, and might be open to an entente with the US. Not full diplomatic relations, not even close, but a slight shift. Which, given how Dunn had walked away from the nuclear agreement, would be seismic for Iran.

Though Aziz had also made it clear that the new American President would start from a very big trust deficit. It would be difficult for Iran to enter into another agreement with oversight because it would make them look weakened and vulnerable.

There was now, Secretary Adams felt, a very, very small opening created by a predatory and unpredictable Russia and an America open to being less confrontational.

It was her job to find that sliver of mutual benefit. And perhaps, over time, expand it into a genuine understanding. So that Iran would no longer be a persistent threat, and the US and its allies no longer targets for attacks.

But they weren't there yet. Far from it. And the bus bombs had made the chasm all the greater. But it had also given her the opening she needed.

"So you'd rather not discuss the murders of the Pakistani physicists," she said, selecting a plump date from the platter of fruit and other treats provided by the Sultan's kitchens. "Never mind the murders of all those people on the buses."

"I'm happy to discuss it, I'm just not happy to be blamed. After all, why would Iran want to kill Pakistanis? And to do it in such a bloody way? It makes no sense, Madame Secretary. Now, India . . ."

He spread out his expressive hands, inviting her to see his point.

"Ahhh," she said, sitting back and spreading out her own hands. "Now, Bashir Shah . . ."

She watched as the man across from her turned to marble. The sun gleaming off the perspiration on his brow.

His smile had faded, and his eyes no longer looked even slightly amused. He glared at her, the mask of civility slipping.

"Perhaps," she said, "we might speak in private?"

When the others had left, Ellen leaned toward Minister Aziz, and he leaned closer to her.

"Havercrafte man pore mārmāhi ast." She pronounced the words slowly, quietly, carefully. And saw his gray brows rise.

"Really?" he said.

Ellen's brows lowered. "What did I just say? My aide looked it up and gave me the phrase. I've been practicing."

"I just hope what you said isn't true. Your hovercraft is full of eels."

Ellen's lips twitched into a smile she was clearly fighting to contain. Finally, giving up, she laughed. "I am sorry. The truth is, my hovercraft has no eels."

Now he laughed. "I wouldn't be so sure. Now, what did you mean to say, Madame Secretary?"

"The English expression I was going for is 'cards on the table.'"

"I agree. A time for honesty."

She held his eyes and nodded. "A message was sent from the home of one of your senior nuclear physicists in Tehran, warning us about the bus bombs. Unfortunately, the FSO receiving it dismissed it as junk and ignored it until it was too late."

"A shame," was all he said.

If the Iranian Foreign Minister was surprised by her candor, he was far too practiced a diplomat to show it.

Time was short, and there was a lot of ground to cover. She'd managed to get him on his own more quickly than she'd expected, but now she needed to cross the finish line.

"That physicist and his family are now in the custody of your secret police."

"There is no such thing," he said. A rote answer for the ears of any eels that might be listening.

She ignored it. "The United States government would consider it a favor if they were released, along with the other two Iranians picked up at the same time."

"Even if we had them, I doubt they could be released. Do you let traitors and spies go?"

"If there is a greater benefit, yes."

"And what would that benefit be to Iran?"

"The thanks of the new President. A private IOU."

"We had the thanks of the old one. And it was substantial. He pulled out of the nuclear treaty, allowing us the independence Iran deserves to develop our peaceful nuclear energy program. Without interference."

"True. He also allowed Bashir Shah to be released. Dr. Shah would be the cobra in your hovercraft, no?"

Aziz stared at her. And she stared back. Waiting. Waiting.

"What is it you really want, Madame Secretary?"

"I want to know how you knew about the Pakistani nuclear

physicists, and what you know about Shah's plans. And I want those people released."

"Why would we do all that?"

"Because to have a friend, you need to be a friend. Why did you agree to meet me? Because you know that Russia is unstable, fickle. You're increasingly isolated. The Islamic Republic of Iran needs, if not friends, then fewer enemies. Shah, with Pakistan's help, is on the verge of providing nuclear weapons capability to at least one other country in the region. Maybe even to terrorist organizations. That's why you had the scientists killed. But there are more physicists out there. You can't kill them all. You need us to help stop it. And we need you."

A few minutes later Secretary Adams and Minister Aziz parted. The Iranian Foreign Minister headed straight to the airport to take the short flight back home, while Ellen requested the Sultan's indulgence that she be allowed to stay in his palace for a little while longer.

Standing at the balustrade, looking out over the ancient, storied port, the American Secretary of State placed her call.

"Barb? I need to speak to the President."

"He's a little busy—"

"Now."

Barb Stenhauser stood back and watched as President Williams took the call.

"Ellen, how did it go?" There was more than a slight edge of anxiety to his voice.

"I need to go to Tehran."

"Right. And I need to be at 90 percent in the polls."

"No, Doug, you want that. I'm talking about a need. Minister Aziz all but admitted they planted the bombs, and I think we have a chance of rescuing our people and getting information on Shah, but there was no way Aziz was going to give us what we need. He can't. Only the President can. And maybe not even Nasseri. It might have to be the Ayatollah."

"You'll never get an audience with the Supreme Leader."

"I won't if I don't try. If I demonstrate a willingness to go to them, that will help."

"What you're demonstrating is desperation. For God's sake, Ellen, have you no sense? How would it look if one of the first places you visit as SecState is a sworn enemy who's bombed tankers, shot down planes, harbored terrorists, and now murdered innocent civilians?"

"No one needs to know. I can be in and out in hours. Take a private jet. Does anyone even know I'm in Oman?"

"No. We've explained your absence by saying you're at a luxury spa in North Korea."

A laugh escaped Ellen before she could stop it.

"Can't this be done virtually?" asked the President. "We can't risk anyone believing we're cozying up to enemies."

Across the room he could see the bank of monitors with talking heads. So-called experts. Most, if not all, wondering where the Williams administration was in all this. How they could not have known about the attacks. What else didn't they know?

The former Secretary of State was on Fox News explaining that, on their watch, no such catastrophe happened or could happen. And who knew what might happen next, on American soil, with such weakness in the Oval Office.

"I understand how this might look," Ellen conceded. "But we finally have a chance to get Shah and stop whatever he has planned. I have to be there in person. I have to show goodwill."

"Do we know that the Iranians even have that information?"

"No," admitted Ellen. "But they have more than we do. They knew about the physicists. What I don't understand is why they felt they had to blow up whole buses. Why not just shoot the scientists? Far easier."

"As a public spectacle?" Williams suggested. "They've done worse."

"It still doesn't make sense. The answers are in Tehran, and so are Zahara Ahmadi and our agents. They've been arrested by the secret police. We have to try to get them out, and find out what the Iranians know about Shah. If they don't know what Shah has planned and where he is, then they might know who does."

"Why would they tell us?"

"Because they want us to stop him."

"Then why didn't they tell us before? If they want our help, why didn't they tell us about the physicists?"

"Look, I don't know. That's why I have to go to Tehran."

"And if it backfires? If the Iranians decide to release photos of you bowing to the Grand Ayatollah or President Nasseri? Or they decided to arrest you? Charge you with spying? Then what?"

"I know what," she said, her voice suddenly cold. "I know you won't negotiate for my release."

"Ellen—"

"Do I have your approval or not? The Sultan has been kind enough to lend me one of his jets, and they need to know. And I need to get there before the Iranians change their mind and go to the Russians for help."

"All right," said Williams. "Go. But if you get into trouble . . ."

"I'm on my own. I did this unilaterally. I did not consult you."

Coward, she thought as she hung up.

Lunatic, he thought as he hung up.

"Get Tim Beecham up here," he snapped.

"Yes, Mr. President."

As his Chief of Staff left, Doug Williams stared at the monitors and felt the walls of the Oval Office begin to spin. Like a centrifuge. That separated liquid from solid.

Leaving only the dense behind.

CHAPTER 24

OK, I'm in," said Pete Hamilton. "What do you need me to find?"

Betsy had installed him in Boynton's office and given him the log-in and password to access classified information, but not before locking the main door into the Secretary of State's suite of rooms, as well as Ellen's own office and her Chief of Staff's.

She'd done everything but shove the couch up against the door, and she was considering that.

"Everything you can on Tim Beecham."

Hamilton's fingers hovered over the keyboard as he stared at her. "Jesus. The Director of National Intelligence?"

"Yes. Timothy T. Beecham. And while you're at it, find out what the *T* stands for."

Two hours later, as the sun was just coming up, Hamilton shoved his chair back from the desk.

"You have something?" she said, walking over to stand behind him. "What's this?"

Hamilton rubbed his face with both his hands. His eyes were bloodshot and his face drawn.

"That's all I could find on Beecham."

"Two hours?"

"Yes. Someone doesn't want us to know more. None of his reports, his emails, his notes from meetings, his agenda. Four years' worth of documents gone. Nothing. None of the things that need to, by law, be kept. They're all gone."

"Gone where? Erased?"

"Or filed somewhere else. In some other department, where no one would think to look. Could be anywhere. Or they've just buried the information so deep I can't find it."

"Why?"

"Isn't it obvious? There's something they want to hide."

"Keep digging."

"I can't. I've hit bottom."

Betsy nodded, thinking. "All right, so far we've been going after Beecham. Maybe we need to look elsewhere, sneak around behind him. Find a back door."

"Shah? Taliban?"

"Bow ties."

"Sorry?"

"Tim Beecham wears bow ties. I remember reading a feature on him that Ellen's DC paper did for their fashion section."

"So?"

"So they must archive all news stories. There's a clipping service, right? Tim Beecham wasn't the Director of National Intelligence in the Dunn administration. He was a high-level intelligence advisor. He wouldn't be quoted in many articles. In fact, he'd make sure he wasn't. But one on fashion? A feel-good article in a paper notorious for criticizing everything Dunn's people did? They must've leapt at the chance."

"Bow ties?"

"They got Al Capone on tax evasion," said Betsy, leaning closer to the screen. "Why not get Beecham on bow ties? The noose around his neck. They wouldn't bother to classify bow ties. Find the article and you'll find him."

Pete Hamilton understood. Bow ties could be the bridge, the one they failed to burn, to a wealth of incriminating information.

"I'll get coffee," said Betsy.

"And pastries," Pete called after her. "Cinnamon buns."

As she left Boynton's office, the sound of fingers pounding on keys following her out, she remembered her promise to call General Whitehead's Ranger and ask for protection.

It seemed silly. Impossible to believe, in the comfortable and familiar and safe environs of the Secretary of State's offices deep in the State Department building, that there could be a threat to their lives. But then, she knew that was exactly what those people on those buses must've thought.

But first, coffee and cinnamon buns.

Riding down to the cafeteria on the first floor, Betsy was comforted knowing that they'd at least found out what the *T* stood for in "Timothy T. Beecham." Though that too was odd.

The older Iranian woman from the Tehran government stepped back and examined Ellen. Then said in English, "You'll do."

They were in the bedroom of the Sultan's jet, now parked in a hangar of Tehran's Imam Khomeini International Airport. The woman then turned her attention to the others in the spacious cabin. Katherine Adams and Anahita Dahir were similarly attired and similarly unrecognizable in head-to-toe burqas.

Before boarding the Sultan's private jet in Oman, Secretary Adams had called Minister Aziz and asked for the traditional dress. He immediately understood why.

Then, while still in the terminal in Oman, she'd taken Anahita aside.

"I think you should stay here. If the Iranians find out who you are, and they probably will, there could be trouble. You might even be arrested as a spy."

"I know, Madame Secretary."

"You know?"

Anahita smiled. "I've lived all my life in fear of what would happen if the Iranians find my family. It seems inconceivable that I'd just walk right into the lion's den. But yesterday I watched my parents, and I saw what all that secrecy and fear has done to them. The lives they've led, afraid all the time. I'm tired of being afraid. Tired of making myself small for fear of being noticed. Enough. Besides, whatever happens, it can't be any worse than what I've imagined."

"I don't know if that's true," said Ellen.

"You don't know what I've imagined. I was raised on stories of the demons who come at night. The *khrafstra*. The ones I was most afraid of are the *Al*. They're invisible. The only way you know they're there is because horrible things are happening."

And horrible things were certainly happening.

Ellen remembered Anahita's face when she first heard that Bashir Shah was behind the bombings.

"And Shah is an *Al*?"

"I wish. He's Azhi Dahaka. The most powerful demon. He commands an army of *Al*s, bringing chaos, terror. Death. Azhi Dahaka is created out of lies, Madame Secretary."

The two women stared at each other.

"I understand," said Ellen.

She stepped aside and watched as Anahita boarded the flight to Tehran.

Just before the plane landed, Ellen had placed a call to the hospital in Frankfurt, to speak to Gil.

"What do you mean, he's left?" she demanded.

"I'm sorry, Madame Secretary. He said you knew."

More lies, thought Ellen, looking out the window at Iran below. Persia. She wondered, if she looked hard enough, if she'd spot the Azhi Dahaka racing toward Tehran to meet the plane. Or was it occupied elsewhere? Was it creeping toward the shores of the United States, grown ever more powerful for all the lies being told?

"But his injuries?" she said to the head physician.

"Are not life-threatening, and he's an adult. He can sign himself out."

"Do you know where he went?"

"I'm afraid not, Madame Secretary."

She then tried his private line, but it was answered by someone else. A nurse. Gil had given her his phone and asked her to hold on to it, the nurse explained.

So that he couldn't be tracked, Ellen knew.

"Did he tell you anything else?" she asked.

"No."

"What is it? There's more, isn't there?" She could tell by her tone.

"He asked to borrow two thousand euros."

"And you gave it to him?"

"Yes. I got it out of the bank yesterday."

Which meant, Ellen realized, he'd been thinking of bolting since then, and hadn't told her.

"Why did you give him the money?"

"Because he was desperate," she said. "And he's your son, and I wanted to help. Did I do something wrong?"

"No, not at all. I'll make sure you get your money back. If you hear from him, please let me know. *Danke.*"

As she hung up, her phone rang.

"A misplaced modifier walks into a bar . . ."

Betsy! Ellen was always relieved to hear that voice.

". . . owned by a man with a glass eye named Ralph. What is it? Have you found something?"

"What we've found is nothing, nothing at all, on Tim Beecham. It's all hidden deep. Which is, in itself, pretty telling, don't you think?"

"Betsy, we have to find something. We have to have proof he's behind all this. He'll just say it's a setup. That someone else is trying to implicate him. I need to warn the President, but I can't do that without proof."

"I know, I know. We're trying. And I think we might have found a way in, through a back door. Thanks to you."

"Me?"

"Well, not you, but your DC paper. You did a fashion feature on power brokers who wear bow ties."

"We did? Must've been a slow month."

"As it turns out, it could've been the most important story your outlets ever ran. All the documents on Beecham have been buried in another file, where we'd never have found them. Wouldn't know where to start looking. Except they also filed the bow tie story, the only interview he gave while working for Dunn. I can't imagine they classified it. Pete Hamilton's looking now."

"When you find that, you find the rest."

"I hope so." Betsy heard a deep sigh down the line.

"You'll let me know if it leads anywhere?"

"You'll be the first. Oh, and we did find one thing about Beecham. What the *T* stands for. You'll never believe it."

"What?"

"His full name is Timothy Trouble Beecham."

"His middle name is Trouble?" asked Ellen, finding it difficult not to laugh. "Who names their child that?"

"It's either an old family name, or his parents had an inkling . . ."

That they'd given birth to an *Al*, thought Ellen.

"Oh, and I called Captain Phelan, the Ranger," said Betsy. "She's on her way."

"Thank you."

"Where are you?"

"Just landing in Tehran."

"Let me know . . . ?"

"I will. You too."

The plane circled Tehran's Imam Khomeini International Airport. Ellen's breath fogged the window as she unconsciously hummed a half-forgotten tune.

And then the American Secretary of State became aware of the song she was humming, by the Horslips.

"'Trouble, trouble,'" she murmured the lyrics. "'Trouble with a capital *T*.'"

When the jet had come to a halt in the hangar, the Iranian woman stepped on board carrying the burqas the Secretary of State had requested.

A few minutes later they left the plane. The women descended the stairs, with Charles Boynton behind.

The Western women were careful not to trip on the long burqas, which covered them head to toe with only a small mesh window at their eyes.

Women in Iran did not normally wear the full burqa—that was mostly in Afghanistan—but enough did that these three would not look completely out of place. Nor would a casual observer, an airport worker, a driver, be able to tell that the American Secretary of State had just arrived in Iran.

Ellen Adams reached the last rung, and she stepped onto the ground. The first senior American official to set foot in Iran since President Carter in 1979.

"Holy shit," said Pete Hamilton, looking over the screen at Betsy. "I'm in."

"In where?" asked Denise Phelan, putting down her cinnamon bun.

Betsy was grinning ear to ear. "Let me tell your boss first."

She dialed General Whitehead and told him.

"Bow ties," said the Chair of the Joint Chiefs with a laugh. "You're a dangerous woman. I'll be right over."

"Dr. Shah, the Secretary of State's plane hasn't landed in Islamabad as planned," the aide said.

"Then where is she?"

"We think Tehran."

"That can't possibly be true. She wouldn't be that reckless. Find out."

"Yes, sir."

Bashir Shah sipped his lemonade and stared into space. He'd grown, over the years, almost fond of Ellen Adams. He'd come to know her quite intimately, and that had bred a curious bond.

"What are you up to?" he whispered to himself.

He knew her well enough to know she considered her moves carefully before acting. Though it was possible he'd rattled her into this mistake.

Or maybe it wasn't one.

Maybe he was the one making the mistake. The thought was so foreign, so unexpected, he realized he was the one who was rattled. It was slight, a small barb of doubt. But it was there.

The aide returned a few minutes later and found Dr. Shah adjusting the cutlery on the table, set for his luncheon guests.

"It is Tehran, sir."

Bashir Shah took in that information, looking out across the terrace to the ocean. So different from all those years under house arrest in Islamabad, where his world was circumscribed by his lush garden.

He would never allow himself to be imprisoned, no matter how comfortably, again.

"And the son?"

"He's exactly where you predicted."

"Not predicted. There was no guesswork. Nor was there free will. He had no choice."

At least one member of that damned family could be counted on to go where pushed.

"Get my plane ready."

"But, sir, your lunch guests will be here in—" A look from Shah shut him up, and he hurried away to place the call.

"He can't cancel," said the woman on the other end. "Who does he think he is? It's an honor to have the former Pres—"

"Dr. Shah sends his sincere apologies. An emergency has come up."

Bashir Shah got into the armored limousine, turning his back on the Atlantic Ocean. He'd seen enough water for a lifetime. He longed, he found, for a garden.

CHAPTER 25

Gil Bahar had left the hospital in Frankfurt as soon as his mother was gone.

As he dressed, the young nurse gave him the money. He suspected it was her life savings.

"I'll be back. I'll pay you back."

"My little sister was supposed to be on that bus. She missed it. I know you're trying to stop something else from happening. Take it. Go."

When he was in the car on the way to the airport, he opened the bag. There were the euros. And some medications and bandages.

He took one of the painkillers and saved the rest.

Hours later, at the moment his mother tried calling his hospital room in Frankfurt, Gil Bahar stepped off the plane and looked around.

Peshawar. Pakistan.

He felt his stomach tighten and his heart race, and he wondered for an instant if he might pass out as blood rushed from his head to his core. As though trying to escape the memory of all the other blood. All the other heads.

He hadn't been back to Peshawar since his kidnapping. Since his horror when he realized it wasn't ISIS or Al-Qaeda, which would have been horrific enough. No, he was in the hands of the Pathan.

Less well-known than other jihadists, probably because people were afraid to even acknowledge their existence, never mind say their name, the Pathan were an extended family whose influence extended into Al-Qaeda, the Taliban, even into security forces. They were the ghosts. And you sure didn't want to be there when they materialized.

But when the sack had been removed from his head and his eyes adjusted, there he was. In a Pathan camp, on the Pakistan-Afghanistan border.

And Gil Bahar knew he was dead. And it would be horrible.

But instead he'd managed to escape. He'd run as fast and as far as he could. And now he was running as fast and as far as he could to return.

He tried to look relaxed as the customs guard at the airport studied him closely. They didn't get many tourists.

"I'm a student," he explained. "Working on my PhD. It's on the Silk Road. Did you know—"

There was a thud as the stamp hit his passport and he was waved along.

Once out of the airport, into the heat and dust and bustle of the city of almost two million, Gil paused. Slender men rushed toward him.

"Taxi?"

"Taxi?"

Gil raised his hand to his brow, to cut down on the glare, then chose one of the drivers, who reached out to take his bag. But Gil kept hold of it, all but swatting the man away.

Getting into the battered taxi, he settled back. Only when the city was in the rearview mirror did Gil speak.

"Salam alaikum, Akbar."

"Your accent is improving, you shit-face."

"'Shithead' is better. 'Shit-face' normally means drunk."

"In your case, it could mean anal," said Akbar, and heard Gil laugh. "And peace be with you, my friend."

Akbar turned off the main highway, and they bumped along increasingly rutted roads. The Silk Road was far from smooth, as Alexander the Great, Marco Polo, Genghis Khan, and others had discovered to their peril.

The face of the Chair of the Joint Chiefs was grim as he sat at Charles Boynton's desk and read the texts and emails.

"So far nothing especially incriminating," he said, looking up and over the computer. "Shah is mentioned, but only in passing. It's almost as though Beecham didn't know who he was."

General Whitehead looked at the others. The office of the Chief of Staff to the Secretary of State smelled of coffee and cinnamon buns. Betsy Jameson and Pete Hamilton stood on the other side of the desk, while Captain Phelan had taken up a strategic position by the door.

The blinds had been lowered, the curtains drawn. It was the first thing the General had done when he arrived. Not to block out the sun, but to block the view of any long-range scope.

They were deep into the hidden files on Timothy Trouble Beecham. But that meant they were also in increasing danger.

"There's a reason someone went through this much trouble with Beecham's documents," said Whitehead, ceding the seat to Hamilton, who went back to work. "Hiding all this must've taken weeks." He nodded in thought. "Yes, there's something in there."

"I'll find it," said Hamilton, scrolling and scanning.

"Is his middle name really Trouble?" asked Whitehead.

"Apparently," said Betsy. "I can see why he never uses it. I thought maybe the *T* stood for Traitor."

Bert Whitehead turned to look with disgust at the computer,

as though it were the quisling. Then he returned his gaze to Betsy. "Where's Secretary Adams now?"

Before Betsy could answer, Hamilton said, "OK, that's enough for now. My eyes are too bleary, I'm afraid of making a mistake. I need to rest."

He shut down the computer.

"I can take over," said Betsy.

"No, you need a rest too. You haven't slept all night. Besides, I know which documents I've been through. I have a system. You'll just screw it up. One hour, then I'll be fresher."

"He's right," said Whitehead, turning to Captain Phelan. "We know the importance of rest. Of being sharp, right, Captain?"

"Yes, sir."

General Whitehead picked his hat up off the desk, glancing at Hamilton as he did, his eyes sharp, assessing. Then he walked to the door.

"Are you sure you can trust him?" he whispered to Betsy. "He did work for Dunn."

"So did you."

"Ahhh, no. I worked for the American people. Still do. But him?" He used his hat to gesture toward Pete Hamilton, who'd folded his arms over the keyboard and laid his head down on them. "I'm not so sure." He turned back to Betsy and suddenly smiled. "Bow ties. You're quite something. When this is over, I hope you'll join my wife and me for dinner. Not at Off the Record."

Betsy smiled. "I'd love to."

When this is over, she thought, watching Captain Phelan accompany the General as he walked down Mahogany Row to the elevators. They talked in voices too low for her, or anyone else, to hear.

When this is over.

That was a nice thought.

"Close the door," said Pete Hamilton when she returned to

Boynton's office. He was wide awake and logging the code back into the computer. "Better still, lock it."

"Why?"

"Please."

She did, then joined him. His fingers were flying over the keys. It sounded like footsteps running, racing. In hot pursuit.

Then he stopped and stood up so that Betsy could take the seat and read what it was he'd found, and trapped, in the black rectangle of the computer screen.

"You got it?" she said, sitting down, though something in his expression, in his pallor, warned her. It wasn't what they'd expected. It was, she could tell, far, far worse.

She had to go over it twice, three times. Then she scrolled down. And back up. Before she trusted herself to look over at him.

"Is this why you turned off the computer?" she asked.

He nodded, staring at the memo on the screen.

It gave full support to the Pakistani plan to release Dr. Shah from house arrest.

Scrolling down, they looked in stunned silence at the second memo. It strongly advised withdrawing from the Iran nuclear pact.

A third went into detail as to why no plan for post-withdrawal Afghanistan was necessary or advisable.

The memos were each flagged high priority and classified top secret. And were signed by the Chairman of the Joint Chiefs of Staff. General Albert Whitehead.

"Oh dear."

"Madame Secretary," the head of her Diplomatic Security team bent down and whispered, "you have a call."

"Thank you," she whispered back. "But I can't take it now."

"It's from your counselor, Mrs. Jameson."

Ellen hesitated. Her eyes never leaving President Nasseri. "Please tell her I'll get back to her as soon as possible."

The Iranian President had met Secretary Adams and her small entourage at the entrance to the main government building, where he had his offices. Ellen had asked his permission to remove the burqas before their meeting began, the better to see him, and the better for him to see her.

"But before I do, Mr. President, I'd like to introduce you to my companions. My Chief of Staff, Charles Boynton."

"Mr. Boynton."

"Mr. President."

"My daughter, Katherine."

"Ahhh, the media titan. You've taken over from your mother." He smiled charmingly. "I have a daughter. I hope one day she'll succeed me, if the people will it."

If the Supreme Leader wills it, you mean, thought Ellen, but did not say.

"I hope so too," said Katherine. "It would be wonderful to see a woman as President of Iran."

"As it will be to see a woman as President of the United States. We shall see who achieves it first. Perhaps you will both serve. Or maybe your mother . . . ?"

He turned back to Ellen and gave a small bow.

"Oh, now, President Nasseri," said Ellen. "What have I donc to offend you?"

He laughed. It was exactly the right response. Acknowledging his comment, while being appropriately self-deprecating.

Now she could leave that charade, and the burqa, behind. But there was one more introduction. Ellen turned to the woman standing to her left.

"And this is Anahita Dahir, a foreign service officer in the State Department."

Anahita stepped forward, very slightly. Her burqa hid her face, but there was no hiding the tension in her body. It emanated from her. Ellen, standing so close, could see the voluminous material trembling.

"Mr. President," she said in English, before switching to Farsi, "my family name was once Ahmadi."

She lifted her chin and stared at him, as he stared at her. One of his guards took a step forward but was waved away.

While Ellen could not understand the Farsi, she heard "Ahmadi" and knew that Anahita had done it.

Secretary Adams stepped closer to her FSO.

"I know who you are," President Nasseri said in English. "The daughter of Irfan Ahmadi. Your father betrayed Iran. He betrayed his sisters and brothers in the revolution. He betrayed his own sister and brother. And how has America treated him? My sources report that he and your mother are in prison. Arrested for the simple crime of being Iranian. They were not afraid of us. They were afraid"—he turned to Ellen—"of you."

This was falling apart much faster than Ellen could have predicted. South Korea was suddenly looking like a triumph.

She opened her mouth to speak, to deny it, but then she remembered the Azhi Dahaka. Who thrived on lies.

How easy it was, Ellen thought, to deny the truth for fear of feeding an even bigger lie. And she realized then how dangerous the Azhi Dahaka was. Not because it was some creature in pursuit of good people. There was no pursuit. It was already there. Inside them. Manufacturing, dictating lies.

It was the ultimate traitor.

"That is true," she said.

Her words temporarily stunned him into silence. He looked at her as though trying to figure out why the American Secretary of State would admit such a thing.

"And he had reason to be afraid," she continued. "Not because he was Iranian, but because he lied about it. Though that's not why we're here."

"Why are you here?"

"Perhaps you'll permit us to remove our burqas before we continue this conversation."

President Nasseri gave a curt nod toward the woman official who'd met the plane with the clothing. She took them into an adjoining office to change and refresh.

Ellen was relieved to be out of the burqa, which she found quite suffocating.

"Are you all right?" Katherine asked Anahita, who looked gray but composed.

"He knew a lot about us," said Anahita. "My father suspected there were spies, but I thought that was just paranoia."

She drifted toward the window that overlooked the old city.

Katherine took her hand. "It's OK."

"OK?" asked Anahita.

"To feel at home here. That is what you're feeling, isn't it? Despite the run-in with Nasseri."

Anahita smiled at Katherine and sighed. "Is it that obvious? How can I be happy and afraid at the same time? Part of me is afraid because I'm happy. Does that make sense? I've been frightened, even ashamed, of Iran all my life. But here I am speaking to the President, of all things. In Farsi. And"—she looked out the window—"I feel comfortable here. Like I belong." She turned back to Ellen. "It doesn't make sense."

"Not everything has to," said Ellen. "Some of the most important things in our lives defy reason."

"'And now here is my secret, a very simple secret,'" said Katherine, squeezing Anahita's hand. "'It is only with the heart that one can see rightly; what is essential is invisible to the eye.'" She smiled at her mother. "When I was a kid, Dad and Mom used to read me to sleep every night. My favorite was *The Little Prince*."

Ellen smiled. How simple those times had felt. With Quinn and Gil and baby Katherine. Like Anahita, Ellen Adams could never have predicted life would lead her here. To Iran. Into the heart of the enemy. Never mind as Secretary of State. How surprised her younger self would have been.

And while she had no proof, Secretary Adams now knew in her heart that Anahita Dahir was loyal to the United States. Ironically it was her saying she felt at home in Iran that finally convinced Ellen.

A spy, a traitor, would never admit that.

She doubted the American President and US Intelligence would accept her reasoning. But the Little Prince would.

Sadly, he did not hold their fates in his tiny hands.

Ellen caught their eyes and then glanced toward the female official standing by the door.

"I'm sorry," said Anahita, in a whisper. "I shouldn't have said what I did to President Nasseri. It just made him angry."

"No." Ellen's voice was also low. "If asked anything, you just keep telling the truth."

"If he knows about my father, he must know that Zahara is my cousin."

"Yes." Now was the moment Ellen had to decide just how dangerous a game she was willing to play. Her next words were spoken in a normal voice. For all to hear. "But he might not realize she sent the warning to you. They might only know that it came from the Ahmadi home and went to the State Department."

"What will they do to Zahara?" Anahita asked.

"They say they'll try her as a spy and traitor," said Ellen.

"And what do they do to spies and traitors?" asked Katherine.

"They're executed."

There was silence.

"And if they find out about Anahita?" Katherine glared at her mother. "What will they do to her?"

Ellen took a deep breath. "Let's just go on what we know, and not speculate."

Though in her gut she knew. And she wondered how big a blunder she'd made in bringing the FSO with them. And, by raising her voice beyond a whisper, how big a fiasco she'd just created.

And now Secretary Adams, in modest Western dress with a hijab over her hair and framing her face, sat across from President Nasseri in the featureless conference room, in a featureless building, designed and built, Ellen suspected, by the Soviets in the 1980s.

She was also going on the assumption the Russians had installed bugs and were listening to everything they said. As were Iranian Intelligence and their secret police. For all she knew, their own intelligence agents were listening in too. Including Timothy Trouble Beecham.

This meeting might have a larger audience than Big Brother.

"You asked why we're here. I'm assuming Minister Aziz"—she nodded toward the older man—"has told you. We know you're responsible for the bombs that blew up those three buses."

When President Nasseri began to speak, she held up her hand.

"Please, let me finish. That tells us a few things, including your desperation to stop those physicists. We also know that Bashir Shah hired them. Which means you got information about those physicists from someone close to him."

"There is also a great deal you don't know," said Nasseri.

"That's why I'm here, Mr. President. To listen and to learn."

Before he had a chance to say more, President Nasseri rose, almost leaping to his feet. As did Aziz. As did everyone else in the room, except the Americans.

Ellen turned to see an elderly man enter the room. He had a long, trimmed white beard and black flowing robes.

She also stood, turned, and found herself facing the Supreme Leader of the Islamic Republic of Iran, the Grand Ayatollah Khosravi.

"Dear God," whispered Anahita.

CHAPTER 26

Gil Bahar gripped the door handle and placed his other hand on the roof of the battered old taxi to steady himself as the car heaved along trails that could no longer really be called roads.

After more than an hour of that, Akbar pulled off.

"We walk the rest of the way. Can you make it?"

It was clear Gil was in pain.

"Let me rest, just a moment."

Akbar gave him a bottle of water and some bread, which Gil took gratefully. He looked at his stash of painkillers. Two left.

Then he looked at the rugged terrain ahead. He knew where they were heading, and that the steep slope and jagged rocks were the least of his worries.

He took a pill, then removed his slacks to change the now bloody dressing over his leg wound.

"Here," said Akbar. "Let me."

He took the roll of bandages from Gil's shaking hands and very carefully, exceptionally skillfully, cleaned the wound, putting antiseptic powder on it before winding the new bandage around the leg.

"Nasty."

"I'm the lucky one," said Gil, not able to hide his agony even if he wanted to. Besides, he and Akbar had been through too much to need to disguise pain, of any sort.

Within minutes, the medication had kicked in and Gil got to his feet. He was pale but had recovered his strength.

Looking ahead, he said to Akbar, "You can wait here if you like."

"No, I'll come. Otherwise, how will I know if he kills you?"

"And if he kills you too for bringing me?"

"Then it is the will of Allah."

"Alhamdulillah," said Gil. Thanks be to Allah.

The two men set off. Along the way up the rocky path, Akbar found a tree limb that could serve as a cane for Gil, who limped along behind, reciting Muslim prayers for strength. And courage.

"She's not answering," said Betsy, her voice low, almost a growl.

She'd asked Denise Phelan, the Ranger captain, to stand out in the hall. When she looked surprised, Betsy had explained that there was highly classified material they needed to go over, and no one else should be in the room.

Captain Phelan, understandably, looked at Pete Hamilton, the disgraced former mouthpiece for Eric Dunn.

"I've deputized him," said Betsy, meeting and holding the captain's eyes.

It was nonsense, of course. She might as well have said she'd given Hamilton a decoder ring or a utility belt. Or Thor's hammer.

She could see the Ranger hesitating. Perhaps even believing it. Who would say such a preposterous thing unless it was true?

Still, even with Phelan in the corridor, they kept their voices low on the assumption the room was bugged.

Denise Phelan was General Whitehead's aide-de-camp. Which meant she'd been sent there to watch, not watch over, them. They had to assume listening devices had been placed in the offices.

Betsy was still reeling from the revelation that it was Whitehead, not Beecham, who was the mole, the one working with Bashir Shah.

The Chair of the Joint Chiefs of Staff was siding with, and providing vital information to, terrorists.

The "why" of it was unfathomable, so she didn't try. That was for later. Right now she needed to warn Ellen.

Betsy couldn't get through by phone, so she shot off a text.

"I think there's a typo," Pete Hamilton whispered when he saw what she'd written.

A synonym strolls into a tavern.

"Where?"

"The whole thing. Didn't you mean to write, *Whitehead's the mole*? You seem to have misspelled it."

"It's our code for trouble," said Betsy, in hushed tones. She nodded toward the computer. "We need to find out what else is in those documents."

Hamilton sat at Boynton's desk and went back to work.

Ellen turned to the cleric. As he moved into the room, guards and officials bowed, touching their palms to their hearts.

"Madame Secretary."

"Your Eminence," said Ellen. She hesitated, fully aware that what President Williams had said was true. If a photograph should get out of her meeting with, never mind bowing to, the head of a terrorist state, there would be hell to pay.

Ellen Adams made to bow anyway. There were more important things than appearances. Like the thousands of lives that hung in the balance. Dependent on the outcome of this meeting.

She'd dropped her head barely an inch before Grand Ayatollah Khosravi reached out. Not touching her. Not even close. But the meaning of the gesture was obvious.

"No," he said, in the slightly reedy voice of a man in his eighties. "Not necessary."

Ellen stood up straight and met his gray eyes. There was curiosity there, and gravity. She wasn't fooled. Here was a man who had almost certainly approved of the murders, over the years, of countless people. And just hours ago, to kill three people, he'd ordered the slaughter of more than a hundred innocent men, women, and children.

But she met courtesy with courtesy.

"May Allah be with you," she said, and placed her hand over her heart.

"And with you." His eyes were steady, holding hers. Assessing her, even as she assessed him.

Ranged behind the cleric was a wall of younger men. In the brief time Secretary Adams had had to do research and talk with experts on modern Iran, she knew that these were the Ayatollah's sons, along with some advisors.

She also knew that the Grand Ayatollah Khosravi wasn't just the spiritual leader of Iran. Over the more than thirty years he'd been the Supreme Leader, he'd privately consolidated power while appearing to be, claiming to be, a humble cleric.

Ayatollah Khosravi oversaw what amounted to a shadow government, with his own people making the important decisions on Iran's future. If there was to be a change of direction, however slight, it would come from him. It was his hand on the tiller. Not Nasseri's.

The Grand Ayatollah wore the flowing black robes and mantle of his office, and an immense black turban that had its own code. The fact that it was black, not white, declared he was a direct descendent of the Prophet Mohammed. And the size of a turban denoted status.

The Grand Ayatollah's resembled the outer ring of Saturn.

He waved a veined hand, and they sat back down. Khosravi taking a seat beside President Nasseri and across from Ellen.

"You are here, Madame Secretary, for information you believe we can give you," he said. "And you think there's a reason we might."

"I think, in this instance, our needs align."

"And those needs are?"

"To stop Bashir Shah."

"But we have stopped him," said the Grand Ayatollah. "His physicists can no longer carry out their mission."

"What is that mission?"

"To build nuclear bombs. I'd have thought that was obvious."

"For whom?"

"It doesn't matter. Giving any other power in this region a nuclear bomb, or nuclear capability, would be against our interests."

"But there are others who can take their place. You can't murder every physicist in the world."

Khosravi raised his brows and smiled very slightly. As though saying that he could and, if need be, he would kill every nuclear physicist in the world. Except their own.

But Secretary Adams also knew that he'd come to this meeting for a reason. There was no way the Supreme Leader of the Islamic Republic of Iran would be there unless he wanted something too. Needed something.

And she suspected she knew what it was. Despite the fact that he looked robust, there were rumors from US Intelligence that his health was declining. Khosravi wanted his son Ardashir to succeed him. But the Russians wanted their own person to ascend. Someone they could control.

Which would mean Iran would be independent in name only. It would, in reality, become a satellite of Russia.

It was a covert power struggle. One this wily survivor of the byzantine and often brutal politics of the Middle East was determined to win. But his presence there told her he was no longer sure he could.

And so he'd decided to play each side against the middle. It was a dangerous game, and the fact that he was willing to play it spoke of desperation and a vulnerability he would never acknowledge.

But he didn't have to. She had done it for him by saying that their needs aligned. She could see that he understood. Neither wanted Russia to win this struggle. And both were more desperate and vulnerable than they cared to admit.

It was better, and worse, than Ellen had thought. Better because there was a chance of success; worse because desperate and vulnerable people, and states, could do unexpected and even catastrophic things.

Like blow up buses filled with civilians to kill one person.

"How did you know about Shah's physicists, Your Eminence?" she asked.

"Iran has friends all over the world."

"A state with so many friends surely doesn't need to commit mass murder. Not only did you kill all those people on the buses, but you then tracked down and murdered the one bomber who escaped. As well as his family, and two senior American officers."

"You mean the head of your Intelligence in Germany and his number two?" the Grand Ayatollah asked.

The fact that he was not pleading ignorance told Ellen he wanted her to know this was important enough for him to personally follow, if not direct.

"And what would you expect us to do," he asked, "when all our warnings went unheeded? Believe me, we did not want to harm all those people. And we would not have, had you answered our pleas. You are as responsible for what happened as we are. More so."

"I beg your pardon?"

"Come now, Madame Secretary. I know there was a change of regime—"

"Administration."

"—in your country, but surely there is some continuity in information. You can't tell me that I, a simple cleric, know more than the Secretary of State for such a great nation?"

"As you know, I'm new to the post of Secretary of State. Perhaps you can enlighten me."

The Ayatollah turned to the younger man sitting on his right. His son and apparent successor, Ardashir.

"We warned your State Department about the physicists months ago," Ardashir said. His voice was soft, almost matter-of-fact, as he delivered this bombshell.

"I see," said Ellen, apparently absorbing the information in her stride. "And?"

He lifted his hands. "And nothing. We tried several times, thinking that perhaps the messages were not getting through. As you can imagine, we could not use official channels. We can show you what was sent."

"That would be helpful." Not that she needed to confirm their existence or the actual wording. What she wanted were the names of the people the warnings were sent to. She suspected Tim Beecham was one.

She was desperately trying to regain her balance, though the advantage had been lost.

"When it became clear to us that the West did not care," Ardashir continued, "we took matters into our own hands, with regret."

"You didn't have to blow up innocent people."

"Except that we did, Madame Secretary. The only information our source could get was that these physicists had been hired to build nuclear weapons for Dr. Shah. But we did not know their names. All we had were their travel arrangements."

"The buses," said Nasseri. "We asked if your network had more information. We begged you. And in the end we had no choice."

"We needed Dr. Shah and the West to know this sort of threat to the Islamic Republic of Iran would not be countenanced," said Ardashir. "We will not allow another country in this region to acquire a nuclear weapon, especially after my father issued a fatwa against all weapons of mass destruction."

"Yes," said Ellen. "And yet you have your own nuclear physicists. I believe you've just arrested the head of your nuclear weapons program, Dr. Behnam Ahmadi."

"No."

"No? No what?"

"No, the program Dr. Ahmadi runs is for nuclear power, not weapons," said Ardashir. "And no, we did not arrest him. We asked him to come in to answer some questions. But the young woman, his daughter? Yes. She's under arrest. She'll be tried, and if found guilty, she will be executed." He turned to Anahita. "You are the person she contacted, her cousin. Is that not so?"

Anahita made to speak, but Ellen grabbed her hand. While she'd advised the FSO not to lie, there was no need to give up more information than necessary.

The revelation that Iran had actually tried to warn the United States about Shah's plans and those warnings were ignored was a political, diplomatic, and moral catastrophe. It did not excuse or create a moral equivalency with what Iran had done, but it threw a giant wrench into the calculus.

Ellen searched for something to say. "The United States is now prepared to act—"

That was met with amusement by the ranks of officials, though it was silenced by an almost invisible movement by the Supreme Leader, who gave her his full attention.

"—albeit late." Ellen turned to Khosravi.

She could see that the Iranians had been prepared for her to attack. To bring up the tragically long list of their own transgressions.

And she was tempted. But she also knew to give in to that desire, however legitimate, would be to once again descend into the same old polemic. Where nothing was resolved, and all came away covered in mud and bile.

"I am very sorry, Your Eminence, that your messages fell on deaf ears. On behalf of the United States government, I apologize and express our deep regret at ignoring your warning."

She heard a gasp. Not from the Iranians, though their surprise was clear.

It had come from Charles Boynton, her Chief of Staff, who whispered, hissed, "Madame Secretary!"

Ellen imagined all those people listening, from the Russians to American Intelligence, also gasping, at the fact that the American Secretary of State had just apologized to the Grand Ayatollah of Iran.

But this was calculated. She knew exactly what she was doing. She was steadying herself on the knife blade. Finding that balance between truth and discretion while sending a subtle message to the Grand Ayatollah.

He was experienced enough to know that the weak blustered, denied, lied, and struck out wildly.

The powerful admitted a mistake, thereby robbing it of its hold on them.

Only the truly formidable could afford to show contrition. Far from displaying weakness, the American Secretary of State had demonstrated immense strength and resolve.

The Grand Ayatollah understood what Ellen Adams had just done.

He tilted his head in acknowledgment, partly of the apology but mostly of the move that had robbed them of the high ground.

"You want information on Dr. Shah," said Khosravi. "And we want him stopped. I think, as you said, Madame Secretary, our needs align. But unfortunately, we cannot give you very much information. We don't know where Shah is. All we know is that he is selling nuclear secrets, along with the scientists and material." He paused to wipe his nose with a silk kerchief. "We also believe that though we stopped it this time, he will continue unless he himself is caught. You let the monster out. He is your responsibility."

"To return him to house arrest?"

"I would not advocate that, Madame Secretary."

Ellen knew perfectly well what he was saying. What he, the Iranian State, wanted the United States to do.

"How did you get your information about Shah and the physicists?" she asked.

"An anonymous source," said the Ayatollah's son.

"I see. Would that be the same source who told you about Zahara Ahmadi?" Ellen asked.

The Grand Ayatollah nodded toward a Revolutionary Guard at the door, who opened it. A young woman, in a brilliant pink robe and hijab, walked in.

Anahita made to get up, but Ellen placed a hand on her leg to stop her.

This did not go unnoticed.

Behind Zahara came an older man. Her father, the nuclear physicist, Behnam Ahmadi.

When both saw the Grand Ayatollah, they stopped. Shocked. It was doubtful either had ever actually seen him in the flesh except, perhaps, at a great distance.

Dr. Ahmadi immediately dropped into a deep bow, his hand over his heart. "Your Eminence."

Zahara followed, but not before staring at Ellen, clearly recognizing the Secretary of State, then at Anahita.

The cousins looked so much alike that it was impossible for Zahara not to know who she was. But she managed to say nothing, instead bowing to the Supreme Leader, her eyes down in modesty and humility.

"We were just discussing you," said President Nasseri. Khosravi had given him a sign to take over. "Perhaps, Miss Ahmadi, you'd like to tell us how you came to know about the bombs on the buses."

"You told me."

Every brow in the room went up, but none higher than Nasseri's. "I did not."

"Not directly, but you sent your scientific advisor to my father, and he told him about the physicists, and that all you knew was that they'd be on those exact buses, at that time. I overheard. My bedroom is over my father's study."

She didn't look at her father as she spoke. It was clear, by her almost robotic tone, that she'd anticipated the question and had prepared, and rehearsed, her answer.

It was also clear that she was trying to protect her father.

"And why did you decide to tell the Americans?" asked Nasseri.

The room became electric. Her answer would decide her future. If she admitted it, she had no future.

"Because, Your Eminence," Zahara stared at the Grand Ayatollah, "I don't believe that Allah, the merciful, the compassionate, would approve of the murders of innocents."

And there it was. A faith declared. A fate sealed.

"You would lecture us, you would lecture the Grand Ayatollah, about Allah?" demanded Nasseri. "You know the will of Allah?"

"No. What I do know is that Allah would not want innocent men, women, and children murdered. Had I overheard that you planned to kill just the physicists in order to protect Iran, I wouldn't have tried to stop it."

She turned to look at her father, whose eyes were still cast down.

"My father knew nothing about this."

"Well," said the Grand Ayatollah, "I would not say that, my child. How do you think we found out what you'd done?"

The room grew very, very still. They'd turned into a tableau. All staring at father and daughter.

"Baba?"

Silence.

"Daddy? You told them?"

He lifted his eyes and mumbled something.

"Louder," demanded President Nasseri.

"I had no choice. My computer is monitored. Every search I do, every message sent is seen. They'd have found out eventually. I had to do it, to protect your brother and sister. To protect your mother."

"He proved his loyalty," said Nasseri.

Though Ellen noted the look of disgust on the face of both the Grand Ayatollah and Minister Aziz. Loyalty to the state might come first, but to betray your family spoke volumes about the character of the person. And none of it good.

Dr. Behnam Ahmadi might survive his daughter, but his character would not.

Zahara turned away from him.

Secretary Adams turned away from him.

The Grand Ayatollah and everyone else in the room turned away from Behnam Ahmadi.

Events were moving quickly now, falling into place even as they fell apart.

Ellen had to think quickly. Had to act quickly if anything was to be salvaged.

"We need to look ahead, not back," said Ellen, dragging their attention away from the young woman. She would figure that out later. "The United States is prepared to act, but to do that I need information on Shah. His location. His plans. How far along he is. I need to know your source."

Ellen held the Ayatollah's gaze, trying to send a message. Trying to tell him she was aware that the Russians were almost certainly listening in. That so much of what was being said in that room was for their benefit. She knew he could not possibly tell her, even if he had the information. But perhaps he could send her some sign.

Something. Anything.

He must know where the information about Shah came from. It

had to be someone close enough to Shah to get it right. But not so close that he had all the information.

The Grand Ayatollah's unwillingness to tell her almost certainly meant the source was Russian. But not the state. If it was, Khosravi would have no trouble telling her. After all, he wouldn't be revealing anything Russian Intelligence didn't already know.

So, thought Ellen. The source was Russian. But not Russia. That left just one other possibility.

The Grand Ayatollah held her gaze. "You read your children *The Little Prince*. I also read to my children."

Ellen was completely, utterly focused. Her nerves tingling. He'd just quietly confirmed that they had indeed overheard everything she, Katherine, and Anahita had said while changing out of the burqas.

Including Secretary Adams's deliberate admission, suspecting they'd be monitored, that Anahita had been the recipient of her cousin's message.

It was a calculated risk, and Ellen was about to find out if her calculations were correct.

Nothing the Supreme Leader said now was without layers of meaning.

The elderly cleric turned to his sons. "Your favorites were always the Persian *Fables of Bidpai*." He lifted his limp right arm with his left, and Ellen remembered that he'd been badly injured in a bomb attack years ago, and had lost the use of that arm. Now he cradled it, as though it were a child, and turned back to her. "Do you know the fable about the cat and the rat?"

"I'm sorry," she said. "I do not." It had not escaped her notice that he'd used the old word for their country, "Persia."

"A large cat, let's say a lion, was caught in a hunter's net." His voice was low, soothing. His eyes sharp. "A rat was just coming out of its hole and saw this. The lion begged the rat to nibble through the ropes and free him, but the rat refused." The cleric smiled. "He was a wise old thing and feared that, once freed, the lion would eat him because that's what lions did. But the cat pleaded, and do you know what the rat did?"

"He—" Nasseri began, but was stopped by Aziz.

"I believe, Mr. President, that was directed at the American Secretary of State."

Ellen thought. She suspected this was the message, the code. But she couldn't work it out.

"I do not, Your Eminence"—and saw, to her surprise, a look of approval.

"The wily rat nibbled through the rope, but not all the way. He left a strand, one bite thick, so that the cat was still trapped. They could hear the hunter approaching. He was getting closer and closer."

The others in the room disappeared, and all that remained were the Supreme Leader of the Islamic Republic of Iran and the American Secretary of State.

Grand Ayatollah Khosravi lowered his voice and seemed to speak directly into Ellen's ear.

"The rat waited until the lion was distracted by the approach of the hunter and then, at the last minute, he bit the final strand, freeing the cat. In the instant before the cat realized he was free, the rat escaped down his hole. Then the lion, freed, escaped up the tree."

"And the hunter?" asked Ellen.

"Was left empty-handed." The Ayatollah shrugged, though his dark eyes never left hers.

"Or maybe," said Ellen, "he was eaten by the lion. Because that's what lions do."

"Maybe." The Grand Ayatollah turned to the Revolutionary Guard. "Arrest her."

Ellen froze. The guard took a step toward Zahara.

"Not her," said Khosravi. "Her. The traitor's daughter. The one who received the message."

Anahita stumbled to her feet. Ellen leapt up and stepped in front of her. "No!"

"You didn't really think, Mrs. Adams," said Aziz as the Revolutionary Guard pushed her aside and ripped Anahita from Ellen's grip, "that we would allow a spy, a traitor, to stroll into Iran, into a meeting with the highest levels of government, without consequence. We know who the rats are."

"I'm sorry," said the Grand Ayatollah, getting to his feet and leaving the room.

CHAPTER 27

AK-47s were pointed at them from the mountain lookouts as Gil and Akbar slowly approached the Pathan encampment. They couldn't see the fighters, but they knew they were there.

Now in regional Pashtun dress, both men held their arms out, and Gil dropped the branch he'd been using as a cane, in case it was mistaken for a rifle.

Beside him, Akbar was breathing heavily from both the climb along the rugged footpaths and fear. Gil's limp was more pronounced, and he winced with every step.

But still, they moved forward.

An armed guard approached, and behind him came a familiar figure. The machine gun was leveled at the two newcomers. Gil and Akbar stopped.

"As-Salam Alaikum," said Gil Bahar. "Peace be upon you."

"Wa-Alaikum-as-Salam," said the man who was clearly in charge, the commander of the Pathan camp. And upon you Peace.

There was a moment's tension. The younger man, holding the rifle, gripped it tighter, awaiting instructions. With his back to the commander, he could not see the slight smile that had appeared on his bearded face.

"You are not looking at all well, my friend," the commander said. "But better, I hope, than when I last saw you."

"Well, you still have your head."

"Thanks to you."

The guard lowered his weapon as the guerrilla commander moved past him and embraced Gil, kissing him three times.

Gil stepped back and held the man at arm's length, studying him.

He'd filled out, grown muscular. In his early thirties, he was no longer the fresh-faced kid Gil had first met. But then, neither was Gil.

The man's face was weathered and careworn, bearded, his hair long and held back from his face. He wore the uniform of the Afghan fighter. A hybrid of Islamic dress and Western military clothing.

"How are you, Hamza?"

"Alive." The commander looked around; then, putting his large hand on Gil's shoulder, he said, "Come. It's getting late, and who knows what appears out of the darkness."

"I thought you owned the night," said Gil as he followed.

"I own nothing." Hamza held back the flap of the tent for Gil to enter while Akbar remained outside.

"Yes, I see you are the same simple man I left behind," said Gil, surveying the boxes of explosives and grenades and long wooden crates with *Avtomat Kalashnikova* stamped on them.

AK-47s. All the boxes had Russian writing.

Hamza ordered the men in the tent to leave, then poured them both tea from a samovar.

"Thankfully, not everything from the Russians is meant to kill," he said, lifting his glass of sweet tea in a toast. Then he grew grave. "You should not have come."

"I know. I'm sorry. I wouldn't have if there was any other way."

Hamza nodded toward Gil's leg, which was weeping blood again. "What happened? Did you try to stop her?"

"The nuclear physicist? No. I followed Dr. Bukhari from the flight out of Pakistan, where you said she'd be, to Frankfurt. I was just hoping to follow her to Shah and find out what he's up to. But the bus she was on was bombed."

Hamza nodded. "I heard about the explosions. They haven't said why it happened, or who did it, but I wondered." He stared at Gil. "Why are you here?"

"I'm sorry, Hamza. I need more information."

"I can't give you more. I've already said far too much. If anyone finds out . . ."

Gil leaned forward on the large pillow on the ground where he was sitting, wincing slightly as he did. "You and I both know that the only way you'll be safe is if Shah is taken out. He must know by now that someone betrayed him. It won't be long before he puts it all together and comes after you."

"A middle-age Pakistani scientist climbing that mountain, past my guards? I think I'm safe."

"You know what I'm saying. And you know who he'll send." Gil looked behind him, at the crates. "I'm sorry."

"I have nothing to do with Shah. I only passed along a rumor about those physicists."

"True, but someone told you about them." When Hamza shook his head, Gil looked around. "I need more."

"You need to leave. It's too late now, but first thing in the morning." Hamza got up. "I have nothing more to say. I helped you escape years ago. Don't make me regret it. Maybe Allah meant for you to be beheaded. I don't want to have to follow through on His wishes."

"You don't believe that," said Gil, remaining where he was. "You let me go because we spent months together studying the Qur'an. You taught me the word of the Prophet Mohammed. That true Islam is about peaceful coexistence. That's why you wanted to stop Shah. And still do."

In his captivity Gil had begun to listen to the guards, began to pick out words, phrases. Began to talk to the guards in their own

Pashto language. Until one night the youngest, the one who brought him his meals, answered.

After a few months the young man sat and, at Gil's request, taught him Arabic phrases, the language of the Qur'an. They talked about Islam. They read the Qur'an together, and Gil learned about the teachings of the Prophet. And over time, he fell in love with what the Prophet, what Islam, had to say as a way of life.

And over time, as they discussed it, Hamza's views softened, and he saw how the radical clerics had twisted the words, the meanings, to their own ends.

In the cover of night, after the French journalist had been beheaded, Hamza had slipped Gil's bonds from his wrists and ankles, and released him. They'd stayed in touch, covertly. Their own bonds strong.

"I know you will not kill innocent men, women, and children," said Gil. "Other combatants, yes, but Allah would not want innocents killed. That's why you told me about Shah and the physicists. A rifle is one thing"—he turned to the crates filled with AK-47s behind them—"but weapons of mass destruction that kill indiscriminately are something else. I need more information. To stop it." Gil leaned forward on the large pillow on the floor of the tent, gritting his teeth against the pain in his leg. "If Shah's clients build a nuclear bomb and it goes off, it will kill thousands. And what will Allah say then?"

"Are you mocking my beliefs?"

Gil looked struck. "No, not at all. They're my beliefs too. That's why I came all this way, up that damned mountain. To see you. To try to stop it. Please. I'm begging you, Hamza. Help me."

They stared at each other. Much the same age, they'd grown up a world apart, but fate had brought them together, like brothers. Like kindred spirits. Perhaps for this very reason, for this very moment.

Hamza was not his real name. He'd adopted it when he'd joined the fighters. It meant "Lion."

And while Gil was his real name, it was not his full name. Most assumed it was Gilbert. But in the dead of night, as the prisoner and his keeper discussed the Qur'an, Gil had told him his secret.

His full name was Gilgamesh.

"Oh my God." Hamza's laugh had bordered on the hysterical. "Gilgamesh? How did that happen?"

"My father studied ancient Mesopotamia at university and would read my mother poetry. Her favorite was the epic *Gilgamesh*."

Gil did not tell Hamza that on his wall growing up was a poster from the Louvre. It was of a statue looted centuries earlier from a site in the ancient Mesopotamian city of Dur-Sharrukin. It was a carving of Gilgamesh, the hero of the epic. He was holding a lion to his chest. Their spirits, their fates intertwined.

That site had been destroyed by ISIS in the recent wars. So what had looked like looting had actually saved many artifacts.

Saviors, Gilgamesh had come to appreciate, came in unexpected forms. And often did not initially appear to be saviors. Just the opposite. Saviors could be quite unsavory, and monsters could be compelling, making the worst seem the best. Like those radical clerics. Like unscrupulous political leaders.

Now the two men, Gilgamesh and the Lion, sat in the tent in the twilight, facing each other. Facing a decision.

CHAPTER 28

Mom, what're we going to do? We can't leave Ana behind."

Katherine was following her mother as Ellen paced the office where they'd been placed and told to change back into burqas. And prepare to leave.

It was the same room they'd used to change out of their burqas a thousand years ago.

"I don't know," said Ellen. That much was true, and probably not a surprise to the Iranians and Russians who were almost certainly listening in.

Secretary Adams stopped her pacing to stare at Anahita's burqa. It was lying on the couch, the flattened form of a human. As though the woman had disappeared so suddenly she'd left her shadow behind.

It reminded Ellen of those terrible images of Hiroshima and Nagasaki after the atom bombs had dropped and the people vaporized, leaving just a dark outline behind.

Dear Lord, Ellen prayed. *Dear God, help me.*

Secretary Adams stared at the black outline of Anahita's burqa and felt herself clutching thin air. Frantic to halt her fall.

She was desperate now. How to stop Shah, and also get her FSO and Zahara Ahmadi released and out of Iran?

Things had not improved with her visit. In fact, they'd gotten considerably worse.

At least on the surface.

Ellen resumed her pacing, around and around the walls of the room, like a great cat trapped. She had the feeling she already had what she needed. That the Grand Ayatollah had given her the information, the tools, to do what needed to be done. Even as he'd arrested her FSO, effectively taking Anahita hostage and tying the Secretary of State's hands.

What was he up to?

Arresting the American FSO had been a surprise. A shock. It was an aggression, a provocation. It made no sense, on the surface.

So why had the Grand Ayatollah Khosravi done it? And what did he want her to do now? She did not have many options. What she couldn't do was leave without Anahita Dahir, and without information on Bashir Shah. He must know that.

And yet he was throwing her out of Iran. Empty-handed.

She stopped her pacing in front of the window and looked out at the Iranian capital.

The cat-and-rat story clearly meant something. It was more than an allegory. But who was the cat in the story, and who the rat?

And why would the one help the other? Because they had a temporary common purpose. To defeat the hunter. To defeat Dr. Bashir Shah.

So why arrest Anahita Dahir?

Why?

Nothing that shrewd man said or did was without layers of meaning and purpose.

"Mom," said Katherine, her voice betraying her growing anxiety, "you have to do something."

"I am doing something. I'm thinking."

There was a tap at the door.

"Madame Secretary," said Steve Kowalski, her Diplomatic Security officer. "You have a text message from your counselor."

Ellen was about to ask him to please leave them alone so she could think. But then she remembered Betsy's call. And now a text. This must be urgent.

Ellen asked for her phone.

"What is it?" Katherine asked.

Ellen, already pale from the stresses of an interminable day, lost what little color she had left as she read Betsy's message.

A synonym strolls into a tavern.

Trouble. Big trouble.

A dyslexic walks into a bra, Ellen typed. The prearranged response to say it was indeed her, and she understood that something terrible had happened.

The reply came within moments. Betsy had obviously been staring at her secure phone, waiting for Ellen.

The traitor isn't Beecham. It's Whitehead.

Ellen sank into a chair. Her free fall had ended. She'd hit rock bottom.

She was tempted to write, *Are you sure?* But knew Betsy would be absolutely certain before sending that.

Instead she wrote: *Are you all right?*

Yes. But Whitehead's Ranger is outside the door.

Ellen felt her heart contract. She'd asked Betsy to contact the officer. And now . . .

Proof?

Memos. Whitehead approved the release of Shah. Approved and supported it.

Ellen exhaled. He'd lied.

She remembered Whitehead's small glance when Tim Beecham had left the Oval Office to make a call. It had helped confirm to Ellen that the Chair of the Joint Chiefs did not trust the Director of National Intelligence.

Now she saw it, and a hundred other little things, for what they were. Not just subtle, but sly. He was quietly undermining, assassinating, Tim Beecham. The death by a thousand artful glances.

What does he know? Ellen wrote.

Everything I know.

Which was pretty much everything. Except what had happened in Iran. And he might know that. He might be listening.

Ellen realized that Whitehead, with his security clearance, must've been involved in hiding all of Beecham's files, knowing how damning that would appear, while at the same time removing anything incriminating about his own role. This plan hadn't just been thrown together. It must have been months, maybe years, in the making. All through the Dunn administration, when there was internal chaos and almost no oversight.

But General Whitehead had missed one reference to himself. An especially damning one. That struck her as odd. So much effort, but they missed that mushroom cloud of a message?

But that thought was overwhelmed and overtaken by the other.

Bert Whitehead? A traitor? In league with Bashir Shah? Giving information to terrorists? Why would the Chair of the Joint Chiefs of Staff do that?

He'd betrayed his country. He'd been a party to mass murder. He'd lied at every turn.

General Albert Whitehead, the Chair of the Joint Chiefs, was the Azhi Dahaka.

Fred MacMurray was the devil.

General Whitehead knew if Shah was successful, thousands, perhaps hundreds of thousands, would be turned into shadows.

Her phone vibrated with another message. This one from Gil.

Have to go, she wrote Betsy. *Be careful.*

She looked closer and saw that the message from her son had come in from a source she didn't recognize, but the subject line read, *From Gil.* Instead of his usual curt text, Gil had written his mother an email.

No, Ellen realized as she opened it. He'd written to the US Secretary of State.

She read it through, and when she finished, the phone slipped through her fingers to drop in her lap.

Gil was in Afghanistan, close to the Pakistan border. In Pathan-controlled territory. Where he'd been held before. Dear Lord.

He had the information they needed.

The three Pakistani nuclear physicists assassinated in the bus bombs were decoys. Diversions. Undistinguished scientists hired by Bashir Shah with the sole purpose of being slaughtered. To make the West believe the danger had passed. Or that, at the very least, they had time.

When, in fact, time had run out.

Gil's source had told him that the real nuclear physicists had been recruited several years earlier. Top-flight scientists, apparently on sabbatical but in reality hired out to Shah, who'd rented them to a third party, almost certainly Al-Qaeda. To set up a nuclear weapons program inside Afghanistan.

Ellen stood up so abruptly the chair fell over. She thought, quickly. Then wrote, *Call me.*

Gil had borrowed the phone from someone he clearly trusted. An Akbar someone. It would not be tapped. And her phone was secure. Still, the room was almost certainly bugged. She had to be careful what she said.

They'd have two, maybe three minutes before the call was intercepted.

"Time two minutes," she whispered to Katherine, who saw the urgency and for once didn't ask questions.

Ellen picked up the call before the first ring was complete. "Tell me where."

"Shah's physicists? I don't know exactly. Someplace along the Pakistan-Afghan border. Wouldn't be a cave or a camp. Would have to be some abandoned factory."

It was a long border, a lot of territory, but Gil could not be more specific.

"Size?" She was trying to keep her voice low, and her statements vague.

"Don't know. Anything from dirty bombs in a knapsack to something bigger. Could take out a few blocks or a whole city."

Katherine held up a finger. One minute gone. One minute left.

"Plural?"

"Yes."

"Where?"

There was what felt like an interminable pause before he answered, "US."

"Where?"

"Cities. I don't know which. More are being made. I think the Russian mafia's supplying the materials to Shah."

That made sense, thought Ellen, her mind racing. Making connections. Not the Russian government. Not officially. But the Russian President and his oligarchs had ties to the mob, and they had personally shared in the billions made from selling everything from weapons to human beings.

The Russian mafia was completely without ideology, without scruples. Without brakes. What they did have were arms, contacts, money. They would sell anyone anything. From plutonium to anthrax. From child sex slaves to organs.

They'd get into bed with the devil, then make him breakfast, if necessary.

Shah had to use a third party to tip off the Iranians about the physicists. Who better than an informant working for both the Russian mafia and Iranian Intelligence?

The Russian mafia was the link, connecting Iran and Shah. The wraith that moved between the two.

"Mom—" said Gil.

"Yes?"

"The chatter is that they're already there. In the cities. The bombs. That's why Shah had the physicists killed in Europe, to shift focus away from the US. To make us think the next attack, the big one, would also be in Europe."

Katherine was circling her finger. It was time.

But there was one more question.

"When?"

"Soon. That's all I know."

Ellen hung up and muttered, "Fuck."

A text came in for Betsy.

She was bleary with the need for sleep and had told Pete Hamilton to break for a few hours' rest. He was curled on the couch in Charles Boynton's office, dead to the world, while Betsy lay on Ellen's couch and stared at the ceiling.

Her body was drained but her mind continued to whirl. Bert Whitehead. The mole. The Chairman of the Joint Chiefs of Staff, a four-star General, a veteran of the bloody Afghan and Iraq wars, a traitor.

And then came the text.

Can't sleep. Any more info on Beecham? I need to tell the President.

For a moment Betsy thought it was from Ellen in Tehran, but quickly realized it was from Whitehead.

Nothing, she wrote, her fingers shaking from exhaustion and rage. *Taking a break to sleep. Suggest you do the same.*

And then, before she could lay her head down again, another message arrived, this time from Ellen. She'd forwarded a message from Gil.

Betsy read it, then muttered, "Darn."

Bashir Shah's plane landed in the dead of night, and he was driven to his home in Islamabad, the little-used back way in, through the garden.

He'd left the US just a day ahead of when he'd planned to. When he had to.

Just over a day ahead of when the world changed forever.

"Is Ellen Adams still in Tehran?" he demanded of his lieutenant.

"As far as we know."

"That's not good enough. I need certainty, and I need to know who she's met with and what she's been told."

Fifteen minutes later, as Shah prepared for bed, his lieutenant came with the information.

"She met with President Nasseri."

"And?" Shah could see there was more, but the man was afraid to tell him.

"And the Grand Ayatollah."

"Khosravi?" Shah glared, and his lieutenant nodded, his eyes wide.

"She was told nothing."

"Nothing?"

"No. And one of her group, the FSO, has been arrested as a spy."

Shah sat down on the side of his bed, trying to see it. This didn't make sense.

"The Grand Ayatollah told her some story about a cat and a rat. It's a fable. Something he read his kids."

"I'm not interested in that. I need to know everything she does."

What, thought Shah as he brushed his teeth, was Khosravi up to? What was Ellen Adams up to?

I should have killed her when I had the chance.

Fortunately her son will soon be dead, and she'll know it was his doing and her fault.

He spat into the sink, then went to his laptop and found the old Persian fable of the cat and rat. It was about unlikely alliances, he saw. That much was obvious. But it was also about the hunt. And misdirection.

Bashir Shah slowly lowered the lid of the computer. He was, he knew, much too experienced a hunter to be tricked. He would get both the cat and the rat.

"We need to leave," said Akbar. "We should do it now."

"Are you kidding?" said Gil. "It's dark. The mountains are crawling with mujahedin. If Hamza's fighters don't kill us by mistake, they will. Look, I want to get out too, but it'll have to wait until first light." Gil took a closer look at his companion. There was no mistaking the fact that Akbar was antsy, nervous. "Why are you so anxious to leave?"

Akbar looked behind him. They were in their own tent. Hamza had arranged for food and drink, and now Gil was settling in for sleep, his whole body aching.

"I just have a bad feeling about this," said Akbar.

He wrapped the woolen blanket around himself and leaned against the tent pole and, for the hundredth time, felt for the long knife hidden in the folds of his clothing.

CHAPTER 29

Madame Secretary," said Charles Boynton. Her Chief of Staff had knocked, then entered. "The Sultan of Oman's jet is ready. The Iranians are insisting you leave."

His lanky form stood by the door, uncertain.

Both the Secretary of State and her daughter were standing by the window, looking as though they'd had the fright of their lives.

"What is it?" he asked, taking another step inside the room and closing the door.

Ellen had forwarded Gil's message, adding some of the details he'd told her on the phone, to both Katherine and Betsy. She'd considered sending it to President Williams and Tim Beecham, but hesitated.

General Whitehead could not be working alone. He had to have collaborators in the highest echelons of the White House, perhaps even the cabinet. If she sent it, and it was intercepted, they'd know that the plot had been discovered. And rather than risk being caught, they might set off the bombs prematurely.

No. Ellen knew she had to tell President Williams privately. In person.

But her work in Iran wasn't done. They had to get more information. Someone was supplying Shah with nuclear materials, probably, as Gil said, the Russian mafia.

And someone had told the Iranians about the physicists.

Again, probably an Iranian informant working with the mafia. They'd deliberately leaked the information so that Nasseri and the Ayatollah would do exactly what Shah wanted. They'd murder his physicists.

That person might know about Shah's larger plans. Maybe even his whereabouts. And that informant was probably still in Iran. If they could just find him, or her.

"What is it?" Boynton repeated. "Madame Secretary?"

"Mom?" said Katherine.

Ellen brought her hand up to her mouth and tilted her head back, staring at the ceiling. Trying, trying to see it.

If she'd figured this all out, so had the Grand Ayatollah. He needed her help to stop Shah. And she needed his help to stop the terrorist attacks.

Did Khosravi know who the informant was? If so, he couldn't possibly tell her. Not outright. Their every word, every action, was being monitored.

So he had to get her the information another way.

That's what the story of the cat and rat had been about. Mutual interests. But it was also about misdirection. Distraction. Looking one way while the important thing was happening somewhere else.

"Did they say I needed to leave?" she asked Boynton. "Or we did?"

He seemed confused by the question. "Isn't it the same thing?"

"Please, humor me. Try to remember exactly what the official said."

Boynton considered. "He said, 'Please inform Secretary Adams that she needs to leave Iran, on the orders of the Grand Ayatollah.' "

"Well, that seems pretty clear," said Katherine.

"I wonder," said Ellen, then turned back to her Chief of Staff. "Hold them off."

He gave a snort of unexpected laughter. "At the pass?" But seeing his boss's serious expression, his face fell.

"Stall them," said Secretary Adams.

"Stall them?" demanded Boynton, his voice almost a squeal. "How?"

"Just do it."

She all but shoved him out the door. As it closed, she heard her Chief of Staff tell the Iranian official that they'd be right out. "Small delay. Women's issues." Then she heard him ask, "Do you have women's issues here?"

We might not have as much time as I hoped, thought Ellen.

She tried to calm her mind. To put aside General Whitehead as the mole.

To put aside what Gil had said. That nuclear bombs were almost certainly already in American cities. Ready to go off. Soon.

Each beat of her heart felt like the ticking down of the clock.

She closed her eyes and took a deep breath in. A deep breath out. *Try to see the next move*, she told herself. *Shut out all the noise, all the interference. See clearly . . .*

"Mom?"

Silence. Then her eyes flew open.

Her heart began to beat more quickly. Pounding against her rib cage. Big Ben, counting the precious moments. Racing toward the chimes at midnight.

Her mind raced alongside her heart. Almost there. Almost there.

And then she had it. What the Grand Ayatollah meant.

Ellen strode across the room and threw open the door. As she did, she heard Boynton and the poor Iranian official talking about what tree the Prophet might have been, had he been a tree.

She suspected she'd interrupted moments before her Chief of Staff was also arrested, for blasphemy.

"Charles!"

He looked at her, like a fish on a hook. "Yes?"

"Come in."

He didn't need to be asked twice.

"I need to leave," she said as she shut the door behind him. "Now."

"Yes, that's what I said," said Boynton.

"And you need to stay."

"Huh?"

"You and Katherine."

They stared at her.

"We can't leave Anahita," Ellen explained, her voice at a normal register. Making sure all those listening in could hear her. "I need to return to DC and talk with President Williams about the situation. Get his instructions. You need to stay in Iran until I return. In the meantime, you should head out sightseeing."

Both looked at her as though she'd lost her mind.

"There'll be people following you. Might as well take them on a wild-goose chase. Make them think you're up to something. Go see Persepolis. Or, wait, better still, ask to see the prehistoric cave art of Baluchestan."

"What are you talking about?" said Katherine.

"I was reading about it on the way here," Ellen explained. "Archaeologists found cave drawings there. Eleven thousand years old. Some believe it proves that thousands of years ago Iranians migrated to the Americas."

"What?" said Katherine, completely lost now, while Boynton took the better part of valor.

"The drawings show the same horse that the Indigenous peoples of North America rode. It makes sense that you'd want to see it."

"Does it?" Boynton spoke at last. "Does it really?"

"Sure, as a nod to the belief that we're all one people. Look, the point is to lead whoever might be following you on a merry chase."

"Merry?" said Boynton.

"Well, a morose chase, if you prefer."

While Boynton looked up the rock art, Katherine dropped her voice to a whispered rasp. "Mom, the bombs. What Gil told you. We can't waste time."

"I'm not." Ellen held her daughter's eyes, and Katherine saw the determination there.

"That site is almost twenty hours away by car," said Boynton, looking up from his phone.

"I'm sure they can fly you to a nearby airport, then drive," said Ellen, reverting to her normal voice once again. Or as normal as she could manage. "You can sleep on the way, and anyone interested in your movements will waste even more time and effort following you."

"But we'll also be wasting time and effort," Boynton protested.

Katherine looked at her mother, whose eyes were bloodshot from exhaustion but gleaming. With brilliance or madness, Katherine couldn't tell. Had Gil's message, and the pressure of trying to stop a catastrophe, pushed her right over the edge?

"Anahita?" Katherine asked. "And Zahara? What do you want us to do to help them?"

"And the two Iranians who were also arrested?" asked Charles.

"I'll see what President Williams wants to do. These decisions go beyond me. I'll get back as soon as I can. Look, make as much noise as you can about going to those caves. That way you'll be followed, and they won't pay attention to what I'm doing."

As she spoke, she typed a quick message to Katherine.

Go. Trust me. I'm on it.

It was pitch black as Secretary Adams boarded the Sultan's plane. Once in the spacious cabin, she removed the burqa and tried to give it to the woman official.

"Keep it," she said, in perfect English. "I believe you'll be returning."

As the plane headed down the runway on the first leg of her long journey home, Ellen sat forward, as though that would get her to Washington faster.

Her last sight of Katherine was her daughter and Boynton getting into another car for their own long journey, to the caves.

She hoped and prayed she'd understood the Ayatollah's story about the cat and rat correctly. She was pretty sure he'd had Anahita Dahir arrested so that someone from Ellen's party would have to stay behind.

When he'd publicly expelled Secretary Adams, but allowed her daughter and Chief of Staff to stay, that had confirmed it for Ellen.

He was playing a game of misdirection. He wanted to tell them something, but Ellen was too closely watched.

So the Supreme Leader had to get her out of the country, while guaranteeing someone from the American contingent would stay behind to meet the informant and get the information they needed.

As the plane reached cruising altitude, Ellen received a text from Katherine.

Plane waiting for us at airport. We were expected.

Ellen lowered her head, heavy with relief.

They were expected. This was what Khosravi wanted her to do.

She sent back a quick thumbs-up, then sat back. Confident. Certain that she'd read the Supreme Leader of the Islamic Republic of Iran right.

But . . .

She tried to push that traitorous thought away.

But . . .

The man was a terrorist. A sworn enemy of the United States. Who'd funded any number of attacks on the West. And she'd just placed her daughter, placed her nation, in his hands? On the basis of some cat-and-rat fable?

She was trusting that the sly old cleric was not the one who'd set a trap, and she had not just walked into it.

That was her last thought before exhaustion overtook her.

Boynton crossed himself as the door to the small turbo prop was closed.

They managed to catch some sleep on the flight to Sistan and Baluchestan Province, which, Charles Boynton informed Katherine in his Eeyore way as they started their descent, was not far from the border with Pakistan. Somehow, in his opinion, that made all this worse.

But then, thought Katherine as she looked out the window, straining through the darkness to see some land, he didn't know about the nuclear bombs already in US cities. He didn't know what "worse" really was.

A grizzled older fellow named Farhad met their plane and explained that he'd be their driver and guide. They got into his battered car, which smelled of tobacco, and he drove them into the desert.

He spoke fluent English, his accent soft and musical. He was used, he said, to taking Western archaeologists to this site. He was clearly proud of it. It was just the three of them in the car, and no other vehicles in sight. None of the ever-present guards and observers. Everyone had lost interest in them.

Charles Boynton had also lost interest, staring out the window in the predawn glow at the endless landscape of sand and tors.

As he drove, Farhad told them about the discoveries of Bronze Age pictographs and petroglyphs, of animals and plants and people.

"Some drawn with vegetable dye," he explained. "Some with blood. There're thousands of them."

This area, he told them, despite the wealth of rock art, was essentially ignored by tourists.

"No foreign traveler ever comes here."

He talked passionately about the need to protect the finds. He looked at Katherine, sitting next to him while Boynton snored in the back seat. Head back, mouth open.

"That's why you're here, right? To protect what's important?"

His gaze was so intense, she nodded. Unsure what she was agreeing to.

They arrived just as the sun was rising. Once Boynton was coaxed awake, they climbed onto a plateau and Farhad set out a breakfast of strong coffee from a thermos, plump figs, oranges, cheese, and bread.

Katherine took a photograph of Boynton and Farhad. The Chief of Staff, still in his suit and tie, looked like he'd stepped through a hidden door at Foggy Bottom and ended up here.

Unexpectedly. Unhappily.

She sent it off to her mother, with a short note to say they'd arrived at the caves and would write when there was something more to say.

Now, perched on the rocks as the sun rose, Katherine looked out over the ancient landscape, unchanged for tens of thousands, perhaps millions, of years. And marveled. Others had sat exactly where she was and etched the figures into the stone, capturing their life. Their beliefs. Their ideas. Their feelings even.

"May I?" she asked, and when Farhad nodded, she reached out her index finger and traced the lines.

"It's an eagle," he explained. "And that"—he pointed to the lines above it—"is the sun."

For reasons she didn't fully understand, Katherine felt a lump fizzing in her throat, and her eyes grew moist. Much like when she heard a piece of music that reached her deeply hidden places. Or read a passage in a book that moved her. These drawings of horses and hunters, camels and sinuous birds soaring. Of joyous sunbursts. They were profoundly human.

The hands that drew them had felt the same ground beneath them, had felt the same sun. Had felt the need to record their rituals. Their lives were not so different, not at all different, from her own.

And not so different from what she did with the newspapers and TV networks she ran. This, in stone, was their news. The events of their day.

It was a comforting feeling, she thought, as she sipped coffee and ate fruit and cheese. And watched the sun rise. And she needed comfort.

She was so afraid about what Shah had planned. What he'd already placed in American cities. She was so afraid they wouldn't be able to stop it.

She was so confused about why her mother had sent them there, what she needed from them. And yet, tracing the sun, Katherine felt a profound and unexpected peace.

These declarations of life had survived millennia.

And while lives would end, life went on.

"Come," said Farhad as he cleared away the breakfast, "the best ones are inside."

Nodding toward what looked like a narrow fissure in the stone, he stood up and handed them each a lantern. They squeezed through, with Boynton muttering, "Shit, shit, shit."

Once in, Katherine brushed red dirt from her jacket and looked around, moving the light in a slow arc. She couldn't see any more drawings.

"They're farther down," Farhad explained. "That's why they weren't found until recently."

He walked ahead of them as Boynton and Katherine exchanged glances.

"Maybe I should stay here," said Boynton.

"Maybe you should come with me," said Katherine.

"I don't like caves."

"When have you ever been in one?"

"You obviously haven't spent much time in the White House," he whispered.

Katherine's laugh tumbled down the caverns and returned to them as a sort of low moan.

She brought out her phone. No reception. She was tempted to video their progress, but her battery was getting low, so she clicked off the phone but kept it, like a talisman, in her hand.

They followed Farhad around a corner and saw that he'd stopped. Then turned to them.

"I think this is far enough." He held a gun in his hand.

They stared at the guide. At the gun.

"What're you doing?" Katherine managed.

"Waiting."

And then they heard it, from even deeper in the cave. Footsteps. The echo made it impossible to tell how many people were approaching. It sounded like hundreds. And Katherine had the wild idea that the ancient figures on the walls, drawn in blood, had come alive. Had stepped out of the stone and were approaching.

They turned toward the sounds, and Katherine saw that Farhad's weapon was now pointed into the darkness. At whatever was coming closer and closer.

She quickly put her lantern on the dirt floor of the cave and motioned Boynton to do the same, and together they quietly backed away from the light, into the darkness.

They'd barely taken three steps when they saw who was coming out of the depths of the ancient cave. At first it looked like a cluster of bobbing lights. Spirits suspended.

But as they got closer, the figures behind the lights became visible.

It was Anahita. And Zahara and her father, Dr. Ahmadi. And

the two Iranian agents, American assets, who'd met Zahara and passed along the message. There were two Revolutionary Guards with them, weapons drawn and pointed not at their prisoners but at Farhad and Katherine and Boynton.

They stopped fifteen feet from each other.

Had her mother made a terrible mistake? Katherine wondered.

Was this how it ended? With her own blood sprayed onto the walls? Joining that of her ancient ancestors? To be interpreted centuries from now by some anthropologist who'd decide the splatters were some attempt to chart the stars?

Seemed that article her mother had read was right after all. Ancient Iranians and Americans did end up in the same place. Only it wasn't Oregon; it was the walls of this cave.

Katherine held Anahita's eyes, which were also filled with terror. The FSO was thinking the same thing.

This was the end.

Katherine clicked on the video on her phone. Whatever happened to them, there would be a record.

"Mahmoud?" One of the Iranian agents who'd been arrested was peering at them.

Farhad lowered his handgun slightly, but not all the way. "I heard they'd picked you up."

"Yes," she said, not smiling. "Someone must've informed." She turned to the guards. "You can lower your weapons. This's who we're meeting."

"Mahmoud?" whispered Katherine. "I thought your name was Farhad."

"When I'm a guide, it is."

"And what are you now?" asked Boynton.

"Your savior."

The woman agent shook her head. "The ego that walks like a man. He's an informant for MOIS."

"The Iranian intelligence agency," Boynton said.

"Mahmoud also works for the Russian mafia," the woman explained, the disdain clear. "That's why we're here, am I right?"

They were still standing fifteen feet apart. While they sounded cordial, collegial, there was about them a tightly coiled tension. Like meat-eaters ready to spring.

Katherine's lantern, placed on the ground, threw its light against the rough stone wall of the cave. Illuminating exquisite drawings.

Graceful, voluptuous. These were of a magnitude finer than the ones outside. There was movement, a flow to them as the blood men on blood horses and camels plunged their spears into a screaming, writhing, catlike creature.

This was a hunt. This was a kill.

CHAPTER 30

Hamza met them at the outer ring of his encampment.

The morning was clear and cold, but by midafternoon it would be stifling hot. Such was life at this altitude and latitude. Life in this atmosphere demanded an ability to adapt.

As Gil and Hamza embraced, Gil felt something slipped into his jacket pocket. At first he thought it was a phone, but it was too bulky, and far too heavy.

"I think you'll need it," Hamza whispered. "Good luck."

"Thank you. For everything."

They locked eyes, each understanding what the other had done. And the consequences. Then Gil followed Akbar down the mountain, along the narrow trail that would eventually take them back to the old taxi. And from there into Pakistan and a flight . . . where?

Home? To DC? Where there was almost certainly one of the bombs?

As he limped along, Gil tried to justify going back there. And tried to justify not.

Akbar, familiar with the route, knew exactly where he would do it. At the place where the path fell away. When they were beyond Hamza's sentries and there would be no witnesses.

He felt in his pocket for his phone. He'd get extra if he could take a picture of the body. Enough to buy a new car.

As soon as Air Force Three landed, Secretary Adams was whisked away in the armored SUV, through the streets of Washington. Lights flashing. Escort vehicles blocking intersections.

And still it felt like a lifetime between Andrews and the White House.

Ellen kept checking her phone. She hadn't had a message from Katherine since the photo she'd sent of her sullen Chief of Staff beside a weathered older Iranian man in traditional dress, accompanied by the text: *Made it. You're right. Well worth coming. But no one followed.*

That had been several hours ago. And nothing since.

She checked again, then sent off a message.

News? You OK? Followed by a heart emoji.

When the SUV rolled up to the side door into the White House, Ellen leapt out. Marine guards opened the door. Officials paused to greet her: "Madame Secretary."

She tried to look composed while pretty much sprinting along the wide halls. She'd texted Betsy to meet her in the President's outer office and to bring Pete Hamilton.

The two women embraced, and Betsy introduced the former press secretary for Eric Dunn.

"Thank you for helping us," said Ellen.

"I'm helping my country."

Ellen smiled. "Good enough."

"I'll let the President know you're here, Madame Secretary," said Williams's secretary in her slow drawl. Ellen half expected to be offered sweet iced tea.

But while the woman sounded relaxed, she moved quickly,

with an economy of motion that proved she knew exactly what this was about.

Well, perhaps not exactly, thought Ellen, as she checked her phone. Again.

Nothing.

The door opened, but they only got two steps into the Oval Office before all three stopped. And stared.

Though she'd asked that this meeting be private, just between them and President Williams, she saw two men get to their feet from where they'd been sitting on the sofa.

The men turned in a kind of synchronized movement.

Tim Beecham and General Bert Whitehead.

Ellen was beyond trying to hide her surprise, or her annoyance. Stepping forward, she ignored the men and spoke directly to Williams.

"Mr. President, I thought I asked that this meeting be private."

"You did. I didn't agree. If you have information on Shah, the sooner we all hear it, the faster we can put a plan in place. Tim delayed his flight to London to be here. So let's have it."

It was then he noticed the other two people with her. Betsy Jameson he knew, but the other . . . President Williams was clearly zipping through the photo album every politician kept in their brain.

And then he had it. His expression grew happier at having placed the man, and more perplexed. Having placed him.

"Aren't you—"

"Pete Hamilton, Mr. President. I was President Dunn's press secretary."

Williams turned to his SecState. "What's this about?"

Ellen stepped closer to the President. "I came back because there's something you need to hear personally. Privately. Please."

If he heard the plea in her voice, he ignored it.

"About Shah?" he asked. "You've found out about his plans?"

There was nothing for it. Ellen Adams squared her shoulders and said, "It's about the mole, the traitor, in your White House. Who approved Dr. Shah's release from house arrest. Who's working with him and elements in the Pakistani government to get the Taliban and Al-Qaeda a nuclear device to use against the United States."

With each word President Williams's eyes widened until he looked like a caricature of a terrified man.

"What?"

"You found it?" said Whitehead. He took a step closer to Tim Beecham. "The evidence we need?"

Williams looked at the Chair of the Joint Chiefs. "You knew?"

Ellen also turned to General Whitehead. Her anger, her fury, was impossible to contain or mistake. She was trembling with rage.

For a moment she couldn't speak, but her expression said it all as she stared at the General.

Whitehead's face opened with surprise. Then his brows drew together. "Wait. You can't possibly think—"

"I know," said Ellen, glaring at him. "We have the evidence."

She nodded to Betsy, who placed the printouts on the Resolute desk. Mrs. Cleaver had driven in the first nail. She turned and glared at Whitehead before stepping back.

The General went to move toward the desk and the papers, but Williams held up a hand and he stopped.

The President picked them up. As he read, his face grew slack. His mouth opened; his eyes grew dull, uncomprehending. It was that moment, that instant, when you tripped going down the stairs. That moment when you realize you won't be able to save yourself. And this was going to be bad.

There was complete silence in the Oval Office. Except for the tick, tick, tick of the clock on the mantel.

Then President Williams dropped the papers and turned to Whitehead.

"You bastard."

"No, it's not me! I'm not the one. I don't know what those papers say, but it's a lie."

He looked around wildly; then his eyes landed on Tim Beecham, who was staring at the Chair of the Joint Chiefs with horror and shock.

"You," said Whitehead, and started forward. "You did this."

He took a step toward Beecham, who backed away, tripping over an armchair and falling to the floor.

"Security," called Williams, and all doors flew open.

Secret Service agents swarmed the President while others drew their weapons, scanning the room for the danger.

"Arrest him."

The agents looked from the President to the man he was pointing at. A four-star general. A war hero. For many of them, their hero.

The Chairman of the Joint Chiefs of Staff.

There was but the slightest pause before the senior agent stepped forward.

"Drop your weapon, General."

"I'm not armed," said Whitehead, spreading his arms wide. Then, as he was being frisked, he shifted his eyes to the President. "It's not me. It's him." He nodded toward Beecham, just getting up off the floor. "I don't know how he did this, but it's Beecham."

"For God's sake," said Ellen. "Give it up. We have the evidence. We have the memos, the notes. The ones you thought you'd hidden. Agreeing to the release of Shah. Destabilizing the region. Setting this whole thing up."

"I never . . . ," began Whitehead. "Releasing Shah was madness. I'd never—"

Betsy cut him off. "We found the memos among the Beecham papers."

"The what?" said the Director of National Intelligence. "Where?"

"General Whitehead here tried to implicate you," explained Betsy. "Tried to frame you as the traitor by, among other things, taking your documents from the Dunn era and moving them from the official archives. He buried them so that it looked like you had something to hide."

"I found the documents," said Pete Hamilton. "They were hidden in the Dunn administration private archives."

"There's no such thing," said President Williams. "All correspondence and documents are automatically sent to the official archives. They can be marked secret, but they're there."

"No, Mr. President," said Hamilton. "The Dunn people were careful to create a parallel archive. They couldn't erase documents, but they could put them behind an almost impenetrable wall. Only those insiders with the password could get in. I had the password, but not the computer access."

"I had the access," said Betsy Jameson, "but not the password. So we worked together."

"You changed all the references of your involvement with Shah and the Pakistanis to make it look like it was Mr. Beecham," Pete Hamilton said to Whitehead. "Except you missed two. And we found them."

Whitehead was shaking his head. Apparently dumbfounded. But Ellen had come to appreciate that of course he'd be a good liar, a good actor. He'd have to be.

She'd been taken in by this Fred MacMurray, everyone's best friend, once. Not again.

"And then you went about quietly insinuating that Tim Beecham wasn't to be trusted," she said. "And it worked. I believed you."

"That young man who was following me from Frankfurt, and was in the park and the bar," said Betsy. "The one I told you about.

You went to talk to him. I was so grateful that you took care of it so easily. Now I know how. He was one of yours."

"No."

"Is that when you got the scan of the note Ellen gave me?" said Betsy. "You didn't get rid of him. You told him to go to the Secretary of State's office and search it while I was in the bar with you. You told him to look for something personal. Something you could send Shah, to freak Ellen out."

"Was it your idea or Shah's?" asked Ellen.

"None of this happened." But his denials were getting weaker and weaker as the net closed.

"Betsy, is that Ranger still with you?" Ellen asked.

"Yes, I left her in the hall outside."

Ellen turned to the President. "There's an Army Ranger—"

"Captain Denise Phelan," said Betsy.

"She's with him. She needs to be arrested too."

"For God's sake, this's gone too far," said Whitehead. "Captain Phelan's a decorated veteran. She's put her life on the line for this country. You can't do this to her. She's not involved."

"But you're admitting you are?" said President Williams, and when General Whitehead fell silent, he nodded to one of the Secret Service agents. "Arrest Captain Phelan."

Whitehead inhaled deeply, realizing, Ellen knew, there was no escape now. He was caught, trapped. Phelan would almost certainly admit everything in exchange for a lighter sentence.

"Wait a minute," said Beecham, trying to catch up. "Just so I'm clear. You thought I betrayed my country?" he said to Ellen. "That I was working with Bashir Shah? Based on no evidence? Just his insinuations?"

"I did, and I'm sorry, Tim," said Secretary Adams.

"'I'm sorry'?" said Beecham, almost shouting. Incredulous. "'I'm sorry'?"

"It didn't help that you're very unlikable," said Betsy. Ellen pressed her lips together. Tightly.

"Why?" said Williams. His eyes hadn't left Bert Whitehead. "For God's sake, General, why would you do it?"

"I didn't. I wouldn't." His brows were furrowed, furiously thinking. The strategist not giving up. Desperate to find a hole in the net.

But there was no way out. Writhe as he might, he was trapped, and he knew it.

"Money," said Beecham. "It's always money. What did they pay you to murder men, women, and children? To give a nuclear bomb to our enemies? How much, General Whitehead?" He turned to the President. "I'll have my people look into offshore accounts. I bet we'll find it there."

Whitehead's eyes remained on Ellen, flickering for a moment to Betsy, then back.

"Captain Phelan had nothing to do with any of this," he repeated to Ellen, quietly.

"And you, you bastard, you tried to implicate me? To set me up?" Beecham was working himself up from rage to hysteria. "I've given my whole life in service to this country, and you try to smear me with your shit?"

Now Whitehead, with unexpected speed, turned and lunged at Beecham, tackling him to the carpet in one swift move. Sitting astride him, Whitehead's fist pumped up and down, smashing into the face of the Director of National Intelligence, as Beecham cried out and tried in vain to cover up.

It took the Secret Service just a moment to react, but it was long enough for the General, trained in Special Forces, to inflict damage.

Two agents grabbed the President, bending him down and protecting him with their bodies while two others went for the General. One swiped his gun across Whitehead's face, knocking him off Beecham and to the ground. Dazed.

They knelt on him, guns to his head.

Instinctively, Ellen had swung her arm across Betsy's body, in a protective movement. Pushing her back. As a mother might with a child when braking suddenly.

Doug Williams stood back up and straightened his clothes.

They dragged Whitehead to his feet, blood streaming down the side of his face.

"It's over, Bert," said Williams. "There's nothing to gain by not telling us everything. We need to know what Shah is up to. Where's the target?" Silence. "Who's buying the nuclear technology? Is it the Taliban? Al-Qaeda? How far along are they? Where're they working?" Silence. "Where are the bombs? Tell us!" the President roared, and took a step toward Whitehead, as though about to attack him.

An agent helped Tim Beecham to his feet and, depositing him in a chair, he handed the DNI a towel. His nose was broken, his blood seeping into the white carpet.

Whitehead turned to Ellen. "I've done my part."

"Oh my God," whispered Betsy. "He admits it. Until this moment . . ."

"What?" Ellen stared at Bert Whitehead. "You have to tell us what you've done."

" 'When thou hast done, thou hast not done,' " he said, staring at Betsy. " 'For I have more.' "

The words sat surrounded by a horrified silence before it was broken by the President of the United States.

"Take him away. I want him interrogated. We need to know what he knows. And Tim, get medical help."

When the Oval Office was cleared, Doug Williams sat heavily in his chair behind the desk and stared down at the printouts. The damning memos.

"I'd never have dreamed . . ."

He looked up and indicated that Ellen and Betsy should sit. Then he got up again. Slowly. Like a man battered.

Walking over to Pete Hamilton, he took the younger man's arm and led him to the door.

"Thank you for your help. Give me a few days, and then I'd like to see you again."

"I didn't vote for you, Mr. President."

Williams smiled wearily and lowered his voice. "I'm not sure they did either."

He tilted his head toward his Secretary of State and her counselor.

But his face held no amusement. Only crushing worry.

"Good luck, Mr. President. If there's anything else I can do . . ."

"Thank you. And not a word to anyone."

"I understand."

When Hamilton left, Williams returned to his desk. "You came all the way back from Tehran to tell me about General Whitehead?"

While he'd been talking to Hamilton, Ellen had checked her phone. Nothing. Still nothing from Katherine. And nothing more from Gil.

She was moving now from worry to panic.

But she had to focus. Focus.

Betsy took her hand and whispered, "You OK?"

"Katherine and Gil. No word."

Betsy squeezed her hand as Ellen turned back to Williams. "You needed to know about General Whitehead, Mr. President, and I couldn't risk the message being intercepted."

"You think others are involved besides the Ranger?"

"I think it's a possibility."

"Is this a coup attempt?" His face was pale, but at least, thought Ellen, he was willing to face the worst.

"I don't know." Then she paused.

Was it? If those nuclear bombs went off killing hundreds, thousands, maybe hundreds of thousands, and gutting major American cities, there'd be chaos. And outrage.

And once a semblance of order was restored, there'd be legitimate calls for accountability. For answers. But also cries for revenge. And not just against the terrorists who'd done it, but against an administration that had failed to stop it.

The fact that this had all started under Eric Dunn would be lost in the frenzy.

Ellen thought Eric Dunn was foolish, but not, she believed, a lunatic. Not actively involved in this plot. It was others, those who'd benefit by the chaos. By a war. By a change of administration. The leeches and minions who had metastasized under Dunn and were still among them.

Maybe this *was* a coup attempt.

Doug Williams could see that his Secretary of State was perplexed.

"We'll get it out of Whitehead," he said.

"I'm not so sure," said Ellen. "But there's something else. Something I also needed to tell you in private."

The President looked at Betsy.

"She knows," said Ellen. "And so do my daughter and son. But they're the only ones. It was Gil who got the information."

The door to the Oval Office flew open and Barb Stenhauser appeared, stopping a few feet in to stare at the bloodstains on the carpet.

"I just heard. Is it true?"

"You need to leave us, Barb," he said. "I'll buzz when I want you."

Stenhauser stood there, stunned. By what she'd heard in the hallways, about General Whitehead, and what she'd just heard from the President.

Her eyes left the President and rested on Secretary Adams before shifting to Betsy Jameson. Her gaze was cold. Chilling.

"What's happening?"

"Please, Barb," said Williams, a warning in his voice not to make him say it a third time.

When she left, Williams leaned forward and said, "Tell me, Madame Secretary."

And Ellen did.

CHAPTER 31

"Let's rest here," said Akbar.

He stopped and looked over the edge, into the canyon below.

Gil paused, grateful to his companion for considering him and his leg. The descent, while easier on the lungs, was far harder on his wounded leg. All the jarring and skidding.

"No," he said. "We have to get down. Quickly. I need to contact my mother."

"What did Hamza say to you? You looked pretty upset."

"Oh, you know him. Drama queen."

Akbar laughed. "Yes. He's famous for it. All the Pathan are."

"I was upset because he either couldn't or wouldn't tell me anything. I think he knows stuff about Shah, but wouldn't say. He was my last hope. I have to get down to tell my mother that I got nothing."

"Didn't you write her yesterday? You borrowed my phone."

"I did, but hoped Hamza would change his mind this morning and I'd have something useful to send her. But he didn't."

Akbar studied his companion. His friend. Well, not, as it turned out, a close friend.

"Too bad. All this way for nothing." Akbar spread out his arm, inviting Gil to take the lead. "You first."

"Actually, probably better if you go. If my leg gives out, I want to be able to land on you."

"Now who's being a drama queen?" But he stepped forward. It made what he had to do a bit more difficult, in that Gil would see it coming. A knife in the back was always easier. As was a shove from behind.

And he wouldn't have that shocked face haunting him. Though Akbar suspected it would disappear as soon as the new car arrived.

As he moved around the corner of the rock wall, the path narrow and littered with rubble from slides, he stopped, turned, and, arms out, reached for Gil.

Seeing this, Gil was, for an instant, baffled. But it lasted just a split second.

He stepped away, knocking his wound against an outcropping. Crying out in pain, he felt his leg buckling. Instinctively, he reached out and grabbed Akbar by his cloth robe, dragging him down with him.

As he hit the ground, he released Akbar and scrambled away, his right hand grasping for the pocket of his robes. Where Hamza had hidden the gun.

"What're you doing?" he shouted as Akbar got to his hands and knees and scrambled after him.

Gil's eyes widened. Akbar didn't answer, but the long, curved blade in his hand did.

"Shit," said Gil, and dug more furiously for the pocket. But the voluminous robe wasn't giving it up so easily.

He reached for a handful of rocks and dirt and threw it into Akbar's face. It barely slowed the man down.

Gil kicked furiously, but Akbar, an adept at hand-to-hand fighting from his years with the mujahedin, grabbed Gil's boot and twisted, so that Gil screamed in pain and terror as his entire body was turned onto its side. Like a calf being roped.

He was completely defenseless. He bucked and cried out and waited for the knife across his throat when, to his horror, he realized what Akbar was doing. He was dragging him over the edge. So that it would look like he'd slipped and fallen. An accident. Not murder.

"No, no!"

He was sliding over the edge. His heavy boots dragging him down. It was happening in slow motion, like the nightmare where he'd try to run but couldn't.

His arms out in front of him, his hands scrabbled frantically for purchase. Something, anything, to cling to.

But it was already too late. He'd passed the point of no return. Any moment now the slide would speed up and he'd be right over the edge, flailing in the air.

And then . . .

His fingers dragged through the dirt, ripping his nails and leaving a trail of blood.

And then there was a shot. A single shot. And in his peripheral vision he saw something, a blur, tumble over the side.

But Gil's problems weren't over. He was still sliding. He struggled even more furiously, grabbing, grabbing.

And then he felt a hand on the scruff of his neck, stopping him. Dragging him back up.

Once safe, he lay on the ground panting, crying. Unable to stop shaking. Finally he raised his head, his face filthy with dirt and muddy tears.

"Now who's the drama queen?" said Hamza.

"Oh shit, oh shit. How did you . . . ?"

"Know? I didn't. But I've never trusted the little bastard. He was always only in it for what he could get out of it. Mostly money. Selling captured arms on the black market so that they'd end up back with those we took them from. He was an asshole."

"Why didn't you tell me?"

"How was I to know you kept in touch with that piece of shit?"

"Who was he working for?" asked Gil. But he knew. "Shah? Oh

Christ. If Akbar was hired by him, that means Shah knows I came here. Spoke to you." As Gil spoke, Hamza was nodding. "He'll know you're the one who gave me the information."

"Maybe not. Around here allegiances are"—he scanned the arid landscape—"fluid. Akbar could've been working for anyone. He'd know that anywhere the son of the American Secretary of State went would be information worth selling."

"But it wasn't just information. Someone paid him to kill me."

"Seems so."

"Which is why the gun." Gil put his hand over the pocket.

"Yeah, for all the good it did. I heard what you said to him. You lied. You said I hadn't told you anything. Why? Did you suspect him?"

Gil looked over the edge, at the splayed and broken body below. Did he? But he shook his head. "No," he admitted. "I'm just naturally cautious. The fewer who know, the better."

Hamza too looked over the cliff, at the dead body he'd created. "I was surprised to see him with you at the encampment."

The sentence sounded familiar. It took Gil just a moment to realize why. " 'I had an appointment with him in Samarra.' "

When Hamza tilted his head, Gil said, "A quote from an old Mesopotamian story. About the impossibility of cheating death."

"Seems you've cheated it twice. I wonder where it plans to meet you?" Hamza stooped and picked something off the trail. "These fell from his pocket." He handed the cell phone and car keys to Gil. But kept the long, curved knife. "I'd stay away from Samarra, if I was you."

As he limped and skidded down the mountain, Gil had the odd feeling that Death was not following him, but had stayed behind. That the appointment was with Hamza. That he'd led Death right to him.

And by the last glance he had of his friend, he could see that Hamza suspected the same thing.

In giving Gilgamesh that information, Hamza the Lion had also given his life. And bloated Death, in the form of Bashir Shah, would take it.

Gil kept checking Akbar's phone for reception. Up at the encampment, there was a signal, but in the valleys and caverns? Nothing.

Once at the car, he turned it toward the porous border, and the rutted back roads across to Pakistan.

His plan now was to return to Washington. He just wanted to get home. To be on hand to help. But he'd go via Frankfurt, to repay the kind nurse and find Anahita.

Since his kidnapping, he'd allowed fear to build a wall around him, and from that fortress he'd viewed the world. Safe, sovereign, and alone. But no more. As he'd slid over the edge, his fortress had fallen. Now, given yet another chance, he was damned if he was going to let fear steal any more precious time he might spend with her. If Death was to find him, it would be with love, not fear, in his heart.

As Anahita took her place beside her cousin, she noticed that Zahara was sitting as far from her father as possible in the cave. With Katherine Adams on the other side of Zahara, the two women formed a supportive embrace.

Once the guns had been lowered, Farhad, or Mahmoud, had led them down an almost hidden side passage to where it opened into a cavern. There he instructed them to put their lanterns in the middle of the stone circle where the floor of the cave had been blackened by a fire that had died out tens of thousands of years earlier.

They sat on boulders, rolled into place by hands long dead and dust.

Had some catastrophe occurred, Anahita wondered, to make these people abandon their home? Was this a place of celebration?

Of ritual? Of refuge? Had they hidden here, deep in the caves, believing they were safe?

As Anahita and the others now believed.

But had something found them anyway?

She looked at the drawings covering the walls and even the ceiling. The gentle flickering of the kerosene lamps gave the figures movement, so that it looked like the hunt was in full and perpetual swing. It also looked, in one sequence, as though the catlike creature they were after had turned. Was now chasing them.

Is that what had happened? Had it found these men, women, children?

Anahita knew her imagination was getting the better of her, and that was not good. Especially when reality was frightening enough.

She stared across the cluster of lamps at her uncle on the far side of the circle. He hadn't spoken to Anahita, but he had glared at her as though she were the enemy. As though she'd lured his daughter into doing something she should never have done.

And, by extension, forced him to do something he should never have done.

Dr. Ahmadi had, though, spoken to Zahara, begging her at every opportunity to forgive him. To understand why he'd turned her in. He'd wept and reached for her hand, but she'd yanked it away, stepping over to Anahita and Katherine, and leaving Dr. Ahmadi alone with his agony.

The nuclear physicist sat with his head in his hands, and Anahita was reminded what Einstein had said: "I know not with what weapons World War III will be fought, but World War IV will be fought with sticks and stones."

But Einstein was being disingenuous. He knew perfectly well, as did those around their circle, what was going to blow them back to the Stone Age.

And none knew better than the father of many of those weapons. Dr. Behnam Ahmadi.

" 'Now I am become Death . . .' " Under her breath she muttered the words of Robert Oppenheimer, quoting from the Bhagavad Gita. " 'The destroyer of worlds.' "

Maybe, Anahita thought as she watched her uncle, *we need to get used to living in caves.*

Katherine turned to Charles Boynton, who'd plastered himself to her side. To protect her? she wondered. But she knew the answer. It was so she could protect him.

Katherine was growing almost fond of this man.

"The Oval Office?" she whispered, looking around the cave.

He smiled. "It's uncanny."

Farhad cleared his throat, and all eyes swung to him.

"I was told by my handler in MOIS to meet the Americans and bring them here. And tell them what I know."

Katherine closed her eyes for a moment. So her mother either knew or suspected that this was the Ayatollah's plan. But she had to figure a way to get them out of Tehran and on their own so that they could get the information they needed to stop Shah without anyone else knowing.

Certainly without the Russians knowing.

The destination didn't matter, as long as no one followed them.

Canny Mother. Canny Ayatollah.

Farhad looked into the darkness that surrounded them, then back to the gathering. "I wasn't told about"—his arm swept around—"all of you."

"Does it matter?" asked Katherine.

"It might. If they were followed." He was clearly afraid. His eyes darted this way and that. "Why're you here?"

"We were told to come here and bring them," said the senior

Revolutionary Guard. "And to hand them over. But not him. He's to return with us."

The guard was looking at Dr. Ahmadi, who'd raised his head.

"Then why bring him?" asked Boynton.

The guard actually smiled. "Were you told why you were really here?"

"Look," said Katherine, her nerves jangling. "The sooner you tell us what you know, the faster we can all get out of here."

Her unease had deepened. If this man had been told to pass along information, and he was clearly anxious to do it and leave, what was with the breakfast? Why waste time preparing a meal?

It now seemed like he was stalling. Waiting even. But if not for Anahita and the others, then who?

"Where are the real scientists working?" demanded Katherine.

"Real scientists?" said Boynton. "What're you talking about?"

She didn't want to waste precious time explaining about Gil's message. All her considerable focus was on Farhad.

"There's an abandoned factory in Pakistan, on the border with Afghanistan," said Farhad, dropping his voice to a whisper.

Everyone in the circle leaned forward. Katherine, her imagination not quite in check, could picture the images on the walls turning. Also leaning in. Sensing bigger game. Sensing fresh blood.

"The Russian mafia has been selling fissionable material and equipment to Shah and sending it there for more than a year," said Farhad.

"They've already built at least three bombs," said Katherine, and Farhad looked at her, surprised she knew. He nodded.

"Holy shit," said Boynton.

"Where are they?" Katherine asked.

"I don't know. All I know is what I heard and that's that they were sent to the States on container ships two weeks ago."

"Holy fuck," said Boynton. "There're nuclear bombs in the

United States?" He jumped to his feet and loomed over Farhad. "Where? You know, don't you. Where are they?"

When Farhad shook his head, Boynton lunged at him, knocking him off the rock to the dirt floor. The bureaucrat, while considerably larger and several years younger than Farhad, was no match for the wiry man trained in physical combat. The most combat Charles Boynton had done was with the vending machine at Foggy Bottom. And even then he lost.

Before he knew it, Boynton was in a stranglehold.

"Stop it," demanded Katherine. "We don't have time for this." She shoved Farhad, who turned angry eyes on her, and for a moment Katherine thought he was going to attack her. But he pulled back and released Boynton, who staggered up, holding his throat.

"Sit," Katherine said, and both did. She also regained her seat and leaned closer to Farhad. "Have you been to that facility?"

Again he glanced around, then gave a small nod. "I delivered something in crates. I don't know what it was."

"Tell me where it is."

"Bajaur District, just outside Kitkot. An old cement factory. But you'll never get to it. The Taliban's everywhere."

"Who knows where the bombs are planted? Which cities and where?" demanded Katherine.

"Dr. Shah."

"And? Others must. He didn't deliver them himself."

"Someone at the factory would know. They'd have to arrange for the shipping. And there'd be people in the US to place them. But I don't know who they are. All I know is what I've heard."

"And that is?"

"It's just rumor. Look, Dr. Shah is like a myth. All sorts of fantastic stories have built up around him. That he's hundreds of years old. That he can kill you with a look."

"That he's the Azhi Dahaka," said Anahita.

Farhad had turned gray with terror and nodded.

"Facts, not myths," demanded Katherine. "Come on. Come on."

She noticed that the flames in the lanterns, whose glass chimneys had been raised, were wavering. And she felt a slight breeze. Enough to raise the hairs on her forearms.

It was, she thought, just the mention of Shah. Her imagination.

But the flames were now unmistakably fluttering. Others had begun to notice it too.

"Tell me," said Katherine, lowering her voice but raising her intensity.

Farhad's eyes had widened, and the Revolutionary Guards had lifted their rifles and tightened their grips. Turning toward the darkness behind them.

The first shot hit Farhad in the chest.

Katherine swung her arms out and knocked both Zahara and Boynton off their boulders, even as she herself rolled off and lay on the dirt floor, trying to shelter behind the rocks as bullets sprayed and ricocheted.

She saw Charles Boynton crawl over to Farhad, grabbing his gun and leaning close as the dying man mouthed words, then coughed blood onto Boynton's face.

Boynton looked over at Katherine, his eyes wide with terror.

Farhad was dead. And others, including one of the Revolutionary Guards, had also been cut down.

"Zahara!" cried Dr. Ahmadi over the gunfire.

The remaining guard had taken position in a crevice of the cave wall and was firing back, into the darkness.

They had to get away from the light, Katherine knew. Or, better still, they had to get the light away from them.

She steeled herself.

Anahita, who'd been watching her, guessed what Katherine was about to do, and prepared herself.

At the next burst of gunfire from the guard, both women leapt back into the stone circle and, grabbing the lanterns, they threw them into the darkness. Toward where the enemy gunfire was coming from. Then they hit the ground, covering up.

The guard had been shot and was slumped against the wall, but the woman agent had reached him and taken the AK-47.

As the lanterns struck the ground and exploded, their attackers were suddenly illuminated.

"Poimet," one of them yelled in Russian. It was the last thing he said as the agent fired. "Fuck."

Boynton also turned his gun on them and kept firing as bullets sprayed the cavern.

In the barrage of gunfire Katherine had rolled back to the dubious shelter of the boulders and now lay with her arms over her head. When it ended, she slowly lifted her head.

There was acrid smoke hanging in the air. As it dissipated, a scene of carnage was revealed.

"Baba?"

Katherine and Anahita turned to see Zahara crawling toward her father, who was faceup, spread-eagle, where he'd fallen. Hit by a burst of machine-gun fire as he'd tried to make his way to his daughter.

"Baba?" Zahara had reached her father and was kneeling beside him.

Katherine went to go to her, but Anahita stopped her. "Give her a moment."

Farhad was also dead, as were the Revolutionary Guards and both of the Iranian agents.

"Charles," said Katherine, going up to Boynton, whose legs had given way and left him sitting like a child on the ground. A child with a gun. "Are you all right? Are you hurt?"

She knelt down and gently took the weapon away.

He looked at her, his lower lip and chin trembling. "I think I killed someone."

She held his hand. "You had no choice. You had to."

"Maybe he's just hurt."

"Yes, maybe." Katherine took out a tissue, licked it, and rubbed Farhad's congealing blood off his face.

"He said"—Boynton looked toward Farhad, who was staring up as though mesmerized by the magnificent art hovering above him on the ceiling of the cave—"'White House.'"

"What?"

"He said, 'White House.' What could it mean?"

CHAPTER 32

President Williams's eyes were bright, focused. Taking it all in.

With every word Ellen uttered, his hands had slowly clenched into fists so tight Betsy believed they would soon weep blood. His nails cutting into the flesh would make stigmata.

The scientists murdered on the buses were decoys.

The real nuclear scientists, far more accomplished than the others, had been in Dr. Shah's employ for a year or more.

Shah had been released, and accelerated work to develop a nuclear weapons program for the Taliban and Al-Qaeda. Certain elements within Pakistan and Russia knew about it.

They'd succeeded in creating at least three bombs, already placed in American cities. And set to go off any day, any moment now.

But they didn't know where. They didn't know when. They didn't know how big.

"Finished?" he asked. When Secretary Adams nodded, he hit a button and Barb Stenhauser appeared. "Tell the Vice President to get herself onto Air Force Two and fly to Cheyenne Mountain in Colorado Springs and await further instructions."

"Yes, Mr. President." Stenhauser looked shocked but disappeared without asking questions.

He turned back to Ellen. "All this came from your son?"

Ellen braced for the innuendo, if not outright accusation: How could Gil know if he wasn't himself in on it? If he hadn't been radicalized while in captivity? He had, everyone knew, converted to Islam. He loved the Middle East, despite what had happened.

How could they possibly trust his information?

"He's a brave man," said Doug Williams. "Please thank him. Now, we need more information."

"I think the Grand Ayatollah was trying to give me some."

"Why would he do that?"

"Because he's looking at succession, at the future of Iran, and he doesn't want it passed out of his hands, to an adversary, or into Russian control. Nor does he want American involvement. But he sees a narrow path forward. Where the cat and rat cooperate."

"Sorry?"

"Never mind. Just a story."

The President was nodding. He didn't need to hear the fable to understand. "If we stop Shah, we both win."

"But Ayatollah Khosravi couldn't be seen to give me the information. I've left my daughter, Katherine, behind, with Charles Boynton, in the hopes I'm right. The Ayatollah had one of my FSOs arrested. Anahita Dahir."

"The one who received the warning message?" The President made a note of her name.

"Yes." No need right now, Ellen thought, to tell him about her family background. "Then he had me ejected from Iran."

"I'll alert our people at the Swiss embassy in Tehran that one of our FSOs is being held illegally."

"No, please don't."

His hand, reaching for the phone, stopped. "Why not?"

"I think the Grand Ayatollah did it so that he could pass the information on to them."

"But why not to you?"

"I'm too conspicuous. He had to get me out of Iran. He knew anyone watching—"

"The Russians—"

"Or the Pakistanis or Shah—would be following me. They'll think I've been humiliated—"

"Well," said Williams, and made a face.

"—and they won't care that my daughter and Boynton have been left behind to try to get the FSO released."

"But you're saying they've been left behind to get the information the Grand Ayatollah wants to pass on. What information?"

"I don't know."

"You don't even know if that's what he has in mind. You're risking a lot, Ellen."

Everything, she thought but didn't say. "There's a lot at stake."

"Boynton," said the President. "Your Chief of Staff. Isn't he the one who lost the battle with the Twinkie?"

"I believe it was a Ho Ho."

"Well, at least no one will suspect him of being a spy. Have they discovered anything?"

Ellen took a breath. "I haven't heard from them in several hours."

Doug Williams bit his upper lip and gave a curt nod. "We need to find out where those bombs are planted. And we need to find out where they're being made."

"Agreed, Mr. President. I don't think General Whitehead will tell you, though I think he knows."

"We'll beat it out of him if we have to."

Ellen, who'd been appalled by the brutality of "enhanced interrogations," now found within herself a deep well of situational ethics. If torture would get the information out of him, might save thousands of lives, then bring it on.

Ellen lowered her eyes to her hands, fingers intertwined, knuckles white, in her lap.

"What is it?" Betsy asked.

Ellen looked up and held her friend's eyes. Betsy gave a small snort of understanding.

"You can't do it, can you. The end doesn't justify the means . . ."

"The end is defined by the means," said Ellen, then looked at Doug Williams. "There are better, faster ways than torture. We know that under torture people will say anything to make it stop. Not necessarily the truth. Besides, Whitehead will hold out too long. We need to search his home. He wouldn't keep that information at his office in the Pentagon, and I doubt he'd keep it on his computer. He'd have notes somewhere in his home."

Williams picked up the phone. "Where's Tim Beecham?"

"At the hospital, sir. His nose has been broken. He should be released soon."

"We don't have time. Send his deputy in here. Now."

"I'd like to go with them," said Ellen, getting up.

"Go," said Williams. "Let me know. I'll get in touch with our allies. See what their intelligence services can pick up about those other scientists working for Shah."

Sirens blaring, the motorcade drove to Bethesda, Ellen checking her phone the whole way.

The dread was almost insupportable. Suppose she never heard? Suppose she'd sent her children to their deaths? And never, ever found out what happened to them?

Maybe she should contact Aziz in Tehran. The Iranian Foreign Minister could send people to Baluchestan, to the caves. To see . . .

But she hesitated.

She needed to give Katherine more time. Contacting Aziz would blow the whole thing.

Instead she forced herself to focus on the job in front of them. Finding the information General Whitehead had hidden away.

"Did he say anything to you?" Ellen asked, for the hundredth time. "Anything at all that could help?"

Betsy had racked her brains. "Nothing except that fucking poetry. And that's no help."

It had been chilling, the way he'd quoted John Donne. Again.

They pulled into the drive of a Cape-style home, with a picket fence and dormers and a wide, sweeping veranda with rocking chairs.

The fact that it looked so typically, almost stereotypically, American made Ellen even angrier. She could feel her bile rising.

Agents pounded on the front door while others swarmed around back.

Just as they were about to knock the door down, a woman answered. Her gray hair was nicely done in a simple but classic cut. She wore slacks and a silk blouse.

Elegant, Ellen thought, but not at all pretentious.

"What is it? What's happening?" she asked. Her tone on the verge of demanding, but not quite. As she was pushed aside, she said, "Where's Bert?"

She looked past them, searching for her husband. Her eyes coming to rest on the American Secretary of State.

She held the collar of a large dog who was looking excited and puzzled. From deeper in the house came the sound of a child crying.

"What's happening?"

"Stand aside," one of the agents said, shoving her.

Ellen nodded to Betsy, who took Mrs. Whitehead's arm and led her in the direction of the crying child.

By now the agents were all over the place. Pulling books from shelves, upending chairs and sofas. Taking paintings off the walls. So that the home, gracious and comfortable moments earlier, was now in disarray. And getting worse.

Betsy followed the General's wife into the kitchen while Ellen found the study, where the Deputy Director of National Intelligence and the senior operatives were searching.

The room was large and bright, with huge windows looking out over the back garden, where a child's homemade swing had been hung. It was a thick wooden plank, with rope attached to the limb of an oak tree.

A football, made for children, sat abandoned on the grass.

The study walls were lined with bookcases, stuffed with volumes and framed photos, all of which were being taken down, examined, then tossed onto the floor.

What the room didn't have were medals or citations.

Just pictures of children and grandchildren. Of Bert Whitehead and his wife. Of buddies. Of comrades.

While the whirlwind swirled around her, Secretary Adams stood against a wall. Wondering.

What made a man do such a thing? Betray his country? Murder fellow citizens? One of the nuclear bombs had almost certainly been placed in DC. Almost certainly in the White House itself.

The President knew it too, which was why he'd sent his VP and senior cabinet, except for Ellen, away. The blast, and the fallout, would be felt for miles. Incinerating, irradiating everything, everyone, in its path.

What had happened to Bert Whitehead? If conspiring with terrorists was the answer, what in the world was the question?

Ellen found Betsy and the others in the kitchen, where Mrs. Whitehead and her daughter were being interrogated.

She listened at the door for a minute or two as the women were peppered with questions from two intelligence agents, while the crying child struggled in its mother's arms.

"Can you leave us, please?" said Ellen.

The agents, annoyed, looked over, then leapt to their feet.

"I'd like to speak with Mrs. Whitehead and her daughter privately."

"We can't do that."

"Do you know who I am?"

"Yes, Madam Secretary."

"Good. I've traveled all night from my son's hospital bed in Frankfurt"—she stretched the truth—"to be here. I think you can give us a few minutes."

They looked at each other, clearly unhappy. But they left.

Before taking a seat, Ellen looked at the crying child, then said to the daughter, "Perhaps you can take him outside. Fresh air."

"Mom?"

Mrs. Whitehead gave a small nod. When the daughter and grandson left, Ellen sat and studied the woman. It was clear that anger was battling fear, was battling confusion.

But Ellen was also perplexed. Mrs. Whitehead looked familiar. Ellen knew her from somewhere.

And then she had it. "It's not Mrs. Whitehead, is it."

She saw Betsy's brows go up, but she remained quiet.

"It is when I'm at home."

"It's Professor Martha Tierney. You teach English lit at Georgetown."

One of the books splayed open on the floor of the study had this woman's face on it. An author photo, albeit from years ago. The book was called *Kings and Desperate Men*, from a poem by John Donne. It was a biography of the metaphysical poet.

"Why does your husband keep quoting, 'When thou hast done, thou hast not done'?"

"'For I have more,'" Professor Tierney finished the line. "It's a play on words. I'm a Donne scholar. That pretty much makes Bert a Donne scholar too. I guess he likes that quote."

"Yes, but why?"

"I don't know. I've never heard him mention it. You're not here to discuss poetry, Madame Secretary. Tell me what's happening. Where's my husband?"

"So if close proximity to you for years made him a Donne scholar," said Ellen, "does that make you a security expert?"

"I want a lawyer," said Professor Tierney. "And I want to speak to Bert."

"I'm not a cop and you're not under arrest. I'm asking you to help us. To help your country."

"Then I need to know what this is about."

"No. You need to answer our questions." Ellen lowered her voice and her tone. "I know this is a shock. I know it's frightening. Just please, tell us what we need to know."

Professor Tierney paused, then nodded. "I'll help in any way I can. Just tell me, is Bert all right?"

"Has your husband ever mentioned Bashir Shah?"

"The arms dealer. Yes. Just the other day. He was ranting about him being released from house arrest."

"He told you that?" said Ellen.

"Is it a state secret?" asked Professor Tierney.

Ellen considered. "No, I suppose not."

"No. Bert has never, would never, tell me anything that was."

"So he was surprised by Shah's release?"

"Shocked. And angrier than I've seen him in a long time."

Ellen felt herself tempted to believe it, but of course, that's what these people, these traitors, traded on. People's willingness to believe the worst, but to dismiss the catastrophic.

If General Whitehead was angry, it wasn't because Shah was free, but because they'd found out.

"Where does your husband keep his private papers?" asked Ellen.

After a slight pause, Professor Tierney said, "There's a safe behind the bookcase closest to the study door."

Ellen was on her feet. "The combination?"

"Let me come. I'll open it."

"No. We need the combination."

The two women stared at each other, and finally the professor gave it to her and explained, "It's the dates of our children's birthdays."

Ellen left and returned a few minutes later. "Let's go," she said to Betsy.

Once in the car, on their way back to DC, Betsy asked, "So? What was in the safe?"

"Nothing except birth certificates for the kids. They'll be analyzed in case there's something hidden in them, but . . ."

Betsy noticed that Ellen hadn't come away empty-handed. She clutched Professor Tierney's book.

Kings and Desperate Men.

And women, thought Betsy.

It was only once across the border into Pakistan that Gil found a signal. Pulling over, he quickly typed a message to his mother.

It wasn't safe to be in a vehicle stopped on the side of the road, so he didn't dawdle. After sending it off, he headed to the airport, still several hours away.

"I'll go," said Anahita.

"I'll go with you," said Zahara. "My father. I have to . . ."

They were at the car Farhad had used to drive them there. But the keys were nowhere to be found. Still with him, they realized.

Katherine, having lost her own father suddenly, understood. She gave a brief nod. "Go, but hurry back. God knows who else is headed here. Someone obviously told the Russians about this meeting."

"Farhad," said Boynton. "He was playing all sides."

Katherine gave Anahita the gun that Boynton had taken from the dead man. "Hurry."

The cousins, so much alike in shape and movement, scrambled up the slope together to the cave entrance. Once in, they ran through the now familiar passages, toward the glow from the broken lanterns.

They hadn't gotten very far when Zahara slowed to a stop and lifted her hand. Ana stood beside her. Tense. Every sense vibrating.

And then she heard it too.

Voices. Russian voices.

"Shit," she muttered. "Fuck, fuck, fuck."

She looked behind her, toward the cave entrance. Then back toward the slight glow and angry brutish voices.

There was no choice. They needed those keys.

Crouching down, Ana inched toward the open cavern. Dark and distorted shadows moved about in the passage on the far side of the cavern. She looked at Zahara, who was staring at the body of her father. He was lying where he'd fallen, partly hidden behind the boulders.

"Go," Ana whispered. "But be quick."

She wasn't sure what Zahara had to do, and now wasn't the time to discuss it.

On her belly, Ana slithered to Farhad's body and, forcing herself to look, she patted him down and found the keys.

Carefully, carefully, carefully she withdrew them, trying not to make a sound.

Clutching the keys tight in her fist, she glanced toward Zahara just as her cousin kissed her father on the forehead, then backed away on her hands and knees.

They'd gotten as far as the entrance to the passageway that would take them back out when there was a shout. And a flashlight beam hit them.

The cousins turned and ran. Not looking back. Not bothering to hide. They sprinted down the passage toward where the sun shone through the narrow opening, like the blade of a knife.

They could hear boots behind them, and shouted orders.

Squeezing through, Ana shouted to Katherine and Boynton, "There're more. They've seen us."

"They're coming," shouted Zahara, scrambling and sliding down the slope.

Katherine ran to meet them, grabbing the keys from Anahita. "Get in!"

They did not need to be coaxed. As the vehicle started, there were shots. Ana rolled down the window and fired back. Wildly. She'd never held a handgun, let alone fired one. But it was enough to make the two men at the cave entrance duck.

Katherine hit the gas and they took off. When Ana looked back, the men had disappeared.

But not for long, she knew. Katherine knew. They all knew.

They would be after them.

Boynton had found old maps littering the back seat, and was trying to figure out where they were and where they were going.

"My phone's out of power," said Katherine, struggling to keep the old car from skidding off the road. "We need to let Mom know what Farhad said about Shah's physicists. Charles?"

"I'm on it," said Boynton, fighting to get the map out of his way. Zahara grabbed it as the car shimmied and bounced.

Charles's phone was in the red. Three minutes of power left.

He wrote quickly but took precious moments to make sure there were no typos. Now was not the time to make mistakes.

He hit send and exhaled.

"Where do we go?" asked Ana.

In the distance, a cloud of dust was pursuing them. The vehicle was silent. They barely knew where they were, never mind where they could go.

"Pull over, please," said Ellen, and the Diplomatic Security agent at the wheel did.

"Madame Secretary?" asked Steve, in the front passenger seat, turning to look at her.

But she was quiet, reading and rereading the two messages that had come in almost simultaneously.

First Gil's, from that Akbar's phone, saying he was heading home to DC via Frankfurt.

Then one from Charles Boynton.

Ellen inhaled deeply, then leaned forward and spoke to the driver. "We need to get to the White House. As fast as you can."

"Right."

The siren was put on, and, lights flashing, they sped through the streets.

"El?" said Betsy. "What is it?"

"Katherine and Boynton got the information. We know where the bombs are being made."

"Oh, thank God. Do we know where they've been placed? Which cities?"

"No, but we will once we raid the factory. Gil wrote too. He's heading back here. I've told him not to."

Betsy nodded and tried to look like her hair wasn't on fire. "At least they're safe."

"Well . . . ," said Ellen. It was clear from Charles's message that they were far from safe. "Can you look up cave art of Saravan? It's in Sistan-Baluchestan Province in Iran."

While Betsy did, she asked, "Why?"

"Because I sent Katherine and Boynton there."

"To get them out of danger?"

"Not exactly." When Betsy had the map of that part of Iran up on her phone, Ellen looked, tracing a line across the border between Iran and Pakistan. Then she shot off a message to her son.

Gil heard the ping and pulled over to read the reply from his mother.

Then he did a quick map search. "Shit."

He considered for just a moment, then sent his reply.

Ellen could see the dome of the Capitol Building when Gil's message arrived.

She forwarded it to Boynton, with a few words added herself. Then she threw herself back in the seat and thought.

There was one minute of power left on Boynton's phone when the message from his boss appeared.

"Pen, paper, quickly," he said, and, grabbing the map from Zahara, he scribbled a few words before his phone died completely.

"Pakistan," he said to the others. "We need to get to Pakistan."

"Are you insane?" said Zahara. "I'm Iranian. They'll probably kill us."

"They certainly will," said Ana, gesturing toward the dust cloud following them, as though the Tasmanian Devil were in pursuit.

Charles leaned forward and spoke to Katherine. "Your brother's in Pakistan. He can meet us. He has friends and contacts there. I have the name of the town. It's not far from the border. We just have to get across."

Katherine glanced in the rearview mirror. The whirlwind was getting closer.

While Zahara and Anahita tried to work out the best way to the border, Charles Boynton sat back and stared ahead.

Something had been bothering him. Something that he'd forgotten. And then he remembered. Quickly pulling his phone out, he clicked and clicked, but there was no juice left. It was dead.

He'd forgotten to tell Secretary Adams what Farhad had sputtered with his last breath.

White House.

CHAPTER 33

Ellen and Betsy were barely through the door to the Oval Office before President Williams said, "Did you find anything?"

"Not at Whitehead's house, but Katherine and Charles Boynton have found out where Shah has installed the physicists. They're pretty sure we'll also find information there about where the bombs are hidden."

"Thank God. Where is this place?"

"In Pakistan, close to the Afghan border." She gave him the specific information.

"That should be easy enough to find," he said. "An abandoned cement factory in the Bajaur District of Pakistan, just outside Kitkot," he repeated, double-checking that he had it right. When Ellen nodded, he hit the intercom. "Get General Whitehead in here—"

Then stopped himself.

"Sir, the General—" Stenhauser said.

"Yes, I forgot. Tell the Commander of US Special Forces Command to meet me in the Situation Room. Now. And tell Tim Beecham to be there too. Is he out of the hospital?"

"I just had a message from him, Mr. President. He's on his way to London for that meeting of the intelligence services. Should I recall him?"

"No," said Ellen, and when President Williams looked at her, she said, "It's important he be at those talks."

Williams narrowed his eyes, but said into the intercom, "No, Barb. Let him go." Then he collected papers from his desk and said, "Come with me."

"I'm sorry, Mr. President, but I want your permission to go to Pakistan to meet with the Prime Minister. I think it's time we had it out."

"Like you and the Iranians had it out, Ellen?"

"We got the information."

"You also got one of your FSOs arrested and yourself expelled from the country."

"We got the information," she repeated. "It wasn't pretty, it wasn't conventional, but we got it."

"But can we trust it?"

"Are you asking if we can trust my daughter?"

"For God's sake, Ellen, let it go. I fucked up with Gil. I'm sorry. I should've stepped in to get him released from his kidnappers."

Ellen waited for more.

All those months, days, hours, minutes. Every excruciating second she'd braced for the news her son had been beheaded. To see it. To see it. No matter how she might try to avoid it, the images would have been on every front page, every newscast. Every website.

Gil's mother would have been forever blinded by that sight. The image would have floated in front of everything else she'd ever see for the rest of her life.

And the man who could have saved Gil that agony, could have saved her, was *sorry*?

She didn't trust herself to speak. Instead she stood in the Oval Office, trying to catch her breath. Staring at the President of the United States. And wanting to hurt him. As he'd hurt her son. Hurt her.

"Imagine," she finally said, "your son had been beheaded."

"But Gil wasn't."

"He was, every night and every day, in my mind."

Doug Williams hadn't considered that, and now an image appeared. Of his own son, kneeling on the ground. Filthy. Frightened. The long blade at his throat.

Williams gasped and stared at Ellen, holding her eyes. Long, long seconds passed before he whispered. "I'm sorry."

And this time, she could see, he meant it. It wasn't an expedient political apology, meant to make a minor mistake go away. The words were wrung from someplace deep down.

He was sorry.

He knew enough not to ask for her forgiveness. It would never be given, nor should it be.

"Ellen, I'm not doubting your son or daughter, but I am questioning their sources."

"People have given their lives to get us that information. It's all we have. We have to go with it. I need to get to Islamabad, and I need to arrive with all the pomp, all the displays of power we can muster. If nothing else, I need to be a distraction while you plan and carry out the raid."

"I don't even want to know what you mean by 'distraction,'" said the President as they hurried down the wide hallway, Ellen running to keep pace with his long strides.

"But . . . ," she said.

Williams stopped, turned, and looked at her. "What is it now?"

She took a deep breath. "I want to stop and see Eric Dunn on the way."

"In Florida? Why?"

"To find out what he knows."

"You think the former President is behind this?" demanded Williams. "Look, I have no respect for the man, but I can't imagine he'd actually allow nuclear devices to be detonated in American cities."

"Neither do I, but he might know something, even without realizing it."

Betsy, listening to this, was reminded of the famous line about President Reagan during the Iran-Contra hearings.

What didn't he know, and when did he know he didn't know it?

What Eric Dunn didn't know would fill archives.

Once they had Williams's consent and were heading to Air Force Three, Betsy looked at the book Ellen still had with her.

Professor Tierney's *Kings and Desperate Men*. The biography of John Donne.

Betsy sat back in the seat and thought of the confrontation to come. *When thou hast Dunn*, she thought, *thou hast not Dunn . . .*

She was propelled forward as though shoved from behind.

"Jesus, El, that's what Whitehead was saying. What he's been saying all along. 'Dunn.' Not 'done.' A play on words. John Donne was doing it. And so was Whitehead. That's why you have the book, that's why we're going to see Eric Dunn. Because Bert Whitehead is telling us to."

"Yes."

"But it must be some trick. He wants us to waste our time. Eric Dunn either knows nothing, or he knows something but would never tell us. Whitehead is messing with us, trying to get into our heads. A bit of psychological warfare."

"Maybe," said Ellen. She leaned forward and asked her security agents to take a detour, to Tim Beecham's home in Georgetown.

"Didn't they say he was on his way to London?" asked Betsy.

"Yes," said Ellen, and left it at that.

Once there, the housekeeper confirmed that he was away, and Mrs. Beecham and their two teenaged sons had left for their vacation home in Utah.

Just as their plane took off for Florida, she asked Betsy, "Why is Bert Whitehead still in DC?"

"Well, he's being held in an interview room in the White House against his will. Maybe that's why."

"And why is Tim Beecham not here?"

"Because he has a meeting of intelligence chiefs in London, to get more intel. You yourself said it was important he be there."

"And it is."

"What're you thinking?" Betsy asked.

But Ellen didn't answer. She was deep in thought. Lost in thought.

Once at cruising altitude, the console on Ellen's desk buzzed with an incoming, encrypted message. The President was on video. Ellen tapped the screen in front of her, and Doug Williams's face appeared.

She looked at Betsy, who smiled and left the compartment. This was top secret. Not even the Secretary of State's counselor could be in on it.

"I'm here, Mr. President," said Ellen.

"Good. We're assembled." President Williams nodded to the Generals around the table.

And so began the most important meeting of any of their lives.

How to get American Special Forces into that abandoned cement factory to stop production of nuclear weapons and, most crucially, find out where they'd already been placed.

For what felt like the hundredth time that day, an assault rifle was leveled at Katherine Adams.

And she realized it was no longer shocking.

For the last twenty-five kilometers, as they'd raced for the border between Iran and Pakistan, Katherine had rehearsed what to say. She and the others, especially Charles, had discussed it.

How to get across. And how to make sure their pursuers did not.

"You claim to be the daughter of the American Secretary of State?" said the Pakistani border guard.

Anahita translated, and Katherine nodded. He had her passport, along with Boynton's. The others did not have passports, or documents of any sort.

For reasons Katherine didn't bother to think too much about, the Pakistani border guard considered their passports far more suspicious than the others' lack of any documentation.

"Why are you crossing into Pakistan? What is your purpose?"

"Safety," said Boynton. "I know your Prime Minister would be very angry to learn that the daughter and Chief of Staff of the American Secretary of State were hurt or killed because you didn't let us in. It would be a political and personal nightmare. For him, and for you."

"But," said Katherine, to the now confused and agitated guard, "can you imagine, when we tell him how you saved our lives, how pleased he'll be with you? What's your name?"

Anahita wrote it down.

Boynton pointed to the approaching dust cloud. "That vehicle is filled with members of the Russian mafia. Those are the ones you need to stop. America is your ally, Russia is not."

The other guard appeared from the hut and showed his colleague a phone. Whatever was on it seemed to confirm their identities.

Charles Boynton stared at the phone, tempted to ask if he could borrow it. The more he thought about it, the more crucial it became to tell Secretary Adams about Farhad's final words, coughed out as though written in blood.

White House.

But even if the Pakistani guard would give him his phone, Boynton could not possibly use it to send a message to the American Secretary of State's private and secure cell. Though Charles continued to stare at it as though it were a rib steak, and he a starving man.

"And them?" The guard pointed his gun at Anahita and Zahara. "Iran is not our friend. These people have no documents. I can't let them cross."

This was the danger. That the guards would agree to let in Katherine and Boynton, but not the others.

"Well, since they have no documents," said Katherine, "how do you know they're not Pakistani?"

"They're not."

"They might be. Look, we won't leave without our friends, so make your decision. Are they Iranian or Pakistani? Do we get across and you're a hero? Or do you turn us away and you're in a world of trouble?"

"They have assigned us to an outpost along the border with Iran, madame," said the new guard, in good English, handing them back their passports. "How much worse could it get?"

"You have a border with Afghanistan, do you not?" said Charles. "That can't be a picnic."

He shrugged. "You'd be surprised." But he could see they would not be. "Are you bringing in any alcohol? Any tobacco?" They shook their heads. "Any firearms?"

He looked directly at the gun in Ana's lap.

They shook their heads, and he waved them through. Not out of love for the US, but fear of his own Prime Minister. And the Afghan border.

As they pulled away, they heard him mutter, "Fucking Americans." But it was without rancor, and almost with admiration. Almost.

Katherine didn't care.

This region, in fact the entire arbitrary border, was a cauldron of factions, of tribal loyalties. Of grievances centuries old. Of mixed, divided, complex allegiances. Almost none of them to the US. But neither were they fans of Russia.

Katherine gunned the car, and as they rounded the corner, she saw, in the rearview mirror, the storm cloud arrive at the border.

Soft mutterings came from the back seat.

Zahara held a string of prayer beads, and with each bead she murmured, *"Alhamdulillah."*

Anahita joined in.

The beads were worn and slightly shiny, from Dr. Ahmadi's fingers repeating the prayer many times a day all his life. Zahara had risked her life to get them. A vestige of a man she loved. Despite what he'd done. One horrible thing did not wipe out a lifetime of devotion.

"Alhamdulillah."

As they raced through the small towns and villages, toward the rendezvous with Gil, first Boynton, then Katherine joined in until the filthy shitbox of a car was filled with the softly muttered word, repeated. Over and over. Bringing with it something close to calm.

Alhamdulillah.

All thanks and praises be to Allah.

Thank God, thought Katherine. Now they just had to find Gil.

Ellen watched as the head of Special Forces bent over a 3-D topographical map of the Bajaur region of Pakistan. He expertly swept it around, exploring, manipulating, searching.

"Back in 2008, there was a battle of Bajaur." He zoomed in and moved on. "Pakistani forces fought to dislodge the Taliban from the region. Eventually they won, driving them out. But it was brutal. The Pakistanis fought bravely, relentlessly. I'm sorry to hear the Taliban are back." He looked up and met the President's eyes. "We had advisors there at the time. Intelligence and military. Bert Whitehead was one of them. He was a Colonel then. He knows the region. He should be here, Mr. President."

"General Whitehead is needed elsewhere," said President Williams.

Looks were exchanged between the military men and women in the room. They'd clearly heard the rumors.

"So it's true?" one of them said.

"Move on," said President Williams. "We need to get to that factory. How do we do it?"

Is that where it had begun? Ellen wondered. Had a hairline fracture formed in Colonel Whitehead's beliefs as the brutal fighting swirled in the mountains and valleys and caves?

As the years went by, had he seen too much? Been forced to do too much? Been forced to be silent as acts he found repulsive were committed?

Had he seen too many young men and women die, while others profited? Had the crack in Colonel Whitehead spread slowly, over time, until it became a chasm in General Whitehead?

Taking out her phone, she looked up the Battle of Bajaur and saw it had been called Operation Lion Heart.

Had the lion escaped the trap, but left his heart behind?

Putting down her phone, she focused on what was happening back in DC, in the Situation Room. She was no expert in military tactics. Her job would be to smooth things over once it became clear to the Pakistanis that the US had conducted a covert military operation inside their borders, without permission, and captured, maybe killed, Pakistani citizens.

With luck, she thought, Bashir Shah would be among the dead. But she doubted it. How do you kill an Azhi Dahaka?

She focused on the map, on the rugged, near-impenetrable terrain. Where she and President Williams saw villages and mountain ranges and rivers, the generals saw something else. They saw opportunities and death traps. They saw landing sites for choppers and paratroopers. And they saw how those troops would be cut down before their boots hit the ground.

"This's going to take some time, Mr. President," said the ranking general.

"Well, we don't have time." Williams looked at Secretary Adams on the screen. She nodded. It had to be done.

"I told you that terrorists are using that factory to create a nuclear program for the Taliban," he said. "But there's something else."

For I have more, thought Ellen.

"We have intelligence that says they've built three devices and have placed them in American cities."

The generals, who'd up until then been bending over the map, stood up as one and stared. Unable to speak for a moment.

It felt like a gorge had now opened, separating those in the room from the rest of the world. An uncrossable space from not knowing to knowing.

"We have to get into that factory," said President Williams. "To stop the scientists, but mostly, right now, to find out where those bombs are hidden."

"I need to call my wife," said one officer, making for the door. "Get her and the children out of DC."

"My husband and daughters," said another, also making for the door.

Williams nodded to the officers at the door, who took a step in front of it.

"No one leaves until we have a plan. We have one shot, and we need to take it in the next few hours."

Ellen watched this, her mind racing. She tried to slow it down, knowing where it was heading and not liking it at all.

She'd been halfway there already, but had been too frightened to go the rest of the way. But now she did.

"Madame Secretary," came the pilot's voice over the speaker. "We have permission from Palm Beach International to land.

We'll be on the ground in seven minutes. I'll need to cut communications."

"No," she snapped before regulating her tone. "I'm sorry, but no. I need more time. If you have to, circle again."

"I can't. I don't have clearance from air traffic con—"

"Then get it. I need five more minutes."

There was a pause. "You have it."

As Air Force Three banked and turned, Ellen spoke for the first time in the meeting.

"Mr. President, I need to speak to you. Privately."

"We're in the middle—"

"Please. Now."

After getting off the call with the President, and letting the pilot know she could land, Ellen looked out at the palm trees and the ocean sparkling in the bright sunshine, and thought of the rustic swing and the football. And the photographs. And the white picket fence.

And she thought of the mothers and fathers at the barrier in Frankfurt, holding photos of their missing children. While staring at the flat, flapping red blankets on the asphalt.

She thought of Katherine and Gil, somewhere in Pakistan.

Ellen Adams thought of kings and desperate men. And wondered if she'd just made the worst mistake of her life. Of anybody's life.

CHAPTER 34

Secretary Adams's motorcade arrived at the tall gold gates at the front of Eric Dunn's Florida estate.

Even though he knew they were coming, even though his private security could see their motorcade arriving down the long, long drive, still they were made to wait.

Secretary Adams smiled and was cordial when the security guards, essentially Dunn's private militia, asked for her identification. And took their time returning it. Unnoticed by Dunn's people, Ellen's knee was bouncing up and down while Betsy went through her treasury of swear words.

Steve Kowalski, Ellen's head of Diplomatic Security, a longtime veteran of the service, turned in the front seat to look at Mrs. Cleaver as she combined and conjugated words that should never, really, have conjugal relations. The ensuing progeny was both grotesque and hilarious, as she turned nouns into verbs, and verbs into something else entirely. It was a display of linguistic gymnastics the agent hadn't thought possible. And he'd been a marine.

It was clear that while he admired Secretary Adams, he adored her counselor.

On the drive from the airport to the gates, they'd watched a news conference Eric Dunn had given while they'd been on the plane. He'd called it knowing they were on their way.

The sole purpose appeared to be to throw filth all over Secretary Adams's son. Not just implying but actually accusing Gil Bahar of being involved in the bombings in London, Paris, and Frankfurt. Of being radicalized. Of whispering in his mother's ear, and perhaps even turning the Secretary of State against the US. A country, he shouted and gestured, now weakened by the change of government. A country where the radicals, the socialists, the terrorists, the abortionists, the traitors and morons were in charge.

"You can go in now," said the guard. He wore an insignia Ellen recognized from their reports on the alt-right.

"Is the Secret Service no longer in charge of the former President's security?" Ellen asked as the SUV drove the rest of the way toward the home that looked like a castle.

"Supposedly they are," said Agent Kowalski. "But he's put his own people on the front line. He thinks the Secret Service is part of the Deep State."

"Well, if that means profoundly loyal to the United States and the position of President but not the individual, then he's right," said Ellen.

Before going in, she checked her phone again. No message from Katherine or Gil or Boynton. No message from the President.

Handing her phone to the head of her security detail, she got out of the car; then she and Betsy stood at the huge double doors and waited for them to open.

And waited. And waited.

The bartender watched with dismay as Pete Hamilton once again made his way across the dim room, to take a stool at the Off the Record bar.

"I thought I told you not to return," he said as Pete sat down.

But there was something different about the young man. He

looked less dissipated. His eyes brighter. His clothes cleaner. His hair unmatted.

"What happened to you?" the bartender asked.

"What d'you mean?"

The bartender cocked his head at Pete and realized, to his surprise, that he cared about this young man. Four years of watching the slow, aching decline did that. He felt bad for the kid.

Politics at any level could be brutal. Here, in DC? It was merciless. And this kid had been pilloried. Run through and placed on a spit to burn.

But now, unexpectedly and suddenly, Pete Hamilton seemed whole again. Healthy again. After only a day. Amazing what a shower and clean clothes could do.

The bartender had been at his job for far too long to be fooled. This was a veneer, nothing more.

"I'll have a scotch," said Pete.

"You'll have sparkling water," said the bartender. He plopped a wedge of lime in and placed the tall glass on a coaster with Secretary Adams's caricature.

Pete smiled and looked around.

No one paid any attention to him. He knew it might be a mistake to be there; he'd been told to go straight home, and he had more work to do tracking down evidence against Whitehead and any of his accomplices in the White House.

But he wanted to hear what was being said, here in the bowels of power.

Not surprisingly, the main topic, the only topic, was Bert Whitehead and the rampant rumors that the Chair of the Joint Chiefs had been arrested.

It was unclear on what charge.

The largest group of patrons was clustered around a young woman who'd just arrived. Someone Pete hadn't seen in the bar before but now recognized from those moments earlier in the day, waiting to enter the Oval Office. She was the assistant to President Williams's Chief of Staff.

She caught his eye and smiled brightly. He smiled back. Maybe, he thought, picking up his glass and wandering over, this might be his lucky day.

It never occurred to him to wonder why, in the midst of the greatest crisis facing the nation, Barb Stenhauser's assistant would be in the bar.

It never occurred to him to wonder if maybe, maybe, she'd followed him there.

It never occurred to him that this could be a very, very unlucky day.

President Williams had left the Situation Room, then returned half an hour later after holding a prescheduled news conference.

He knew if he canceled it would look strange. The news conference had only lasted ten minutes. He'd spent the rest of the time doing something else.

There had been a few questions from the journalists about General Whitehead, but they were vague. The storm clouds were gathering, but so far nothing had broken. There were only distant rumblings.

"What've you got?" Williams asked after rejoining the generals around the map.

They had, by then, come up with two plans.

"We don't have confidence in either of them, sir," said the head of Special Forces. "But they're the best we can come up with on short notice. If we had more time . . ."

"We don't," said Williams. "In fact, we have less and less time." He listened to their suggestions. "What're the chances of success?"

"We estimate 20 percent for the first plan and 12 for the second. If the Taliban is as well entrenched as reported, it's a near certainty that our team won't even make it to the ground."

"We could bomb the hell out of the factory, though," said one of the generals.

"It's tempting," admitted the President. "But if there are other bombs, we'd risk setting them off. And we'd destroy any information they have on where in the US the nukes have been placed. That's the priority right now."

"Is there no other way to get the information?"

"If there was, we'd be doing it." The President leaned over the map. "Maybe this is foolish, but I'm seeing another possibility. Suppose we put down here—" He pointed to a place the generals hadn't considered.

"The area's too rugged," said one of the generals.

"But there is a plateau. Just big enough to land a couple helicopters."

"How do you know there's a plateau?" one asked, leaning closer.

"I can see it." President Williams manipulated the 3-D image to zoom in. Sure enough, there was a flat area. Not large, but there.

"I'm sorry, Mr. President, but what good would that do? It's ten kilometers from the factory. They'd never make it there."

"They're not supposed to. They're a diversion. We can support them with air strikes, so they keep the Taliban fighters busy, while the real force drops onto the factory."

They stared at him as though he'd lost his mind.

"But that's insane," said the Vice Chair of the Joint Chiefs. "They'd be cut down immediately."

"Not if we create a diversion. If the Taliban is occupied somewhere else. That's possible, isn't it?" His eyes searching theirs. "In the hours before the raid, we spread rumors through our network of informants that we've heard of the Taliban presence in the area, and we might be planning an assault. That will get their attention. The raid would be far enough away that they won't suspect the factory is the real target, but still in the heart of Taliban-controlled territory, so it's believable. In fact, I'll speak with Prime Minister Bellington in the UK. Make it sound like it's an SAS assault in retaliation for the bombings. It's believable and gets the focus away from us."

He looked at them as they looked at each other.

"Is it possible?" he asked.

There was silence.

"Is it possible!" he shouted.

"Give us half an hour, Mr. President," said the acting Chair.

"You have twenty minutes." Williams made for the door. "And then I want the Special Forces in the air. While they're on their way, you can work out the details."

Once out the door, he leaned against it, closed his eyes, and brought his hands to his face muttering, "What have I done?"

"Kings and desperate men," whispered Betsy as they walked through the vast entrance hall, gawking at what would have been splendid had it been an actual palace and not a monument to overcompensation.

"The President is waiting for you on the terrace," said his personal assistant.

There was actually a series of terraces, Italianate in design, leading down to an Olympic-size pool, with a fountain in the middle. Making it both impressive and useless for actual swimming.

All this was surrounded by manicured lawns and gardens. And, at the very end of the property, the ocean. And, beyond that, nothing . . .

The world ended for Eric Dunn, Ellen suspected, where his own property ended. Nothing mattered beyond his sphere of influence.

Which remained, she needed to admit, surprisingly large.

She had to get this meeting over with quickly, but knew if she gave him that impression, he would prolong it.

"Mrs. Adams," he said, getting up and coming toward her, his hand out.

He was large. Immense in fact. Ellen had met him many times, though only in passing at social events. She'd found him amusing, charming even. Though uninterested in others and easily bored when the spotlight shifted to anyone else.

She'd had her media outlets do profiles on Eric Dunn as his empire had grown, then crumbled, then rose again. Each time more audacious. More bloated. More fragile.

Like a bubble in the bath, it was ready to burst at any moment and release a stink.

And then, unexpectedly, he'd turned to politics and won the highest office in the land. But not, she knew, without help from people and foreign governments who planned to profit from it. And had.

It was the strong shadow that accompanied the bright light of democracy. People were free to abuse their freedoms.

"And who's this little lady?" Dunn asked, turning to Betsy. "Your secretary? Your partner? I'm open-minded, as long as you don't do it in public and scare the horses."

While he laughed, Ellen made a guttural sound, warning Betsy not to react. It just fed this hollow man.

Ellen introduced Betsy Jameson, her lifelong friend and counselor.

"And what do you counsel Mrs. Adams to do?" he asked, waving them to chairs already set out.

"Secretary Adams makes up her own mind," said Betsy, her voice so sweet it terrified Ellen. "I'm just there for the sex."

Ellen blinked and thought, *God, if you're listening, take me now.* There was a pause before Eric Dunn started laughing.

"OK, Ellen, what can I do for you?" he said, reverting to his hail-fellow-well-met persona. "Nothing to do with the explosions, I hope. That's Europe's problem, not ours."

"Some intelligence has come our way that is . . . disturbing."

"More shit on me?" he asked. "Don't believe it. Fake news."

Ellen was sorely tempted to mention the crap he'd just smeared all over her son, but knew that was exactly what he wanted. Instead she pretended, to herself and him, that she hadn't seen it.

"Not directly, no. But what can you tell us about General Whitehead?"

"Bert?" Dunn shrugged. "I never had much use for him, but he did as he was told. All my generals did."

Did he say that to provoke her into pointing out they were not actually his generals? Or did he believe it?

"Is it possible he was doing more than he was told?"

Dunn shook his head. "No way. Nothing happened in my administration without my knowing, without my approval."

Well, that statement's going to come back to bite him in the ass, thought Betsy.

"Why did you agree to the release of Dr. Shah from house arrest?" Ellen asked.

He leaned back and his chair creaked. "Ahhh, so that's it. He told me you'd be asking."

"He?" said Ellen. "General Whitehead?"

"No, Bashir."

While Ellen could control her tongue, she could not control her blood flow. Now it raced from her face to her core. Regrouping there, amassing there, and leaving her face deathly pale.

"Shah?" she asked.

"Bashir, yes. He told me you'd be annoyed."

Ellen held her tongue until she could talk civilly. "You spoke to him?"

"Sure. Why not. He wanted to show his gratitude for my help. He's a genius and an entrepreneur. We have a lot in common. Look, haven't you done enough damage to him? He's a Pakistani businessman wrongly accused by, among other places, your media organization of being an arms dealer. He explained it all to me. The Pakistanis explained it. Your problem is that you confuse nuclear energy with nuclear weapons."

Betsy mumbled something barely audible.

Dunn turned to her, his face suddenly suffused with blood. The bubble about to surface and burst.

"What did you just say?"

"I called you . . . astute."

Dunn continued to glare at her, then turned back to Ellen.

She almost leaned away. There was no denying the force of this man. Ellen had never experienced anyone, anything, like it.

Most successful politicians had charisma. But this went way beyond that. To be in his orbit was to experience something extraordinary. There was a pull, a promise of excitement. Of danger. Like juggling grenades.

It was exhilarating. And terrifying. Even she could feel it.

Ellen Adams was in no way attracted to this; in fact, she was repulsed. But she had to admit that Eric Dunn possessed a powerful magnetism and animal instinct. He had a genius for finding people's weaknesses. For bending them to his will. And if they didn't bend, he would break them.

He was dreadful and dangerous.

But she would not back away. She would not run for cover.

She would not bend. And she sure as hell would not break.

"Who in your administration suggested getting Dr. Shah released from house arrest?"

"No one. It was my idea. I'd met with the Pakistanis privately at a summit, to do damage control. It came up then. They were complaining about the interference of the previous administration and saying how relieved they were to have someone in power who knew how to lead. They'd had a terrible time with the last president. Weak and stupid. They mentioned Dr. Shah. He's a hero in Pakistan, but the then President listened to bad advice and forced the Pakistanis to arrest him. It's caused huge damage to relations. So I fixed it."

"By agreeing to the release of Dr. Shah."

"Have you met him? He's sophisticated, intelligent. He's not what you think."

As tempting as it was to argue, she did not. Nor did she ask how Shah showed his gratitude. She didn't have to.

"Where is Dr. Shah now?" she asked instead.

"Well, I was supposed to have lunch with him yesterday, but he canceled."

"I'm sorry?"

"I know, can you believe it? Canceled. On me."

"He was here? In the US?"

"Yes. Has been since January. I arranged for him to stay at the home of a friend, not far from here."

"He had a visa to enter the US?"

"I guess. I flew him over just before moving here myself."

"Can you give me the address?"

"He's not there anymore, if you thought you'd drop in. Left yesterday."

"For where?"

"Not a clue."

Ellen shot a glance at Betsy, warning her not to rise to that lobbed ball. But Betsy was staring, appalled, and in no mood or condition to indulge her personal feelings. Instead she glanced down at her phone, where a flagged message had come in from Pete Hamilton.

HLI

It was clearly a typo, so Betsy replied with a question mark, then returned to the conversation.

"Mr. President," Ellen was saying, "if you know, or know of anyone who does know, where Dr. Shah is, tell me. Now."

Her tone actually stopped Eric Dunn. His face became suddenly serious. His brows drawn together as he studied her.

"What is it?"

"We think Dr. Shah's involved in a plot to give Al-Qaeda nuclear weapons." It was as far as she would go.

Dunn stared at her, and for a moment she thought she'd shocked him into actually helping. But then he began to laugh.

"Perfect. He said you'd say that. You're paranoid. He told me if you did say that to ask how you liked the flowers. I have no idea what that means. He sent you flowers? Must be love."

In the silence all Ellen could hear was her own breathing. Then she got up.

"Thank you for your time." She held out her hand, and when he took it, she yanked and pulled the immense man right up to her, so that their noses were touching and she smelled his breath. It smelled of meat.

She whispered, "I think under all that greed and stupidity you actually love your country. If Al-Qaeda does have a bomb, they'll use it here, on American soil."

She pulled back and stared at his now slack face before continuing.

"You've made it clear time and again that nothing happened in the White House without your approval. You might want to either rethink that claim or help us stop this. If there is a disaster, it will be dumped at your big gold door. I'll make sure of that. If you know where Shah is, you need to tell us."

She saw fear in his eyes. Fear of the impending disaster, or being blamed for it? Ellen didn't know and didn't care.

"Tell us. Now," she demanded.

"I can tell you where he stayed. I'll have my assistant give you the address. But that's all."

But she knew that was almost certainly not all.

"For I have more . . ."

"General Whitehead. What role did he play in the release of Shah?"

"Is he trying to take credit? It was my idea."

Ellen stared at him. He couldn't help taking credit, even for a catastrophe.

Secretary Adams and Betsy Jameson waited in the entrance hall for Dunn's assistant to give them the address of Shah's villa in Palm Beach. When she arrived, she handed Ellen the slip of paper saying, "I hope you know that President Dunn is a great man."

Ellen almost asked if he'd told her to say that, but instead she said, "Perhaps. It's a shame he's not a good one."

Interestingly, the young woman did not argue with her.

When they were back in the SUV, Betsy nodded toward the paper in Ellen's hand.

"Are we going there?"

"No, we're going to Pakistan." She asked for her phone and sent the address Dunn's assistant had given them to President Williams, who would, she knew, order immediate action.

"Mr. President." The crisp businesslike voice of the UK Prime Minister came down the secure line. "What can I do for you?"

"Jack, I'm glad you asked. I need to spread the rumor that your SAS is planning an assault on Al-Qaeda–controlled Pakistan, in retaliation for the bombings."

There was a pause.

To his credit, the UK PM did not immediately hang up.

Williams clutched the phone, hand tightening. Knuckles bloodless.

"What are you up to, Doug?"

"Best not to know. But we need your help."

"You know this could put my country in the crosshairs of every terrorist."

"I'm not asking you to do it, just not to deny the rumor. Only for the next few hours."

"Perception is reality. It doesn't matter if the UK is responsible, the terrorists will believe it. They want to believe it."

"The reality is, you're already in the crosshairs. Twenty-six dead, Jack."

"Twenty-seven. A little girl died an hour ago." There was a long sigh. "All right. Do it. If asked, I won't deny."

"No one must know the truth. Even your own people," said Williams. "I know there's an urgent meeting of international intelligence leaders in London."

He heard a long exhale as Bellington considered. "You're asking me to lie to my own people?"

"I am. I'll be doing the same thing. If you agree, I'm going to start with my own Director of National Intelligence. Tim Beecham's at that meeting in London. I'm going to let him know the rumor of an SAS attack. He'll ask your people. They'll ask you."

"And I need to lie."

"You need to not tell the truth. Be cagey. Be vague. It's your strong suit, isn't it?"

Bellington laughed. "You've been talking to my ex-wife."

"So what's it going to be, Jack?"

Williams saw that an urgent message had come in from Secretary Adams. He waited, waited, for Bellington's answer.

"The girl was seven years old. My granddaughter's age. Yes, Mr. President, I can keep the wolves at bay for several hours."

"Thank you, Mr. Prime Minister. I owe you a drink."

"Great. Next time you're here, Doug, we'll go to a pub and have pie and a pint. Maybe watch a football match."

Both men paused, imagining it. Wishing it were possible. But those days were gone for both, forever.

When he hung up, Williams read the message from Ellen, then ordered the FBI and Homeland Security to the villa in Palm Beach.

He also told them to find out what private jets had left Palm Beach the day before, who the passengers were, and where they were headed. Then he put in motion the SAS rumors.

The buzzer on his desk sounded.

"Mr. President," said the Vice Chair of the Joint Chiefs, "they're in the air."

President Williams looked at the time. In a matter of hours, Special Ops would be flying into Taliban-controlled Pakistan, arriving in the dark.

The raid was underway. The offensive had begun.

CHAPTER 35

Ellen slept fitfully on the flight to Islamabad, waking often and checking for messages.

All the aircraft—the Chinook helicopters and refueling planes—had taken off from a secret base in the Middle East, and the commanders were going over final plans for the assaults.

By the time Air Force Three arrived in Pakistan in early evening, the Rangers had been split into two units.

She looked at the time. Three hours and twenty-three minutes to first boots on the ground. The diversion unit first. Then, twenty minutes after that, the factory raid.

Another message confirmed that Bashir Shah had left Florida for parts unknown. The villa was empty. No people. No documents. And there was no log of any flight with his name.

Disappointing, but no surprise.

They were tracing every private flight and had now expanded the search to commercial aircraft out of the area.

Bashir Shah, like some wraith, had vanished.

She looked at her desk, where the bouquet of sweet pea still rested. She saw, with satisfaction, that they were wilting. Drooping. Dying.

The steward had tried to take it away, but Ellen wanted it left there. It gave her an odd satisfaction to watch his offering die.

A poor substitute for Shah himself, but better than nothing.

"Before we leave the plane, I want to show you something," said Betsy.

She hadn't heard back from Pete Hamilton and had decided to show Ellen his message anyway.

"*HLI*?" said Ellen. "What does it mean?"

"I think it's a typo."

Ellen's brow furrowed. "But it's flagged. You don't flag a typo. If it's that important, you'd make sure it was accurate, wouldn't you?"

"I would, but he must've been in a hurry."

"Has Hamilton explained?"

"I asked but no reply."

They both stared at the letters. Did he mean to write *HIL*? But if so, what would that even mean? The hill? Capitol Hill? Was that where one of the bombs was? But again, it made no sense. Why leave off the second *L*? And yet Hamilton had marked it urgent.

"Let me know when he replies."

Ellen looked at herself in the mirror. No burqa this time. Just conservative, modest dress. Long sleeves, a pantsuit. A beautiful silk scarf her Pakistani counterpart had sent when her appointment as Secretary of State had been announced. It was in the design of a peacock feather and was exquisite.

She almost felt bad for what she was about to do. But there was no choice. If those brave operators could do what they were about to do, so could she.

"You up for this? Would you rather stay here? Get some sleep?" she asked Betsy, who looked tired and stressed but was trying to hide it for her sake.

"Are you kidding? Compared to teaching *The Tempest* to ninth graders, this's nothing. Jesus, I'd rather parachute into Al-Qaeda–occupied territory any day than face thirty fourteen-year-olds."

"O brave new world," Betsy thought, looking at her friend, *"that has such people in it."*

"We've got this," said Ellen.

"Hell is empty," she thought, *"and all the devils are here."*

Or at least not far from here. She hoped Shah was at the factory, unaware of what was approaching. She looked at the time again.

Three hours and twenty minutes . . .

The Chinook helicopters flew in staggered fashion.

The sun was just setting as they rose and, tipping their noses down, they surged forward, carrying the Rangers who would drop onto that plateau. And hold it.

The captain looked at their determined faces. Most in their twenties. Already hardened veterans. But this mission would be harder than anything they'd faced. And some, if not many, would not return.

Her own commander knew it, even as he'd given her the assignment. And she knew it as she'd looked at the plan. But such was the importance of this mission that she hadn't argued. Or hesitated.

"Strange to think that Katherine and Gil are in Pakistan too," said Betsy as they prepared to leave Air Force Three. "Though quite far away. I wish they could join us." She paused, to let Ellen say they could. And would. But there was silence. "Still," Betsy went on, "I'd rather have them here than in DC."

"So would I." It was, Ellen knew, the first instinct of anyone who knew about the nuclear bombs. Get the family out of DC. Out of any major city likely to be a target.

Outside the plane a military band had struck up and was going through its ceremonial drill while playing martial music.

"Did you see this?" Betsy held out her iPad.

Ellen bent down and saw a clip from President Williams's news conference.

A reporter had asked him about former President Dunn's statements on Gil Bahar and his role in the bus bombings.

"I will answer that once, and only once," said President Williams, looking straight at the camera. "Gil Bahar risked his life, and almost lost his life, trying to save the men, women, and children on that bus. He is an extraordinary young man. He makes his family proud, he makes his country proud. Any attempt to sully his name, his reputation, or that of his mother comes from people who are both ill-intentioned and ill-informed."

Ellen raised her brows and wondered how she'd never noticed that Doug Williams had a nice voice.

"Still nothing from Pete Hamilton?" she said.

Betsy double-checked and shook her head.

"Madame Secretary," said her assistant. "It's time."

Ellen looked at herself in the mirror one last time. She took a deep breath. Stood up tall. Shoulders squared. Chin up. Head high.

We've got this, Ellen repeated to herself as she stepped out into the warm evening, to cheering and waving American flags. To the National Anthem, which never failed to stir her heart. " 'Twilight's last gleaming,' " she sang.

Dear God, help us.

The second wave took off, the helicopters filled with precious cargo. The sons and daughters of parents who would be terrified to know what their country was asking of their children. The young men and women clutched M-4 rifles and stared across the aisle at each other.

The young men and women clutched M-4 rifles and stared across the aisle at each other.

They were the tip of the spear. The Rangers. Elite troops. A decade earlier, Navy SEALs had also dropped into Pakistan, that time to get Osama bin Laden. And they had.

These soldiers knew their mission was at least as important, if not more.

And they knew it was at least as dangerous, if not more.

"This can't be it," said Charles Boynton when the car shuddered to a halt in the tiny Pakistani village. "It's a shack."

"What did you expect?" asked Katherine. "The Ritz?"

"There's a lot between the Ritz and—" He gestured toward the wooden structure, which was leaning slightly. "Is there even electricity?"

"For your electric toothbrush?" asked Katherine as she got out of the car. Though privately, she had to admit, she was a little surprised and disappointed.

"No," said Boynton. "For this." He held up his phone. "I need to get it charged and send a message to your mother."

White House. White House.

Katherine was about to say something snarky but bit her tongue. She was hungry and tired and had hoped their destination might solve both those issues, but clearly it would not.

White House. White House, thought Boynton. Why hadn't he sent that message along with the rest? Because people had been trying to kill him. Because he'd killed a man.

Because he'd temporarily lost his mind, and all he could think of was getting the information about the real physicists and their location to his boss before he himself was killed.

White House. All the way there he'd asked himself what it meant. Or, really, he'd tried not to accept what seemed obvious.

Someone in the White House was collaborating with Shah. It could have meant General Whitehead, but he was not the White House. He was the Pentagon.

Still, Farhad might not make the distinction.

But in his heart, Charles Boynton knew that was not true. If Farhad spewed "White House" in blood with his dying breath, he meant it.

Katherine knocked on the door. It shuddered as she rapped. And then it unexpectedly opened, and Gil was standing there.

"Oh, thank God," he said.

Katherine went to embrace her brother, but noticed Gil was looking past her.

To Anahita Dahir.

Then she felt herself nudged aside as Anahita went to Gil and hugged him tight.

"Well," came a voice behind Katherine, "that was unexpected."

She turned and saw Ana. Then she looked more closely and realized it was Boynton, not Ana, who was clutching Gil and pretty much sobbing.

Charles pulled away and said, "Phone, do you have a phone?"

"Yes—"

"Give it to me." Gil did and moments later Boynton hit send.

There. It was no longer his responsibility. And yet he found that while the words had been sent, the meaning lingered. Stuck like a barb in his mind.

White House.

"Madame Secretary, this is an unexpected pleasure."

The Prime Minister of Pakistan, Dr. Ali Awan, extended his hand, though he did not look altogether happy.

"I was in the neighborhood," said Ellen with a warm smile.

Dr. Awan's smile was strained. This was an inconvenience, but when the US Secretary of State suddenly drops in for dinner, you cannot send a surrogate.

He'd met her at the entrance to his official residence inside the grounds of the Minister's Enclave. Floodlights illuminated the gracious white buildings and spilled onto the lush gardens.

Majestic palms soared overhead, and Ellen, a lover of history, could only imagine how many people over the centuries had stood where she was and also marveled.

The evening was warm and fragrant. Scents both sweet and spicy rose from the flowers in the heavy humid air. Secretary Adams's motorcade had driven past the chaotic and exuberant street life of the Pakistani capital, down the long Constitution Avenue, and arrived at this venerable enclave, a haven of peace in the center of the vibrant city.

It was strange in the extreme to be in such a serene setting, given what was about to happen a few hundred kilometers away.

She looked up at the stars and thought of the Rangers sailing through the night sky.

The helicopters were approaching the landing zone, but in the mountains and canyons it was impossible to actually see the plateau until they were right upon it.

The pilots were on night vision, hoping, hoping the Taliban and their antiaircraft guns would not spot them before they reached the LZ. Though the Chinooks had been heavily modified, the pilots and operators knew that stealth technology was far from perfect in helicopters.

There was no talking. The pilots strained to see while the soldiers in the belly of the chopper were staring out at the stars, lost in their own thoughts.

After cocktails, which Ellen was relieved to see were made up of fresh fruit juices and contained no alcohol, the guests were seated at an oval table, beautifully set for dinner.

Ellen had given her phone to Steve Kowalski, her chief of security. It was protocol, but she also wanted it out of her hands. She was far from sure she could resist checking it every two minutes.

Across from her, Betsy had engaged a young Army officer in conversation, while Ellen turned to the Prime Minister, who was seated on her left.

Men and women had been hastily called to attend this dinner, including, Ellen was relieved to see, Dr. Awan's Military Secretary, General Lakhani, who sat on the other side of the Prime Minister.

The Foreign Minister was also there, in the hopes, Ellen assumed, the new American Secretary of State would prove as inept as the last.

She realized the recent debacle in South Korea had had unexpected benefits. It had proven, at least to some, that she was indeed incompetent. And, therefore, easily manipulated.

That was exactly what she wanted these people to think. For the next few crucial hours, anyway.

"I was hoping Dr. Shah would be here."

Might as well confirm her ability to be indiscreet.

There was a clatter as two or three government officials dropped their forks. But not Prime Minister Awan. He remained perfectly composed.

"Do you mean Bashir Shah, Madame Secretary? I'm afraid he is not welcome in my home, or in any government building. He's viewed by some as a hero, but we know the truth."

"That he's an arms dealer? Selling nuclear technology and

material to anyone willing to pay?" Her gaze was innocent, her voice neutral, as though she were confirming a rumor she'd only just heard.

"Yes." His voice was clipped. Had he not had such self-control, his tone would have verged on rude. It certainly held a warning. Bashir Shah was not to be mentioned in polite, certainly not in foreign company, in Pakistan.

"The fish is delicious, by the way," Ellen said, letting Dr. Awan off the hook.

"I'm glad you like it. It's a regional specialty."

They were both working hard to remain cordial and relaxed. Ellen suspected he was as anxious as she was to have this charade over. In her research, which included speaking with Pakistani scholars and intelligence officials who'd studied the turbulent state, Ellen had concluded that Dr. Awan was deeply conflicted.

He'd been an early supporter of Shah but had publicly turned on him. A Pakistani nationalist, Prime Minister Awan believed that his country's only hope of survival when living next to the giant that was India was to get stronger and stronger. Or at least appear to.

Like a puffer fish, it made itself seem larger, more intimidating. And it did so by filling itself with fissionable material.

Bashir Shah provided that. But the nuclear physicist also brought along all sorts of unwanted and dangerous attention. Another maniac juggling weapons, only his weren't grenades; they were nuclear bombs.

"I don't suppose you know where he is, Mr. Prime Minister. I think his home isn't far from here."

American agents had his house under surveillance, but he might've snuck in before all this happened.

"Shah? Not a clue." Dr. Awan had resigned himself to getting this conversation over with, since she seemed determined to talk about this unpleasant and even perilous topic. "Your previous President asked that he be released from house arrest, and we complied. After that, Dr. Shah was free to go wherever he pleased."

"You don't consider him a threat?"

"To us? No."

"Then to who?"

"If I was Iran, I might be worried."

"I'm glad you brought that up. I'm hoping we can work together, Mr. Prime Minister, to get Iran back into the nuclear treaty, and to give up any nuclear weapons they might have. It worked for Libya."

She got the reaction she'd expected and wanted. His brows went up, and General Lakhani, the Military Secretary, leaned across the Prime Minister to stare at her, as though she'd said something monumentally stupid.

Which she had.

Sometimes, Secretary Adams thought, you were the cat. Sometimes the rat. And sometimes the hunter.

She could see what they were thinking.

Here was an opportunity that had fallen out of the sky, almost literally, and into their laps. It was not to be wasted. They could take the new Secretary of State in hand. Offer to be her teachers, her mentors. To, in effect, inculcate her with the Pakistani view of the region. Where they wore white hats, and India, Israel, Iran, Iraq, everyone else wore black and were not to be trusted.

But she also knew there were elements within Pakistan, within the government and even the military, probably around that table, who saw the American withdrawal from Afghanistan as an opportunity to assert even more power and influence in the region.

By essentially making Afghanistan another province of Pakistan.

With the Americans gone, the Taliban, after being given safe haven for years in Pakistan, would again take power in Afghanistan. And with them would come their allies, in some ways their international military arm: Al-Qaeda.

It was an Al-Qaeda intent on hurting the West. Specifically intent on revenge against the United States for the killing of Osama bin Laden. They'd pledged it, and now, with the help of Bashir Shah and the Russian mafia, with the American withdrawal from Afghanistan and the reemergence of the Taliban, they'd be in a position to carry the threat through, and in a more spectacular, more destructive fashion than they'd dreamed possible.

A terrorist organization could do what a government could not. A government was subject to international scrutiny and sanctions.

A terrorist organization was not.

Dr. Awan, a good man, if not a great one, was hardly a jihadist. He was far from a radical. Terrorist attacks sickened him. But he was a realist. He could not control those radical elements within Pakistan. Once the Americans left, once the Taliban returned and Shah was freed, there was almost no stopping it.

The Pakistani Prime Minister had been privately shocked when the former American President, at the summit meeting, had asked for Shah's release. He'd tried to explain to President Dunn the possible consequences, but it fell on deaf ears.

Despite liberal doses of flattery, which usually worked with the American President, he was adamant that Shah be released. It was Awan's only failure. Clearly someone else had gotten to Dunn first, with even more flattery. He could guess who.

And now Bashir Shah was out in the world, and Prime Minister Awan found himself back on the tightrope, balancing between keeping the Americans close and the radical elements within his own country closer.

As for Al-Qaeda? Awan just wanted to keep his head down.

His life, both political and physical, depended on his ability to do that.

They'd been worried when Dunn lost the election, but now it seemed this new Secretary of State was just as ignorant, just as arrogant. And therefore, just as malleable.

The fish was tasting more and more delicious.

CHAPTER 36

It was a rough landing.

The wind whipping through the canyons made it near impossible to control the helicopters. But the pilots of the two Chinooks held them steady long enough for the Ranger platoon to leap out and race clear.

Just as the helicopters lifted off and were turning for cover, a strong gust pushed the lead copter toward the rock face.

“Shit, shit, shit,” muttered the pilot, as she and the copilot fought for control. But the rotor clipped the rocks. There was a jolt.

She felt the control stick shaking and shuddering. And the craft tilting.

Seeing where this was heading, she looked at her copilot and her navigator. They looked back at her, and nodded.

Then she steered it away from the troops on the plateau. Away from the other helicopter.

There was silence in the cabin as the helicopter slipped over the edge and out of sight.

“Oh God,” the pilot whispered.

And then came the fireball.

It was followed seconds later by contrails from the Taliban positions.

“Incoming,” the Ranger captain yelled.

A string quartet was playing Bach's Concerto for Two Violins as the salad course was served.

It was one of Ellen's favorite pieces of music. She listened to it most mornings, to ease herself into her day. She wondered if it was a coincidence, but suspected it was not. She also wondered who in the room had arranged for it to be played.

The Prime Minister? He seemed oblivious to any hidden message. The Foreign Secretary? Maybe.

The Military Secretary, General Lakhani? From what she'd read in the confidential briefings, he was the most likely. A man with one foot in both the establishment and the radical camps.

But someone would have had to have told General Lakhani. And Ellen knew who.

The same person who'd sent the sweet peas.

Who'd sent the cards on her children's birthdays, who'd undoubtedly poisoned her husband.

Who'd arranged for the bombing deaths of so many men, women, and children.

Bashir Shah put the plate of greens and fresh herbs in front of Secretary Adams.

This was the moment. He felt an odd sensation and realized it was excitement. It had been a long time since the cynic had felt anything at all, never mind this frisson.

He'd never met Ellen Adams in person, but he'd studied her from a distance. Now, as he bent down, he was so close he could smell her eau de toilette. Clinique, he knew. Aromatics Elixir. It might even be from the bottle he'd sent her for Christmas. Though he suspected she'd thrown that right into the trash.

He knew this was a ridiculous risk to take, but what was life without risk? And what was the worst that would happen? If found out, he'd claim it was just his little joke. To dress up as one of the waiters. At worst, he was trespassing, but no charges would be laid. Of that Shah was certain.

Part of him, the reckless part, hoped he would be discovered, and would get to see Ellen Adams's face when she realized who he was. How close he'd gotten. And that there was absolutely nothing she could do about it. He was, thanks to the Americans themselves, a free man.

He could kill her now. Snap her neck. Or plunge one of the sharp knives into her. He could put poison, or ground glass maybe, into her food.

He had that power of life and death over her.

Instead he'd slipped a piece of paper into her jacket pocket. It wouldn't kill her, but it might come close.

Yes, he'd play with her a little longer. Watch her reaction when the bombs went off. When she realized her failure had caused the deaths of thousands. And a seismic shift in her country.

As he inhaled her subtle scent, he wondered if he hadn't developed a macabre crush on this woman. A sort of reverse Stockholm syndrome. So close were hatred and love linked, apparently.

But no, he knew his strong feelings were rank. This woman had ruined his life. And now he'd return the favor. Slowly. He'd take all that was precious away from her. True, her son had escaped the assassination attempt, but there'd be other days, other chances.

For now, at this moment, he was enjoying himself. He even allowed himself to speak to her.

"Your salad, Madame Secretary."

Ellen Adams turned.

"Shukria," she said in Urdu.

"Apka khair maqdam hai," the server said, and gave her a warm smile.

He had nice eyes, she thought. Deep brown and gentle. Her father's eyes. That must be why he seemed slightly familiar.

He also had a pleasant scent. Jasmine.

The server moved on to the Prime Minister, who also thanked him but did not look up. The Military Secretary seemed in a good mood, almost jovial. He said something to the server, and the man smiled politely before continuing on his rounds.

Now what did General Lakhani have to be so happy about? Ellen couldn't shake the feeling that whatever it was, it did not bode well.

As Bach continued softly in the background, Ellen realized this was a far more complex dance than she'd anticipated.

Where were the Rangers now? The diversion must have begun. Had they reached the factory yet?

"You talk about getting Iran to give up its weapons program," Prime Minister Awan was saying, dragging Ellen's mind back to the conversation. "I believe, Madame Secretary, the Grand Ayatollah is too canny for that. He doesn't want to become another Muammar Gaddafi."

Ellen almost said, *Remind me*, but thought that would be a step too far. Prime Minister Awan would never believe she was that ignorant. He was examining her closely, watching. Analyzing. She could feel the intensity of his stare.

She decided to remain quiet and let him wonder just how naïve she was. She also fought the temptation to look at her watch, which would be considered the height of rudeness, and perhaps signal to anyone watching that she was expecting something to happen.

Which she was.

Once again her mind went to the assault forces. To how the operation was going. And how much *merde* would hit the fan when her hosts discovered what was really going on while they enjoyed their fresh herb salads and listened to Bach.

"Colonel Gaddafi was convinced to give up his nuclear weapons," the Military Secretary explained, while Dr. Awan continued to watch Ellen. "And the next thing you know, Libya's invaded, and Gaddafi's overthrown and killed. No one in this region has missed that lesson. Any country with a nuclear weapon is safe. No one would dare attack. Any country without nuclear capability is vulnerable. It is suicide to give up their weapons."

"The balance of terror," said Ellen.

"The balance of power, Madame Secretary," said the Prime Minister with a benign smile.

An aide had bent down and was whispering to General Lakhani, who turned and stared at the aide, then said something to him before he hurried off.

The Military Secretary then spokc quietly to Dr. Awan.

This was it, Ellen realized. She forced herself to relax. Breathe. Breathe. Across the oval table, Betsy had also noticed this exchange.

Prime Minister Awan listened, then turned to Ellen. "We've just received word that the British are planning an attack, tonight, on Al-Qaeda positions inside Pakistan. Do you know anything about that?"

Fortunately, Ellen was genuinely surprised by this news, and showed it.

"No, I don't."

Awan studied her with his singularly intense stare, then nodded. "I can see that's true."

"But it makes sense, I suppose," said Ellen, slowly. "If they believe Al-Qaeda is behind the bombings in London and the other cities."

While her carefully chosen words came slowly, her sharp mind was moving rapidly, examining all the possibilities.

Was it possible that what the PM said was true? The Brits had decided, perhaps from a suggestion coming out of that intelligence meeting Tim Beecham was attending, to launch their own attack? Were the skies over Pakistan crowded that night?

The other possibility was that it was not true. That President Williams had put out this false rumor. If so, it was brilliant. Ellen just wished she knew which was which.

"What doesn't make sense," snapped Awan, as all conversation in the room stopped, "is not informing us. It is an attack on our sovereign territory. Do we know where?"

"My aide is finding out," said General Lakhani, who was now looking a lot less jovial. Just then the aide returned and bent down to whisper to him.

"Out loud," he said. "Everyone knows now. Where's the attack supposed to happen?"

"It's already underway, General. In the Bajaur region."

"What are they thinking?" demanded the Prime Minister. "Another Battle of Bajaur? As though the first wasn't bloody enough."

He'd been there. A mid-level officer who barely escaped with his life. And now he was listening to music and eating salad while the second one raged. God help him, he was relieved to be here and not there. He spared a thought for the British commandos engaging the Taliban and Al-Qaeda in their mountain fortress.

The Battle of Bajaur. Operation Lion Heart. The trauma was never far away. That event was just one of many reasons Prime Minister Awan hated war and longed for a peaceful and secure Pakistan.

Dr. Awan saw that his Military Secretary looked relieved, which didn't make sense. How could he be pleased that the British had launched a covert attack within Pakistani borders? The General should have been enraged.

What was he up to? the Prime Minister wondered. He also

wondered, as he felt himself wobble on the tightrope, if he really wanted to know.

Prime Minister Awan harbored no illusions about General Lakhani, and had only appointed the man to appease the most radical elements in his party. It was a problem, having a Military Secretary he could not trust.

At that moment Secretary Adams's head of security whispered to her and handed over her phone.

"If you'll excuse me, Mr. Prime Minister. An urgent message."

"From the British?" he demanded, the sting of national insult still smarting.

"No, from my son."

"Almost there, sir," said the pilot. "Ninety seconds."

The Colonel gave the order, and the assault troops stood and lined up at the door.

Out the windows they could see in the distance the night sky lit up with artillery fire, and then huge explosions as their jets dropped bombs on Taliban positions.

The Rangers on the plateau had engaged the enemy. The diversion had begun.

"Forty-five seconds."

Eyes swung from the windows to the door that was about to open. They had their own job to do. To rapidly, with lightning speed, secure the factory before those inside could scatter. Before those inside could destroy documents.

Before those inside could set off a nuclear device.

"Fifteen seconds."

The door was yanked open, and there was a great whoosh of cold, fresh air.

They hooked their cords onto the wire overhead and braced.

Ellen read the short text. Not from Gil but from Boynton.

The informant Farhad, who worked for both Iranian Intelligence and the Russian mob, had been killed by the Russians. Just before he died he'd said two words.

"White House."

The incoming fire from the Taliban positions was brutal. Worse than expected. The Captain recognized the weapons fire as Russian-made, and passed the information back to HQ, along with the report that they were holding their ground. Returning fire.

She was about to ask where the air support was, when there was a mighty roar overhead, then earth-shattering explosions as American fighter jets dropped bombs on the mountainside.

It gave them temporary reprieve from the withering fire.

And then it began again.

Hunched behind a rock, the commander looked at her watch. The other platoon must be at the factory. They just had to draw fire for another twenty minutes.

Just hold on. Just hold on. Whatever happens, just hold on.

She was the only one of her platoon who knew why they were really there. If they were captured, none of her soldiers could be tortured into revealing what the true nature of the mission was.

But she knew she would never allow any of them to be captured.

President Williams sat in the main Situation Room on the bottom floor of the White House, surrounded by his intelligence and military advisors. They'd been there for the past hour. It was windowless. Stuffy. But no one noticed or cared.

They were completely focused on the monitors, watching and listening to the Rangers about to rappel onto the factory.

"Fifteen seconds," came the voice of the pilot. Surprisingly clear.

President Williams braced, clutching the arms of his swivel chair.

The head of Joint Special Operations Command was beside him, while the Vice Chair of the Joint Chiefs of Staff was next door, monitoring the troops on the plateau.

"Mr. President, we've lost one of the helicopters," the Vice Chair reported.

"The Rangers?" asked Williams, trying to keep the alarm out of his voice.

"Are out. But the three Special Ops crew members are lost."

Williams gave a brusque nod. "The others are holding?"

"Yes, sir. Drawing fire, drawing attention."

"Good."

"Go, go, go!" came the order.

In the Situation Room, thousands of miles away, the President of the United States leaned forward.

He could see exactly what was happening through the night vision cameras on the helmets the Rangers wore. It was like being there, only not.

Doug Williams gave a small thrust as he rappelled from the chopper with the commander in charge of the raid. It was eerily quiet, almost peaceful, as the President watched the others descend.

There was a thump and grunt as his boots hit the ground.

Not a word was spoken. The Rangers knew exactly what to do.

The agent knocked on Pete Hamilton's door and looked around at the grimy hall.

The place stank. He looked at his partner, who was grimacing.

"Hamilton?" he shouted, pounding on the door with his fist.

They'd traced him back here from the Off the Record bar. He'd arrived more than an hour ago but had not answered any messages since then.

The lead agent, a veteran of the Secret Service, looked around. This wasn't right. If someone was working with the White House, they'd make sure to answer their texts, emails, calls. If it was three in the morning, then maybe . . . but it was only midafternoon.

He felt the hairs on the back of his neck go up.

Bending over the lock, he needed just a few seconds with his tools before there was a soft click. Bringing out his handgun, he nodded to his partner.

Ready?

Ready.

With his foot, he nudged the door open.

And stopped.

The dessert was placed in front of Ellen, this time by a different waiter.

The dinner in Islamabad had never been exactly jocular but had now turned downright sullen with news of the apparent British raid in Bajaur.

General Lakhani had excused himself, though the Prime Minister had stayed behind. Perhaps indicating how important Dr. Awan considered his American guest. Or more likely, thought Ellen, indicating who was really in charge. And who should just enjoy his sweet gulab jamun.

Secretary Adams realized the rumor about the SAS was indeed a ruse. It was American Special Forces who'd landed in Bajaur and engaged Al-Qaeda. It was just a matter of time, minutes now, before the Pakistanis realized what was really happening. And who'd really orchestrated the raid. Raids.

She moved the balls of cake around in their syrup. A slight scent of rose and cardamom wafted up from the fine bone china bowl.

She'd heard nothing from President Williams since forwarding the warning from Boynton.

White House.

Actually, it was simply confirmation of what they already knew. There was a traitor in the White House. Close to the President.

Just then Ellen's phone buzzed with a red-flagged message.

The agents who had been sent to check on Pete Hamilton had found him in his apartment. Shot dead.

They'd traced his movements to Off the Record, where he'd been chatting up a young woman, who left shortly after he did. They were finding out who she was.

"Are you all right?" Dr. Awan asked, seeing her pale.

"I think the fish might not have agreed with me. Would you excuse me, Mr. Prime Minister?"

"Of course." He rose as she got up and nodded to Betsy to join her. Everyone else around the table also got to their feet and watched as the two women hurried out, led to the restroom by a female aide.

It seemed this awkward, interminable evening was drawing to a close. When the guest of honor threw up, that was generally a signal that it was over.

But they were wrong.

The Rangers literally hit the ground running, racing for the factory. Now, as the President and others watched, they breached the gates and poured inside.

"Clear!"

"Clear!"

"Clear!"

Seven seconds since getting in. And so far, no resistance. Not a shot fired.

"Is this normal?" Williams asked the head of Special Operations.

"There is no 'normal,' Mr. President, but we had expected that the facility would be defended."

"And the fact it isn't?"

"Could mean we have taken them completely by surprise." And yet he seemed disconcerted.

President Williams almost asked what else it could mean, but decided to just watch. They'd find out soon enough.

The moments ticked by, elongating almost to breaking. Williams had never realized a second could be so elastic, and so long.

Heavy boots pounded up concrete steps two at a time, M16 guns at the ready. One group headed up, another down, another raced into the huge open area filled with industrial equipment.

Twenty-three seconds.

"Clear!"

"Clear!"

"Clear!"

"What's that?" Williams pointed to one of the screens.

The commander was given an order to get closer, and as he did, *that* became obvious.

"Oh, fuck," said the President.

"Oh, fuck," said the head of Joint Special Ops.

"Oh, fuck," said the commander on the ground.

That was a line of bodies. All in white lab coats. The physicists were slumped to the floor. The wall behind them pockmarked with bullet holes and streaked with blood.

"Get their IDs," the leader said. "Search them for papers." Gloved hands reached out and searched the bodies.

"When did this happen?" the head of Special Ops demanded of the commander of the elite force.

"Looks like they've been dead a day, maybe longer."

Shah had killed his own people. Their usefulness was at an end. He had what he needed, Williams knew. The bombs had been assembled and sold to Al-Qaeda, who were now under the protection of the Taliban.

Shah was just tidying up.

"Find the documents," the President commanded. "We need that information."

"Yes, sir!"

Please God, please God.

"More bodies up here," came another voice. "On the second floor."

"And in the basement. Jesus, it was a massacre."

"Watch for IEDs," the commander ordered as he and the others ransacked the facility, looking for documents. For computers. For phones. For anything.

President Williams brought his hands up and held his face as he stared at the screens. His eyes wide. His breathing rapid.

"We need to know where the bombs were sent," he repeated.

Ninety seconds in, and nothing.

Two minutes and ten seconds. Nothing.

"Nothing so far," the commander reported. "Will keep looking. No sign of any booby traps."

The head of Joint Special Operations Command turned to the President. "That's strange."

"But good, right?"

"I guess." But the man seemed uneasy.

"Tell me."

"I'm worried that whoever did this wants our people to move deeper into the place before they trip them."

"What can we do?"

"Nothing."

"Shouldn't we warn them?" President Williams nodded toward the screen.

"They know."

Those in the Situation Room turned grim faces to the screens and watched as the Rangers moved deeper into the factory in search of vital information. Knowing full well what was probably awaiting them.

"Mr. President."

Williams startled, his focus interrupted, and looked over to the door where the Vice Chair of the Joint Chiefs was standing. He was grasping the doorframe and looked ill. Behind him were the men and women who'd been monitoring the events on the plateau.

Williams stood up. He could see by their faces that the news wasn't good. "Yes, General?"

"They're gone."

"I'm sorry?" said Williams.

"They're all dead. The whole platoon."

There was a deathly silence. "All?"

"Yes, sir. They tried to hold back the insurgents, but there were too many. It looks like they might've been warned."

Williams looked at the head of Special Ops, who was stunned. Then back to the man at the door.

"Go on, General," said the President, standing taller and bracing.

For I have more . . .

"When it became clear that the Pathans and Al-Qaeda forces would overwhelm them and there was no escape, the Captain in charge of the operation ordered that they grab whatever terrorists they could reach as shields and fight to the end."

"Oh God." Williams closed his eyes and bowed his head and tried to imagine . . .

But could not.

Then he straightened up, took a deep breath, and nodded. "Thank you, General. The bodies?"

"I've sent in helicopter gunships to try to recover them, but . . ." The General looked physically sick.

"Yes. Thank you. I want their names."

"Yes, sir."

Time enough to grieve later. President Williams returned to the factory, where the other Rangers were moving deeper and deeper into what was almost certainly a trap.

But they needed that information.

Which American cities were sitting on nuclear devices that were about to go off?

Betsy searched the women's restroom, then locked the door.

They were alone, though that didn't mean they weren't being overheard.

"What is it?" she whispered. "What's happened?"

Ellen sat on the silk settee and stared at her friend, who sat down beside her.

"Pete Hamilton's been murdered," Ellen whispered. "His laptop and phone and papers are missing."

"Ohhhhh." Betsy slumped. Every bone in her body had dissolved as the eager face of the young man came to her. She'd recruited him. Convinced him to help.

If she hadn't—

"That last message from him, when did it come in?" asked Ellen.

Betsy gathered herself and checked, then told her.

"And nothing since? No explanation?"

Betsy shook her head. Suddenly *HLI* was less a mystifying typo and more a last, urgent message from a young man who might have been afraid for his life.

"But there's more," said Ellen. She looked ghastly. "The diversion force . . . the Rangers . . ."

"Yes?"

Ellen took a deep breath. "They've been killed."

Betsy stared at Ellen. She wanted to look away. To close her eyes. To retreat, just for a few seconds, into darkness. But she couldn't abandon her friend, even for one precious moment. Instead she reached out and grasped Ellen's hand.

"All?"

Ellen nodded. "Thirty Rangers and six Special Ops air crew. Gone."

"Oh God," sighed Betsy, then asked the question she dreaded. "And the others? At the factory?"

"No word."

There was a knock on the door and the handle jiggled.

"Madame Secretary," a woman's voice called. "Are you all right?"

"Just a moment," Betsy replied. "We'll be out soon."

"Do you need help?"

"No," Betsy snapped, then pulled herself in. "Thank you. We just need a bit of time. Upset stomach."

Which was now true.

They both stared down at the phone clutched in Ellen's hand. Waiting, waiting for another message from the White House.

White House, thought Ellen. That was the message from Boynton. It was what the Iranian double agent had said with his dying breath.

"Let me see Pete Hamilton's message again."

Another message from a man about to die. And knowing it. Not *White House*, but might as well have been.

HLI

Just then a message, flagged urgent, appeared on Ellen's phone. From the White House.

President Williams stared at the screens as the Rangers in the factory finished their second sweep of the place. Then he turned to the head of Joint Special Operations Command.

"Bring them home."

"Yes, sir."

Ellen Adams went into the cubicle and, sinking to her knees, she threw up while Betsy stared at the few lines on the phone, sent by President Williams.

Factory empty. Physicists and technicians dead. No papers. No computers. No idea where bombs were sent. Evidence there had been fissile material there. Analyzing signature. No info on destinations.

Nothing.

Betsy knew she should go over to Ellen. To help her. Should get cold cloths for her face.

But she couldn't move, except to finally close her eyes. Covering them with trembling hands, she felt her cheeks wet beneath her palms.

Pete Hamilton was dead. The Ranger platoon sent in as a diversion was dead.

The physicists were dead, and the factory was empty.

It was all for nothing.

They still had no idea, absolutely no idea, where the nuclear bombs had been planted. Or when they would go off. Except it was almost certainly soon.

CHAPTER 37

Madame Secretary?"

This time the voice at the door belonged to Agent Kowalski, the head of Ellen's Diplomatic Security team.

"Do you need help?"

"No, no. Thank you. Just another minute. Just splashing water on our faces."

Which they had been doing, but Ellen had kept the taps running to help cover what she was about to say to Betsy.

"I think I know what Pete Hamilton meant," she whispered.

"Pardon?"

"The message. *HLI.*"

"Then it wasn't a typo, sent in a panic?"

"I don't think so. Years ago, just after Dunn took office, Alex Huang came to me."

"Your senior White House correspondent," said Betsy.

"Right. He'd picked up chatter from some of the more marginal conspiracy theorists on the Web. Vague references to a Web room, a site called HLI. He looked into it and concluded this HLI was either a joke or wishful thinking circulated by far-right extremists. Fantasists. Either way, it didn't exist."

"Are you sure it was HLI? How can you remember that detail from years ago?"

"Because of what 'HLI' stood for. Because of what the story could be, if true."

"What did it mean?"

"'High-level informant.' In the White House."

"But imaginary, right? Some fictitious senior official who was, what? Passing secret information to the ultra-right?" asked Betsy. "Area 51? Aliens among us. Vaccines have a tracking device. Finland doesn't exist. That sort of thing? They made up stuff and attributed it to this HLI?"

"That's what Huang thought at first. Weird but probably harmless. He even asked Pete Hamilton about it at a White House briefing. Pete denied knowing anything, and Huang decided it was just another conspiracy theory rabbit hole. But I asked him to keep at it a little longer."

"Why?"

"Because most rabbit holes end at the fringe, but this one went beyond that."

"Into the dark web."

"I don't actually know."

"But Alex Huang finally stopped?"

It had always amused her that journalists covering the government were called "correspondents," as though it were some foreign land. But now she saw why. It was a country within a country, with its own rules of behavior. Its own gravity and stifling atmosphere. Its own shifting borders and boundaries.

The national animal of that country was a rumor. The White House was infested with them. Veterans who'd survived many changes of administration had done so by knowing which rumors were true. And which were not. And, perhaps even more importantly, they'd learned which false rumors could still be useful.

"Yes. He couldn't get far. And that's what he found strangest of all. Most of the people who peddle conspiracy theories want as much publicity as possible. They want their 'secret' spread far and wide. But those who knew about HLI did not. In fact, they seemed desperate to keep it quiet."

"A great silence," said Betsy.

Ellen nodded. "He finally stopped looking and quit not long after."

"Where'd he go? Another paper?"

"No, I think he moved to Vermont. Maybe to a paper there. Quieter life. Being a White House correspondent is a burnout job."

"OK, I'll try to find him."

"Why?"

"Because I want to follow up. If this HLI really does exist, and is involved, we need to find out. For Pete's sake."

It was not an expression. It was the reality. Betsy felt a duty to that young man.

"Fine, but not you," said Ellen. "I'll get someone else to do it."

"Why not me?"

"Because Pete Hamilton got himself killed asking questions."

"And you think, dear one, if those bombs go off, we're not all going to be put against a wall?" said Betsy. "I'll look into it. Now what were those initials again?"

Ellen smiled slightly. "You're a silly, silly woman." She turned off the taps. "Ready?"

"Once more unto the breach, dear friend," said Betsy, checking her lipstick in the mirror.

They walked out of the restroom straight into the furious face of the Pakistani Prime Minister.

Ali Awan was standing in the splendid hallway, his hands behind his back. Every man and woman from the dinner was ranged behind him, including the string quartet.

All glaring at Ellen Adams.

"Madame Secretary, when were you planning on telling me?"

He held up his phone, where a message about the true nature of that night's Special Ops raids had just come through.

Ellen had had enough.

"When were you planning on telling me, Mr. Prime Minister?" If he was angry, she was incandescent. "Yes, our Special Forces engaged the Taliban and Al-Qaeda at Bajaur tonight, at terrible cost, while another force attacked the abandoned cement factory. It wasn't the British, it was us. And yes, it was deep into Pakistani territory. And do you know why?"

She took two steps toward him and only just stopped herself from grabbing his long embroidered kurta.

"Because that's where the terrorists are. And why are they there? Because you gave them a safe haven. You allowed enemies of the West, of the United States, to operate inside your country. Why didn't we tell you about tonight's raids? Because we couldn't trust you. You've not only allowed Al-Qaeda to operate bases inside Pakistan, you've allowed Bashir Shah to use an abandoned factory for his weapons. You." She took another step toward him as he backed away. "Are." Another step. "Responsible."

She was right up against him now, looking up into his glistening face.

"And how are we supposed to trust you now?" he said, rallying. "You lied, Madame Secretary. You came here with the sole purpose of distracting us."

"Of course I did. And I'd do it again."

"You have violated our national honor."

She leaned close and whispered, "Fuck your honor. Thirty-four members of our Special Forces lost their lives tonight, trying to prevent a catastrophe you allowed."

"I—" The Prime Minister was on the back foot, figuratively and literally.

"You what? You didn't know? Or you didn't want to know? When you released Shah, what did you think would happen?"

"We had—"

"No choice? Are you kidding me? The great nation of Pakistan capitulated to an American madman?"

"An American President."

"And how are you going to explain this to the current American President?" She glared at him.

Prime Minister Awan looked shell-shocked. He'd fallen off the high wire but was still clinging to it with one hand. Holding on for dear life. Hanging over an abyss.

"Come with me." Ellen took his arm and practically shoved him into the women's restroom. Betsy followed and locked the door before anyone else could follow.

"Mr. Prime Minister," his head of security shouted. "Stand back."

"No," Awan called. "Wait. I'm not in danger." He looked at Ellen. "Am I?"

"If I had my way—" Ellen began, then heaved a deep breath. "Look, I need information. Shah hired nuclear physicists to build bombs and used that factory in Bajaur to do it."

"Bombs?"

She studied him. Was it possible Dr. Awan didn't know? She thought, by the appalled look on his face, that he probably didn't. Maybe they'd found, finally, a moral line he would not cross.

"There's evidence of fissile material in the factory."

"Nuclear?" Trying to grasp the situation. His expression had gone from appalled to horrified.

"Yes. What do you know?"

"Nothing. Oh my God." He turned away from her and began pacing the luxurious space, weaving around large silk-covered poufs. His hand on his forehead.

"Come on, you must know something," Ellen said, following

him. "Our intelligence tells us the bombs were sold to Al-Qaeda and have already been delivered to their targets."

"Where?"

"That's the problem." Ellen reached out and stopped him, turning him around to face her. "We don't know. All we know is that they're in three American cities. We need to know their exact location and when they're set to go off. You need to help us, Mr. Prime Minister, or so help me God . . ."

Prime Minister Awan's breathing had become rapid and shallow, and Betsy was worried he was about to pass out.

It was clear that while he might have suspected some of this, the specifics were a shock.

He sat down heavily on one of the ottomans. "I warned him. I tried to warn him."

"Who?" Ellen took the one next to him and leaned forward.

"Dunn. But his advisors were adamant. Dr. Shah needed to be released."

"Which advisors?"

"I don't know. All I know is that he listened to them and wouldn't be persuaded."

"General Whitehead?"

"Of the Joint Chiefs? No, he was against the idea."

But then, thought Betsy, he would be. Publicly. She thought of Pete. Of his excitement, mixed with horror, when he'd found those documents buried in the private archives pointing to the Chair of the Joint Chiefs of Staff.

Was Whitehead the HLI? He must be. But there was a chance he wasn't acting alone. He was the Pentagon. Suppose there was someone else, in the actual White House?

"Where's Shah now?" Ellen demanded of Awan.

"I don't know."

"Who does?"

Pause.

"Who does?" Ellen demanded. "Your Military Secretary?"

Dr. Awan dropped his eyes. "Possibly."

"Get him in here."

"Here?" He looked around the women's restroom.

"Your office, then. Anywhere. But fast."

Awan brought out his phone and called. It rang. Rang. Rang.

The Prime Minister's brow furrowed. He sent a text, then called another number.

"Find General Lakhani. Now."

While he did that, Ellen sent a message to President Williams suggesting Tim Beecham be recalled from London.

She received an immediate reply. Beecham would be flown to DC on a military jet.

And I want you back here too, wrote the President.

Ellen paused before composing her text. *Give me another few hours, please. I might have answers here.*

She hit send, and his reply came within moments.

You have one hour, then I want you on Air Force Three.

Ellen went to put away her phone, then reconsidered. She had one more question.

Ordnances used to kill physicists?

Russian.

She looked at Prime Minister Awan and asked, "How deeply are the Russians involved in Pakistan?"

"Not at all."

She considered him. And he considered her. Somehow Secretary Adams's calm was more unnerving than when she was shouting at him.

And where the hell was General Lakhani? He'd gotten them into this; he should be the one facing this wrath.

"I know you thought that I was an incompetent idiot," she surprised him by saying, "who you could manipulate."

"You did give that impression, Madame Secretary. On purpose, I now see."

"Do you know what I thought of you?"

"That I was an incompetent idiot that you could manipulate?"

Listening to this, Betsy thought that it was hard not to like this man. It was, however, harder to trust him.

"Well, maybe a little," admitted Ellen. "But mostly I thought you were a good man in an impossible position. And I still do. But the reckoning has come. You need to make a choice. Now. Us or the jihadists? Do you side with terrorists or with your allies?"

"If I choose you, Ellen, if I help you—"

"You might be their next target. I know." She looked at him with some sympathy. "But if you choose the terrorists, they'll kill you eventually anyway, when your usefulness has passed. And I'll tell you, Ali, you're at that line. After tonight, you might have crossed it. It looks like Shah is cleaning up, and you're now part of the waste. Your only hope is to help us find him." She watched him struggle. "Do you really want Pakistan to fall into the hands of terrorists and madmen? Of the Russians?"

Kings and desperate men, thought Betsy. Only now they were the desperate ones.

"I don't know where Shah is, I really don't," said Awan. "General Lakhani might be able to tell you, but I doubt he will. You asked about the Russians. They're not our allies, but elements within Pakistan are associated with the Russian mafia."

"Including General Lakhani?"

The Prime Minister looked deeply unhappy and nodded. "I think so."

"He traffics weapons from the Russian mafia to Shah?"

Nod.

"Including fissile material?"

Nod.

"And from Shah to Al-Qaeda?"

Nod.

"And guarantees the terrorists safe haven."

Nod.

Ellen almost demanded to know why Awan hadn't stopped it, but it wasn't the time. If they survived this, she would. But she also knew that the American government had crawled into bed with its share of devils over its history. It was sometimes a necessary evil. It was rarely an even bargain.

As Secretary Adams watched, Prime Minister Ali Awan made his choice. Letting go of the high wire, he went into free fall.

"If Bashir Shah has fissile material," he said, "he must be in touch with the highest level of the Russian mafia."

"And who's that?"

When Awan hesitated, Ellen whispered, "You've come this far, Ali. One more step."

"Maxim Ivanov. It's never admitted, but nothing happens without the Russian President having a hand in it. No one could get those weapons, that fissile material, without his approval. He's made billions."

Ellen had had suspicions, had even assigned the investigative unit at one of her major papers to look into Ivanov's connection to the Russian mafia, but after eighteen months of trying, they'd gotten nowhere. No one would talk. And those who might disappeared.

The Russian President made the oligarchs. He gave them wealth and power. He controlled them. And they controlled the mob.

The Russian mafia was the thread connecting all the elements. Iran. Shah. Al-Qaeda. Pakistan.

There was a ping as another red-flagged message arrived. From President Williams.

The fissile material detected at the factory had been identified as uranium-235. Mined in the South Urals and reported missing by the UN nuclear watchdog committee two years earlier.

Ellen absorbed that; then, gathering her courage, she sent a reply.

But she had one last question for Prime Minister Awan.

"Does 'HLI' mean anything to you?"

"'HLI'? I'm sorry. No."

Secretary Adams was on her feet. Thanking him, she left, but before she did, she asked him to not mention anything they'd talked about to anyone.

"Oh, don't worry. I won't."

That she believed.

In the Oval Office, President Williams looked at his phone and muttered, "Oh, shit."

The night had just gone from horrific to even worse.

According to the message from his Secretary of State, the Russian mafia was probably involved. Which meant the Russian President was probably involved.

Doug Williams had absolutely no doubt that he was sitting on top of a nuclear bomb. And he was terrified. He didn't want to die any more than anyone did.

But more than that, he did not want to fail.

He'd ordered the White House be all but evacuated, keeping only the most essential staff.

Specialists were now sweeping the place for traces of radiation from the uranium-235, but President Williams knew there were ways to mask it. And he knew the White House had many, many places to hide.

A dirty bomb, if that's what it was, could fit into a briefcase. And there were plenty of those in the rambling old building.

Williams looked again at Ellen Adams's message.

She would not be returning to Washington. Not just yet. Instead she was taking Air Force Three to Moscow. And could he arrange a meeting with the Russian President?

For a brief moment, President Williams entertained the idea that the traitor in their midst was his Secretary of State. That that was why she was getting as far from the nuclear bombs as possible.

But he dismissed that thought. That was one of the great dangers, he knew. That in their panic, they turned on each other. Suspected each other.

If they were to succeed, they needed to stay together.

While he might be sitting on a nuclear bomb, Ellen Adams was hardly better off. His Secretary of State was heading for a showdown with the Russian Bear.

Which was the better way to go? Incinerated or torn apart?

He folded his arms on the Resolute desk and laid his head down. Closing his eyes just for a moment, he imagined a wildflower meadow and a brook sparkling in the sunlight. His golden retriever, Bishop, was leaping after butterflies he could not hope to catch.

Then Bishop stopped and looked into the sky. Where a mushroom cloud had appeared.

President Williams raised his head, wiped his face with his hands, and placed a call to Moscow.

God, he thought, *don't let me make a mistake now.*

On her way to the airport, Ellen put her hand into her jacket pocket to take out her phone. It was instinct. She kept forgetting that after each use, she gave it to her head of Diplomatic Security.

But . . .

"What's this?"

"What?" asked Betsy. She was both wound up and exhausted. Fried. She wondered how much longer they could go on like this.

Then she thought of Pete Hamilton. And the Rangers on the plateau.

Longer, as long as it took, was the answer.

Ellen held a slip of paper between her thumb and forefinger. "Steve?"

He turned in the front seat. "Yes, Madame Secretary?"

"Do you have an evidence bag?"

The tone of her voice made him look at her closely, then at what she was holding. He reached into a compartment between the seats and took out a baggie.

She dropped the paper in, but not before Betsy had taken a photo of what was written on it, in careful, even elegant script:

310 1600

"What does it mean?" Betsy asked.

"I don't know."

"Where did it come from?"

"It was in my pocket."

"Yes, but who put it there?"

Ellen had been going back over the evening. It hadn't been there when she'd put the jacket on, in Air Force Three, an eternity ago. Any number of people could have slipped it into her pocket later. Though most of the dinner guests had kept a respectful distance. She didn't think Prime Minister Awan or the Foreign Secretary had come close enough.

And neither had General Lakhani.

Then who?

A set of eyes came to mind. Deep brown eyes. And a softly accented voice as he bent close. Close enough for her to smell his cologne.

Jasmine.

"Your salad, Madame Secretary."

And then he'd disappeared. Had not been there for the rest of the service.

But he had been there long enough to slip this paper into her pocket. She was sure of it.

And she was sure of something else.

"It was Shah." Her voice was barely audible.

"Shah?" Betsy was fully awake now. "He had someone give it to you? Like the flowers?"

"No, I mean it was Shah himself. The waiter who gave me the salad. It was Shah."

"He was there tonight? Oh God, Ellen."

"Quick, Steve, I need my phone." As soon as he gave it to her, she placed the call. "This's Secretary Adams. Put me through to whoever's on the Intelligence desk."

After an excruciating minute of trying to convince the overnight switchboard operator at the American embassy in Islamabad that she really was the Secretary of State, Ellen finally hung up and just called the Ambassador.

"I need the address for Bashir Shah," she said. "And I need security and intelligence personnel to meet me at his home immediately. Fully armed."

"Yes," he mumbled, struggling up from a deep sleep. "Just a moment, Madame Secretary. I'll get you the address."

He did, and within minutes they were in a leafy suburb of Islamabad. While they waited for the embassy personnel, Betsy began trying to track down Alex Huang, the former White House correspondent who'd unearthed HLI.

Ellen made another call. This one to Prime Minister Awan, bringing him up to speed.

"Dr. Shah was there tonight?" said the dumbfounded Prime Minister. "General Lakhani must have arranged for it. I saw him joking with the waiter and wondered . . ."

"So did I. Any word on the General?"

"No. We're looking. He might be with Shah."

"Do I have your permission to enter Shah's residence?"

"You'll do it anyway, won't you?" he said.

"Absolutely. But I'm giving you a chance to do the decent thing."

"All right. You have my permission, though I'm not sure our courts would agree that I have the authority." He paused. "But thank you for trusting me."

She hadn't trusted him completely. Not yet. But now she took that leap.

"Do the numbers '310 1600' mean anything to you?"

He repeated them, then paused, thinking. "Isn't 1600 the address of the White House?"

Ellen paled. How had she not seen that? 1600 Pennsylvania Avenue. "Yes."

But what could the other numbers mean? *310.* Was it a time? Was the bomb set to detonate at the White House at 3:10 in the morning?

"I need to go."

"Good luck to you, Madame Secretary."

"And to you, Mr. Prime Minister."

When she'd hung up, she told Betsy what Awan had said about the numbers.

"Yes, that could be it," Betsy agreed. "One of the bombs is in the White House. We suspected as much. But if there are three bombs, why would Shah just warn you about one? I think it's simpler than that. I think they're the same as the other ones."

"What other ones?"

"The buses. The numbers your FSO got and figured out."

Ellen looked more closely at the figures. "Buses? Al-Qaeda's put the bombs on number 310 buses somewhere in the States and they're set to go off at 1600 hours?"

"Four p.m. I think so. Suppose those explosions in London, Paris, and Frankfurt were not only meant to kill the decoy physicists but were a kind of dry run."

"But there's no way we can figure out which cities," said Ellen. "And four p.m.? But in which time zone?"

Betsy stared at the slip of paper. Then she noticed something. "Ellen, it's not *310*. It's *3*, space, *10*. There are three number 10 buses that are going to explode at four in the afternoon, in whichever time zone they happen to be in."

"But that doesn't make sense either," said Steve, turning around in the front seat. "I'm sorry, but I can't help listening." He looked pale, clearly shocked by what he was hearing. "If we know there are dirty bombs on three number 10 buses somewhere in the States, all we have to do is send out an alert to every transportation department to stop them and search. It wouldn't be easy, but it could be done. And we have time."

Ellen heaved a sigh. "You're right. That can't be it."

They stared at the numbers. Ellen's blurry, sleep-deprived eyes hadn't noticed the small space between them, but it was there. Unmistakable once seen.

3 10 1600

But they still had no idea what it meant. Which made finding Shah all the more vital.

As she looked toward the dark house, Ellen felt dread, like ice water, moving up her body. Creeping toward her mouth, her nose. She was, she feared, in over her head.

She didn't know. She didn't know. She didn't know what this message meant.

It could be buses. Or it could be about the White House.

Or it could be random numbers. Bashir Shah messing with her. Having her waste precious time.

What Ellen did know was that she was far too exhausted to work it out herself, even if she could. She'd missed the space between the numbers—what else was she missing?

"Send me the photo you took." When Betsy did, Ellen forwarded it.

"To the President?" Betsy asked.

"No. He can't figure it out any more than we can, and if there really is an HLI, we can't risk anyone else in the White House seeing it. I sent it to the person who solved the first code."

Then she did send a message to Doug Williams, warning him that if there was a nuclear bomb in the White House, it might be set to explode at ten minutes past three that morning.

Williams looked at the clock.

It was just after eight p.m. That gave them seven hours.

CHAPTER 38

Gil and Anahita had ventured out into the small town and found food and bottled water to take back to the others.

They'd talked the whole way there and the whole way back, carrying the fragrant food in string bags.

They started tentatively, by telling each other what had happened to them in the past twenty-four hours.

Anahita listened closely as Gil described the meeting with Hamza and Akbar's attack. She asked questions, sympathized, her attention complete. Then he asked about what she'd been through.

Anahita knew him well enough to know it was a polite inquiry. A quid pro quo. Nothing more. Her mother had often said that anyone can ask the first question. It was the second, the third that counted.

In their time together, as they'd lain in bed after making love, Gil had often asked how her day was. But he rarely asked the second, and never the third question. And while somewhat interested in her day, he rarely, if ever, asked how she herself was.

Ana had learned the limit of his interest in her. She'd also learned not to volunteer personal information. Not to someone who didn't really care. And yet she couldn't help caring about him. Like Othello, she loved not wisely but too well.

But Othello actually had been loved in return. His tragedy was not knowing it.

As they'd walked through the dark alleyways of the small Pakistani town, enveloped in the warm scent of the spicy food, she'd given Gil the most superficial of answers. The headlines. What she'd tell anyone. No more. Not enough to let him inside her actual thoughts and feelings.

Though the door wasn't locked. She was just on the other side, longing to admit him. The key was asking that second question. The third would get him across the threshold, to where she kept her heart.

"That must've been awful," he said when she'd finished; then he lapsed into silence.

Despite herself, Anahita waited. One step. Two. Three steps down the alley, in silence.

She felt Gil take her hand. She knew what that was. A prelude to an intimacy he hadn't earned and no longer deserved. She paused for a moment, feeling the warm familiar flesh against hers. Feeling it, for just a moment on that hot and sticky night, inside her.

Then she let him go.

He opened his mouth to speak, but just then a message came in on his phone.

"It's from my mother. Bashir Shah gave her a piece of paper with numbers on it. She wants you to see what you can make of it."

"Me?"

"It seems to be a code. You solved the last one, she thinks you can solve this one."

"Let me see."

As he turned the phone around for her to read the message, he said, "Ana—"

"Just let me read it," she said, her voice businesslike. Curt.

3 10 1600

Her young eyes had immediately seen the space between the numbers. The FSO was now completely engaged in this work.

She would not be so slow on the uptake this time. It had taken her far too long to see the significance of the message from her cousin Zahara, and then even longer to work out what it meant.

The delay had cost more than a hundred people their lives. That would not happen again. She would not be distracted. All the way back to the safe house, she went over the numbers in her head.

3 10 1600

Once there, she wrote them out on slips of paper and gave one to each of them.

"Bashir Shah sent these," she said. "We need to figure out what they mean."

"This's about the dirty bombs?" Katherine asked.

"Your mother thinks so."

As they shared the food, their heads bent over the table lit by oil lamps, they tossed out ideas, thoughts. Speculation.

1600. The White House?

Three number 10 buses?

It didn't take them long to arrive at the same theories as Secretary Adams. Including the possibility that the numbers were a ruse, a madman's joke. But they had to assume they were meaningful.

Gil glanced across the table at Ana. Her face was illuminated by the soft flame. Her eyes bright, intelligent. Her focus complete.

On their walk he'd wanted to ask her, longed to ask her, about watching her parents being interrogated.

About when she'd found herself in Tehran. When she'd been arrested. What had happened, how she'd felt.

When she'd described, in a few brief sentences, the attack in the caves, he'd felt himself go light-headed at the thought of losing her.

He'd wanted to ask what had happened next. And next. And next. He'd wanted to sit on a doorstep and listen to her. Forever. Lose himself in her world. Find himself in her world.

Instead he'd been silent.

His father had ingrained in him that it was rude to ask personal questions unless he was on a story. As a journalist. But he should wait for friends, especially women friends, to open up. Asking questions could be considered, his father said, a violation. Could be interpreted as inappropriate curiosity.

But there was a reason his mother had divorced his father. And there was a reason his father had gone on to any number of failed relationships.

And there was a reason his mother had married Quinn Adams. Who did ask how she felt. And who listened to the answer. And asked more questions. Not because he was curious, which he probably was, but because he cared.

Instead of speaking, Gil had communicated his caring in the only way he knew how. He reached for her hand. But she'd pulled away. Into silence.

Two black SUVs glided to a stop behind Secretary Adams's vehicle, and agents clad in assault gear jumped out.

After Diplomatic Security, their hands on their weapons, checked IDs, they opened the doors and Ellen and Betsy got out.

"You know whose house this is?" Ellen asked.

"Yes, Madame Secretary. Dr. Bashir Shah," said the senior agent. "We've had it under surveillance. No sign of him."

"Yes, well, we have reason to believe he's in Islamabad. We need to find him and pick him up, alive." She held the agent's eyes. "Alive."

"I understand."

"Are you familiar with the layout of the place?"

"I am. I've studied it, on the assumption we might have to go in one day."

Ellen gave an appreciative nod. "Good." She looked at the dark home. "There might be important papers too. Ones detailing his next target."

"Next?"

"He's responsible for the bus bombs in London, Paris, and Frankfurt. And we think he's planted more. We need to know where."

The senior agent took a deep breath. This had just gone from raiding the home of a prominent physicist and arresting him to something far, far more serious.

"We can't announce ourselves and ask to be admitted," said Secretary Adams. "We can't risk them burning the documents. We need complete surprise."

"That's our specialty, ma'am." He looked at the tall walls. "I imagine it's guarded."

"I expect so. Will that be a problem?"

"No, ma'am. We always expect trouble."

"Trouble with a capital T. I'm coming with you," she said.

"I don't think so," he said just as Steve Kowalski said, "No."

"I won't interfere, but I need to look for those papers."

"No, I can't allow it. Not just for your safety, Madame Secretary, but you'll just get in the way. Endanger the whole operation."

"I'm not suggesting I lead the assault." She turned to her own head of security. "Look, Steve, you've been listening to our conversations. You know what's at stake. You know how many lives have been lost trying to get this information." When he went to object again, Ellen said, "You know as well as I do that there is no longer any safe place. Not until we get Shah and that information. If he's successful, this won't stop with these bombs. It'll go on and on. So, I suggest we divide duties. You find Shah and secure the place while I go through his papers." She looked from Steve to the head of the assault team. "I won't go in until you tell me to. All right?"

Very reluctantly, they agreed.

Ellen turned to Betsy. "Stay here."

"OK."

As they made their way to the tall gates securing the home, Betsy followed.

"Trouble, trouble . . ."

At a signal from Steve, the two women sprinted across the courtyard. With every step closer, closer to the dark house, Ellen felt the hairs on her forearm go up.

"Trouble with a capital T."

There was no resistance. No guards. Secretary Adams had a sinking feeling she knew what that meant.

"Wait a minute, wait a minute, wait a minute." Zahara Ahmadi put up her hands for silence.

They'd been going around and around different theories about the numbers, each more far-fetched than the last.

"This Bashir Shah leaked the information about the nuclear physicists to my government," she said. "Right?"

"The Iranians, yes," said Boynton.

"Because he wanted us to kill them. And to be blamed."

"Yes," said Katherine. "What're you getting at?"

"Who's to say he's not doing the same thing here? Manipulating us?"

"He probably is," agreed Charles Boynton. "But this time we know it."

"That's not the only difference," said Zahara. "I think we've been focusing too much on Shah. Because he wants us to. Why would he give this message to Secretary Adams?"

"Because he's an egotistical maniac who can't help toying with us?" suggested Boynton.

"He's all that," said Gil. "But he's also a businessman. If this fails, he'll have his buyers to answer to, and I doubt he wants that. I think he's just a little afraid it will fail. Time is tight, and we're getting closer than he thought possible."

"I think so too," said Zahara. "This's insurance. The man's practically jumping up and down and waving at us to look at him."

"And away from where we should be looking," said Katherine.

"But where's that?" asked Boynton.

"At his clients," said Anahita. "Shah's the arms dealer. The middleman. He arranges for the bombs to be made, but he's not the one using them. He's not the one choosing the targets and the timing."

"Exactly. But he probably knows," said Zahara.

"Yes, he probably does," said Anahita. "He might've even arranged for their delivery."

"But it's his clients who decide where and when," said Katherine, her eyes widening as she grasped what they were getting at. "We've been looking at these numbers from Shah's perspective, but we need to change—"

"To Al-Qaeda's," said Zahara.

Anahita turned to her cousin. "We've been thinking with Western minds. You're saying we need to start seeing these numbers with Islamic minds."

"Not Islamic. Jihadist," said Zahara. "What would these numbers mean in their world? What significance could they have? Al-Qaeda and other terrorist organizations rely heavily on mythology, not just religion. They repeat and repeat grievances, wrongs done to them, ancient and new. They keep the wounds open. So what wound might those numbers belong to?"

3 10 1600

"We have a body!"

As the agent approached the man, lying facedown in the basement of Shah's house, he saw that there were wires just visible beneath the corpse.

"It's wired," the agent reported, and backed away.

They'd known the place was deserted before they'd put the second step into the courtyard. There was no resistance, and a man like Shah would surround himself with a private army.

No. There was no one there. No one living, that was.

Ellen and Betsy were on the main floor in Shah's study, rifling through his papers. The area had been swept for devices and was deemed safe.

"You need to leave, Madame Secretary," said Steve. "They've found a body in the basement, wired with explosives."

"Is it Shah?" Betsy asked, though she knew the answer.

Steve was shepherding them out of the house. "We don't know. They want to defuse the bomb before turning him over and identifying him."

Ellen was all but certain she knew whose body was in the basement, and five minutes later it was confirmed. General Lakhani, the Pakistani Military Secretary.

The Azhi Dahaka had been busy that night. Cleaning up, using blood and terror as the solution.

When the all-clear was announced, Betsy went to return to the house and their search through the documents, but Ellen stopped her.

"There's nothing there. He's taken it all. And anything we might find will have been planted to misdirect us. We need to go."

"To Moscow?" asked Betsy. She looked like she'd have preferred to go back inside and risk the bomb.

"Moscow."

It was, Ellen knew, the last house on the road. After Moscow, there was nowhere else to go. Except home, to wait.

Though there was one more avenue to pursue. When they'd boarded Air Force Three, Betsy continued her search for the missing journalist. The one who'd unearthed HLI.

Somewhere over Kazakhstan, she found him.

CHAPTER 39

It was ten past nine on a late Fabruary morning when Air Force Three landed in a snowstorm at Sheremetyevo International Airport in Moscow.

The sky looked like it had been punched. Bruised clouds blocked out the winter sun, weak at the best of times. Betsy remembered what Mike Tyson had once said.

"Everyone has a plan until they get punched in the mouth."

She felt more than a little punch-drunk. And if they had a plan, she no longer remembered what it was.

Neither Ellen, nor Betsy, nor their Diplomatic Security agents had brought coats. Or gloves. Or hats. A quick call had been placed to the American embassy and several armored SUVs were waiting for them on the tarmac. But they hadn't thought to ask for heavier clothing.

Taking a deep breath, Ellen stepped out of the plane with only an umbrella over her head to protect her. It was immediately turned inside out, hit by a wind that had started in Siberia and raced across Russia, picking up snow and ice and speed, before slamming into her. She stood at the top of the stairway, momentarily shocked. Unable to breathe. Unable to move except to blink away the snow as it pelted against her face and into her eyes.

Handing the now useless umbrella to the agent behind her, she reached out to steady herself. Her hands grasped the cold metal of the banister, and she immediately let go, for fear the warmer flesh of her hand would freeze to it and she'd have to tear her palm off.

"Are you all right?" Steve had to shout into her ear to be heard above the buffeting.

All right? How wrong could a day go? But then she thought of the Rangers. Of those on the buses. Of the mothers and fathers and children, holding photographs.

Of Pete Hamilton and Scott Cargill.

"Fine," she shouted back and saw, out of the corner of her eye, Betsy's nod of agreement.

For Christmas that year, Betsy had given her a copy of the latest work by her favorite poet, Ruth Zardo. The slim volume was called *I'm F.I.N.E.*

It stood for "Fucked up, Insecure, Neurotic, and Egotistical."

Secretary Adams clamped her teeth together to stop the shivering and turned back to the people waiting below. She forced herself to smile, as though she'd just landed on some Caribbean island for a holiday.

President Williams had, she knew, specifically asked that her visit be confidential. No attention. No fuss. And definitely no media.

Just a private meeting between his Secretary of State and the President of Russia.

Now she stood at the top of the stairs, and waved at the journalists with their cameras. Ask Ivanov to do something and you were practically guaranteed he'd do the opposite. Maybe, she thought as she was racked by another shudder, she should demand that he not, under any circumstances, tell her where Bashir Shah was.

Nor should he tell her where the bombs were hidden.

She started down the steps, hoping she'd reach the bottom before she froze to death. By halfway down, she was finding it difficult to walk. Her legs and feet, in low heels, were beginning to freeze, and she could no longer feel her face.

The stairs were covered in snow and ice, and with each step she slid a little. She wondered if Ivanov had done this on purpose. Surely it wouldn't be that hard to clear the stairs? Did he hope she'd break her neck?

Well, she damn well would not, she decided, even as her foot went out from under her again. She just managed to right herself.

Ellen could see the vehicles, parked farther away than necessary. Warmth. She wanted to leap down the last few steps and run toward them. Hoping to get there before she turned into an ice sculpture.

Instead she forced herself to slow down and stop just before the bottom stair, waiting for Betsy, who was a few steps behind her. She knew it by the muttered "Fuck, fuck, fuck."

If Betsy slipped on the icy stairs, Ellen wanted to be able to break her fall. As Betsy had cushioned hers, all her life.

Finally, after a descent that felt like Everest, her feet touched the snow-covered tarmac.

Ellen forced herself to nod and smile toward the greeters. At least she hoped she was smiling. It was possible her face had simply cracked.

All those assembled to meet her wore parkas so heavy, with fur-lined hoods pulled up, they could have been men or women. Polar bears or mannequins.

She skidded on her way to the car, but Steve caught her arm. Once in the vehicle, Ellen began shaking uncontrollably. She rubbed her arms, then held her hands to the heating vent.

"You all right?" she asked Betsy, though it came out as an unintelligible mumble.

Betsy's frozen face and chattering teeth meant she was reduced to answering with a series of grunts. Though she did somehow manage to make even those profane.

"What time is it?" Ellen asked Steve once her mouth would work again.

"Twenty-five to ten," he said, his words barely formed through still-frozen lips.

"And in DC?"

He looked at his watch. "Twenty-five to"—a spasm of cold went through him—"three in the morning."

"May I have my phone, please?" Once she had it, she typed a short message to President Williams. Her fingers were shaking so badly she had to go back a few times to correct her mistakes. And to correct the autocorrect, which had changed "bombs" to something that should never appear in a message to the President of the United States.

Doug Williams read the message.

He was in the Oval Office. The security team had swept the White House and found no trace of uranium-235, or any radiation. Though they had informed him that didn't mean there really was nothing. Just that they hadn't found it.

The Secret Service, aware of what was happening, asked, demanded, then begged him to leave. They knew, as did he, that if there really was a nuclear device in the White House, it would be placed as close to the President as possible.

But he refused to go.

"It's an empty gesture, sir," his senior agent snapped, tired, stressed, and exasperated.

"You think?" Williams studied the woman. "You've been around presidents long enough to know that no gesture, no word, no action or inaction, is without impact. What would be worse? To die here, or to let the terrorists know they've chased the President out of his own house?" He smiled at her. "Believe me, I'd love to leave. I've realized in the past few hours that I'm not a brave man. But I can't go. I'm sorry."

"Then neither can we."

"I'm ordering you to. Your deaths really would be an empty gesture. Listen, I know it's your job to protect me, but that means trying to stop an attack. Or even taking a bullet to protect the President. But you can't take a bomb. If it goes off, you can't protect me. My death would be a statement to the world that we will not be intimidated. Your deaths would be meaningless. You have to leave. And I have to stay."

They, of course, refused. But the agent in charge made a concession to her Commander-in-Chief. Agents with young children were reassigned to the outer fence. Where they might be safer.

Only when Williams was alone did the General come out of the private bathroom.

The two men stood at the window and gazed across the South Lawn.

"Just so you know, Mr. President, you are a very brave man."

"Thank you, General, but tell that to my shorts."

"Is that an order, sir?"

Williams laughed and looked at the Chairman of the Joint Chiefs of Staff. As long as he lived, President Williams would not forget the look on the man's face as he'd stood in the doorway. When he realized all the Rangers on the plateau were dead. Including his own aide-de-camp, whom he'd personally chosen to lead the assault. An assault, a diversion, that had been the General's idea.

Even now, hours later, the look of horror was still there, like a caul visible only to someone standing very close.

Williams suspected it would be there as long as the General lived.

It was a quarter to three.

So that could be another twenty-five minutes.

Through the snow squalls Ellen could see the brutal postwar Soviet buildings slipping by and the people, heads bowed, also slipping by. Leaning into the blizzard. Trudging to work. Not bothering to look up as the motorcade passed.

While not enamored of the leadership, Secretary Adams very much liked the Russian people. At least those she'd met. They were more than resilient; they were vibrant, full of life and laughter. Always generous and hospitable. Ready to share a meal, a bottle. Ellen could never deny the fortitude of the Russian people. Though it struck her as a crying shame that they'd valiantly fought off the Nazis and fascism from the outside, only to see it creep toward them from within.

Ellen was more than a little afraid that if her mission failed, the same thing would happen in the United States. Was, in fact, already happening.

They'd scored a victory over the despot, deposing him in a fair election. But the victory was fragile. Still, her job wasn't to convince the electorate. Her job was to make sure they got to the next election.

She looked at the time. Five to ten in the morning, Moscow time.

Five to three in DC.

She saw the remarkable onion domes of the Kremlin up ahead, appearing and disappearing through the blowing snow. Ellen and Betsy had warmed up, at least enough to stop shivering, though their clothes were sodden and their shoes wet and stained from the oily slush of the tarmac.

Ellen longed, longed, for a long hot shower. But it wasn't to be.

Betsy checked her phone. She'd found the former White House correspondent living in Québec, in a small village called Three Pines. He'd changed his name, but it was him.

She'd sent a message, asking for his help.

Despite the late hour, he replied. He'd started a new life, he explained. Had fallen in love and was now living with the owner of a bookstore, a woman named Myrna. He worked in the shop three days a week and did volunteer jobs around the village the rest of the time.

Clearing snow, delivering food. Cutting lawns in summer.

He was happy. Go away.

He hadn't asked what it was about, though by his reply Betsy suspected he had guessed.

Still, best she was clear.

HLI, she wrote, and hit send.

There had been silence ever since, though she thought she could feel his terror pulsing through the phone, as though fear were an app and she'd just triggered it.

"Madame Secretary."

Ellen was met at the door of the Kremlin by President Ivanov's junior aide, who smiled and led them inside, where Ellen's security team was asked to surrender their weapons.

"I'm sorry, ma'am," said Steve. "But we can't do that. I believe we have diplomatic exemption to carry weapons." He showed her his credentials.

"*Spasibo.* Yes, under normal circumstances that's true, but since this is a last-minute visit, we haven't had time to do the paperwork."

"What paperwork?" On the surface Steve Kowalski was perfectly calm, but Ellen could see the vein throbbing at his temple.

"Oh, you know democracies," the aide said with a smile. "Always forms to fill out."

"Not like the good old days," said Betsy and got a steely look.

"It's all right," Ellen said to Steve, softly.

"No it is not, Madame Secretary. If something happens . . ."

"You'll still be with me. And nothing will happen. Let's just get this over with and get out."

It was two minutes past ten.

Eight minutes left.

Doug Williams sat on the couch in the Oval Office. Across from him was the General.

They'd known each other for years. The President had met the General's wife and son, who'd done a stint in the Air Force in Afghanistan. Williams felt he should tell the General to leave, but the truth was, he was glad of the company.

Both held glasses of scotch. They'd downed the first, toasting each other's health, and now nursed the second.

Williams didn't know if it was petty on his part, but he'd ordered Tim Beecham back from London. The thought of his Director of National Intelligence sitting in Brown's Hotel enjoying a full English breakfast while he sat on a nuclear bomb was too much for the President.

Beecham wouldn't arrive for another few hours, but it still gave President Williams some small satisfaction.

As the two men chatted, Williams couldn't help feeling they should be talking about things that were of historic significance, of vital importance either politically or personally. But they ended up talking about dogs.

The General's own dog was a German shepherd named Pine.

He was, he told the President, a gift from a close friend in a small village in Québec. The General had visited his friend, a senior officer with the Sûreté, one summer. They'd sat on the bench on the village green, in the shadow of the three huge pine trees. He'd listened to the birds and the breeze and the children playing and felt at peace for the first time in decades.

So much so, he'd named the dog after the village.

Williams talked about Bishop, a golden retriever named not for an ecclesiastic, but a school the President had attended and especially liked. Probably because it was where he and his late wife had met. Bishop normally sat, or slept, under the desk in the Oval Office, but Doug Williams had asked a White House butler to get Bishop far away from the White House.

And to take care of him. If need be.

Five minutes left.

"Madame Secretary."

Maxim Ivanov stood in the middle of the room, not moving. Forcing Ellen to go to him, which she did. These petty gestures, meant to insult, had no effect on her. Once they might have gotten up her nose, but not today.

"Mr. President."

They shook hands, and Ellen introduced Betsy, while Ivanov introduced his own senior aide. Not, Ellen noticed, an advisor. No one gave this man advice. Not twice, anyway.

Ivanov was much smaller than she'd expected. But his personal presence was intense. Standing close to him felt like being next to an explosive whose trigger was held in place by a tightly strung elastic, stretched to breaking.

There was almost nothing between the Russian President and

bedlam. He had that, and so much more, in common with Eric Dunn. What was different, and immediately obvious, was that Maxim Ivanov was the real thing.

A ruthless tyrant, schooled in oppression both subtle and cruel.

While Eric Dunn had a natural instinct for other people's weaknesses, what he didn't have was calculation. He was far too lazy for that. But this man? This man calculated everything, with a coldness that would have given Siberia a chill.

But what Ivanov hadn't counted on, what he didn't see coming, was Ellen Adams. He had not expected the American Secretary of State to hop on Air Force Three and come to Moscow. To the Kremlin. Right into his parlor.

For her part, Ellen could see that beneath the steely gaze there was rare confusion. And with it, some fear, and with that, anger.

He didn't like this. He didn't like her. Never had, and never more than now.

But she could also see that, faced with her, his confidence was returning. And Ellen knew why.

It was because she was a mess. Her hair was askew, bouffant on one side and plastered to her head on the other. She'd gotten ready on the plane, but the blizzard had blown all that away.

Her clothes were damp and soiled. Her shoes squelched as she'd approached.

This was not a formidable representative of a superpower. This was a drowned rat of an American Secretary of State. Pathetic. Weak. Like the country she represented. Or so he thought. Or so she wanted him to think.

"Coffee?" he asked through an interpreter.

"Pozhaluysta," said Ellen. Please.

She could have asked to freshen up before meeting President Ivanov but had chosen not to. She knew that men like Ivanov and

Dunn would always undervalue and underestimate women. Especially one who was disheveled.

It was a very small advantage for her. And it was best not to make the same mistake and underestimate Ivanov. Bad things happened to those who did.

Time was ticking down, and now that the impression had been made, she could ask.

"Do you mind, Mr. President, if my counselor and I freshen up?"

"Not at all." He motioned to the junior aide, who led the women to the restroom.

It was rudimentary but had the necessities. And, most of all, it was private.

Once in, the first thing Ellen did was place the call.

Ninety seconds left.

President Williams's phone rang. He looked at it. Ellen Adams.

"Do you have something?" he asked, allowing his hopes to rise.

"No, I'm sorry."

"I see," he said, the disappointment, the acceptance, obvious in his voice. There would be no deliverance. The cavalry would not arrive.

3 10 1600

Fifty seconds left.

"We've just arrived at the Kremlin and I wanted . . . ," Ellen began, then petered out. "I didn't want you to be alone."

"I'm not." He told her who was with him.

"I'm glad," she said. "Well, glad isn't . . ."

"I know what you mean."

Thirty seconds left. Betsy stood close enough to hear. Both their hearts were pounding.

In the Oval Office, Doug Williams stood up. As did the General.

Twenty seconds.

The women locked eyes.

The men locked eyes.

Ten seconds.

Williams closed his. The General closed his.

There was a meadow with wildflowers. A bright sunny day.

Two.

One.

Silence. Silence. A great silence.

They waited. The timing might be off by a few seconds. Even a minute.

Williams opened his eyes and saw the General staring at him. But still they didn't talk. Didn't dare.

"Oh my God," said Anahita. "I think I have it. What '3 10 1600' means."

"What?" said Boynton as they crowded around her.

"What you said about thinking from a jihadist's point of view," she said to Zahara. "When we say '9/11,' we all know what that means. Suppose '3 10' is the same for Al-Qaeda."

"Why?" asked Katherine. "What could it mean?"

"Osama bin Laden was born on the tenth of March. Three ten." Anahita turned her phone around for them to see the bio she'd brought up. "See? It's his birthday. Today. Al-Qaeda has vowed to avenge his death at the hands of Americans. That's why the bombs are set to go off today. They're making a point. It's symbolic."

"It's revenge," said Boynton.

Katherine was looking it up and nodded. "It's true. He was born March 10th, 1957. So what does '1600' mean?"

"It's the time he was killed," said Zahara.

“No,” said Katherine. “According to this, he was killed at one in the morning.”

“In Pakistan,” said Gil. “That’s four in the afternoon on the American East Coast.”

“We know that from working in Islamabad and reporting back to DC,” said Anahita, holding Gil’s eyes. “We have to get word to your mother.”

“Here.” Gil handed her his phone. “You cracked the code, you send the message.”

Ellen quickly scanned the text, then immediately read it to the President.

Doug Williams exhaled.

“Looks like we have another thirteen hours, General. Then we do this all over again.”

When he explained about the code, the General nodded. “We have time to find the goddamned things. And we will.” He called to Ellen, still on the phone. “Thank you, Madame Secretary. And be careful.”

“You too. I’ll see you in the White House. I’m coming home as soon as I finish here.”

“You might want to take your time,” said Williams. “Tomorrow is soon enough.”

CHAPTER 40

As they freshened up, Betsy told Ellen about finding the journalist.

"He's afraid," she said. "That's why he not only left the paper, he left the country and changed his name."

"So he might actually know something?" asked Ellen.

"I think so."

"We need to get to him."

"Kidnap him?" asked Betsy. She seemed almost pleased at the thought.

"Jesus, Bets, I think we can leave one person unkidnapped."

"I'm not sure that's a word."

"I'm not sure that's the point. No, we need someone who can reason with him. Can you find out if he has family or close friends? Someone we can send there, fast?"

On leaving the restroom, Ellen handed her phone to Steve, who searched her face. Knowing what could very well have just happened back in DC.

"All's well," she said, and saw the relief.

"I was getting worried that you'd left, Mrs. Adams," President Ivanov said when they returned. "Your coffee is getting cold."

"I'm sure it's delicious." She took a sip, and indeed it was. Rich and strong.

"Now, I have to admit, I'm curious why you came here." Ivanov leaned back in his armchair and opened his legs wide. "Directly from Pakistan, which you traveled to from Tehran. And before that you were in Oman visiting the Sultan, and before that Frankfurt. You've had a busy time."

"And you've kept a close eye on me," said Ellen. "Nice to know you care."

"It passes the time. And now you're here." He stared at her. "I think, Madame Secretary, I can guess why."

"I wonder if that's true, Mr. President."

"Shall we place bets? A million rubles says it has to do with the bombs that went off in Europe. You've come to me for advice. Though why you think I can help is beyond me."

"Oh, I think very little is beyond you. And you're partly right. Perhaps we split the winnings."

His smile flattened. When he spoke again, his voice was hard, his words clipped.

"Then let me specify."

The only thing more important to Maxim Ivanov than being right was not being wrong. And certainly not to be told he was wrong. And certainly not to be told he was wrong by what he saw as a disheveled, frumpy, middle-aged woman. A neophyte in a game he had mastered.

Every meeting with another state was a war, and he would win. There was never a tie.

"Yes?" Ellen cocked her head as though he amused her.

"You've discovered that the scientists killed in those explosions were not the same ones Bashir Shah hired to work on the nuclear bombs he's selling to his clients. You're here in the hopes I can help you find those bombs before they too explode."

"What a lot you know about it, Mr. President. And again, you're partly right. I'm here about a bomb, but not the nuclear type. We have that well in hand. I've come as a courtesy. To help you disarm something about to explode closer to home."

He leaned forward. "Here? In the Kremlin?" He looked around.

"In a manner of speaking. As you know, my son works for Reuters. He sent me a story he's about to file, and I thought, as a sign of respect, that I should show it to you first. In person."

"Me? Why me?"

"Well, it has to do with you, Maxim."

Ivanov sat back again and smiled. "You're not still chasing that story about me and the Russian mafia, are you? There's no such thing, and if there was, I'd put an end to it. I won't stand for anyone undermining the Russian Federation or hurting its citizens."

"Very noble. I'm sure the people of Chechnya will be happy to hear it. But no. Not the mafia."

Betsy sat very still, her face placid, though all this was news to her. On the flight over, Ellen had spent time on her computer, but not communicating with Gil. So what had she been doing?

Like Ivanov, Betsy was curious to see where this was going. Though, judging by his face, by his coiled body, he might be slightly more curious.

"Then . . . ?" said Ivanov.

"Then . . ." Ellen nodded to Steve, who brought her her phone. After a few clicks and swipes, she turned it around.

Betsy could not see the screen, but she could see Ivanov's face, which was suddenly red. Then purple.

His gray eyes narrowed, and his lips were compressed. And there pulsed off him a fury she'd never felt before. It was like being hit in the face with a brick. And Betsy found she was suddenly afraid.

They were deep in Russia. Deep in the Kremlin. Ellen's Diplomatic Security had been disarmed. How difficult would it be to disappear them? Put out word they'd taken an internal flight, and it had crashed.

She looked at Ellen, whose face was a cipher. But a tiny throb at her temple gave it away. The American Secretary of State was also afraid.

But was not going to back down.

"What the fuck is this!" Ivanov shouted.

"What?" said Ellen, her tone no longer mildly amused. Now there was a coldness, a harshness to it, that Betsy had rarely heard. "It isn't the first time you've seen photos like these, is it, Maxim? You've used them before yourself. And if you swipe right, you'll see a video. But I wouldn't. It's pretty awful. Not nearly as good as the ones where you're bare-chested on that horse, though Gil tells me the horse does figure in another video."

Now Betsy was really curious.

Ivanov was glaring at Ellen, unable to speak. Or, more likely, all the words were piling up, like a logjam in his throat.

Ellen began to draw the phone back, but Ivanov's hand whipped out and, grabbing it, he threw it against the wall.

"Now, Maxim, no need to have a tantrum. That won't get you anywhere."

"You stupid, stupid bitch!"

"Bitch, maybe, but is it really all that stupid? I learned it from you. How many people have you blackmailed, how many have you ruined with doctored images of pedophilia? When you calm down, we can talk like adults."

Betsy noticed, with relief, that Steve and the other Diplomatic Security agent had moved considerably closer to them. Steve had retrieved her phone and now gave it back to Ellen, who checked it.

Still working.

"You know," she said, balancing it on her knee, as though taunting Ivanov with it, "you're lucky. If you'd broken the phone, and I couldn't contact my son, that story would run. As it is, you have five minutes to disarm this bomb." She nodded toward the phone. "Before it goes out, and off."

"You would not do that."

"And why wouldn't I?"

"It would destroy all hope of peace between our nations."

"Really? And is that the peace that comes with not one, not two, but three nuclear bombs?"

He went to talk, but she held up her hand and cut him off.

"Enough of this. We're wasting time that neither of us has." She leaned toward him. "You not only run the Russian mafia, you created it. You're the father of that obscenity and it does what you say. The Russian mafia has access to Russian uranium. How? Through you. Specifically, uranium-235, mined in the South Urals. Fissile. Its signature was found in the factory US forces raided last night in Pakistan. The uranium was sold by the mafia to Bashir Shah, who hired nuclear physicists to turn it into dirty bombs. He then sold them to Al-Qaeda. Who placed them in American cities. All this under your aegis. I need to know where Shah is, and I need to know exactly where those bombs are."

"This is fantasy."

She picked up her phone and composed a message. Then her finger hovered over the send button. There was no mistaking her resolve, or the revulsion she felt when looking at him.

"Go on," he said. "No one will believe it."

"They believed it when you doctored similar photos to frame your opponents. It's your favorite go-to move, isn't it? The neutron bomb of political assassinations. A charge of pedophilia, complete with photographs. A sure thing."

"I'm too well respected," said Ivanov, though he'd drawn his knees together. "No one would believe it. No one would dare."

"Ah, and there we have it. Fear. You rule by fear. But what you create isn't loyalty, it's enemies-in-waiting. And this"—she held up the phone—"is the fuse that will start the revolution. Pedophilia, Maxim. Believe me, they're images not easy to forget. But you're probably right. Let's just see."

Before he could say anything, she hit send.

"Wait," he shouted.

"Too late. It's gone. Gil will get that message, and within thirty seconds he'll post the story. In one minute, it'll be around the world on the Reuters newswire. In three, it'll be picked up by other agencies. Seconds after that, social media will have it and you'll be trending. In four minutes, your career, your life as you know it, will be over. Even those who say they don't believe it will hide their children and lock away their pets when they see you coming."

He glared at her in unvarnished hatred. "I'll sue."

"Absolutely. I would too. But sadly, the damage would be done. There's always a chance, Mr. President, that in the next few seconds I can stop Gil from posting."

"I don't know where the bombs are."

Ellen stood up. Betsy stood up with her, clutching her hands into fists to stop them from shaking. Until they were on Air Force Three, they'd be at this man's mercy. And mercy was in short supply in Ivanov's Russia.

"It's the truth," he shouted. "Kill the story."

"Why? You've given me nothing. Besides, I really don't like you. I'm happy to see you go down." She headed for the door. "We'll have a much better chance at peace when you're off tending roses in your dacha."

"I know where Shah is."

Ellen stopped. Stood still. Then turned. "Tell me. Now."

Ivanov wavered, then finally said, "Islamabad. He was right under your nose."

"Once again, you're wrong. He was there, but he's gone. He left the body of the Military Secretary behind, wired to explode. Did you know that? Must've taken you a long time to groom General Lakhani as an asset, and now you have to begin again, though I think you'll find Prime Minister Awan less blind than he once was. All thanks to Shah. Not a very stable ally, is he." She glared at him. "Where is he?" She raised her voice. "Tell me."

"The United States."

"Where?"

"Florida."

"Where?"

"Palm Beach."

"You're lying. We have his villa under surveillance. No one's arrived."

"Not there," said Ivanov. Now he was smiling.

"Tick tock, Mr. President. Where in Palm Beach?"

Though by then both Ellen and Betsy knew the answer. Still, it came as a shock to hear it from the thin lips of the Russian President.

CHAPTER 41

"I refuse to believe it," said President Williams. "All we have is the word of a tyrant. Eric Dunn's an arrogant fool, a useful idiot for the far right, never mind Ivanov and Shah, but he'd never knowingly protect a terrorist. Ivanov's lying, he's playing you."

Ellen exhaled, exasperated, and looked across at Betsy. They were on Air Force Three, on their way home.

"He's not wrong," said Betsy. "You saw the look on Ivanov's face. If he could've skinned you alive, he would have. There's no guarantee he's telling the truth, even with you blackmailing him with the photographs. Especially then. At this stage he'd do just about anything to destroy you."

Ellen had put her hand over her phone, but she could still hear the President of the United States' tiny, tinny voice, as though trapped in the device. "Blackmail? What photographs?"

She lifted her hand off the phone and explained.

"Holy shit. You did that? The child . . . ?"

"The little boy was computer-generated. He doesn't exist," said Ellen.

"Thank God for that. But you doctored photographs, then blackmailed a head of state?" Williams demanded.

"He's the head of a criminal organization that's helped put nuclear bombs on American soil. Yes, I did all that, and I'd do more if it came to it. What did you expect me to do? Waterboard him? Look, you might be right, he might've lied about Shah being at Dunn's home. There's only one way to find out."

"I'm guessing you're not suggesting ringing the doorbell."

"No. I'm suggesting a commando raid on the home of a former President to kidnap one of his guests."

"Oh Jesus," he sighed. "Listen, Ellen, Ivanov is clever. If this is a coup, we might be playing right into his hands. Even if we find Shah and the bombs, and manage to disarm them, we'll be thrown out for not just breaking the law but attacking a political rival. Literally attacking, with actual weapons. Good God, if I authorize a raid on his compound, Eric Dunn could even be injured. Then what?" They sat in silence for a few moments before President Williams asked, "Do you believe Dunn's a Russian asset?"

Ellen took a deep breath. "Maybe not intentionally, but I think he might be unwittingly. Not that that matters. It comes to the same thing. If Dunn gets back in, he'll be a pawn. The US might as well be a Russian state. Maxim Ivanov will be calling the shots. He'll then install his own person as Prime Minister of Pakistan and make sure the next Grand Ayatollah of Iran is a Russian loyalist. Ivanov will really become the hyperpower he always claims to be."

"Shit," sighed Betsy.

"Shit is right," said Williams. "I think our only hope is to ask Dunn if Shah is there and, if so, appeal to him to give him up voluntarily. If he does, great. If he doesn't, then we at least have proof we tried."

"I'm sorry, Mr. President, but are you crazy? Have you forgotten who we're dealing with? That might work with any other former President, but any other former President would never have Bashir Shah as a houseguest. We can't risk it. To ask Dunn is to warn Shah. Our only hope is surprise."

"It didn't work in Bajaur last night."

"No." That was not only tragic; it was worrisome. To say the least. The insurgents seemed to know the Rangers were coming.

"White House," Farhad had said. *HLI*, Pete Hamilton had written, almost certainly knowing what was about to happen to him.

They'd both died trying to communicate the same thing. *Traitor.*

That person had warned Shah about the raid, who'd warned the Taliban. Who'd killed the Rangers.

This same person would know about the bombs. Probably even had planted one in the White House. They had to find out who it was. And to do that, Ellen had to take a chance.

"There's something I haven't told you, Mr. President."

"Oh God, don't tell me you kidnapped Ivanov."

"No, though—"

"What is it?"

"Before Pete Hamilton was killed, he sent Betsy a message. Three letters. *HLI.*"

She waited. There was silence.

"That actually sounds vaguely familiar," said Williams. "HLI. But I can't place it. What does it mean?"

"High-level informant."

"Ahhh," he laughed. "That's it. It was a joke around Congress a few years ago. Some journalist was asking questions. All part of a vast right-wing conspiracy." He made it sound ludicrous.

"Yeah, hilarious."

There was silence again. "I guess it's not that funny now," he admitted.

"You think? Pete Hamilton died because he found out about it. The last thing he did was send that message. And for the record, I don't think it's just a right-wing conspiracy. I think it goes way beyond that."

"So you believe there is an HLI?"

"I do."

"Then why didn't you tell me this before?" he demanded.

"I couldn't risk anyone else finding out. Anyone close to you."

"You mean my Chief of Staff."

"Yes. Barb Stenhauser's as high-level as it gets. And then there's her assistant, who we've discovered was the young woman with Hamilton at the bar. She's now missing. You have to admit, it's strange."

"What I have to admit is that anyone smart enough, patient enough, to organize all this would also make sure to have scapegoats. Don't you think?"

Ellen was silent.

"And don't you think my Chief of Staff makes a pretty obvious target? Perhaps too obvious?"

"You might be right. The only way to find out is to track down this HLI site," said Ellen. "Get the name. And that means finding Alex Huang."

"Who?"

"The correspondent who was asking questions."

"How do you know his name?"

"Because he was my correspondent. He quit before getting the whole story. He said at the time that HLI amounted to nothing. Probably just something manufactured by conspiracy theorists. They could make up any crazy thing and attribute it to the mysterious HLI."

"That actually sounds about right."

"I never gave it another thought until Pete Hamilton died getting that information to us. And the Iranian informant said 'White House' just before he died. We can't ignore it."

"Where is he?" asked Williams. "This journalist?"

"Betsy's found him. He's changed his name and is hiding out in a village in Québec. A place called Three Pines. But he's refusing to talk. I want to try to get someone there who can convince him. Someone he trusts. If we've found him, Shah won't be far behind."

"And if he won't tell us what he knows about HLI?" asked Williams. "Do we kidnap him too? Why not? Might as well invade yet another sovereign country, another ally. I'm sure Canada won't mind."

He could feel himself getting giddy and pulled back. He had to keep his head if he was going to come out of this day alive, having found the bombs and disarmed them.

"Look," he said. "Shah's our main target, our priority. If we have him, the rest is moot. But to get him I need to authorize a black op. In broad daylight. Against our own people. Against a former President. Just so we're clear. That's illegal."

"Yeah, well, planting nuclear bombs probably is too," said Betsy.

"Doug, the chances of you or me surviving the day physically, never mind politically, are pretty small," said Ellen. "A prison term should be the least of our worries. If Shah knows where the bombs are, and we have"—she looked at the clock, ironically an atomic clock, on her desk in Air Force Three—"ten hours to find and disarm them, then my vote is we break every law going to do it. And let the chips fall where they may."

"Those chips are going to crush us, Ellen." He sounded not just exhausted but drained. And resigned. "I'll start it rolling. This had better work. Shah had better be there."

Air Force Three was just approaching Andrews Air Force Base as Eric Dunn approached the first tee. And the commandos approached the villa.

President Dunn's tee time had been moved up due to, the secretary of the club explained to Dunn's annoyed assistant, an unexpected computer glitch.

The Special Operators watched him leave the compound, then took up their positions.

They could see the security guards. Private contractors with assault rifles and festooned with so many belts of ammunition they not only clanked when they patrolled; they could barely move.

By contrast, the Delta Force operators relied on stealth and speed. They carried knives, guns, ropes, and tape. That was it.

Any real commando knew that people were more important than hardware. The success of a mission rested more on the training and character of the soldier than on their weapons.

The far-right militia members, on the other hand, valued an Uzi over mental stability.

The Secret Service agents who would normally guard a former President had been marginalized by the private security force brought in by Dunn. And that morning, after a quiet word from HQ, the Secret Service had retreated even further into the background.

It took the leader of the black ops team just a few minutes of watching the private contractors to work out their routine.

When he gave the signal, his people surged over the wall, dropping catlike to the other side, then silently sprinted for the villa. Scans had identified where the people were in the house, and while they could make an educated guess as to which one was Shah, they could not be certain.

The order was no casualties. No one gets hurt. Get the guy and get out.

It was a near-impossible task, but those were the only ones these commandos took on.

While one group swept through the upstairs, a second took the main floor, a third the basement, while two crept into the back garden, where a man was sitting on the patio.

"Not him," he reported and backed away before he could be seen. Then went on to his secondary target.

"Not him."

"Not him."

"Not him."

One by one they reported, while back at the White House and on Air Force Three, Williams and Ellen and Betsy watched the body cams. Barely breathing. If Shah wasn't there . . .

"Not him," the last commando reported.

"He's not here," said the second-in-command.

There was silence for a beat before the leader spoke: "There're people in the kitchen."

"All staff," said another. "A cook, a dishwasher, and a server. Confirmed."

"My scans show four people. One must've been in the walk-in fridge." It was metal-lined, and people inside wouldn't show up. "Check again."

Two Special Operators ran silently down the back stairs to the basement, ducking into a side room and narrowly missing an aide returning upstairs with her breakfast.

As they approached the kitchen, there was the unmistakable scent of coriander and frying bread. And a voice in softly accented English.

"This's called paratha," the man at the stove was saying as he prodded a triangle of bread in the cast-iron pan. "Once it's almost done, we add the egg mixture."

Delta Force entered the kitchen. The cook had just begun to register the intruders, and the man had just begun to turn to look, when tape was put over his mouth and a sack over his head.

"Got him."

One of the commandos slung him over his shoulder; then they turned and ran. They were gone in seconds, vanishing before the cook or dishwasher could react.

They raced up the stairs, the body kicking and squirming and moaning. The commandos were guided by tech support telling them where the people were.

Ducking into a room, they waited until staff and security ran past, converging on the kitchen, reacting to the shouts.

The Deltas were in and out of there in minutes.

Twelve minutes later a civilian helicopter took off from a private field and headed north.

Air Force Three had landed, but Ellen and Betsy stayed on board to watch the operation.

"Please, dear God," said Ellen when the helicopter took off, "let it be Shah and not some poor cook."

"Take his hood off," President Williams ordered, and the Delta commander did.

Staring at them was the face of the waiter from the dinner in Islamabad.

Staring at them was the face of a notorious nuclear physicist.

Staring at them was the most dangerous arms dealer in the world.

Dr. Bashir Shah.

"We got him," sighed Ellen. "We captured the Azhi Dahaka."

Down the line she could hear Doug Williams laughing, an edge of hysteria in his relief. Then the laughing stopped. "Azhi who? It isn't Shah?"

"Oh, I'm sorry. Yes, yes. It's Shah. Congratulations, Mr. President, you did it."

"We did it. They did it." Williams spoke into the earphones to the Delta commander. "Congratulations. One day I hope to be able to tell you just how important this action is."

"You're welcome, Mr. President."

On hearing that, Shah's eyes widened. His mouth was still taped, but his eyes said it all. He was pretty sure he knew where they were taking him.

And what was waiting there, besides the American President.

Doug Williams bowed his head and brought his hands up to his face, feeling the rub of stubble.

Before he went into his private bathroom to shower and shave, he looked up "Azhi Dahaka." It took him a few tries to get the spelling right, but there it was.

A three-headed dragon of destruction and terror, born of lies and spawned to wreak havoc on the world. A serpent tyrant whose appearance ushered in chaos.

Yes. Bashir Shah was all that.

But as Doug Williams splashed water on his face and looked at himself in the mirror, he wondered who the other two heads belonged to.

Ivanov, yes. But who was the other? Who was the HLI?

It was only when he was in the shower, the hot water flowing through his hair, over his head and face, down his body, it was only as he felt himself almost human again that it came to him.

What Ellen said about her journalist. The one who, like so many others before him, fled to Canada in hopes of finding safety. She'd mentioned some village in Québec. It was the second time someone had recently talked about such a thing.

As he toweled himself off, he remembered. Those dreadful moments waiting to be incinerated.

The General said something about his dog. Pine.

Three pines. Three Pines.

Hurrying out of the bathroom, a towel around his waist, he called the Chair of the Joint Chiefs of Staff, listened, then called his

Secretary of State, who was on her way to her own home for a quick shower and change of clothes before heading to the White House.

"Have you sent anyone to Québec to talk to the journalist?" he asked.

"Not yet. We're trying to find someone he trusts."

"Don't bother, I think we have someone."

It was now nine in the morning. If they were right, the nuclear bombs would go off at four that afternoon.

Seven hours. They had seven hours.

But they also had Shah. And now, maybe, they had a lead on the third head of the Azhi Dahaka.

"How's Pine?"

"Great. Though his ears are kinda big," said the General over the phone.

"Really?" Armand Gamache looked down at Henri, his own German shepherd, who'd trip over his ears if they hung down. As it was, they stood straight up. The dog looked constantly astonished. "I've been hearing rumblings out of DC. Everything all right down there?"

"Well, as a matter of fact, that's why I'm calling. You know a fellow named Alex Huang?"

"Sure. Not personally, but I used to read his reports from the White House. He retired, didn't he?"

"Quit, yes. He now lives in Three Pines."

"I don't think so. No one here by that name."

"No, but you do have an Al Chen. An American. Arrived two, three years ago?"

"Two years ago, yes." Gamache's voice had grown wary. "Are you telling me he's Huang? Why would he change his name?"

"That's why I'm calling. I need you to do something."

Ellen stepped inside the shower. Finally.

She closed her eyes and let the warm water hit her face and cascade down her exhausted body. She felt bruised all over, even though she had no injuries. None visible, anyway. But she knew she would never fully recover from the shock, the pain, the terror of the past few days.

The injuries were internal. Eternal.

There was no time to think of that. There was still a distance to be run. The final sprint.

She and Betsy had stopped in at her home for quick showers and to change into clean, fresh clothes. A pit stop. For her. For Betsy?

Once out of the shower, Ellen smelled fresh coffee and maple-smoked bacon.

"You're making breakfast?" she asked as she entered the bright and cheery kitchen. "The world is literally about to explode and you're frying bacon?"

"And I'm warming up those cinnamon buns you like."

Yes, now she could smell that as well.

"Are you trying to torture me? I can't stay. Have to get to the White House."

"I've made them to go. We can eat and drink in the car."

"Betsy—"

Her counselor stopped, the spatula in her hand, and looked at her. "No, don't say it."

"You're not coming with me."

"Like hell I'm not. We've been best friends since kindergarten. You saved my life more than once, supporting me emotionally, financially. After Patrick died . . ." She took a breath, a gasp, teetering on the edge of that bottomless wound. "You're my best friend. I won't be left behind."

"I need you here. For Katherine. For Gil. For the dogs."

"You don't have any dogs."

"No, but you'll get some, won't you? If . . ."

Betsy's eyes began to sting, and her breath came in jagged gasps. "You. Can't. Leave. Me. Behind."

"I need you," said Ellen. *Please*, she begged herself. *Say it. Say the last words. "With me." With me. I need you with me.* "Here. Promise me you'll do as I ask. Please. For once in your life. I'll video-call you. But if you're not here, I'll hang up, so help me God."

"I'll be here."

"I'll leave a number by the hall phone. Use it if you need to."

Betsy nodded.

Ellen grabbed her, hugging her tight. "The past, present, and future walk into a bar . . ."

Betsy gripped her friend and tried to speak, but nothing came out. Ellen pulled back, kissed Betsy on the cheek, turned, and left.

As she walked quickly to the door and the waiting vehicle, she passed the framed photos of the children, of the birthdays and Thanksgivings and Christmases. Of her wedding to Quinn.

Of Betsy and her as kids. Betsy all dirty and snotty and Ellen pristine. Two halves of a splendid whole.

Ellen Adams left her home and stepped into the waiting SUV. To take her to the White House, where the President and a nuclear bomb were waiting.

"It was tense," Betsy whispered as she watched the vehicle pull away. Then she slowly, slowly sank to her knees. Ellen's perfume hung softly, subtly all around her, as though there to keep her safe. Aromatics Elixir.

She bent over so that she was as tiny as she could get. Closing her eyes. Rocking.

Betsy Jameson wasn't just afraid; she was in a state of terror.

Chief Inspector Gamache, the head of homicide for the Sûreté du Québec, walked into the bookstore.

"Still hasn't come in, Armand," said Myrna.

"What hasn't?"

"The *Charlotte's Web* you ordered for your granddaughter. You look distracted."

"A little. Is Al around?"

"He's shoveling snow at Ruth's."

"Shoveling her out, or in?" asked Armand, and Myrna laughed.

"Out this time."

"Merci," said Armand and walked through the brilliant, crystalline winter day, over to Ruth Zardo's small home just off the village green. He saw puffs of snow rising from behind the tall drifts, and the flash of a shovel blade.

"Al?"

The man, in his late forties, his face flushed from exertion and cold, stopped and leaned on the shovel. "Armand, what's up?"

"Can we talk?"

Al stared at his neighbor. By the look on Gamache's face, he could guess what this was about. He'd been contacted a few hours earlier by someone named Betsy, from the State Department. He'd refused to talk. He had a new life, he explained. A good life. A peaceful life.

Finally.

Though not altogether peaceful. There'd been a shadow over it, every day and every night. Al Chen had known this day would come, when the shadow moved off and the creature itself appeared.

Chen gave a long, long exhale, his breath coming out in a stream of steam. Thrusting the shovel into the snowbank, he said, "OK. Let's talk."

The two walked over to the bistro, their feet crunching on the packed snow. Their eyes squinting into the brilliant sun that was bouncing off the deep drifts.

Up ahead, Gamache saw the bistro. Chen saw the end of his peaceful life.

Once inside, they found seats by the fire and ordered cafés au lait.

"Merci," said Gamache when the drinks had arrived; then he turned to Al, studying him for a moment. When he spoke, his voice was hushed. "I know who you are and why you came here. It was to hide, wasn't it?"

Al didn't speak. So Gamache went on.

"And I know why you stay here." He looked at the door that connected through to the bookstore. He leaned close to Chen and dropped his voice still further. "If he finds you, he'll bring all manner of hell here. Not just to you, but to Myrna and anyone else he wants."

"I don't know who you're talking about, Armand. Who's 'he'?"

"The person you're hiding from. Do you want me to actually say it? Look, if we found you, so will he. I don't know how much time we have, but I suspect it's not much."

"I can't go back, Armand. I just barely got out." His hands were trembling, and Armand remembered the man who'd arrived two years earlier.

Shaking anytime there was a loud noise. Unable to go into a crowded room. Trembling when anyone looked his way, never mind spoke to him. It was all they could do to coax him out of his room at Olivier and Gabri's B&B. Finally it was Myrna, with her warm melodic voice and chocolate cake, who did it.

Suspecting he liked books, she'd invited him over to her store one summer evening, after it had closed. Every three days after that, she'd open the door and let him browse, privately. He bought all sorts of books, sometimes new, often used.

Then she'd coax him onto the patio out back, where they'd sip beer and watch the rivière Bella Bella flow by. They'd talk. Or not.

Then she got him onto the front patio. Where he could see village life, slow but never stagnant, flow by.

Little by little Al Chen had emerged.

And now he was fully a part of the community. Though not fully honest with them.

"Does Myrna know who you really are?"

"No. She knows I have a past I don't want to discuss, but not who I am."

"I won't tell her. But you need to go back. You need to tell them what you know about that website. HLI."

Al shook his head. "I won't. I can't."

"Look," Gamache said. "They have Bashir Shah. He's on his way to DC now, in custody. But they need to know who the high-level informant is. You can see that, right?"

"They have Shah? For real? You're not just saying that?"

"They have him. But you know how dangerous he is. What he and his people are capable of. President Williams needs to know Shah's informant in the White House."

Armand hadn't been told about the bombs, didn't have to be. He knew about the bus bombs in Europe, of course. And he'd heard the chatter about other explosives. More powerful ones. Somewhere.

"If you can't go back, then tell me. Who's the high-level informant? Who is he?"

Instead of yelling, Gamache's voice had softened. From vast experience, he knew that people naturally put up their defenses when yelled at. But if spoken to gently, they, like a frightened wounded animal, might just come to him.

Al Chen shook his head, but this time it was different. He wasn't refusing to talk, Gamache could see. He was disagreeing with him.

"Not a he."

"She?"

"Them. That's what I found out. HLI isn't a single person. Or it might be, someone's obviously directing it, but what I found out is that HLI is a group. An organization."

"What's its purpose?"

"To return America to what they think it should be. From what I could tell, it's made up of powerful people who are disaffected."

"With?"

"With government. With the direction of the country. With changes in the culture. Having what they see as real American values eroded and disappearing. These aren't just decent conservative people who miss the way it once was and want it back. These are ultra-right extremists. Fascists. White supremacists, militias. They feel the United States is no longer America, so they don't feel they're being disloyal. Just the opposite. They mean to right the ship."

"By sinking it?"

"By purging it. They feel it's their patriotic duty."

"Members of the military?"

Chen nodded. "High-ranking. Respected. Members of Congress too. The Senate."

"*Mon Dieu,*" whispered Gamache, leaning away for a moment and staring into the fire.

"Who? We need names."

"I wish I knew. I'd tell you, but I don't."

"Supporters of the former President?"

"On the surface, but only that. These are people who hate the government. Even his."

"But some are members, politicians themselves."

"If you were going to bring down a huge system, wouldn't you start the rot from the inside?"

Gamache nodded. "HLI is a site on the dark web, right? Where these people share information."

"Beyond the dark web."

Gamache raised his brows. "I didn't know there was such a thing."

"The web is like the universe. It never ends. There are all sorts of wonders, and all sorts of black holes. That's where I found HLI."

"I need the address."

"I don't have it."

"I don't believe you."

They stared at each other. Gamache could see fear and anger in Al Chen's eyes. And Chen could see irritation, impatience in Gamache's. But he could see something else.

Deep inside those eyes, there was sympathy. And there was understanding. This man knew fear.

Al Chen took a deep breath, glanced toward the bookstore where Myrna was sorting the volumes that had come in, and did something Gamache had not expected.

He unbuttoned his shirt.

There, above his heart, was scar tissue. "I told Myrna it's a shorthand my mother used, for her favorite quote."

"And she believed you?"

"I'm not sure. She accepted."

"What is it really?"

"The address of HLI."

Gamache tilted his head and looked at the scar tissue, then into Chen's eyes. "It's not like anything I've seen before."

"Then count yourself fortunate. This will take you to the black hole. But it won't get you in. You need an entry code for that."

"And that is?"

Chen shook his head. "I never got it. This's as far as I got before they sent their people after me. And I came here."

He looked out the mullioned windows, etched with frost, to the three pine trees soaring over the village, pointing up to the heavens.

"We need the entry code," said Gamache. "Do you have any idea who has it?"

"Well, obviously any member of HLI. And probably Bashir Shah."

"Do you mind?" Gamache held up his phone, and when Chen shook his head, he took a photo of the short string of numbers and letters and symbols.

Not obviously a web address. At least not to any normal site. Not in this world, anyway.

"Who did that to you?"

"I did. Drunk and high one night."

"Why?"

"I think you know why, Armand."

Al rebuttoned his shirt, and together they left the bistro. Though bundled in a heavy parka, Alex Huang still felt the biting cold. No amount of insultation could warm him. The cold came from within. But maybe now he could feel warm again, fully human again.

Before they parted Armand thanked him and asked, "Did your mother really have a favorite quote?"

"Yes. It was '*Noli timere.*' "

Armand put out his hand. *"Noli timere."*

While Huang went back to digging out the ungrateful poet, Armand went home to send the photo to his friend. The Chair of the American Joint Chiefs of Staff. A photo not just of a web address, but of a man's self-loathing. Cut into his flesh as an accusation, a daily reminder of cowardice.

Noli timere, Armand thought as he hit send. Be not afraid.

Now, maybe, Al Chen, Alex Huang, could see the scars as something else. A hallelujah, a blessing. That he'd put the dreadful letters and numbers and symbols over his heart, where he'd never lose them. And that he ran to this village, where he actually did lose his heart.

Armand looked out at the splendid day and whispered, “Be not afraid. Be not afraid.”

But he was.

CHAPTER 42

This was the endgame.

Everyone in that room knew it.

It was 2:57 in the afternoon, DC time. 1457. They had until 1600, an hour and three minutes to find and disarm the bombs. They'd come a long way since that first coded message had arrived at Anahita Dahir's station in the State Department, an eternity ago.

But had they come far enough?

Teams were standing by in each major city. Every intelligence organization, internationally, was poring over communication intercepts from Al-Qaeda and its allies and had been since this began. But so far, nothing.

Their only real hope was the middle-aged Pakistani scientist sitting in the hard-backed chair in the Oval Office, glaring across the Resolute desk at the President of the United States.

"Tell us where the bombs are, Dr. Shah," said Williams.

"Why should I?"

"You don't deny it, then?"

Shah cocked his head, amused. "Deny it? I spent years under house arrest because of you Americans, thinking about this moment. Dreaming of it. Watching what was happening here in the States. Watching you make a balls-up of democracy. Very entertaining. Best reality show ever, though it's not actually reality, is it? Most of politics, of so-called democracy, is an illusion, staged for the great unwashed."

"Are you saying the bombs aren't real?" said Ellen.

"Oh, no. They're real."

"Then unless you want to go up too, you'll tell us where they are. We have"—she looked at the clock—"fifty-nine minutes."

"So you worked out the code I slipped into your pocket. Yes, fifty-nine. Ah, fifty-eight minutes, and then all this goes away. Given a choice between bedlam and a dictatorship, what do you think the American people will choose? Driven by fear of another attack, in a state of terror, they'll do the terrorists' work for them. They'll destroy their own freedoms. Accept, even applaud, the suspension of rights. Internment camps. Torture. Expulsions. The liberal agenda, women's equality, gay marriage, immigrants, will be blamed for the death of the real America. But thanks to the bold action of a patriotic few, the white Anglo-Saxon Christian, God-fearing America of their grandparents will be restored. And if they have to slaughter a few thousand to achieve it, well, it is war, after all. The beacon that was America will die, by suicide. Frankly it was coughing up blood anyway."

"Where are they!" shouted President Williams.

"I've seen a lot of coups, though never quite this close." Shah leaned forward. "They all have one thing in common. You want to know what that is?"

Williams and Ellen glared at him.

"I'll tell you. They're all so . . . sudden. At least, to the person being coup'd. All those about to be toppled, and perhaps even shot or hanged, look like you do, Mr. President. Shocked. Appalled. Perplexed. Frightened. How could this happen? But if you'd been paying attention, you'd have seen the tide turning. The water rising. The uprising. This's as much your fault as anyone's."

Shah sat back, crossed his legs, and brushed an invisible piece of lint off his knee. But Ellen noted a slight quiver in his hand. A quiver that had not been there when the waiter had given her her salad.

This was new.

This man was afraid after all. But of what? Of dying, or something else? What would an Azhi Dahaka fear? Only one thing.

A bigger monster.

And judging by the tremble, one must be close.

"While you were looking outward, scanning the horizon for threats," he continued, "you missed what was happening in your own backyard. What was taking root right here, on American soil. In your towns, your shops, in your heartland. Among your friends, in your families. The sensible conservatives moving to the right. The right moving far right. The far right becoming alt-right. Becoming, in their rage and frustration, radicalized thanks to an internet filled with crazy theories, false 'facts,' and smug politicians allowed to spew lies.

"I saw from a distance what you could not see close up. The unhappiness here growing into outrage. The so-called patriots had the rage, the intent, the financial backing. They had the fuse, all they were missing was the one thing I could provide."

"A bomb," said Williams.

"A nuclear bomb," said Ellen.

"Just so. All I needed was to be released, and your useful idiot of a President provided that. I could then put the two halves together." He lifted his hands. "International terrorists in Al-Qaeda and domestic patriots." He placed his hands together. "And voilà. Yes, I had years to think about this moment. Time and patience, time and patience. Tolstoy said those are the strongest of warriors, and he was right. So few have both. I do. True, I'd assumed I'd be watching this from my home in Islamabad, but now I get a front-row seat."

"You're actually on the stage," said Ellen.

He turned to her. "As are you. I'm in a lucrative but dangerous profession. I have no illusions about that. I've considered the different ways I might die, and honestly, quickly in a flash of light is probably the best. I'm ready. Are you?" He turned back to the President. "Besides, if I did tell you, my clients would make sure my death was a lot less quick and a lot less light-filled."

"That's probably true," said Williams. "You're fortunate you're in our custody and they can't get at you. Unless there happens to be an HLI in the household."

That rattled the physicist for just a moment but long enough for Ellen to realize who Bashir Shah was afraid of. Who the bigger monster was. The high-level informant.

"HLI?" Shah said. "I have no idea what you're talking about."

"That's a shame," said Williams. "Not for you, of course. But maybe for others."

The smile froze on Shah's face. "What do you mean?"

Fifty-two minutes left.

"Well," said Williams, "you've left a trail of bodies behind you, some to clear up loose ends and some to act as a warning to others. I suspect your friends will do the same thing when they find out we have you. Now, who might Al-Qaeda, who might the Russian mob, go after as an object lesson not to betray them?"

Ellen bent down and spoke into Dr. Shah's ear. She could smell jasmine and sweat. "I'll give you a hint. Who did you go after when my news agencies started reporting on your black market arms sales? Who poisoned my husband? Who terrorized my children? Who tried to kill my son and daughter just yesterday?"

"My family? You'd hurt my family?"

She stood up. "No, Dr. Shah, that's one of many differences. We would not harm your family."

He exhaled.

"Unfortunately, all our agents and operatives in Pakistan and beyond are busy trying to track down information on the bombs, as are our allies. And so while we absolutely will not harm your family, neither can we protect them. Who knows what Al-Qaeda has been told about why you're at the White House? Who knows what Ivanov and the Russian mafia think?"

"It's even possible," said President Williams, "there are rumors that you're cooperating. That you're an American asset. Democracy. Free speech. It is entertaining, isn't it?"

"They know I'd never betray them."

"Are you so sure? When I was in Tehran, the Grand Ayatollah told me a Persian fable about the cat and the rat. Do you know it?"

Shah nodded.

"But there's another one you might be interested in. The frog and the scorpion."

"I'm not."

"The scorpion wants to cross a river, but he doesn't swim. He needs help. So he asks a frog to take him across on his back," said Ellen. "The frog says, 'But if I do, you'll sting me and I'll die.' The scorpion scoffs. 'I promise not to sting you because we'd both drown.' So the frog agrees and the two set off across the river."

Shah's face was turned away, but he was listening.

"Halfway across, the scorpion stings the frog," said Ellen. "With his last breath, the frog asks, 'Why?' "

"And the scorpion answers, 'I can't help it,' " said President Williams. " 'It's in my nature.' " He leaned across the desk. "We know who you are. We know your nature. As do your so-called allies. They know you'll betray them in an instant. Tell us where the bombs are, and we'll protect your family."

Barb Stenhauser entered the Oval Office at that moment and crossed to President Williams.

"Tim Beecham's back, he's waiting in the outer office. Should I show him in?"

"Please do, Barb."

"And President Dunn's on the phone. He sounds angry."

Williams looked at the time. Fifty minutes left.

"Tell him to call back in an hour."

Katherine Adams, Gil Bahar, Anahita Dahir, and Charles Boynton sat in silence around the rickety table. The sole light in the room was off in the corner so that their faces were mostly in shadow.

Which was just as well. They could sense each other's increasing terror. No need to also see it.

Boynton touched his phone, and the time lit up. Ten minutes past midnight in Pakistan. Fifty minutes to the time when Osama bin Laden was killed.

Fifty minutes to when hundreds, perhaps thousands, would be killed. Including Katherine and Gil's mother.

And there was nothing they could do.

Bashir Shah looked toward the door as Tim Beecham walked in.

The President's DNI stopped in his tracks and stared at the man sitting upright in the chair. Beecham looked unwell. Though the bruising around his eyes and the splint on his nose didn't help.

"You got him?"

But no one was paying attention to the DNI. All eyes were on Shah.

"Where are the bombs?" the President repeated.

"All I can tell you is that they're in DC, New York, and Kansas City. Protect my family. Please."

"Where in those cities?" demanded Williams as Ellen picked up the phone and made the calls.

"I don't know."

"Of course you do," said Beecham, quickly picking up on the situation and striding across the floor to where Shah sat. "You must've arranged delivery."

"But only to agents in each city."

"Their names!"

"I don't know. How can I remember?"

"The shipments weren't labeled *Nuclear Bombs*," said Beecham. "What were they supposed to be?"

"Medical equipment, for radiology labs."

"Shit," said Beecham, reaching for another line out. "If radiation is detected, it's explainable. When did they ship?"

"A few weeks ago."

"A date," Beecham shouted. "I need a date." He spoke into the phone. "It's Beecham. Get me Homeland Security. I need international shipments traced. Now!"

"February 4th. By ship via Karachi."

Beecham relayed the information.

Ellen, off the phone now, was listening. Something was wrong. "He's lying."

Beecham turned to her. "Why do you say that?"

"Because he's volunteering information."

"To save his family," said President Williams.

Ellen shook her head. "No. Think about it. His family must be safe. He said himself, he's had years to plan this. He wouldn't leave them, or himself, vulnerable like that. He doesn't trust Al-Qaeda and the Russian mafia any more than they trust him. He's messing with us."

"Why?" demanded Beecham.

"Why do you think? Why does Shah do anything? He'll take it to the wire, won't you? Then demand something extraordinary for the information we need. But only about the bomb you're sitting on. You'll let the others explode. You set this whole thing up. Even going to Dunn's. Any sensible person would hide out in some remote château in the Alps until this blows over—"

"Don't you mean 'blows up'?" said Shah. No longer looking anxious, afraid. Now he was shaking his head, smiling.

"You mean he wanted to be brought here?" said Beecham.

"You are a bright one," Shah said to Ellen, then looked at Tim Beecham. "You, not so much." Shah turned back to Ellen. "I probably should have poisoned you too, but I've enjoyed our little relationship."

Barb Stenhauser appeared at the door. "The General's here, with security. Did you want—"

"Send him in," said President Williams. "And come in yourself."

Ellen brought out her phone and pressed the video call button.

Thirty-six minutes left.

This was it.

Betsy picked up on the first ring.

She could hear voices, could see the Oval Office. But not Ellen. She was obviously holding her phone in front of her. Betsy was about to speak, then changed her mind.

There was a reason Ellen hadn't said anything. Best to remain quiet until Ellen did speak.

What Betsy did do was hit record. The camera swung around to the door, and Betsy's eyes widened in surprise.

Tim Beecham's eyes widened in surprise.

Bashir Shah's eyes widened in surprise.

General Whitehead's face was bruised; his uniform was stained with blood from the fight with Tim Beecham. Two Army Rangers stood on either side of him.

"Glad you could join us, General," said Williams, and turned to the others. "I think you know the Chairman of the Joint Chiefs."

"Former," said Beecham.

"Someone here is 'former,'" said Whitehead. "But it's not me."

He nodded to the officers who walked forward to take up positions on either side of the former Director of National Intelligence.

CHAPTER 43

What is this?" demanded Beecham.

"Anything yet, Bert?" asked President Williams, ignoring Beecham.

"Still waiting."

"Waiting?" Beecham looked from one man to the other. "For what?"

Thirty-four minutes.

Ellen walked up to Beecham. "Tell us."

"What?"

"Where are the bombs, Tim?"

"What? You think I know?" He looked stunned and afraid. "Mr. President, you can't think—"

"We don't think, we know." Williams glared at Beecham. "You're the high-level informant. The traitor. The one not just leaking information, but actively working with our enemies, with terrorists, to set off nuclear bombs. It's over. I've written a statement to be sent to Congress and the media at 1601 today, naming you as the traitor. Even if you somehow survive, you'll be hunted down. You've failed. Tell us where they are."

"No, God, no. It's not me. It's him." He gestured toward Whitehead.

Thirty-three minutes.

Williams came around the desk and made straight for his DNI. He put his hand around Beecham's throat and thrust him all the way back across the Oval Office until Beecham's back pounded into the wall.

No one tried to stop him.

"Where're the bombs?"

"I don't know," he sputtered.

"Where's your family?" demanded Ellen, striding across the room to stand right beside the President.

"My family?" Beecham croaked.

"I'll tell you. They're in Utah. You took your children out of school and sent them far away from any fallout. You know where General Whitehead's family is? I do. I met them. His wife, daughter, grandson are here in DC. What's the first thing anyone does if there's danger? They get their family to safety. Even Shah did. And so did you. Then you got yourself out. But Bert Whitehead stayed. As did his family. Because they had no idea what was about to happen. That's when I began to realize who the real traitor was."

"Tell us!" Williams demanded, and had to will himself not to squeeze the life out of Beecham.

Thirty minutes.

"We have it," called Whitehead. "It just came in. I'm forwarding it to you, Mr. President."

Williams let go and Tim Beecham slid to the floor, clutching his throat.

The President ran to his desk and, not bothering to read the text, he clicked on the photograph, then grimaced. "Is that human skin? What is this?"

"According to my friend, it's the internet address of the HLI site."

"Cut into someone's skin?" demanded Williams.

"Not someone's," said Ellen. "It's Alex Huang."

"Huang?" said Barb Stenhauser. Up until that moment she'd

been hanging back, by the door. Now she stepped forward to look at the monitor. "The White House correspondent? Wasn't he one of yours? He quit a few years ago."

"He went into hiding," said Ellen, glaring at Shah, who was watching this as though it was a play. "He'd been investigating rumors of something called the HLI. He thought it was just another fringe conspiracy theory site for the far right, but then he dug deeper. Pete Hamilton found out too. But Pete didn't get away."

"What did they find out?" asked President Williams.

"My friend in—" But Whitehead managed to stop before giving away Huang's location.

Ellen looked at Shah, who'd leaned slightly forward.

"Huang says HLI isn't one person," the General continued. "It's a group, an organization. All highly placed in different branches of government. Including, God help me, the military." He shook his head, then continued. "There're elected officials. Senators, members of Congress, and at least one Supreme Court Justice."

"My God," whispered Williams.

"There it is," said Shah. "The coup face."

"You fucking ass—" began Williams, but stopped himself.

Twenty-eight minutes left.

The President turned back to the photograph on his screen. "What're we supposed to do with this? It's gibberish. Just a series of numbers, letters, and symbols."

Ellen bent closer, making sure her phone faced the screen. He was right. It was unlike any internet address she'd ever seen.

"The address apparently takes members to a place beyond the dark web," said Whitehead.

"That's bullshit," croaked Beecham, still on the floor and holding his throat. "There is no such place."

"Let's just see." Williams put them into his laptop and hit enter.

Nothing happened.

The computer was thinking, thinking. Thinking.

Twenty-six minutes.

Come on. Come on, thought Ellen. Prayed Ellen.

Betsy sat at Ellen's kitchen table, in the pool of sunshine streaming through the windows, and watched.

Come on. Come on, she prayed.

In the Oval Office, President Williams stared at the screen. At the thin blue line pulsing forward, retreating. Pulsing. Retreating.

Come on, he prayed.

"It isn't working," said Stenhauser, panic in her voice. "We need to leave." She stepped closer to the door.

"Stay where you are, Barb," commanded the President.

"It's twenty-five to four."

"You're staying. We're all staying," he said.

General Whitehead nodded to one of the Rangers, who took up position at the door.

Come on. Come on.

Just then the computer stopped thinking. It went to black.

No one blinked. No one breathed. And then a door appeared on the screen.

President Williams took a deep breath and whispered, "Oh, thank God."

He pushed the cursor to the center of the door and prepared to click.

"Wait," said Ellen. "How do we know it's not a trap? How do we know clicking on it won't set off the bombs?"

He looked at the time. "It's twenty-two minutes to four, Ellen. At this point, does it matter?"

She took a deep breath and gave a curt nod, as did General Whitehead.

"Noooo," whispered Betsy. "Don't do it."

Williams clicked on it.

Nothing.

He tried again. Nothing.

"Is there a knocker? A doorbell?" asked Ellen. It sounded ludicrous, but no one laughed.

"No," said Williams. Now he was moving the cursor around and clicking at random. "Shit, shit, shit."

Twenty minutes left.

Whitehead picked up his phone and looked again at the message from Gamache in Québec.

"Damn, I didn't read the whole email. Too anxious to get the photograph. He says Huang told him we need a code to get in."

"What?!" demanded Williams. "Does he say what it is?"

"No. Huang couldn't find it and stopped trying when he realized they were after him."

Eighteen minutes.

They looked at Beecham.

"What is it? What's the code?" Whitehead strode over and lifted him off the floor by his lapels, pounding his back so hard against the wall, the portrait of Lincoln tilted. "Tell us!"

"I don't know. For God's sake, I don't know. Ask him!" Beecham waved toward Shah, who was smiling.

"Time and patience. I'm enjoying myself. Why would I tell you?"

"But you know it?" demanded Ellen.

"Maybe. Maybe not."

"What're we supposed to do?" Williams demanded. "What could it be?"

Ellen was staring at Shah. Her eyes drilling into him until he shifted slightly.

"Al-Qaeda," she said.

"You want me to try 'Al-Qaeda'?" asked Williams, and before Ellen could say no, he did.

Nothing.

"What I mean," said Ellen, "is that Al-Qaeda chose today for the bombs for a reason. To mark Osama bin Laden's birth and death. Symbolic. And we all know symbols are powerful. Three, ten, sixteen hundred. These people"—she waved toward Beecham—"think of themselves as patriots. True Americans. What would they use as a code?"

"Independence Day?" suggested Williams. "But the words? The numbers?"

"Try both," said Ellen.

"But we might only get one or two tries," said Whitehead.

Williams lifted his hands in exasperation. Then wrote *IndependenceDay* and hit enter.

Nothing.

He tried caps, no caps, the numbers. A space.

"Shit, shit, shit."

Fifteen minutes.

"Wait," said Ellen. She turned to Shah. "I'm wrong." She stared at him for one beat. Two. Time and patience. Three beats.

All sound, all motion, stopped as she stared at the Azhi Dahaka, and he stared back.

"Try three, ten, sixteen hundred."

President Williams did.

Nothing.

Ellen's brows drew together. What could it be? She was sure, when she'd given those numbers, she'd seen Shah's eyes widen.

"Try three, space, ten, space, then sixteen hundred."

As soon as Williams hit enter, there was a sound. A creaking. And the door slowly, very slowly, opened to reveal three screens, each showing a bomb.

"Oh my God," said the President of the United States, as they all stared.

"You fool. You gave it to them."

Everyone looked at Shah, then at the person who'd spoken.

General Bert Whitehead was pressing a gun to the President's head.

CHAPTER 44

Betsy Jameson couldn't see the Oval Office, but she knew something terrible had just happened.

What she could see was the laptop screen.

Ellen was holding her phone absolutely rock steady, pointing at the opened door and what it revealed.

"You fucker," rasped President Williams as he was hauled backward out of his chair. The handgun at his temple.

The Army Rangers started forward.

"Everyone back away," commanded Whitehead.

"That's why you sat with me this morning," said Williams. "You knew the bomb wasn't going to explode at ten past three."

"Of course I knew. Beecham, get their guns." He indicated the Army Rangers, who looked more shocked than anyone. "Stenhauser, they have zip cuffs. Cuff them to the legs of the desk."

"Me?" said Stenhauser.

"For God's sake, you think I don't know who you are? I recruited you, and you recruited your assistant. Where is she, by the way? I'm assuming she's the one who killed Hamilton. I hope you looked after her too."

Tim Beecham had disarmed the Rangers and offered one of the

guns to Stenhauser. She looked at it, clearly knowing what accepting it would mean.

"Oh, what the fuck," she said, and took it. Then she slowly turned until the weapon was pointing at the Chair of the Joint Chiefs of Staff. "Who are you?"

The General gave a snort of derision. "Who do you think I am?"

She looked at Shah. "Do you know him?"

Shah was watching this and shaking his head. "No. But then, I don't know you either. Identities were closely guarded. But the fact that he's holding a gun to the President's temple is a clue, don't you think?"

Bert Whitehead smiled. "You want to know who I am? I'm a true American. A patriot. I'm HLI."

The third head of the Azhi Dahaka was the Chair of the Joint Chiefs of Staff after all.

The military coup was underway.

Betsy's eyes widened. At what was being said, but mostly at the images on the laptop.

The open door had revealed the locations of the bombs.

On one side of the screen were shots of the devices themselves, and on the other, a live video of their location.

Twelve minutes left.

She could see the huge concourse of Grand Central Terminal in New York City, crammed with rush hour commuters. And the bomb in the station's infirmary.

She could see families lining up for Legoland in Kansas City. And the bomb in the first aid office.

But in the White House, the location of the bomb wasn't clear. The image was too close up to see anything else around it. It could be anywhere in the vast building.

There was, however, a live shot of the Oval Office. She could see that Bert Whitehead had taken the President hostage. They'd been right after all.

Eleven minutes and twenty-five seconds.

Someone should do something, she thought. Someone should be told.

Someone should make a call.

"Oh dear," she sighed. "It's me. Ellen wants me to do it."

But who to call?

Betsy was paralyzed. Who could defuse the bombs? Even if she knew, she couldn't use her phone. She needed to keep up this connection to the Oval Office. To the President's laptop screen. To Ellen.

But there was another phone. A landline in the front hall. She ran to it and found the number Ellen had placed beside it. Grabbing the phone, Betsy dialed.

"Madame Vice President?"

Ten minutes and forty-three seconds.

"No, you're not HLI," said Beecham. "She is." He pointed to Stenhauser. "She set the whole thing up. She's the high-level informant."

"Shut up, you idiot," Stenhauser snarled.

"They know," said Beecham. As he stared at the President's Chief of Staff, his eyes widened. "You're the one. You tried to set me up. Hiding my documents. Making it look like I was behind all this. So I'd take the blame if anything went wrong. You're working with Whitehead."

"He's not involved," said Stenhauser. "I have no idea who he is."

"Good," said Whitehead. "That was the idea. You think I wanted anyone to know? Think back, Stenhauser. Was it really your idea, or were you led to it? I needed a front, someone who could approach

Senators, members of Congress. Supreme Court Justices. How many of them have you recruited now? Two? Three?"

"Three," said Beecham.

"Shut the fuck up!" said Stenhauser.

"Oh my God," whispered Ellen, as the extent of the plot became clear. "Why? Why would you do this? Allow terrorists to set off nuclear bombs here? On American soil?"

"America? This isn't America!" Stenhauser shouted. "Do you think Washington, Jefferson, any of the Founding Fathers would recognize this country? Jobs for hardworking Americans are being stolen. Prayer is banned. Abortions are happening every hour of every day. Gays can marry. Immigrants and criminals are flooding in. And we're letting it happen? No. It stops now."

"This isn't patriotism, it's domestic terrorism," Ellen shouted. "For God's sake, you helped in the slaughter of a platoon of Army Rangers."

"Martyrs. They died for their country," said Beecham.

"You make me sick," said Ellen. She turned to General Whitehead. "And you started all this?"

Six minutes and thirty-two seconds.

"I don't know who he is," said Barb Stenhauser. "But he's not one of us. Drop the gun."

She stepped toward Whitehead just as the General, in one swift movement, swung his weapon away from President Williams and toward Barb Stenhauser.

Williams saw that this was the moment. He thrust his elbow back, hitting Whitehead in the solar plexus, doubling the man up.

He then dove for Ellen, knocking her to the floor.

As the fusillade went off, Ellen curled into a ball and covered her head.

Betsy listened in horror.

Ellen's phone had dropped facedown onto the floor. She couldn't see anything, but she heard the shots. The shouts.

And then, silence.

She stared, openmouthed, wide-eyed. Not breathing. Finally she managed to whisper, "Ellen?" Then screamed, "Ellen!"

A commanding voice said, "Mr. President, are you all right? Madame Secretary?"

Betsy thought it must be a Secret Service agent, arrived to restore order.

"Ellen! Ellen!"

The blank screen disappeared, and she saw her friend's face. "Did you make the call?" Ellen demanded.

"Call?"

"The Vice President. Did you tell her where the bombs are?"

"Yes. The shots—"

"Blanks," came the President's familiar, though strained, voice.

Five minutes and twenty-one seconds.

"On the floor," a man said, his voice forceful. "Hands behind your head."

Ellen swung around, taking her phone with her so that Betsy could see Bashir Shah, Tim Beecham, and Barb Stenhauser facedown on the floor, hands behind their backs. Bert Whitehead, gun in hand, was kneeling beside the Rangers, cutting the zip cuffs off them.

"The bombs—" said Williams.

"Betsy's alerted the Vice President," said Ellen. "They're on it."

"But the one here," said Whitehead. "Where is it?"

They looked at the screen.

Four minutes and fifty-nine seconds.

"It could be anywhere," said Williams. He turned to the captives. "Where is it? Tell us! You'll die too."

"It's too late," said Stenhauser. "You'll never defuse it in time."

Williams, Adams, and Whitehead stared at one another.

"Where's the infirmary?" Ellen asked.

"I don't know," said the President. "I can barely find the dining room."

But General Whitehead's eyes had widened. "I know where it is." He looked down. "It's directly beneath the Oval Office."

"Oh, shit," said the President.

General Whitehead was already making for the door.

Four minutes and thirty-one seconds left.

The President of the United States and the Secretary of State took the back stairs two at a time, a few steps behind the Ranger and the Chairman of the Joint Chiefs of Staff.

"I hope to God you're right," said Williams.

"I am. The others were in infirmaries. This one must be too." But Ellen sounded far more confident than she felt.

Secret Service agents were close behind them. In the basement they found the door to the medical unit locked.

"I have a code to get in." The President punched the keypad, but his hands were shaking so badly he had to do it twice. It was all Ellen could do not to scream at him.

Instead she glanced at the countdown.

Four minutes and three seconds.

The door thumped open and lights automatically went on.

"You have your tools?" Whitehead asked the Ranger.

"Yes, sir."

They stood in the middle of the room and looked around.

"Where is it?" demanded Williams, turning full circle, his sharp eyes scanning.

"The MRI machine," said Ellen. "If the bomb missed detection, it's because they expected to see radiation from the MRI."

Three minutes, forty-three seconds.

The Ranger, a specialist in bomb disposal, carefully opened the panel on the MRI.

There it was.

"It's a dirty bomb, sir," he said. "A big one. This would take out the White House and spread radiation over half of Washington."

He bent over it and got to work while Whitehead turned to Williams and Ellen and said, "I'd tell you to run, but . . ."

Three minutes, thirteen seconds.

Whitehead stepped away and placed a call, Ellen suspected to his wife.

Betsy stared at her phone. She could see Ellen. Ellen could see her.

It was, Betsy thought, perhaps some small consolation that she would not have to grieve the loss of her friend for long. She'd go too, eventually, from radiation poisoning.

There was, thought Ellen, great comfort in knowing Katherine and Gil were far away.

Katherine and Gil, Anahita, Zahara, and Boynton huddled together in the near dark and stared at the phone in the middle of the table. On it was the live feed from Katherine's television network.

She knew if nuclear bombs went off, it would be reported live within minutes.

Right now the anchor was interviewing some talking head about whether a tomato was a fruit or vegetable. And what did that make ketchup in the dietary charts for schools?

Two minutes and forty-five seconds.

Gil felt a familiar hand slide into his and looked at Ana, who, with her other hand, held Zahara's. He reached out for Katherine, who reached out for Boynton's hand.

The tight circle stared at the phone and watched the countdown.

As the Ranger worked, and the General spoke on the phone, Ellen felt Doug Williams beside her. When she took his hand, he smiled his thanks.

"I can't work it out," said the Ranger. "It's not like any mechanism I've seen before."

One minute, thirty-one seconds.

"Here." Whitehead thrust his phone at the Ranger. "Listen."

They stared at the Ranger, working frantically.

Forty seconds.

He grabbed another tool and dropped it. General Whitehead stooped and picked it up, handing it to the wide-eyed Ranger.

Twenty-one seconds.

Still working. Still working.

Nine seconds.

Betsy closed her eyes.

Eight.

Williams closed his eyes.

Seven.

Ellen closed her eyes. And felt a calm come over her.

CHAPTER 45

All networks were carrying the news conference live.

The monitor in the Secretary of State's office was tuned to the James S. Brady Press Briefing Room in the White House. Reporters were milling around, awaiting the President.

"He didn't invite you to join him?" Katherine asked her mother.

"Would you expect him to?" asked Betsy, taking a swig of Chardonnay.

"He did actually. I declined." Ellen looked at her family. "I'd rather be here with you."

"Aww." Gil looked at Betsy. "You're drinking from a glass."

"Only because she's here." Betsy pointed to Anahita.

They sat on the sofa and in armchairs, their stocking feet up on the coffee table. Bottles of wine and beer and a tray of half-eaten sandwiches sat on a sideboard. Gil twisted the top off a beer and handed it to Anahita before taking one himself.

"What's he going to say?" he asked his mother.

"The truth," said Ellen, collapsing onto the couch between her children.

They'd arrived back in DC in the early hours to find their mother asleep, still in her clothes.

Thank God for swift military transports, Ellen thought.

When she woke up, she gave them most of the story, though the details would have to come out over time. And with patience.

Now Katherine watched the monitor. She had journalists at the news conference, but of course she also had the inside story. She'd written up her own account of events they'd been through, and sent it to her senior editor, embargoed until after the President spoke.

Even with all they knew, it would take months, maybe years, to untangle all that had happened. And to ferret out all the members of HLI.

Two Supreme Court Justices and six members of Congress had been arrested, with more arrests expected in the coming hours and days. And probably weeks. And months.

"Yesterday," said Gil. "In the Oval Office. Did you know when General Whitehead took the President hostage that he was bluffing?"

"I wondered that too," said Betsy. "You left the number for the Vice President and told me I had to stay home. You did that so that I'd be there to call. You must've known something."

"I hoped, but I didn't know. I thought if I couldn't call, you had to. But for a brief moment when Whitehead held the gun to Williams's head, I believed he really was the traitor."

She was back there in a flash, that moment of horror when she'd known they'd failed. All was lost. She'd woken up at two thirty that morning, sitting bolt upright in bed. Her eyes wide and staring. Her mouth open.

Ellen wondered if the terror would ever completely go away. It brushed up against her even now as she sat on the couch, between her children. Safe and sound. Her heart pounded and she felt lightheaded.

I'm safe, she repeated. *I'm safe. Everyone's safe.*

Or at least as safe as anyone could be in a contentious democracy. Such was the price of freedom.

"Did the President know that the General was acting?" asked Anahita.

"Turns out he did. They'd worked it up together. I'd also wondered why the Secret Service hadn't burst in right away. Williams had ordered them to stay outside the Oval Office."

Ellen smiled remembering how the bomb had been defused. Turned out Bert Whitehead hadn't called his wife. He'd called the squad disarming the dirty bomb in New York.

They'd had more time and managed to figure it out and were able to quickly walk the Ranger through what to do.

The timer had stopped with two seconds left.

Once they'd regained their composure, General Whitehead had turned to Doug Williams. Rubbing his solar plexus, the Chair of the Joint Chiefs had asked if the President had to hit him quite so hard.

"Sorry," said Williams. "Too much adrenaline. But good to know I could take you."

"You might not want to test that, Mr. President," said the Ranger, still bending over the bomb.

Now Secretary Adams and the others watched as journalists began to take their seats in the Brady Press Briefing Room.

"Mom?" said Katherine.

"Sorry." Ellen came back to the present.

"How did you know the General wasn't the HLI?" asked Katherine.

"I thought he was, at first. I believed those documents Pete Hamilton found in the Dunn administration's hidden archives. But then a couple of things began to bother me. When he was arrested, he attacked Tim Beecham. Beat him. Just before being taken away, he said to me, 'I've done my part.'"

"I remember that," said Betsy. "Gave me chills. I thought he was confessing that he'd gotten Shah released and cleared the way for the bombs to be planted on American soil."

"His job was done," said Ellen. "I thought so too. But the more I thought about it, the more I realized he could have meant something else entirely. It was so far out of character for General Whitehead to lose control like that. He'd been in combat, led operators on dangerous missions. To have command like that, first he needed command of himself. I began to wonder if he hadn't actually lost control. If he'd attacked Beecham on purpose."

"But why would he do that?" asked Gil.

"Because he suspected Beecham was the traitor but had no proof, so he did what he could to get him out of the room when we discussed strategy. It worked. Beecham was in the hospital when we were coming up with a plan."

"That's what he meant when he said, 'I've done my part,'" said Betsy. "Now it was our turn."

"But there was something else?" said Katherine.

"Yes. Something far more obvious and far simpler. Bert Whitehead's family was still in DC. Beecham's wasn't," said her mother.

There was a question Betsy had been afraid to ask, but did now.

"Did General Whitehead design the factory raid?"

"Yes. I'd told Williams that I thought we'd gotten it wrong. That Whitehead had been set up. I have to admit, he didn't buy the 'I've done my part' explanation, but when he heard about the families, he was convinced. When the head of Special Forces and the Generals couldn't come up with a good plan to get into, and out of, that factory, Williams went to Whitehead. He'd been one of the American observers at the Battle of Bajaur. He knew the terrain."

"And he designed the diversion," said Katherine.

"And the factory raid. The two went together. He wanted to lead it himself," said Ellen. "But Williams wouldn't let him. We couldn't risk others finding out that Whitehead had been released. Beecham had to believe he'd convinced us."

"So you knew even then it was Beecham?" said Gil.

"We thought so, but had no proof. When he asked to go to London, Williams agreed. Again, to get him far away."

And now it came to the question Betsy had been afraid to ask.

"Then who did lead the diversion?"

Ellen looked at her and said, softly, "Bert chose his aide-de-camp. She'd served three tours in Afghanistan with the Rangers. She was his best officer."

"Denise Phelan?"

"Yes."

Betsy closed her eyes. She didn't think she had any more sighs left in her, but she had at least one more, a long deep sigh of sorrow for the young woman standing in this very room, holding the coffees and smiling.

She saw Pete Hamilton, hard at work.

Digging, digging. Deeper, deeper. He hadn't stopped after finding the information planted about the Chair of the Joint Chiefs of Staff.

He'd kept digging. Past the normal internet. Past the dark web. Past the fringe. To the vast emptiness, the vacuum. Where no light could penetrate. And there he found HLI.

And in digging so deep, he'd dug his own grave.

And now both were gone.

Bert Whitehead tossed the stick and watched as it disappeared into a snowbank. Pine leapt after it. Burying her head. Bottom in the air. Tail wagging.

Her huge ears lay on top of the pristine snow, like wings.

Beside Pine, the other shepherd was dancing excitedly, then plunged his head into the next snowdrift. For no discernable reason.

"Henri, it must be admitted," said the man beside Whitehead, "keeps very little in his head. It's really only there to support his ears. Everything important, he keeps in his heart."

Bert's laugh came out in a puff of steam. "Smart dog."

Both men looked toward the Gamache home in Three Pines, where their wives would be sitting by the television waiting for the President's news conference.

"Would you like to go inside and watch?" Armand asked.

"No. You go if you want. I already know what the President will say. I don't need to hear it."

He sounded exhausted, wrung out. Bert and his wife, along with Pine, had flown up to Montréal, then driven down to the peaceful little Québec village in the countryside. For exactly this.

For peace.

The two men walked in silence, their boots squeaking on the snow as they made their way around the village green. Old fieldstone, brick, and clapboard homes faced them, smoke rising from chimneys, warm lights at mullioned windows.

It was just after six o'clock and already dark. Polaris, the North Star, was bright overhead. It held steady, always there, while the rest of the night sky moved around it.

Both men paused and looked up. It was comforting to have something that did not alter. One constant in an ever-changing universe.

The cold scraped their cheeks, but neither was in a hurry to get inside. The air was refreshing. Bracing.

It had been just over a day since the events, but they seemed a lifetime ago and a world away.

"I'm sorry about Denise Phelan. About all of them."

"Merci, Armand." The General knew that the Chief Inspector understood the grief of losing people, most of them appallingly young, under his command.

He too kept what was most precious in his heart. The young men and women would live there, safe, for as long as their own hearts beat.

"I just hope we get them all," said Whitehead.

Armand stopped. "Is there any doubt?"

"With someone like Shah, there's always doubt."

"When you put the gun to the President's head, you already knew where the bombs were. The President had opened the HLI site, and it gave you their exact locations, including the one in the White House. Why not send bomb disposal experts down to defuse it? Why waste precious time pretending to hold the President hostage?"

"Because we didn't know where the White House bomb was. The feed showed the Oval Office, but the one showing the bomb itself was too close up."

"Then how did you figure it out?"

"It was a guess."

Armand looked at the Chair of the Joint Chiefs of Staff, appalled. "A guess?"

"We knew the others were in infirmaries; we guessed that one was too. But that only came later. What we didn't have were Beecham and Stenhauser's confessions. It wasn't enough to get the bombs. We had to get the bombers and we had to have proof."

"Did you know Secretary Adams was livestreaming it to her counselor? That her counselor was calling in the information?"

"I could see what she was doing with her phone, yes. I hoped . . ."

"So close," said Armand. "Why did they do it? I can see being disenchanted with where the country is going, but nuclear bombs? How many would have been killed?"

"How many die in a war? They saw this as another American Revolution."

"With Al-Qaeda as their ally? The Russian mafia as an ally?" said Gamache.

"We all make deals with devils, at times. Even you, my friend."

Armand nodded. It was true. He'd made such deals.

Their walk took them past the bistro, whose windows threw

buttery light onto the snow. They could see villagers sitting by the fire, having drinks and talking animatedly. They could guess what about. What everyone around the world was talking about.

They paused at the darkened bookstore. Up above, there was a light in the loft. It flickered softly as Myrna Landers and Alex Huang watched the news conference.

"It's very peaceful here," said Bert Whitehead, turning away and looking into the mountains and forests. And star-filled sky.

"Well," said Armand, "it has its moments." He saw a long sigh escape his companion. "Why don't you retire? Move here? You and Martha can stay with us until you find a home."

Bert was silent for a few steps before answering. "It's tempting. You have no idea how tempting. But I'm an American. As flawed as it is, those are the scars of a democracy worth fighting for. It's my home, Armand. Just as this is yours. Besides, until we're sure we have all the conspirators, I'm staying on the job."

"Ladies and gentlemen, the President of the United States."

Doug Williams walked slowly to the podium. His face grave.

"Before I give my prepared statement, I would like us to observe a moment of silence for those who gave their lives to save this country from possible catastrophe, including six Special Ops air crew members and an entire Ranger platoon. Thirty-six brave men and women."

In the Secretary of State's office, they bowed their heads.

In Off the Record, they bowed their heads.

In Times Square, in Palm Beach, in the streets of Kansas City and Omaha and Minneapolis and Denver. Across the vast plains, and the mountain ranges, in towns and villages and great cities, Americans bowed their heads.

For the true patriots who gave their lives.

"I will read a prepared statement," President Williams said, breaking the silence. He then paused and seemed to consider. "Before taking questions."

There was a slight murmur through the crowd of journalists. They hadn't expected that.

In the Secretary of State's office, they listened.

President Williams had invited Ellen to the Oval Office that morning to discuss what should and should not be said to the American public. He also invited her to join him at the news conference, but she begged off.

"Thank you, but I feel the need to be with my family right now, Mr. President. I'll watch it along with everyone else."

"I need your advice, Ellen." He waved her to the armchair by the fireplace.

"That shirt does not work with that suit."

"No, no, not that. I'm trying to decide whether to take questions at the news conference."

"I think you should."

"But you know they'll ask questions that are sensitive. Almost impossible to answer."

"I do. Tell them the truth," said Ellen. "We can handle truth. It's the lies that do damage."

"If I do that, you know I'll be blamed for allowing it to get that far." He looked at her closely. "Is that why you're suggesting it?"

"Consider it payback for South Korea."

"Oh." He grimaced. "You know about that?"

"I guessed. Isn't that why you appointed me Secretary of State? So that I'd not only have to give up my media platform but I'd also be out of the country most of the time, and out of your hair. You could make sure I'd fail. I'd be internationally humiliated, and you could fire me."

"Good plan, no?"

"And yet here I am. Doug, what's going to happen in Afghanistan? You know that with our pullout, the Taliban along with Al-Qaeda and other terrorists will take over."

"Yes."

"All the progress made for human rights could be wiped out. All the girls, all the women, who went to school, got an education. Got jobs. Became teachers and doctors and lawyers, bus drivers. You know what will happen to them if the Taliban has its way."

"Well, I guess we'll need a strong, internationally respected Secretary of State to let any Afghan government know that rights must be respected. And that Afghanistan must not once again become home to terrorists." He looked at her long enough for her to begin to blush. "Thank you. For all that you did to stop the attacks. You risked everything."

"You know, don't you," she said, "that the conspirators aren't the only ones who feel we've lost our way. They're the most obvious, but there are tens of millions who agree. Good people. Decent people. Who might not share our politics but who'd give us the shirt off their backs if we needed it."

He nodded. "I know. We have to do something. Give them the shirt off our backs."

"Give them jobs. Give their children a future, their towns a future. Stop the lies that feed their fears."

The lies that had created and fed their own homegrown Azhi Dahaka.

"There's a lot of reckoning. A lot of healing," he said. "More than I realized. You were right in many of your editorials. I have a lot to learn."

"I actually think I said you had to get your head out of— "

"Yes, yes, I do remember that." But he was smiling, and the way he was looking at her made her cheeks burn.

Now, hours later, with the sun setting, she sat in her office with her daughter and son, with Betsy and Charles Boynton and the FSO Anahita Dahir. Who was, Ellen suspected, judging by the look on Gil's face, maybe going to be so much more than her FSO.

They watched as Doug Williams introduced the bomb-disposal experts who'd defused the nuclear devices; then he described what had happened since the bus bombs had gone off.

"That's a nice mention of you, Mom," said Katherine. "He's changed his tune."

And, Ellen noticed, his suit.

Betsy leaned over and handed Ellen something. "Madame Secretary, a little recognition for your public service."

It was a coaster from the Off the Record bar. With Ellen Adams's face on it.

When the news conference ended, Gil asked Anahita if she'd like to grab some dinner.

In the restaurant, she listened as he told her about the book deal he'd been offered. She asked how he felt about it. How long it would take to write.

Since all the facts were out, there was no issue of breaking any confidences. He was excited about telling the full behind-the-scenes story. Though he'd leave out the part about Hamza, the Lion. The member of the terrorist Pathan family who was his friend.

Gil asked if she'd write the book with him.

She declined. She still had her job as a foreign service officer with the State Department.

"How are your parents?" he asked.

"They're back home."

Gil nodded. And Anahita looked out the window. To a Washington, DC, still there.

"How are they feeling?" he asked.

Anahita turned astonished eyes on him. Then told him.

"And how are you feeling?" he asked.

"Madame Secretary."

"Yes, Charles."

"You asked me to look into fissile material missing from Russia."

He stood a few feet from her desk.

It was well after dark. Betsy was at her desk in her own office, writing up notes and answering questions from US Intelligence relating to the video she'd recorded.

"What did you find?" Secretary Adams asked.

He was looking at her in a way that was deeply disconcerting. It was fairly clear that her Chief of Staff had not found a basket of kittens.

She put out her hand for the paper he held, then indicated a chair beside her. She'd never done that before, preferring he stay on his side of the desk. Standing.

But the world was new, and they'd begun again.

She put on her glasses and looked at the paper, then at him.

"What's this?"

"There's fissionable material missing not just from Russia but also from Ukraine, Australia, Canada. The United States."

"Where'd it go?" Even as she asked that, she knew how ridiculous it was. After all, it was missing.

Still, he answered, rubbing his forehead with his hand. "I don't know. But it's enough to make hundreds of bombs."

"How long's it been gone?"

Again he shook his head.

"And from our own storehouses?"

He nodded.

"But that's not all." He pointed farther down the page.

"When thou hast done," she thought, *"thou hast not done, for I have more."*

She dropped her eyes. As she read, she took a long, slow gasp.

Sarin gas.

Anthrax.

Ebola.

Marburg virus.

She turned the page over. The list continued. Every horror known to man. Every horror made by man was there. And not there.

Missing. Unaccounted for.

Ellen looked at the long, lost list.

"I think," she whispered, "we have our next nightmare."

"Yes, I think you're right, Madame Secretary."

THE END

Acknowledgments

We are both grateful for the chance to work together, an experience that has added to the joys and surprises of our friendship. And we each have lots of people to thank, so here goes:

Louise:

This book started for me, as so many things do, unexpectedly.

I was at the family cottage by a lake north of Montréal in spring 2020. The pandemic was in full swing and I was sheltering in place when a message came in from my agent: *I need to speak to you.*

Now, in my experience, that almost never means good news.

The middle of a worldwide pandemic (as it turned out it was not the middle, but just the beginning), isolating by an already isolated lake, and some disaster is about to befall my literary career.

I grabbed a bag of jelly beans and called my agent.

"How would you feel about writing a political thriller with Hillary Clinton?"

"Huh?"

He repeated it. As did I.

"Huh?"

Now, while this question came as a complete surprise, it did not come out of the blue. Hillary and I know each other. Are, in fact, close friends (and still are—I think that could be considered a miracle).

Our friendship happened, as so many things do, unexpectedly.

Hillary was running for President. It was July 2016 and her best friend, Betsy Johnson Ebeling, gave an interview to a Chicago reporter about their relationship. In that interview she was asked what they had in common. Among the things Betsy mentioned was their love of books, specifically crime novels.

Then the reporter asked the question that changed all our lives.

"What are you reading now?"

As fate would have it, they were both reading one of my books.

My amazing publicist with Minotaur Books, Sarah Melnyk, saw the interview and excitedly contacted me.

My upcoming tour for the new Gamache book would start in Chicago—how did I feel about meeting Betsy there before the event?

To be honest, it's quite stressful before big events, and meeting a stranger beforehand is not ideal. But I agreed.

A week or so later I was backstage, heard a sound, turned, and fell in love. Just like that.

I'd expected Hillary's best friend to be some intimidating power broker. Instead I saw a slight woman, gray hair in a bob, with the warmest smile and kind eyes. I lost my heart then and there.

I loved Betsy then, and I love her now.

A few weeks after I got home from tour, my beloved husband, Michael, died of dementia. In struggling to get a handle on life without him, I found comfort in opening all the cards of condolence.

One day, sitting at the dining table, I opened one and started reading. It talked about Michael's contributions to research into childhood leukemia. His position as head of hematology at the Montreal Children's Hospital. His work as a lead investigator with the international pediatric oncology group.

The writer talked about loss and grief and offered heartfelt condolence.

It was from Hillary Rodham Clinton.

Secretary Clinton, in the last stages of a bruising brutal campaign for the most powerful job in the world, took time out to write to me.

A woman she'd never met.

About a man she'd never met.

A Canadian who couldn't even vote for her. It was a private note, not meant to help her in any way, but offering comfort to a stranger in profound grief.

It was an act of selflessness I will never forget, and one that has inspired me to be kinder in my own life.

I'd kept in touch with Betsy, and when November rolled around she invited me to the Javits Center in New York City to see Hillary win the presidency. I will never forget looking across the vast room and seeing tiny Betsy sitting and staring. That thousand-yard stare of someone who has just seen too much.

In February of 2017, Hillary invited Betsy and me to Chappaqua for the weekend. It would be our first meeting.

And I fell in love again, though part of the magic of those extraordinary few days was sitting quietly and watching the two friends who'd met in sixth grade. Who'd stayed close all their lives. One going on to be a lawyer, First Lady, Senator, and Secretary of State, and, if votes counted instead of the electoral college, winning the presidency, while the other became a high school teacher, then a community activist. Raising three children with her wonderful husband, Tom.

It was so clear that Betsy and Hillary were soul mates that it was almost a spiritual experience to see them together.

Betsy and Tom, Hillary and Bill came to visit me in Québec that summer for a week's vacation.

By then it was clear that the breast cancer that Betsy had battled for many years was winning. But still, she leaned into life, with the support of the huge circle of close friends that she and Hillary shared.

In July 2019 Betsy died.

If you've read *State of Terror*, you'll know that it was written as a political thriller, as an examination of hate, but finally, ultimately, a celebration of love.

Hillary and I felt strongly that we wanted to reflect the profound female relationships we both have. That unshakable bond of friendship.

And we wanted Betsy to figure large.

While Betsy Ebeling in real life was far gentler, without quite that mouth on her, she shares many qualities with Betsy Jameson. Her luminous intelligence, her fierce loyalty. Her bravery. Her bravery. Her bravery. And her boundless capacity for love.

So, yes, when my wonderful agent, David Gernert, asked if I'd write a political thriller with my friend H, I agreed, though not without trepidation.

I'd just finished the latest Chief Inspector Gamache, so felt I had the time, but while there are similarities, I'd only ever written crime novels. A political thriller on this scale was so far beyond my comfort zone as to belong on another planet.

But how in the world could I let fear of failure steal this opportunity? I had to at least try. I have a poster up where I write. On it are the final words of the Irish poet Seamus Heaney.

Noli Timere. Be not afraid.

Truth is, I was afraid, but often it's not a case in life of less fear, but of more courage.

So I closed my eyes, took a breath, and said yes. I'll do it. As long as Hillary was happy too. It was so clearly going to be an even greater risk for her.

I won't go into the details of how this particular plot developed except to say it came out of one of our many phone calls that spring, when Hillary talked about what, as Secretary of State, woke her up with a start at 3 a.m. There were three nightmare scenarios. We chose this one.

The actual idea of us writing this book together was the brainchild of my friend, one of the great publishers of his generation or any, Stephen Rubin. Thank you, Steve!

He approached David Gernert, who approached me. Thank you, David, for shepherding this book through the labyrinth and always being so wise, so positive, so warm, and so protective.

I want to thank my own publishers at Minotaur Books/St. Martin's Press/Macmillan for taking, as we say in Québec, *le beau risque*. Don Weisberg, John Sargent, Andy Martin, Sally Richardson, Tracey Guest, Sarah Melnyk, Paul Hochman, Kelley Ragland, and the woman who edited *State of Terror*, the great publisher of SMP, Jennifer Enderlin.

Huge thank you to the team at Hillary's publisher, Simon & Schuster, for your ideas and collaboration.

Thank you to Bob Barnett.

Thank you to my assistant (and wonderful friend) Lise Desrosiers. None of this would be possible without your support, my dear one.

Tom Ebeling, for letting us put a fictionalized version of Betsy into the book.

To my brother, Doug, with whom I was sheltering in the winter/spring of 2020, who listened to all my angst and ridiculous ideas.

To Rob and Audi, Mary, Kirk and Walter, Rocky and Steve.

To Bill, for your input and support. (It was difficult to argue when Bill Clinton read an early draft and said, "A President is unlikely to do. . . .)

We had to keep this collaboration secret for more than a year, but so many friends helped without realizing it just by always being there. This included the friends Hillary and I share, all of whom are in my life because of Betsy.

Hardye and Don, Allida and Judy, Bonnie and Ken, Sukie, Patsy, Oscar and Brendan.

And Hillary—thank you. You made what could have been a nightmare a pleasure. You made the book so smart and the experience so easy and such fun, except when I'd receive five hundred pages (literally) of manuscript—scanned. With her scribbles in the margin.

Thank God for my magic jelly beans.

The laughs we had writing this book, amid the long pauses as we stared at each other over FaceTime, having literally lost the plot.

And, of course, I want to acknowledge my dear Michael. Oh, how happy and proud he'd be. He so admired Secretary Clinton. It would have given him such joy to get to know her as Hillary. And to see what a lovely woman she is.

Michael adored thrillers. Indeed, when it became clear he had one more book in him before the dementia stole his ability to read and understand, I chose a political thriller. Every day I imagine him holding *State of Terror* and beaming.

There is nothing I see, feel, smell, hear that does not owe its existence to the day I fell in love with Michael Whitehead.

And now you know the genesis of another character.

State of Terror is about terror but, at its core, at its heart, it is about courage and love.

Hillary:

I was at home in Chappaqua, sheltering with my family during the pandemic, when Bob Barnett, my lawyer and friend, called to report that Steve Rubin had suggested that Louise and I write a book.

I was dubious but listened as Bob made the case based on his prior experience working with two other clients, my husband and James Patterson, who've written two thrillers together.

I admire Louise as a writer and love her as a friend, but the prospect seemed daunting. I've only written nonfiction, but then I thought, my life is the stuff of fiction, so maybe it was worth a try.

Louise and I began talking and produced a long, detailed outline, which our prospective publishers liked, so we dove into our long-distance collaboration. And what a joy it was to create our characters, refine our plot, and trade drafts. Much on my mind as I wrote in 2020 were the losses of two close friends and my brother, Tony, in 2019.

Betsy Johnson Ebeling had been my best friend since sixth grade, when we met in Mrs. King's classroom at Field School in Park Ridge, Illinois. We'd weathered six decades of life's ups and downs together and I miss her every day.

Ellen Tauscher, former member of Congress from California and Under Secretary of State for Arms Control and International Security when I was Secretary of State from 2009–2013, had been my dear friend for over twenty-five years. After the 2016 election, she came often to stay with me to figure out What Happened.

Ellen died on April 29, 2019.

Then my younger brother, Tony, died on June 7 after a year of illness. It breaks my heart whenever I think of him as a little boy, and the three children he left behind.

And on July 28, Betsy lost her long fight with breast cancer.

Any one of these loses would have been painful, but the combination was devastating, and still hard for me to fully accept.

Both Betsy's husband, Tom, and Ellen's daughter, Katherine, supported our desire to model our fictional characters on their wife and mother respectively.

They carry no responsibility for the differences we created.

When Louise and I decided to construct our story around a

Secretary of State, I suggested Ellen as our inspiration, along with her real-life daughter, Katherine, as the names for our fictional versions.

And, of course, Betsy would be the model for the best friend and counselor, by the Secretary's side.

I want to add my thanks to the people Louise mentions in her acknowledgments, and add that Oscar and Brendan helped in countless ways, including solving a computer glitch with our manuscript at the end.

Thanks also to Heather Samuelson and Nick Merrill for their fact-checking help.

This is the eighth book I've done with Simon & Schuster and the first without the indomitable Carolyn Reidy, who is missed but not forgotten. Thankfully, her legacy continues under the leadership of Jonathan Karp, who continues to encourage me.

I'm grateful to him and the entire team: Dana Canedy, Stephen Rubin, Marysue Rucci, Julia Prosser, Marie Florio, Stephen Bedford, Elizabeth Breeden, Emily Graff, Irene Kheradi, Janet Cameron, Felice Javit, Carolyn Levin, Jeff Wilson, Jackie Seow, and Kimberly Goldstein.

And my thanks to Bill, a great reader and writer of thrillers, for his constant support and useful suggestions, as always.

Finally, this is a work of fiction but the story it tells is all too timely.

It's up to us to make sure its plot stays fictional.